Fires of Justice

Marc A. Beausejour

Fires of Justice

Copyright © 2018 by Marc A. Beausejour

For information contact : www.shepublishingllc.com | info@shepublishingllc.com | Tel: 219.515.8032

Edited by D.A. Goodwin | Front Cover photo by ID 48584570 © Ammentorp | Dreamstime.com | Book Photo by LaTisha Guster

Library of Congress Control Number: 2024932788

ISBN: 978-1-953163-93-6 (*paperback*)

Second Edition : February 2024

1   2   3   4   5   6   7   8   9   10

To the memory of my late pastor,

Reverend Pierre T. Leonidas (*July 26, 1932-April 3, 2017*),

who not only exemplified the true example of a loving physical father

but was the epitome of a spiritual father.

Addition of worries

Subtraction of meals

Multiplication of crimes

Division of communities

Problems without solutions

No fathers, no welfare

No Medicare,

Utopic Workfare

Ugly Mathematics

--Pierre T Leonidas

Excerpt from the poem Missing Fathers

Acknowledgment

First, I would like to thank the Lord for allowing me to get the opportunity to write and publish my fifth book and my third drama novel. After all these years of writing, I would have never imagined in my wildest dreams, that I would get to this point. I want to thank those who have supported this journey, from *Words On High,* all the way to this installment, including my family, friends, co-workers, and close acquaintances. I also want to extend my gratitude to professor, friend and fellow author, D. A. Goodwin; who has taken the time to edit this book. Lastly, I want to thank all the spiritual leaders and social activists who had a hand in inspiring the creation of this novel and it is my sincerest hope that this book ignites the spark that will change the world for future generations.

Introduction

For many years as a society, we were taught that America was formed from the throes of rebellion when the original colonies freed themselves from the British Empire. The Founding Fathers, including George Washington, Thomas Jefferson, John Adams, and John Hancock, helped develop what would one day stand as the foundation of the law. This foundation bestowed each American the freedoms of religion, expression, and the right to bear arms, which has been the backbone of the United States military force. Unfortunately, the education system failed to emphasize the fact that these freedoms were not granted to every living being that landed on American shores. The African Americans, indigenous citizens who were taken from their homeland by slave traders and who were brought under extreme conditions to the newly formed United States, weren't granted the same freedoms and opportunities as their white counterparts.

For years, African American society has been striving to receive the same measure of equality that was bestowed to others during that time. Our African ancestors were enslaved, hanged, castrated, dismembered, and disenfranchised throughout the years, and although America has strived to educate our children about their origins, many details about the devastation of white supremacy have fallen through the cracks of history. As a result, America— whether intentional or not—has created a financial and economic caste system that started when the slaves built the majority of structures and national landmarks that are viewed today. Yet, it was the so-called "dominant society" that reaped the benefits and the financial rewards of the African American's labor. Thus, the term "white privilege" was coined, and to this day, we constantly see this privilege at work.

Although slavery was abolished, the government and justice system has found another way to profit from black suffrage and misery, and it's been through the prison system. Per CNN.com/money, the U.S. prison system has made over $37 billion dollars in its industry. With the understanding that justice must continue to be served to protect the citizens, one must ask, how many of those prisoners were imprisoned for crimes in which they stood accused but never actually committed? How many men and women were driven to insanity, knowing the very precious gift of freedom was stripped from them simply for being in the wrong place at the wrong time?

This is the story of a public educator who finds himself in such a predicament, and not only must he fight to prove his innocence, but he must also fight, in a race against time, the racial element that strives to destroy all he holds dear.

The warden of the Smyrna State Prison facility paced the cell corridors on numerous occasions as he watched the activities of the inmates. Struggling to stifle his fatigue and sense of boredom, he let out a huge yawn. Reaching into his pocket, he pulled out a pack of gum, removing the silver wrapper before putting the stick inside his mouth.

One of the inmates noticed him chewing. "What's the hap, Cojack? Lemme get a piece of that," he said to the warden.

The warden, whose real name was Joseph Vries, looked at the inmate addressing him. "Keep it down, McKinley," he replied.

Sam McKinley was not the most popular inmate in the division by any stretch. Accused of armed robbery and battery, he went out of his way to make everyone's life around him a living nightmare. He would delay in waking up during the morning head count. He would purposely arrive late to the mess hall during mealtimes, and he would slack off during the inmates' work obligations, which included sanitation duties on the highways, roadways, and bridge overpasses.

The other inmates, attempting to stay on the straight and narrow path to freedom, did not want to be associated with a man who would jeopardize their chances at exoneration. Not to mention, McKinley might also receive an early parole, and not because of good behavior. While the other inmates weren't envious, they couldn't escape the obvious truth that McKinley would receive the reprieve because of his color. He was a Caucasian who grew up privileged with a great family upbringing, and money was never an issue for him. Even though he gambled his freedom by being an accomplice to a crime in which he robbed his former employer and held him at gunpoint, he was still guaranteed somewhat of a second chance.

The same couldn't be said about the inmate in the cell across from him. Inmate number 02369 as was written on his jail attire, just stared at the cracked ceiling for hours, not addressing anything or anybody. Unlike McKinley, he was not certain of his future. He might be released the next day, or he might be in the facility for the next ten to fifteen years. He spent countless sleepless nights tossing and turning on his cot, which he referred to as his bed.

But it was nothing more than a cot. In fact, the inmate was convinced a regular camping cot was more comfortable than this piece of wood and cloth that he was lying on. For many people, including McKinley, this was nothing more than a bump in their road of existence.

But for the reflective inmate number 02369, this wasn't a bump. It was a cliff, and he just fell right off it, leaving his life, his family, and his career in shattered remains at the bottom. Lying face up, the inmate heard someone saying his name, in hushed tones.

"Thomas, remember what we talked about yesterday? We can do you it, just you and I. Break outta this hellhole...you know what I mean?" McKinley insisted, whispering so that Cojack wouldn't hear him.

Levell Thomas looked at McKinley's dead serious face.

"Shut up, McKinley," he replied, shaking his head. "How we gon' get outta here? How do you propose that? Oh, we just gon' try to jump that huge fence, huh?" Levell sarcastically asked in the same hushed tones.

They whispered because the main agenda of the watchful guard was to make sure there was no plotting or planning taking place. In addition, the prison had extra security installed, so the possibility of escape was next to impossible.

The thought of escape was especially infuriating to Levell because, where could he go without being easily noticed? He stood at about 6-foot-4 with a bald head and a beard that came down from his sideburns. A former football and basketball player in his time, Levell was used to all the tall jokes wherever he went. But he also had another reason not to talk about escape. He was a black man. Any other ethnic group could discuss the prospect of escape, draw up a plan, and it would work to perfection. Levell, however, knew that if he stepped out of line, he would never see his wife, Caliya, and his four-year-old daughter, Patrice, again.

Stories circulated among the jail unit about inmates who attempted to escape. All attempts had been immediately thwarted, and the ones who tried were dealt with, sometimes by physical force. The last thing Levell needed was for his possibility of parole to be taken away by him joining McKinley's impossible mission.

"Nah, man. Hear me out," McKinley countered. "We ain't gotta worry about the damn fence. We could try digging. Or during the next workday, we could sneak out while everyone else workin'. I got a cousin that stay out by Marietta, and once we get access to a phone, she'll pick us up, and it's all good from there."

Levell thought about the plan for a moment, and he looked at McKinley with the same glowering expression. He was not going to fall for any of the white man's tricks this time.

Ya was the one that got me locked up in the first place.

Levell didn't have a huge issue with McKinley, but he considered people who looked like him to be lower than dirt. Levell was one of those people who was born and raised to give everyone the benefit of the doubt. It just seemed as if whenever he tried to do right by himself and by his family, he was the one who ended up on the short end of the noose. All he ever tried to do was to give his family a better life and put his daughter in a position where she could go to the best schools in the U.S. All those plans now appeared to be dashed as he took a crumpled piece of paper from his pocket.

Before his unexpected incarceration, Levell was a high school English teacher at Kennesaw Mountain High School in Kennesaw, Georgia, where he was residing and where his wife and daughter still lived in a middle-class two-story home down Kennesaw Due West Road. Since his teaching career began in Queens, New York, Levell had the habit of reading old literature books and printing the quotes to store in his pocket. Whenever he felt stressed out during the day, or he felt defeated, he took the quote out and read it, attempting to decipher the message and apply it to his current situation. He found it to be ironic that it worked wonders for him in one of the most difficult places to teach in: Queens. And yet it hadn't succeeded in Georgia, where he resided for only a year.

In his pocket, he had the same quote that he remembered reading before the whole incident occurred. The charges and the accusations that he faced ruined not only his career, but his marriage and his life also. And the person who was responsible for ruining his life had only one name: Raven.

He should have seen it coming. He should have known it was coming. He should have prepared for the upcoming storm.

But how did I know that she would send my world into a tailspin? How could someone so sweet and innocent turn out to be so manipulative and evil? Why did I give her so many chances to come at me? What should I have done? Should I have fought back? Should I have reported her and her friends? How could I have never seen it coming?

All the questions Levell had internalized also revealed a simple answer. They attacked him and sought to destroy him because, although he was the son of Haitian immigrants who came to America and lived in low-income housing, he had graduated high school and college with high marks and had become one of the best teachers in the county. He was educating people the right way, through encouragement and discipline. Raven and her family humiliated him because of their hatred of him and his accomplishments.

Levell looked at the excerpt from William Shakespeare's "The Tempest." It read, "That, if I then had waked after long sleep/Will make me sleep again/And then, in dreaming, The clouds methought would open and show riches/Ready to drop upon me, that when I waked I cried to dream again."

While reading, Levell looked out into the corridor beyond his jail cell. His life had been a dream, a very blissful dream that held promises of fruitful prosperity and a bright future for his family...a dream that would one day turn into a nightmare: from Teacher of the Year to inmate number 02369 in less than a year.

Chapter 1

E LATED HIGH SCHOOL STUDENTS MADE THEIR WAY across the busy highland Avenue intersection to enter Hillcrest High School in Queens. It was June 2014, and the students, more so the seniors, were overjoyed that it was the last week of school before summer break. The hallways were crowded as usual with students going in and out of classrooms, cleaning out their lockers, and taking the time to savor their last few days at the institution. Senior Vijay Singh was one of those students.

As the son of Nazr and Pari Singh, Indian immigrants who moved to America shortly before he was born, Vijay couldn't wait for the day he got to walk across the stage and receive his high school diploma. His parents had been eagerly anticipating the occasion, and for Vijay, it was surreal. He thought about the stories they had told him over the years about the struggles they endured in India and how their main goal was to migrate to the United States in search of a better life and opportunities for their child.

As Vijay started to clean out his locker, he noticed all his graded assignments and papers from the past four years at Hillcrest High. The papers that stood out most were the ones graded by Mr. Thomas. Out of all the teachers that Vijay had at Hillcrest, there was nobody like Mr. Thomas. He had a unique style of teaching his classes, and he loved interacting with students in a way that other teachers wouldn't. Vijay had Mr. Thomas for three classes: American Literature, British Literature, and World Literature. Thanks to Mr. Thomas and his innovating teaching methods, Vijay aced all his classes and earned an academic scholarship to

Stony Brook University. As Vijay cleaned out his locker, his friend Darrell walked up to him.

"What's up, man?" he greeted.

"What's up, Darrell? Yo, this is it, man," Vijay replied as he continued to clean.

"No doubt, bruh. Last week of school, and we graduate this Saturday. Yo, can you believe this is Mr. Thomas's last year ova hea'?" Darrell asked.

Vijay knew Darrell was going to ask about Mr. Thomas leaving Hillcrest, but part of him didn't want to believe it. If he asked other kids in his class, they would agree, in part, about their shock upon receiving the news. Their beloved teacher was leaving Hillcrest High to transfer to another school in a different state.

"Yo, I still can't believe it, man. I got cousins that are gonna be here next year, and I've been tellin' them about Mr. Thomas. Then he dips out on us. All for some prep school in Alabama or South Carolina, one of them country road schools down there," Vijay said.

Vijay wasn't sure of where Mr. Thomas was going, and he didn't care. What better place was there to stay than in the Mecca? He couldn't figure it out. As the warning bell rang, Vijay got up after finishing cleaning. He dapped Darrell and made his way over to Mr. Thomas's classroom, which happened to be both his homeroom and first block class.

As he entered the room, he saw Mr. Thomas seated in his chair. Decorated all around the classroom were titles and illustrations of literary works throughout the centuries from Geoffrey Chaucer's Canterbury Tales to Harper Lee's To Kill a Mockingbird. But the posters that Vijay admired the most were the socially conscious ones that Mr. Thomas hung on his wall such as the writings of Dr. Marcus Garvey, W.E.B. DuBois, Langston Hughes, Alex Haley, Zora Neale Hurston, and other African American figures of the twentieth century.

Mr. Thomas was of Haitian descent, a first generation Haitian American who, like Vijay, had come to America in hopes of a better life and opportunity for his family. Mr. Thomas often showed pride in his Haitian heritage by hanging his native flag on the side of the room adjacent to the other posters he had. At first, the administration at Hillcrest didn't fully agree with the flag because of fear that it would offset the patriotic symbolism of the American flag mounted in the front of the classroom on top of the marker board. But Mr. Thomas never bent over backwards to please the masses. This trait made Vijay admire his teacher.

A 34-year-old man who stood 6'4" with a baldhead and a shaped goatee at the bottom, Mr. Thomas also showed his individuality through his style and wardrobe. He didn't conform to the way normal teachers dressed. In fact, he would teach class in a t-shirt, jeans, and a pair of Nikes or Reeboks, especially on Fridays. The aspect that made Mr. Thomas much more unique was how he wore clothes matching the historical period he was teaching about that day. For instance, when he taught classes about the Renaissance period, he managed to find a piece of garment from back then and wore it to class.

Vijay remembered it so well because he was in class that day before Mr. Thomas arrived, and he remembered talking to his classmates, wondering about their teacher's whereabouts. Finally, a confident Mr. Thomas strode into the room, draped in fourteenth-century garment. All the students, including Vijay, roared with laughter at how absurd their teacher looked in the symbolic frilled shirt, jeans, and sneakers. He had succeeded at grabbing the students' attention to teach the lesson that day.

Many students didn't understand Mr. Thomas and thought his methods were unorthodox, but to Mr. Thomas, it was all a part of learning. Graduating from Queens College with a bachelor's degree and a master's degree in English and minor in education, Mr. Thomas learned that the important part of education was to grab the students' attention, not in a personal manner, but in a way that would instruct and educate students. Therefore, he took those lessons and applied them when he taught at Bayside High School for three years, before teaching at Hillcrest for the past four years.

As Mr. Thomas watched Vijay and the others make their way inside the classroom, he couldn't help but reflect on what would be his last week at Hillcrest High. When the final bell rang, he stood up from his chair and closed the door. Any student who walked in late had to open the door, which always compelled Mr. Thomas to mark them tardy in his grade book. They liked teasing him about how outdated the grade book was because everyone supposedly graded online those days. But Mr. Thomas didn't care what people thought. He was from the old school, and he was going to carry a grade book for as long as he could. If he could stand and teach a whole class with that uncomfortable Renaissance-Era shirt on while taking the criticism, he could surely still carry his grade book.

In retrospect, he was quite pleased that the school year was over. Finally, no more grading papers for two months, and no more worrying about having to fail students.

While there were many advantages that came with teaching sophomore, junior, and senior students, failing them was not one. Mr. Thomas hated to fail students. He hated knowing that the students he failed had potential and resources to succeed, yet they chose not to apply themselves and chose not to come to class. And while he would warn students on the first day of each new semester that he would give a failing grade to anyone who didn't attend class or missed assignments without remorse, deep inside he would have a sense of regret and inner failure when it happened. He was once a student, so he knew the odds were stacked up against some of his students, just as the odds had been stacked up against him.

A Haitian-American, black male living in New York, Levell Thomas didn't have any advantages granted to him. He had to go out and make everything happen for himself. His parents never graduated college, and they had to work different jobs to make ends meet. Unfortunately, Levell was headed down the same path to potential poverty, but reading saved his life. Education saved his future, and he strived to pass his work ethic onto his students. But with the rising cost of living in Queens and the high cost of public transportation, not to mention the rising crime trend in certain areas, Levell was forced to make a difficult decision. He would move out of New York and teach in Kennesaw.

It wasn't a decision that he came to on his own. Caliya insisted upon the move earlier in the year when Levell flew down to Georgia to visit his uncle Max, who lived in Marietta. Max, his wife Vicky, and their two children, a son and a daughter, also lived in New York a few years ago but decided to move to Georgia. One day Max invited his nephew to visit him.

While in Georgia, the first thought that came to Levell's mind was that it was nothing like Queens. People couldn't walk to go shopping because all the stores were in squares, and every place was distant. In New York, Levell could walk to the corner store in fifteen minutes and make it back at about half an hour. And he never had to use his car to run basic errands. In Georgia, on the other hand, the stores were a forty-five minute to an hour walk. Levell quickly realized that if a person didn't own a car or have friends with cars, then he or she wouldn't go anywhere.

But while staying with his uncle, Levell started to see the benefits of living in Georgia. He loved the weather, and he loved the mansion-like houses. He loved that the house and mortgage payments were so much cheaper than the small home he had lived in for years in New York. Even his wife immediately fell in love with the state. After some table meetings and strong consideration, Levell, who was planning on moving after the school year ended, decided to move to Georgia.

Before Levell flew back to New York, Max helped him search for a home. Using the same realtor who sold Max his home, Levell and Caliya settled for a cozy ranch in Kennesaw. The house had three bedrooms, two bathrooms, a garage, and a small basement. After negotiating with the realtor, Levell flew back up to New York to finish the school year and to begin packing for the big move. He set the moving date for July 10, 2014, since school starting in August at Kennesaw.

Unfortunately, Mr. Thomas's students still couldn't grasp the reality that he was leaving.

"Dang, Mr. Thomas, do you really have to go?" a black girl named Alicia asked.

"Yeah, I figured I'd change it up a little bit to experience the southern life. I'm tired of y'all anyways," Levell joked.

"Whatever, Mr. Thomas. You know you love us. We the best class you ever gonna have," Alicia replied as the other students laughed.

It was virtually the last day of class. There were no more lessons, so the students who still attended class just relaxed and talked to each other. Most of the seats in the classroom were empty. The students had all taken their final examination, and to Mr. Thomas's pleasant surprise, they had all passed. But since other classes hadn't issued their finals yet, some students still had to attend school. As a result, the few who were in Mr. Thomas's class were studying for their other finals. Vijay was one of those students.

"So, Mr. Thomas, where you moving to again?" he asked.

"I'm moving down to Georgia, Vijay," Mr. Thomas replied. "Teaching in the city of Kennesaw, the place where one of the Civil Wars took place," he added.

"Doesn't that scare you a little bit though?" Vijay asked.

Mr. Thomas laughed at the question. "No. Why would I be scared?"

"I mean, it's the South. You know what I'm sayin'?" Vijay replied. "The place where they allowed slavery and had segregated places for years. It just sounds...I don't know...just a little risky to me."

Mr. Thomas waved his hand, shaking his head to dismiss the notion entirely. "Look, Vijay, I know where you're going with this, but trust me. All of that stuff was history. I know racism still exists, but the place I'm moving to, they say it's one of the most peaceful places to live in."

"Yeah, but I'm still tight though." Alicia interrupted the conversation before asking, "You leavin' us for a bunch of southern, white-bred kids?"

"Hey, hey, Alicia, come on now. They're still students like you. Different skin—most of them—but same blood...same veins, same heart. They're not all as different as you think," Mr. Thomas replied.

"Says you," Alicia replied slyly. "Besides, they don't have our swag, our slang, or our style. We got the best looking jawns hea' too, while they probably have some snaggletoothed, hillbilly, banjo-playing country girls down there," she cracked, while Vijay laughed.

Mr. Thomas glared at Alicia for a second, but laughed also. "Alicia, you got a ruthless mind, you know that?" he laughed. "What if they talk about us too? What if they said that all New Yorkers were cocky, arrogant, city slickers with too many sports teams that talk with a Jersey or Boston accent?"

Alicia shrugged. "Yo, deadass, it wouldn't even faze me, to be honest, cuz I think deep down all them Georgia cats wanna be like us. Look what they do every New Year's Eve, droppin' a big peach, tryin' to emulate us. Maybe we should go to Times Square and watch an apple drop instead of the ball," she joked, laughing.

"Laugh all you want, Alicia," Mr. Thomas said confidently. "Trust me, I'm always gonna be who I am. I ain't changing for nobody. Levell Thomas is always gonna be Levell Thomas, regardless of where I'm going, so they gonna have to get used to me at some point."

"Yeah, just don't let them use you, Mr. Thomas," Vijay said.

Mr. Thomas looked at Vijay, questioningly. Use me? Use me for what? How are they gonna use me?

It would be a year and a half later before Levell would realize what his student had warned him about.

Graduation day finally arrived, and all the Hillcrest High School seniors were in their violet and gray caps and gowns, sitting on stage at Queens College as the superintendent and principal took the stage to say encouraging words about the class of 2014 and what the future had to offer each graduate. Levell Thomas was one of the teachers dressed in the black and gold cap and gown as he sat with the other Hillcrest instructors.

After the diplomas were certified by the state of New York, the seniors finally stood up, row by row, to receive their diplomas. It was bittersweet for Mr. Thomas as he watched them take the next step in another chapter of their lives. He was going to miss all his students. He had watched them grow up over the years, especially Alicia and Vijay, who sat in their row, patiently waiting for their names to be called. Mr. Thomas had told himself earlier that day that he wasn't going to cry, no matter how touching the ceremony was, and he was going to remain as stoic as possible.

But when his row of students was finally called, Levell Thomas stood next to the table with the stack of diplomas. He handed each student his or her diploma, and despite his best efforts to hide his emotions, he felt a tear roll down his right eye. He hugged Vijay and Alicia as he gave each his or her diploma.

After all the students were given their diplomas, the principal stood up on the podium. "I would like to thank all our parents, relatives, and faculty for attending today's ceremony. Before I present the class of 2014, I would like to present this plaque to one of our instructors here at Hillcrest High

School. For four years this man has been diligent in educating our students and has been effortless in his perseverance for excellence. As he prepares to take his new post as an instructor at Kennesaw Mountain High School in Georgia this fall, we would like to take this time to recognize him for his outstanding work and commitment to our students. Ladies and gentlemen, I would like to award this plaque to Mr. Levell Thomas!" the principal announced enthusiastically as Levell, still in shock, rose up from his seat to accept the plaque.

Mr. Thomas stepped up to the podium. Taking a deep, nervous breath, he looked out at the vast audience. He loved teaching a classroom of twenty to thirty kids, but speaking in front of a crowd was uncomfortable. Still, he worked up his nerve.

"I would like to thank all the students and staff here at Hillcrest High School for this award. When I first took the job, I thought I was just teaching boys and girls, but now that I've been led to another opportunity, I now realize that I was teaching young men and women. It was a pleasure teaching here, and I will never forget the lessons I learned as I was teaching your sons and daughters. It is the satisfaction of preparing them for life that I will miss here at Hillcrest. Thank you," Mr. Thomas concluded as the audience erupted in cheers.

As the principal presented the graduates, and the seniors tossed their caps in the air, Vijay and Alicia hugged Mr. Thomas tightly and celebrated with their class.

Chapter 2

AKING UP AT 6:20 IN THE MORNING, LEVELL MADE his way over to the bathroom at the end of the short hall. After showering and brushing his teeth, he looked around at the empty corridor that used to bear all his portraits, teaching certificates, and his wife's nursing certifications. It was almost surreal that all his belongings, packed away in various boxes, were on their way to Metro Atlanta. Levell had arranged for a U-Haul truck to carry all their items to his uncle's house in Marietta. His wife and baby daughter would board a Delta jet to fly down to Atlanta, where they would meet Max, and he would take them to their new home.

Levell walked over to the side of the bed and reached for his briefcase. He began searching through his school papers, past assignments, and teacher workday papers. He had to make sure he found the literary quote he needed for his day. Looking at the clock, he sped up his search. His family had to be at the airport in about two hours. Finally, he pulled out a quote by Confucius: "Wherever you go, go with all your heart."

Smiling to himself, Levell pocketed the quote before waking his wife. "Caliya baby, wake up. It's time to get ready," he said, while nudging his wife of nine years.

Caliya, who had been sleeping with her back turned, opened her hazel brown eyes while turning to face Levell. Smiling at her husband, she arched her head up and kissed him on the lips. "Good morning, baby. Is it time to go already?" she asked in a groggy voice as she got up.

Caliya was petite, about 5'5" with a light skin tone and long black hair that she kept straight at times or curled whenever it suited her.

"Yeah, baby, it's almost seven. Flight leaves at 9:30, so we got to get a move on," Levell replied as he started to dress.

"Did you wake Patrice up yet?" Caliya asked as she headed over to the bathroom.

"I'm actually headed to her room now," Levell replied from the hallway as he walked over to Patrice's room. He smiled at the sound of his three-year-old daughter's steady breathing as she slept blissfully. Levell did not want to wake her from her peaceful sleep, but they didn't have much time ahead of them. Walking over to the side of her bed, Levell slightly nudged her.

"Tricee? Time to wake up," Levell said as he coaxed Patrice out of sleep.

Startled at first, his daughter looked around, her brown eyes shifting left and right. She smiled, however, when she saw her father standing over her. "Hey, Daddy."

"Hey, sweetie, good morning. Time to wake up, okay? Let me take you to Mommy so she can dress you up. We are gonna fly the big plane today, remember?" he reminded Patrice.

Patrice's eyes suddenly lit with excitement. For weeks she had been thrilled about flying for the first time, and now that the day had arrived, she seemed to be more excited than ever. Jumping out of her bed, she trotted over to Caliya in the bathroom.

"How's my big princess today?" Caliya asked as she picked up her daughter and kissed her.

"Hey, Mommy, Daddy said we get to fly the plane today!" Patrice exclaimed.

"Yes, today is the day we fly the big plane!" Caliya replied. "Are you ready?"

"Yeah!" Patrice yelled.

"Well, before we go, we need to clean up first. That's very important. Are you ready for bath time?" Caliya asked.

Patrice, who was normally reluctant about taking baths, cooperated this time. While Caliya took her daughter's shirt off, Levell checked his watch. They were down to two hours before flight time.

"Baby, we gotta make it quick. Remember to bring your itinerary and ticket with you," he reminded Caliya.

Levell knew that in a few minutes, Avis would arrive to pick them up. Since the Thomas family didn't own a car yet, they had to call for transportation to get them to the airport where they would wait for their flight at the gate. A few minutes and a toddler bath later, Caliya, Patrice, and Levell were all packed and ready as they waited outside the door of their duplex home that they shared with their neighbor, Mrs. Alreeda.

Alma Alreeda was an elderly black lady who had been living next door since before Levell and his wife moved in. Over the past few years, Mrs. Alreeda had been more than a neighbor to Levell and Caliya. She was a motherly presence to them, and she would often help babysit Patrice whenever Levell or Caliya worked late into the night. Levell had grown to love Mrs. Alreeda immensely, and it was a love that was mutual since her husband, Glen, passed away three years ago.

While they were still packing, Levell took one of his family portraits that he had with Caliya and a baby Patrice aside, promising to give it to Mrs. Alreeda as a gift before he left town. Walking outside, they rang Mrs. Alreeda's doorbell. For the first few minutes, there was no response.

"Do you think Alma's home?" Caliya asked.

"I hope so," Levell replied. "She didn't tell me if she had any plans for today. She was supposed to see us off," he added.

After ringing the doorbell again, Mrs. Alreeda finally opened the door. Walking with a cane, she smiled when she saw Levell and his family. Tears started to well up in her eyes. "So is it really that time, Levy?" she asked.

Levell smiled. If anyone could get away with calling him "Levy," it was Mrs. Alreeda.

"Yeah, Alma, we're on our way to the peach state. We want to thank you for everything, from watching Tricee, to helping us sell. We can't thank you enough, and unfortunately this is all we can give to show our appreciation," he said, handing her the family portrait.

Mrs. Alreeda took the portrait and smiled serenely as she looked at them.

"I wish we could give you something more, but-" Levell started, but Mrs. Alreeda shook her head and waved her hand as if indicating that they didn't need to do anything more.

"Thank you so much, Levy. I will hang this on my front hall with my other sons and daughters because that's who you were to me. You're my son, and Caliya's my daughter. So I guess that would make Tricee my granddaughter," she said while bending over slightly to tickle Patrice, who laughed.

"Thanks, again. You were so much more than a neighbor to us. You're like a second mom to me, and I'm sure the feeling's mutual with Caliya," Levell replied.

"Yes, Alma, you mean so much to us. I wish we could take you with us," Caliya said.

Mrs. Alreeda smiled. "Yeah, I wish I could go, but my place is here. My family needs me here, and the good Lord always has a way to serve His purpose through anyone, no matter where they are," she replied, hugging Levell and his wife.

At the same time, the Avis van arrived to take them to JFK Airport. "Okay, honey, let's go," Levell said as he ushered his wife and daughter down the small steps of the house with their luggage.

As they entered the van, Levell waved back at Mrs. Alreeda, who stood at the edge of the stairs and watched the vehicle until it turned right into the busy intersection. While the van drove down the freeway, Caliya and Patrice played a game on an I-Pad. But all Levell could do was stare out the window at all the buildings, corner stores, and public schools, reflecting on his childhood and how all the public parks, basketball courts and public schools played a significant role in his early life. But none stood out more than one of the buildings they passed with an orange and blue sign in the front that read SOUTH JAMAICA HOUSING. While the building wasn't tall, it was wide. Many of the windows had bars on them, and graffiti was sprayed on the side of the building. It was significant to

Levell because it was where he grew up.

He remembered different events from his time in the housing projects, from battles on the basketball courts in the nearby park, to summer days riding bikes in and out of Jamaica Avenue with friends. Those were the memories he cherished. Then there were the less happy memories of living in the housing projects, not having enough money to eat certain days, living on welfare and food stamps, and having to walk over five miles to the laundromat just to wash clothes because his family couldn't afford a washer and a dryer. There were days he had to run home because he had seen kids being harassed my neighborhood gangs and days where he couldn't run but had to stand his ground.

Levell never considered himself a fighter, but he was a survivor. He fought for his family, he fought to stay alive, and he fought for respect. That was how rough the neighborhood was. Even though Levell and his family no longer lived in the south Jamaica housing projects, they applied survival tactics in their everyday lives, especially Levell, who used his persistence toward his schoolwork. Up until this day, he never regretted the choice to stay in school and get his degree. He remembered the peer pressure he received from many of his friends to drop out and join their gang or set, but he didn't want to waste his life.

Kennesaw, Georgia, would present another challenge for him, and it was one that he vowed he would be ready for...

Delta flight 8638 finally landed in Hartsfield Jackson Airport in Atlanta at 12:35. They took the airport concourse trains to the baggage claim area to pick up their luggage. Looking around, Levell saw no sign of his uncle.

"Honey, what time did you say Max would arrive?" Caliya asked.

"Well, he said he would be here a little after noon, so he should've been here already," Levell replied. "Let's walk towards the door. He probably never left his car. He did say that it's hard to find parking out here."

But no sooner as those words left his mouth, Levell saw his uncle, who seemed to be searching for them as well. Max wasn't as tall as Levell although he was slightly husky. Levell nudged his wife and pointed to

Max. Caliya laughed as well upon seeing that Max was unable to spot them. Gesturing to his family to follow, Levell walked over to Max.

"Uncle Max, as tall as I am, you mean to say that you couldn't see me?" Levell asked as Max turned around.

Realizing that it was his nephew, Max hugged Levell, Caliya, and Patrice. "What can I say, man? My eyesight's goin' bad. Call me Ray Charles in a few years," Max laughed.

"Yeah, it must be that," Levell laughed. "So where's Vicky and the rest of the fam?"

"Well, Vicky's at home with Jennifer, and I got Percy in the car waiting outside. As a matter of fact, we gotta go now cuz I'm in a no-park zone right now," Max replied as he helped Caliya with her bags and walked outside to the awaiting Chrysler minivan.

Max was the youngest brother of Levell's mother, Marie. When Levell was born, Max was only ten years old, so they weren't vastly apart in age. Percy, Max's son, helped pack the luggage into the minivan before they drove out onto I-75.

"Man, Percy, you gettin' taller every time I see you, son," Levell said as he patted the twelve-year-old's head on the front passenger seat. "You play any sports?"

"Yeah, I play basketball at Marietta Middle School," Percy replied.

"You should've seen him too, nephew," Max said as he drove down the interstate. "He was droppin' buckets last year in sixth grade. He was averaging almost thirteen points a game," he proudly added.

"Fourteen points a game," Percy corrected his father.

"Oh, okay. Fourteen points a game. My bad," Max replied sarcastically, as if there wasn't a huge difference in thirteen or fourteen points averaged in a season.

"Really?" Levell asked. "Sounds like I'm gonna have to put that to the test one day," he added, laughing.

Looking out the window of the minivan, right away, Levell could see the difference between Georgia and New York. There were more trees and less road lights. The highway roads were wider than those in New York. Atlanta was, indeed, a huge city. As they passed through, Levell saw the gigantic buildings, similar to those in Manhattan. But he quickly noticed that Atlanta was not as big as Manhattan. Levell only saw about eight tall buildings. Manhattan probably had twice, maybe three times, that amount.

As they were passing Atlanta, Max was busy explaining all of the city's trademarks.

"Over there is Centennial Park—you know, the place where they held the '96 Olympics. And right over there is Philips Arena where the Atlanta Hawks play. Right across there is the Georgia Dome where the Atlanta Falcons play."

"That's cool. What I'm wondering is how do ya get around? I mean there are hills and mountains everywhere down hea', and yeah, Atlanta ain't that big," Levell said, laughing.

Laughing too, Max replied, "Well, you still fresh out the city, so it ain't gonna be too big for you right now. But just give it a couple months, and go visit Atlanta, including Underground, CNN Center, and Georgia Aquarium. You'll forget about New York soon enough."

"Sorry, Uncle, no chance of that happening. Not even down here," Levell said. "I'll say this though. It's mad clean down here. No garbage, no bus exhaust smell every five minutes, or no subway tunnel smell. By the way, do ya even have subways down here?"

"Well, we got Marta, and that's something like a subway system," Max replied.

"That's it?" Levell asked.

"Yeah. But look, man, don't even worry about that. After we get you and Caliya and Patrice settled in, we gon' go car shopping, and we're gonna fix you both up with a nice whip," Max replied.

"I thought we were gonna wait a while before we went car shopping, or did the plan change?" Levell inquired.

"No, I just thought we would get your car before school started because, I'll just keep it real with you, the bus system in Marietta and Kennesaw has a lengthy wait time. You'll be late to work every day waiting on your bus. You'd probably be better off drivin' every day," Max said.

Levell agreed. He and Caliya both had a driver's license, but they just never owned a car. They had planned to pull their money together to buy one in New York, but with other expenses, rising sales taxes, and a mortgage, they were forced to hold off. However, when Levell applied for the teaching position at Kennesaw Mountain High School, he knew that they could no longer delay purchasing a car, even if they would have to pay a monthly car note.

As they arrived at Max's two-story home in Falcon's Landing, a subdivision in Marietta, Max unloaded all of Levell's luggage and brought them inside his house. The U-Haul truck was already in the driveway, and Levell couldn't wait to get to their new home and start unpacking.

It was a pain in the butt to pack when we were leaving New York, but it's a bigger pain in the rear to start unpacking once we get down here.

The Thomas family entered Max's home and greeted Vicky and Jennifer, the couple's nine-year-old daughter. They marveled over Patrice and how much she had grown since their last visit when she was just becoming a toddler. Max took them over to his guest room where Vicky had made all the arrangements for his nephew and his family.

Levell turned to Max. "Thanks again, Max. I hope we're not imposing on you. I promise, this is only temporary. As soon as we finalize the lease and move in, we'll be outta here," Levell said.

"Nonsense!" Max exclaimed. "Stay as long as you like, man. Once you get squared away, and you get settled in that nice new home of yours, we're just a phone call away. Unless you'd like to trade houses...I'll give you this old brick home for free, and I'll move to Kennesaw," Max laughed, winking slightly.

"Nah, I'm good. Besides, after the car and getting settled in, I got other things to do. I got to create my lesson plans for this semester, and then they have teacher's workdays for about three days before the first day of school. I guess I gotta go for a meet and greet," Levell replied.

"That sounds like fun," Max sarcastically rolled his eyes as he left the room.

Levell walked to the back door leading to Max's backyard. Max didn't have acres, but his backyard was vast. *Must be a pain when it comes to mowing the lawn.*

Birds chirping and singing to each other filled the air as Levell walked across the yard. Normally, he wasn't used to hearing birds chirping and leaves rustling. He was used to the bustling sounds of cars honking, pigeons flying around, and buses leaving their stops, along with other sounds he had heard growing up, like gunshots firing off at night.

But for the first time in many years, Levell heard what he'd always wanted to hear from New York and never did: silence. The serene silence was what drew him to Georgia and compelled him to take this new challenge of living in the South. But as he inhaled in a deep breath and released, he began thinking about the peace and tranquility that surrounded him. This peace had him wondering for the first time...

Maybe it's just too quiet.

Chapter 3

ITH MAX AND PERCY'S HELP, LEVELL BEGAN THE moving process as soon as the U-Haul truck was driven to his place. As Levell moved into Pine Mountain Club Subdivision, he took the time to take in the beauty of the area: no graffiti on building walls, no cars parked all over the street, and the home looked brand new. It was the fulfillment of a personal goal. If anyone would have told him five years earlier that he would be a homeowner, he would've laughed at the messenger's face. Not only was his credit history questionable at best, but he had also been so accustomed to renting and paying a landlord every month. It was that expense, among others, that irritated him. Levell considered himself an avid taxpayer and a public servant as an instructor in the New York Education System.

After all the tax payments over the years, Levell would have expected New York to cut the cost of living, improve conditions in public schools, and manage the gentrification of the area by opening more programs. However, none of those modifications came to fruition, which spurred the decision for Levell and Caliya to move down to Georgia. Through his uncle and another connection to his family, and upon learning that Kennesaw Mountain High School was looking to fill teaching vacancies in the English department, Levell decided to apply for the position.

Levell was beside himself with delight when he received the email confirming his hiring at the school. Unfortunately, the most challenging part of the process was carrying box after box of items they brought from New York. He blamed his wife in that regard for storing too many unnecessary items that he felt were perishable.

"Honey, I understand the chinaware, and I understand the dressers, but do we really need to take the plastic table fruit?" Exasperated, he'd asked his wife about it as he carried more boxes inside the home.

"Of course, Levey. Why not?" Caliya replied as she took the box and began adjusting the kitchen table.

They had agreed upon taking the furniture and coffee tables, as they did not want to spend an abundance of money buying completely new tables or dining room chairs. Besides making sure their credit was acceptable for the purchase of the home, they also had to put extra money aside to purchase vehicles. At first, Levell wanted to buy only one car for the whole family, but Caliya—a healthcare receptionist—would be working at Kennestone Hospital in Marietta. Neither the school nor the hospital was in walking distance from their home. Therefore, she insisted on buying a car as well.

Levell shook his head while thinking to himself. *Good thing I decided to put all my bonuses and extra, invested money in a separate account. Otherwise, we'd be walking to Kennesaw Mountain and Kennestone.*

While the men were busy at work, Caliya walked upstairs. Although she had taken a tour with the realtor and had seen the home, she still took in the spacious surroundings in the master bedroom. They had decided they would purchase a new mattress for it and a twin-sized bed for the guest room. The only bed they decided to keep from the move was Patrice's, which was brought over to her room. Holding her interactive toddler tablet in her hand, Patrice took a break from the games she was playing and began to watch intently as the men carried more items into their home. After what seemed like hours, they finally emptied out the truck.

"I'll tell you what, nephew," Max said as they unloaded the final box. "Forget paying the movers. You can pay me in advance so I can get a head start on the mortgage," he added, chuckling.

"Yeah right," Levell snickered.

With his money virtually going into his home and needed appliances, the last thought Levell had in his mind was giving family money. However, he did plan on paying Max once he was settled.

"I got you, Uncle Max," he replied. "Without you, I probably wouldn't have been able to get this done."

After Max and Percy left, Levell spent the day with Caliya setting up all their items in their rooms and bathrooms. Walking up to the master bedroom, he heard a song playing through his wife's I-Pad. She had raised the volume just loud enough for it to be heard downstairs. A young woman sang: "I'm starting a new life, I'm not looking back/Forgetting all the things that I lack/I know in the end, it works out for good/I never know how, but I knew you would."

"Baby, who's that on the radio?" Levell asked his wife, who was hanging up all the picture frames on the wall.

"Oh, that's Adia, the gospel singer. She was on I-Tunes, and you know I gotta have my music to work well," Caliya replied as she hung up their wedding picture.

Looking at the picture, Levell couldn't believe that it had been nine years since they got married. The wedding photo displayed a much younger Levell, with hair, standing next to a young, vibrant Caliya.

"I hear you. She got a real nice voice too," he replied as he walked over to help his wife straighten the picture.

After a few more minutes, they managed to perfectly align the picture and proceeded to set up more of their belongings. Once their room belongings were set up, Caliya prepared to go downstairs to the kitchen but before she could leave the room, Levell's hands wrapped around her waist from behind.

"Baby, c'mon we got more work to do. Quit playin'!" Caliya said laughing.

"We can take a break," Levell replied as he kissed his wife's neck. He was tired and sore from all the box-carrying and organizing of heavy furniture.

"A break huh?" Caliya asked. "Let's work on getting a bed first, before we get into bed activities," she added, smiling. Levell laughed as he faked an exasperated sigh.

"Oh ok, I guess I can wait, but you owe me," he replied as he released his wife from his hostage embrace.

"Besides, we also have to get the mattresses and the cars so we can be finished with the move completely," she said.

"Yeah, we need to get those things done. Max is coming by to take us to a car dealership tomorrow and we're going to Aaron's after that to look for a fridge and washer. Looks like we need a dryer too," Levell said after observing an empty space behind a door in the wall which would serve as his laundry room in his home.

While organizing kitchen silverware and putting the table mats in place, Caliya said, "Baby can you check on Patrice? She's been real quiet these last couple minutes. Either she's asleep or she's vanished," she added.

"Yeah, I got you. I'll go check on her right now," he said, stepping out of the kitchen and walked into Patrice's room.

Although not as big as the master bedroom, Patrice's bedroom was still bigger than the bedroom they had living in Queens. Levell walked up the stairs.

"Patrice? How are you? You ok?" Levell asked. Noticing that her door was still open, he looked in and smiled upon seeing his daughter, tablet in hand, fast asleep in her bed which was set up earlier by Max and Percy. Observing his beautiful daughter sleeping on her bed, Levell looked at her peaceful slumber.

Oh, what it would be like if I was a kid again. No worries in the world. Here we are, new residents in a new state and we're trying to adjust, but she's focused on just growing up and is sleeping soundly. She's sleeping a lot better than I probably will tonight.

Levell turned to leave, but not before taking a glance at the window facing his daughter's bed. He could've imagined it, but he saw a flash of what appeared to be black strands of hair or feathers flying quickly in his view. Walking towards the window, which remained shut, he looked outside. Facing his daughter's bedroom window was a huge pine tree, which towered over twenty feet high. From the thickness of its trunk,

Levell surmised that the tree had to be over a hundred years old. He didn't have a problem with the tree, but he knew that when fall and winter came, the tree would present problems if branches started hitting the window. It would startle his daughter who would run over to her parents and sleep in their bed, rather than to sleep alone. The black streak that Levell saw earlier had vanished.

Must've been a crow or some type of bird.

Levell walked away from the window to go downstairs, not realizing that he was being watched and that what he saw wasn't a crow.

"Nephew, you really outdid yourself on this one!" Max said enthusiastically as Levell brought a 2012 red Nissan Versa Sedan. They were at the car dealership on Cobb Parkway in Kennesaw where Levell closed the deal on his new vehicle. Just a few hours earlier, Caliya purchased a white 2011 Toyota Camry.

"Well, I needed something that said, 'Levell you gotta get around in style," Levell replied laughing.

"I see. Always the snazzy one, huh? My sister always said you liked the fancy stuff," Max said.

"Hey man, I'm not your regular teacher. I walk to the beat of my own drum," Levell replied, as they took a good look at the inside of the car.

Since it was a used car, they didn't have much to pay in terms of a car note. The dashboard looked clean, and the tires looked to be in fair condition. The car was confirmed to have passed all emissions' tests and had checked out. Once Levell and Caliya got their cars, the next order of business was to get their tags, which they obtained at the tag office. Once they had them in hand, they drove home. It was amazing that after a few trips up and down Cobb Parkway, Levell and Caliya were already familiar with Marietta, Kennesaw, and Acworth. Thankfully, it wasn't a hard area to memorize.

When it came to New York, whenever they took the bus or train, they always had to look at maps to visit certain places because of the vast population, except when it came to places they were familiar with, such as school or work. Normally, if there were appointments that required them to go to the city, they had to map subway and bus routes that would get them to the location. In Kennesaw, which was about an hour north of Atlanta, all the public places were contained in the city, and now since they were equipped with automobiles, Levell and Caliya didn't have to travel too far to go anywhere.

As they arrived home, Max's wife who was at their home, babysitting Patrice as they went to the car dealership, opened the garage for them. Vicky was nothing short of a God-send for Levell and Caliya because not only did she request vacation days from her job to help watch Patrice while they handled affairs for their new home, but she has offered to show them a tour of historic Marietta City, and went out her way to make sure they knew where to go whenever they needed to schedule doctor's appointments whenever they needed. The Marietta Primary Care center was very reputable, with great doctors and great staff. They worked with almost every insurance company offered and Levell was fortunate that he had the Blue Cross Blue Shield insurance to aid them. She also helped them locate an early education daycare for Patrice, which was the Primrose School in Kennesaw. The hours that the daycare operated fitted Levell and Caliya's schedule since they both worked daytime hours at school and the hospital.

After a few minutes in the house, Levell walked outside for some fresh air. Looking around, he saw people walking their dogs and a few houses down, kids were riding bikes, skateboarding, playing basketball in their driveways. In the house facing his own, there were a group of young white women talking on the front of their porch. They were laughing at some joke and Levell happened to notice that when he glanced at their direction, one of the girls shot him a look back in return. She smiled and waved at Levell and he waved back at her.

This southern hospitality thing never stops down here. Everybody's nice down here. I could get used to this.

The girl looked to be no more than eighteen or nineteen years of age. Her body was fully developed, and she had jet-black hair. The image of the black streak that he saw outside Patrice's window flashed in Levell's mind, but after thinking it over, he shook his head.

There's no way that girl was outside my window this morning. My daughter's on the second floor. She would've had to climb that tree.

Maybe he was starting to lose it. All the stress of moving had him seeing illusions. Turning to re-enter his home, Levell heard one of the girls calling him.

It was the girl with the jet-black hair.

"Hi!" she greeted in a bubbly voice that had a slight southern drawl to it.

Normally, Levell was weary of strangers who came to greet him directly. He always considered anyone outside his immediate family and inner circle of close friends, strangers. But this girl appeared harmless. In fact, she was a bit quirky and maybe a bit too happy.

In less than a minute, she had crossed the street over to Levell's front yard and introduced herself. As she made her way over, Levell couldn't help but notice the girl's shapely figure. She had what guys back in his old hood called "that hourglass figure." She was wearing a pink t-shirt that appeared to be a couple sizes too small and small green shorts with flip-flops. For a moment, Levell had to remind himself that he was out of the game and was married, so he couldn't be scoping the girl like he was doing at that moment. But he couldn't deny it. If he wasn't married, and if he was about fifteen years younger, he would've tried to court the girl. But to be polite, he allowed her to proceed to his front yard.

"My name's Raven Roberts. I live right there," she said pointing to the house facing Levell's home. "You must be my new neighbor," she added.

Levell shook her hand and realized that Raven had a beautiful smile. She didn't have a snaggle tooth at all, so Alicia was incorrect about that assessment.

"Yeah, I'm Levell Thomas," he replied.

"Nice to meet you Mr. Thomas," Raven said. "So how do you like it down here so far?"

Levell looked around as if he was studying his surroundings again. "It's peaceful. Very quiet. I'm still not used to it yet, but I'll get there."

"Where are you from?" she asked.

"I'm from New York," he replied.

Raven's eyes widened, as if in amazement. "Really? That's so cool.

So, did you ever go to the Statue of Liberty?"

That's a strange question. How come when people learn that I'm from New York, they automatically assume that I visited the Statue of Liberty?

Levell recalled a similar incident during his first visit to Georgia. He went to a Publix supermarket on Cobb, and as he was talking to Caliya, a man walked up behind him. Based on his green apron and the Publix logo, Levell knew that the man stocked groceries there.

"Y'all sound funny. Y'all not from 'round here, ain't cha?" he asked.

Levell remembered turning to look at the guy as if he was smoking substances. What did he mean by "sound funny?" Levell started to feel his blood boil, but Caliya answered the man.

"We're from New York," she replied.

"Oh so y'all are Yankees, huh?" he asked.

Levell didn't know if the guy was trying to be funny or not. All he knew was that he was getting more impatient and annoyed by the second. The only Yankees he knew normally played in a diamond field in the Bronx, but he never really followed baseball.

"I guess," was all he could reply at the time.

Later that day, Max explained what the grocer meant by his statement. "Nah, don't sweat that, Levell," he'd replied. "He meant to say that you're from New York, New Jersey, Massachusetts, whatever. It just means you're from up north."

Levell was grateful that his uncle modified and translated what the man tried to say because, if it wasn't explained, Levell might've taken it as an insult. At the end of it, he concluded that some of these people probably never left Georgia, much less flown up to New York, and they were not familiar with certain tones and accents.

But Raven didn't seem to be that oblivious to reality. She seemed merely curious.

"Well, I've been to the Statue of Liberty before, but that was such a long time ago," he answered.

Looking behind her, Levell saw Raven's friends waiting for her on the porch. They seemed to be watching her conversation intently, which Levell thought was quite odd.

"I think your friends are waiting for you back there," he pointed out.

But Raven waved her hand dismissively in their direction. "Oh, don't mind them. They can wait a little while longer. I saw you move in with your wife and your daughter," she continued, abruptly changing the subject. "She is such a little cutie! How old is she?"

"Thanks, and yeah she's three years old, going on thirty," Levell laughed.

Raven laughed also.

"She's a little adult, and she picks things up very early, like folding napkins, doing some cleaning, and she's very savvy with technology. She's growing up too fast for my good," he continued.

"Well it sounds like she's got awesome parents, and she'll grow up to be a very bright young lady," Raven replied.

"Thanks. Caliya and I do our best to raise her to be respectable and responsible," Levell said.

At the same moment, a tall thin white man with a mustache and goatee emerged from Raven's house. Standing behind Raven's friends, he glared intently at Raven and Levell.

"That's my father," Raven said as she turned to cross the street to walk home. "I'll talk to you later," she added.

Levell looked at Raven's father and smiled at him, waving his hand. However, the man did what Levell didn't expect him to do and turned around and entered the house without so much as a smile or nod, shutting the door behind him.

What was that all about? I guess southern hospitality's not contagious.

Levell also turned and went inside his home. Walking into the kitchen, he saw Caliya with Vicky and Patrice, who ran to hug him. "How's my big girl doing?" Levell picked his daughter up.

"I'm doing great, Daddy! Me and Tati' Vicky colored today. See?" Patrice held up a piece of paper from a coloring book. Although she had colored all over the page, as was expected, most of her coloring stayed in the lines.

"This looks great. You are gonna be a great artist," he said, kissing her cheeks.

"So, Levey, who were you talking to outside?" Caliya asked.

"Oh, I was talking to our neighbor Raven. She lives right across the street from us hea'," Levell replied, pointing outside to the porch where the girls were sitting just moments before although the porch was currently empty.

"You know, something weird happened out there. So, I see her father walking out the door, and me and Raven were making conversation. Then once she saw her father, it was like a light switch. She ran back over there quicker than lightning," he said.

"Well, maybe she had to go home for dinner," Caliya rationalized.

"But that's not the end of it though," Levell said abruptly. "When I waved to her father, he acted as if he ain't seen me and then just went back in the house."

"Well then maybe he didn't see you, baby. Don't worry about it," she assured him.

"I mean, I'm not worried, but the guy saw me, Caliya. He made eye contact with me. Then he just turned around and slammed the door behind him as if he was mad that I was talking with his daughter. He had all her friends staring at me, like I was the devil or something," he said.

Caliya walked over to Levell and rubbed the top of his head, which he liked. "Baby, you are reading too much into this. I'm sure there's a logical explanation," she said, turning to Vicky.

But Vicky, who seemed unsure of what to say at that moment, could only shrug.

"Well, I'm gonna go take a shower and catch a nap," Levell said as he turned around and headed upstairs to the bathroom.

Chapter 4

O NOT GO WHERE THE PATH MAY LEAD; GO INSTEAD where there is no path and leave a trail.

Placing the Ralph Waldo Emerson quote in his pocket, Levell headed to the bathroom. Only a few minutes after the alarm clock on his phone woke him up shortly after 6:00 a.m. This day was the first day of school for students in Cobb County, and Levell was keen on meeting his students.

The moving process took weeks, but when Levell and Caliya finally finished settling in, there were only a couple boxes remaining, and Levell thought it was best to place the remaining box in the attic located above the hallway corridor upstairs. With his stuff packed away, he found time to focus on creating the lesson plan for the semester, marking off his calendar where he had pre-planned for the school year. The lesson plans normally never changed for Levell, besides adding a couple more reading assignments for students, and there would be a mandatory project for the students to complete before final exams.

In his mind, Levell wanted to make the project a venture that the students would embark on as a group, but the curriculum requested that the project be a research paper with instructions given on how to write a paper in MLA style. He could already hear the sighs of his students as he imagined them finding out that they had to complete a research paper. It was not so much that Levell had issues with the research paper, but he was an interactive professor and didn't see the benefit of assigning a school paper to his students just so they could retain what they learned in class. After showering and brushing his teeth, Levell walked over to his wife.

"Wake up, baby. Time to go to work," he whispered in his wife's ear.

Caliya stirred but turned her back towards Levell as she tried to stay in bed. When he nudged her again, she finally woke up, annoyed.

"Levell, I don't gotta be at work for another hour," she groaned as she stood up from her bed.

"You're gonna need that hour, baby, or did you forget how Atlanta traffic gets down?" Levell replied.

Upon realizing what Levell said, Caliya ran to the bathroom, concerned that she was running late.

"Luckily, the hospital is just about fifteen minutes away, so you might still make it," Levell assured Caliya.

After they got dressed, Levell walked over to his car, after opening the garage gate. As he made his way out, Caliya soon followed with Patrice in her hands. Caliya had planned to drop her off at Primrose School for early education.

Wearing his favorite blue pastel shirt with a white and blue tie, Levell anticipated starting work in the new school. He couldn't think of any more ways to thank Max for all his assistance in helping him settle and giving him bits of advice about Atlanta and Kennesaw, including shortcuts on getting to work and to the hospital as well as pharmacies to use to pick up essential medicines.

All these pharmacies and drugstores down here, and they don't even have a Duane Reade.

Levell chuckled to himself as he remembered one of the most popular pharmacies in Queens, New York.

Finally arriving at Kennesaw Mountain High School, Levell couldn't help but to look in awe at the structure of the school. The school building was not as tall as it was vastly wide. Having visited other high schools during his time in New York, Levell normally saw tall buildings, maybe four or five stories high, when it came to certain schools that he visited, but Kennesaw Mountain High was a league of its own when it came to building structure. Instead of focusing on height, the committee that funded the construction of this institution had focused on the length and the extra space on campus.

The first time Levell visited the school, he was in the office being interviewed for the position before he moved down to Kennesaw permanently. It was so huge, it almost reminded him of a college campus. Even some colleges in New York that he had seen didn't compare to Kennesaw Mountain High School. York College on Guy R. Brewer Road in Jamaica was huge, but nothing compared to KMHS at the high school level.

After locating the staff parking lot, Levell got out and walked inside the school, showing his ID to the security guard on duty. The ID's were provided during the teacher workday meetings that took place a few days before the first day of school.

During the teacher-workday meetings, Levell met other ambitious professors, including Mr. Finn, the World History teacher, and Mrs. Minick, the freshman Algebra teacher. He also met Mr. Caldwell, the health teacher, and Mrs. Wellington, the band instructor. All the professors were great people with different personalities, most of whom had lived in Georgia for a greater majority of their lives.

Picking up the attendance sheets at the office, Levell walked over to his classroom. The workday had also allowed teachers to decorate their classrooms, should they choose to do so. Levell posted his usual posters of literary figures, such as William Shakespeare, Alexander Dumas, and Edgar Allen Poe, among others, that he bought over from Hillcrest High School. Looking at his attendance sheets, Levell realized that he would be teaching three periods straight before his free period when he normally ate lunch. Then he had two more periods in the afternoon. Normally during a school day, there were six class periods before 3:15 when school ended. It would be quite a workload for Levell but nothing that he wasn't accustomed to before.

Suddenly hearing loud engines roaring outside, Levell looked out his window. The yellow buses had begun arriving and parking while students began to exit them.

These kids got it so made down here. They got buses that they can take for free while children in New York still have to pay bus fare or get a student Metro-Card on top of it.

Even when students didn't have bus fare, they always took the subways, which unfortunately was not an option in Georgia.

Waiting on the first warning bell that would ring at about 8:20, Levell looked over his agenda for the day. First days of school were always light. All they would do was go over the class syllabus, the school rules, and the whole spill on discrimination and how it was against school rules and the laws of behavioral conduct. It wouldn't be until the second day of class when they would dive into their lessons. He taught the upperclassmen, which meant that his students would be no younger than sixteen and no older than nineteen.

Levell selected to teach World Literature because, although he was perfectly capable of teaching ninth-grade level Literature as well as American Literature or British Literature, he simply did not have too much patience to deal with many freshman and sophomore students. It wasn't that he hadn't taught them before, as was the case in Hillcrest High School where a couple of sophomores would be sitting in his classes after completing their English credits earlier. Overall, Levell felt comfortable about the decision to teach the junior and senior class. He felt that he was guiding his students one step closer to graduation, and that was his goal. Just as he had done for so long at Hillcrest, he wanted to contribute assistance to the students and faculty.

With the wall clock displaying 8:27, Levell began to watch the students file in his classroom. He made sure that he had at least twenty-seven chairs, just in case there were a few stragglers or procrastinators who missed registering for classes and would walk in a few minutes late. As the class continued to fill up, Levell picked up his attendance sheet and began to write his name on the marker board.

Finally, the final bell rang. The students who had filed in earlier were talking among themselves, no doubt asking each other about their summers. The seniors were always talking about some party that occurred the previous weekend.

Levell rolled his eyes. These kids were no different than he was when he attended high school, but the only difference was the improvements in technology, which was more to their advantage.

Growing up, Levell remembered a time when his classes didn't even have computers in every room like they did nowadays. If they had to do any type of research, they had to go to the library and pick up books or search the website that would have the information that was needed. But now, I-Phones and I-Pads were coming along, and with access to the World Wide Web, the demand for books had decreased rapidly.

Seeing his room nearly full, Levell decided to start the class off.

"Good morning, everyone. My name is Mr. Thomas. Welcome to World Lit," he said, introducing himself to the students.

Internally, Mr. Thomas was pleased to see students from many different cultures in his classrooms. He still had more white kids in his class, which he didn't have a problem with, but he would've loved to have seen more black kids as well. But on this day, he saw some black kids, some Hispanic kids, and a few who were potentially from other cultures.

"For those who don't know me or haven't met me, I'll give you a little background," Mr. Thomas continued. "Attended and graduated from Bayside High School, class of 1998. Then I attended Queens College and got my degree in English and decided to pursue a teaching career. I taught at Hillcrest High School in Queens, New York, for a few years before moving down here," he finished.

Picking up the attendance sheet, Levell began to call roll. He knew that it would take him a few days to memorize all the names, maybe longer, since he did have five total classes to teach.

"We're going to do it a little different today," Levell said. "When I call your name, I would like for you to stand up and tell me one thing that you like to do the most," he added.

Some kids rolled their eyes as if the whole process was pointless, but others laughed among themselves. Although he was new to the school, Levell was determined to show his students right away that he was not like other professors, and he was cut from a different cloth. One by one, all the students stood up and introduced themselves and told the class what they loved to do.

Levell started to notice a trend. The boys who were in the class seemed to show interest in two activities: sports and video games. Levell couldn't even count on one hand how many had replied that they loved to play their PS4 or their Xbox game sets. The girls, on the other hand, were avid viewers of drama TV shows and those unrealistic "reality shows" that were popular.

Throughout all the responses that Levell received, he was quite alarmed at the fact that none of his students expressed an interest in reading books. That told him that he was going to have his work cut out for him. He had textbooks, slides, and video presentations of the stories they would be covering, but if they didn't show any type of desire to read or develop critical thinking and analytical skills when it came to discussing books from different eras, he feared that it might not be a great semester for most of them. There were a few boys that expressed interest in other activities though.

One student that stood out to Levell was a black student by the name of Xavier Jones. "What's up y'all?" he introduced. "My name's Xavier, and I like to be a pimp," he said in his laid-back manner, causing some students to laugh loudly.

"A pimp? Really?" Levell asked Xavier, while other students watched intently to see how Levell would react.

Normally, teachers they were familiar with wouldn't entertain certain types of crude humor. But they didn't know Levell Thomas too well.

"So, you mean to tell me that you would send out a bunch of women to make money for you, by doing what you probably can't do," he said, while the other students laughed when they realized Mr. Thomas made a crack on a student's sexual ability.

Xavier was a good sport about the joke and laughed as well.

Another student that stood out was a white girl with blonde hair by the name of Brooke Wilder. "Hi, my name is Brooke, and I want to be a pediatrician when I get older, but I love to model," she said.

"Oh okay, so we got a model in the house. Nice. Do you do runway modeling?" Levell asked.

"Yeah, I performed in a couple shows this past summer," Brooke replied.

"Excellent," Levell replied. "Why don't you give us a demonstration? Show us what you got," he added encouragingly.

Brooke's eyes darted left to right, and she shifted in her chair uncomfortably.

"You mean, right now?" she asked nervously.

"Yeah, sure. Why not? That way, if you get that casting call from America's Next Top Model, I can say that she used to model in our class," Levell replied while other students laughed, but a few joined Levell in encouraging Brooke to do an impromptu runway model walk down the classroom desk aisle.

Some students moved their desks, and Brooke took a deep breath and walked down the aisle, model-style, even turning left to right as if she was attempting to impress some judges on the side. As she walked back to her seat, Levell clapped and others joined him. This was all part of Levell's strategy of breaking the ice with his students. He couldn't be a stiff stick-in-the-mud teacher that students complained about. The learning experience should be as enjoyable as possible in Levell's point of view, and past teaching experience has shown him that the more engaged students are in the classroom, the more most of them would pass his classes.

Glancing at his attendance sheet, he was certain that he read all his students' names, but at the very last moment he realized he missed calling a student's name. In fact, it was a name that he was introduced to before.

How did she end up in my class?

Levell looked around the room but didn't see her until he heard the door open. In she walked, twenty minutes late.

"Sorry I'm late," Raven said, her eyes cast downward before looking at Levell, not recognizing him at first, before doing a double take and looking at him again, her eyes wide open, smiling.

"Hi, you're…" she started to state, pointing at Levell before realizing that the whole classroom was staring at her, hanging at her every word, waiting for what was about to come out of her mouth.

"And you're late, Ms. Roberts," Levell said in his best stern voice.

"Please find a seat"

"Sorry," Raven whispered furtively as she made her way through the aisle to sit at one of the empty desks in the back.

Levell began handing out copies of the syllabus to everyone in the class. When he got to Raven, he handed her a copy as well. Raven tried smiling at Levell to ease tension, but he continued handing out the copies.

"Okay folks, this syllabus is detailed with all the rules and regulations regarding assignment deadlines, dates of exams, honor code, and tardiness," he said, looking at Raven's direction upon the word "tardiness." Going over the syllabus in detail, he explained the percentage of all exams and tests that would be taken during the semester.

"Please also be aware that I don't give any extra credit," Levell said. "If you miss an assignment or an exam, there are only three make-up dates. If you fail to show up on those make-up dates, you will receive an automatic zero for the assignment or test."

He went over the parameters of the research assignment that would be counted as a project paper.

"Yes, there is a research paper due the week before finals," he said, while the other students groaned. "C'mon guys, it's not that bad. Just make sure you follow the MLA format example that is listed on the syllabus, and you should do just fine," he added, pointing to a section on the assignment.

"In this paper, you will pick one of the stories that we go over this semester, whether it be Geoffrey Chaucer's *Canterbury Tales* or Miguel Cervantes' *Don Quixote*. I want you guys to pick a story and choose one out of the six essay questions that involves analyzing and breaking down the characterization and significant view points of the story," he finished.

A few hands raised as Levell completed his explanation of the project. "For those of you who're going to ask if you can use Sparknotes or Pink Monkey, the answer is no. I want you to go online and look up actual links to aid you in writing the paper," he said firmly, satisfied that a couple hands lowered upon explaining that detail.

As he continued to explain the layout of his plan for the semester, the bell rang, signaling the end of the period.

"Okay guys, for next class I want you to read chapter one, which talks about early literature, and get started on reading *The Epic of Gilgamesh*," he said as the students started to file out.

Levell sat down behind his desk and took out the attendance sheet for the next class.

One class down. Four to go.

Levell secretly hoped that he could keep up the pace. He was sure that once he'd had his morning coffee, it wouldn't be an issue. While thinking of the next class, he didn't realize that Raven stood over him with a look of dismay on her face.

"Levell, why'd you embarrass me like that in front of everyone?" she asked.

What did she call me? The nerve of this girl. Doesn't she know where she's at?

Levell looked up at Raven, her eyes seemingly goring into his own. "Listen, Raven, when we're in class in a student-teacher environment, you're to address me by Mr. Thomas. You understand? Besides, I didn't embarrass you. You did that on your own by coming in late."

"I know, I know. I'm sorry, okay? I just got busy at home at the last moment, and I didn't think I would be this late coming to class," Raven explained. "But there was no reason to put me on blast like that in front of people. You seemed so cool when we spoke that other day."

Yeah, but that was before I knew that you would be a student in my class. Now I gotta burn that bridge.

Sighing deeply, Levell looked at Raven, her long black hair was flowing behind her back, and her blue eyes filled with what he thought was remorse. "Okay, Raven. I apologize for my tone towards you when you walked into class."

"It's just that I set such a high bar for my students, and I expect nothing less than effort when it comes to my classes, and that goes for everyone. Just because we live next to each other, doesn't mean I'm gonna give you any preferential treatment over everyone else," he explained. "I know the school says they don't penalize you for being late on the first week of school, but I expect that from freshman and sophomores. If I'm correct, you're a junior, aren't you?"

"Yeah, I'm a junior," Raven confirmed.

"So being at that level, I expect all my students to learn how to develop some inner-discipline to start coming to class early. Create a habit for yourself," Levell explained.

Raven nodded to confirm that she understood. "Okay, and I promise I won't be late to any more classes," she said.

Levell smiled at her. "Great! Now I gotta prepare for my next class. You should get going too before you arrive late for your next period, and you'll have to hear the same boring tardy lecture I just gave you," he said, laughing.

"Yeah, I should go. Thanks. Bye!" she said, waving at him before she left. As she walked out, she turned back around and watched Levell work at his desk, unable to take her eyes away from his broad shoulders, chiseled muscles, and that great smile.

And that bald head and goatee is definitely a plus. She pictured running her fingers over his head repeatedly, the smooth sensation of his skin against her own.

"Raven, what's up? Who you lookin' at?" her friend Sarah Whittman said, shaking Raven from her thoughts.

"Nobody. Let's go. I think you got Spanish II with me," Raven said, abruptly changing the subject as she walked down the hallway to her next class.

Chapter 5

OVER THE NEXT TWO WEEKS, LEVELL STARTED TO settle into his new surroundings and continued cementing what he believed to be an early teaching legacy at Kennesaw Mountain High School. He started to shake off his prior feelings of apprehension and appeared to be more comfortable teaching his classes. He hated to admit it, but he found out the students in Georgia were much more receptive than the students he'd had in New York. He didn't want to disparage the students he left behind in Queens, but if he had to be truthful, he would say that the classes he taught at Hillcrest High School had one or two students who were difficult to teach in class, which annoyed him at times. There was no such student in Kennesaw Mountain High, and he was grateful for that aspect.

Level Thomas got acquainted with the other teachers in Kennesaw Mountain. Mrs. Yvette Turner taught social studies at the next class over from him. When they met, he was surprised to find that she was born and raised in New York as well, although not in Queens. She was born in Brooklyn. There was Mr. Andre Price, the math teacher, who taught various levels of math, including Algebra I, Algebra II and Geometry. Unlike Mrs. Turner, Mr. Price was born and raised in Georgia, in Decatur to be exact. There was Mr. Simmons, a health and wellness teacher, who was a no-nonsense type of teacher.

There were other teachers in the school, but Levell frequently spoke with those three, in particular, during their lunch breaks or free periods, and some of the conversations they had were very amusing. If students didn't think teachers talked about them, Levell would be the first to debunk that theory. Once in the confines of the teacher's lounge or at their table at the cafeteria, the teachers would discuss their students, especially the difficult ones. Levell would often listen while Mr. Simmons complained about a few of his students who often acted out in class.

"Hey, Thomas, how about we change places? You teach health and PE, and I'll teach English," Mr. Simmons said, laughing while they were in the break room on one of their free periods.

"Sorry, man, I don't the patience to teach your kids. Hell, I barely have the patience to teach my own," Levell laughed.

"Really? I wouldn't have noticed it. You're the man 'round here brother," Mr. Simmons said. "I would be walking down the hallway and whenever I glance inside that classroom, I see you doing your thing."

"Well, I got a good crop this year. Maybe next semester the roles will be reversed and you'll be the one with the nice senile kids, and I'll be teaching a class full of rebels," Levell said.

"Well when that time comes, let me know, and I won't feel twice as bad," Mr. Simmons laughed. "Anyway, Thomas, we got a football game this coming Friday. We gotta play Harrison High School which is our first home game of the season. You in?" he asked Levell.

But Levell wasn't sure if he wanted to attend the game. It wasn't as if he hated football. Quite the contrary, he loved watching football, from the NFL to certain college teams on ESPN. Levell had never watched a football game at the high school level, and he wasn't eager on attending, but he didn't want to turn down the invite. So, he accepted the invitation to go to the game.

"Okay, so kick-off starts at 7:00 p.m. I'll see you there," Mr. Simmons said as he excused himself to head over to prepare for the next class.

Levell also vowed to bring Caliya to the game along with Patrice, as they both loved sports. Heading back to his class for the next period, Levell reviewed his notes. In all his classes, he was schedule with the lesson plan. All his students were currently in the middle of reading *The Epic of*

Gilgamesh, and their assignments had been to write a synopsis of the story and answer character traits shown by the main characters. It was not a difficult assignment, and many of the students already handed in their papers. Levell graded a few of the assignments that were brought in by the students who didn't wish to wait till the submission date to turn in their work.

One of the students who handed in her assignments early was Raven. She submitted a complete diagnosis on Enkidu, the partner of Gilgamesh who, according to the tale, died during their conquests and journey to find the meaning of life and death. When Levell graded the papers, he was pleased and quite surprised by Raven's complete analysis of Enkidu. Levell chuckled as he recalled the first day of class when Raven had strolled into his classroom almost thirty minutes late. At first, he thought that she was going to be one of those troubled students that he feared. But, thankfully, she had proven him wrong. Raven had come to class on time every day for the past two weeks. She was an active participant during class discussions, sometimes getting so impassioned that she would spark up debates in the classroom at times. Levell had no problem with her inside or outside the class.

There were times when she would be a bit unbearable, sticking around after class to engage in certain small talk over the subject matter or to ask about the assignments. But Levell was never one to turn any student down. And no matter how many times Raven stayed after class, he answered all of her questions. Today was no exception.

"So, Mr. Thomas, are you gonna go to the game tonight?" she asked him.

"Yeah, I wasn't gonna go at first, but I guess I'll check this team out," he replied.

At once, Raven's eyes lit up. "That's great!" she said enthusiastically. "My daddy always sayin' that our football team ain't shit. Hopefully, this will be the year where we prove him wrong."

Levell shrugged his shoulders. "I don't know. I guess we'll see tonight," he replied as she walked out his classroom door.

As the sun began its descent and the sky held its setting glow, hundreds of Kennesaw Mountain parents, alumni, and students made their way over to the football field where the fans were awaiting their team to run out of their locker room tunnel onto the field. The Kennesaw Mountain High School marching band was playing different songs, some of which were popular current ones. Others were more outdated, but the sounds of trumpets, trombone, drums, and other instruments rang through the night.

Levell, Caliya, and Patrice made their way to the field and stood among the crowd of students, most of them with green and black painted across their faces and chests. The "Mustang Stampede," as it were known across the county, had some one of the most raucous fans that were appreciated by the home team, yet hated by their opposition. It was no secret that Kennesaw Mountain High School had developed athletic rivalries with neighboring schools Harrison and North Cobb. After Levell paid for the tickets, he walked over to the stands. His mouth dropped in shock as he saw how vast the field was and how many people were in the stands. On one side of the field, the stands were reserved for the Harrison Hoya fans who shouted and yelled their support for their team while jeering the Mustang fans.

Levell looked at the stands and the amount of people who came out to watch the game. *Man, when they told me that football was king down here, they weren't joking.*

Levell attempted to find a place to sit along with Caliya and Patrice. The football game was no joke in the South as he soon found out. They played football in New York all the time, but high school football in New York City was not hyped up as much as the football games in Georgia. It was a different world down in Georgia when it came to football. Levell even saw the local news sports affiliate van parked at the other end of the field with cameras were out, taping the event. The Harrison Hoya players were out on the field warming up and the Kennesaw Mountain players were still in their locker rooms. Levell was eagerly waiting for Kennesaw Mountain to emerge from their tunnel.

One of their best players, a wide receiver by the name of Adriel Branch, was regarded as one of the fastest players in the county, racking up about 225 yards a game. He also happened to be a student in one of

Levell's classes. The Kennesaw Mountain quarterback, Lee Hampton, was a savvy senior veteran player whose connections with Branch on the field were precise, swift, and on their way to becoming legendary, as they had more passes completed between them than any other quarterback-wide receiver combo in Mustang history.

At last, it was game time. The Harrison Hoya squad, being the road team, ran on the field first, bursting through their banner as they did. Then, only a few minutes later, the band played Kennesaw Mountain's fight song. Emerging from their tunnel bursting through their banner was the Mustang squad.

"Daddy, look! Here they come!" Patrice yelled in excitement as they ran out into the cool Friday night.

After the coin toss was completed, the Mustangs elected to punt to Harrison to start the game. Right from the first snap of the football, Levell already knew the game was over. Harrison seemed unable to crack the Mustangs' defensive sets, so it only took a few plays before Harrison's freshman quarterback threw a pick-six, picked off by a Mustang cornerback who ran to the end zone for a touchdown. At the end of the first quarter, Mustangs were leading fourteen to zero. By this time, the other Mustang fans were yelling themselves hoarse, celebrating every touchdown, shouting support for the defensive players. The noise was so ear-piercing, that Patrice covered her ears, attempting to block the sounds out.

During the second quarter, a group of young white boys and girls made their way over to the stands, passing through people in the same row as Levell. Upon seeing him, one of the girls stopped in her tracks. The identity of this girl was no surprise to Levell.

"Hi, Mr. Thomas!" Raven waved and greeted her teacher. She was wearing jean shorts that hiked all the way up to her thighs. She was also wearing a regular Nike t-shirt, but the t-shirt was rolled all the way up to her upper chest, exposing her bare midriff.

Judging by the way her upper chest moved, Levell could tell right away that Raven was not wearing a bra. He was thankful that it wasn't raining, or it would've been reminiscent of his college days when he and some fraternity brothers held wet t-shirt contests. Practically every woman from every walk of life at that college showed up in all white tees, ready to be doused with water and expose their breasts that became saturated through their white shirts.

"Hey, Raven, what's up?" Levell greeted casually.

"I'm good!" Raven replied brightly. Turning to her friends, she introduced them, starting with a red-headed girl, short and petite, but very much well-endowed like Raven.

"This is Ginger Grant, and this is Haley Settle," she said, pointing to another girl with brunette brown hair who joined them.

Levell recalled seeing Tammy sitting on the stoop the very same day that he met Raven for the first time.

"And this is my boyfriend Tex Brown and his friend Ron Holder."

While the girls kindly greeted Levell, the two boys made no attempt to shake Levell's hand and only nodded at him as if they were acknowledging his presence for the first time. To divert the growing tension between the boys and Levell, Raven walked over to Patrice, who held her mother's hand nervously.

"Oh my God. Mr. Thomas, is that your daughter? She's so cute," Raven gushed as she went to shake Patrice's hand. "How are you?" she asked.

Patrice was so shy that Levell had to coax her to reply to Raven. "I'm fine," she replied.

"I bet you are. You're a beautiful little girl. How old are you?" Raven asked.

"Three," Patrice replied, holding up three fingers.

"Wow, that's amazing!" Raven replied.

"Yeah, she's a little adult," Levell replied. "Oh, by the way this is my wife, Caliya," he added, introducing his wife.

Raven's joviality disappeared immediately, unbeknownst to Levell, but she still greeted Caliya respectfully. "Well, we're gonna go find our seats. See you in class on Monday!" Raven said as she continued to make her way to her seat near the student section.

"On time, I hope?" Levell asked, laughing.

Raven turned back around. "Mr. Thomas, you know good and well I've came to class early since the first day. Don't try to play me," she laughed as she walked away.

As Raven walked out of earshot, Caliya turned to Levell, staring at him intently. Raven's strange behavior did not go unnoticed.

"What?" Levell asked innocently.

"Did you see how that girl looked at me?" she asked indignantly.

"What do you mean?" Levell asked.

"I mean, when she was talking with you and Patrice, she was all happy and bubbly and laughing. Then when she saw me, she turned her face down. Don't you find that weird?" she asked.

Levell looked at his wife, certain that her insecurity had driven her to temporary paranoia.

"What are you talkin' about?" he asked. "I was right here, and she introduced herself to you, like she did to me and Patrice," he said.

Before Caliya could reply, the crowd around them cheered loudly. Kennesaw Mountain had scored another touchdown, and by this time the score was twenty-eight to zero, which was virtually a rout.

"I don't know, Levell. I just don't have a good feeling about this girl," Caliya said.

"Come on, Caliya. Just because she won't say 'hi' to you? Don't you think you're overreacting a little bit?" Levell asked, his eyes still trained on the game.

"I just don't know, baby. I don't trust her," Caliya said flatly.

This time Levell stared at her.

"Look, Caliya, I know you're probably jealous and hating, but I have eyes for you only. Listen, we'll talk about it after the game, okay?" he asked.

"Okay, fine," Caliya answered reluctantly.

As the game clock wound down to zero, signaling half time, Levell told his wife that he was going to the restroom, and on his way back he would stop at the concession stand. Walking through the throng of overjoyed Mustang fans and dejected Hoya fans, Levell made his way to the restroom door just outside the football team's locker room, but the stalls were all being used, and there was a line. Levell decided to open the side school doors, which had been left open, and use the school restrooms. He was relieved to find empty stalls. As he finished he washed his hands and turned the light off before exiting the restroom.

While he made his way back to the stands, passing many classrooms in the dark school corridors, Levell heard a sound. It wasn't the loud screaming heckling voices of the fans outside, but as he listened closely, he realized the sound he heard was moaning. It was a sound of a girl who was either moaning in pain or moaning for a different reason: pleasure.

As he passed the classrooms, he leaned his right ear closer to the classroom doors. The more he walked, the louder the moans were. Nothing but sheer instinct drove him to look through one of the classroom doors where the source of the sound was. Before he saw anyone, he knew he had stumbled across a scene that he was not meant to witness.

Two figures were on the ground, their nude bodies intertwined and moving in rhythmic motion. A young girl and boy were in the dark moonlit classroom having sex on the floor. All their clothes were removed and were piled in a heap just a few inches away. They were lying on what looked like a blanket and next to the blanket was a condom packet, opened at the tip.

At first, Levell couldn't make out the identity of the young couple, but as he looked closer, he finally recognized them. Tex Brown was lying on his back, his arms enveloped around a female companion—a girl who, to Levell's shock did not resemble Raven at all. As the girl flipped her red hair back, Levell recognized Ginger, who was with Raven earlier when she introduced them. Levell knew it would only be a moment before he would be seen by them. Certainly, he couldn't allow this to continue. This was not college, and Levell was a school official, and he had a feeling that Tex and Ginger were underage. He wasn't too sure about Tex, the more he thought about it, but Ginger was a junior just like Raven was, so she was underage, which made a case against Tex for rape.

Man, this guy is a dog. Going behind his girl's back to fuck her best friend. He's gone beyond too far.

Before he made up his mind on whether to expose the cheating couple, a third girl emerged from the dark corner of the classroom. Her black hair fell in curls behind her shoulders, and her bare breasts gleamed in the moonlight. "You like that, baby?" she asked Tex as Ginger continued to go down on him.

"Hell yeah, baby. She moves just like you do," Tex replied in an absolute lustful bliss.

As she made her way to the middle of the sheet where her boyfriend and her best friend were making love, Raven kissed Tex ravenously.

Levell couldn't believe what he was seeing. It was like a real-life flick taking place in front of his very eyes. Leaving them to their nightly activities, one thought burned his mind: *What have I gotten myself into?*

Chapter 6

LEVELL MADE HIS WAY BACK TO THE STANDS WHERE HIS family sat, as the images of the three teens having sex still swam around his mind. Internally, he punished himself for not interrupting their little rendezvous. Why didn't he stop them? Levell had always suspected Raven's boyfriend as a shady character due to the aloof attitude he displayed during their initial introduction. The way he greedily licked away at Ginger's body indicated that he had been longing for physical excitement and thrill outside of any relationship he had with Raven. But what further bothered Levell was Raven's part in the whole affair. She was in the same room and even joined in their provocative activity. The fact that Raven seemed comfortable with a third partner didn't sit right with Levell. But then again, they were hormonal teenagers.

Looking over at Caliya, still enjoying the game with Patrice, Levell just couldn't imagine seeing another man sitting near her or having so much as a conversation without his blood boiling, much less another man lying down with her. If a man ever approached Caliya with the notion to make a romantic advancement towards her, he would have snapped his neck.

Caliya saw that her husband seemed distant and attempted to get his attention. "Baby, are you okay?" she asked.

"Yeah, I'm fine," Levell answered, his eyes on the game clock.

The fourth quarter had just started, but the game was out of reach for the visiting team. The frustrated Harrison Hoya fans grudgingly started to make their way to the parking lot, their once-jubilant night turned sour by the performance of their team. Watching Harrison fans exit, Levell thought it was best for him to leave as well.

"Baby, let's go. I think this game's over anyway," he told Caliya.

"You don't want to stay and congratulate the players? You teach some of them, don't you?" Caliya asked.

"Yeah, but I can congratulate them in class on Monday. They played their butts off tonight," Levell replied.

Making his way over to the parking lot with his family, Levell started to walk out of the field, thinking about what he witnessed at halftime, when he inadvertently bumped into Mr. Landon Scott, the U.S. History teacher making his way over to his car as well. Levell was so deep in thought that he didn't see Mr. Scott in front of him.

"Sorry, Landon, didn't see you there," Levell apologized.

"It's okay, man. Trust me that game was so wild, it made me bump into people too," Mr. Scott replied, laughing.

But it wasn't the game that distracted Levell. It was the x-rated halftime show that took place in one of the classrooms. *Why didn't I say anything to them?*

Here he was, a teacher and an extension of the principal, administrators, other staff members and more. He could've stopped the show with Tex, Ginger, and Raven and had them suspended in the blink of an eye, but he just walked on and remained silent. He wasn't sure how this would come back to haunt him, but he knew that his failed opportunity was going to cost him at a certain point.

I don't know why I'm trippin' over that. They're just kids. At their age, sex is about the thrill and excitement of the ride. I was never there. I didn't see anything.

He would've been lying to himself, if he said that sex never took up most of his thoughts during that time, next to sports and reading. The whole drive back home was mostly silent, and as they arrived, Caliya tried once again to engage her husband in conversation.

"Levy, what's going on?" she asked. "You've been quiet since we left the game. Is something bothering you?" she wondered, as they pulled up to their driveway.

Shifting the car into park, Levell turned to look at his wife. He was determined not to tell his wife what he saw that night. "I'm good, baby," he replied.

Caliya eyed her husband suspiciously. It wasn't like her husband to be unusually silent like her. "I don't believe you," she said. "If something was wrong, would you tell me?"

Levell smiled as he approached his wife and kissed her on the top of her head. "I would tell you anything. You know that," he answered as he looked at Caliya.

Staring at his beautiful black wife, Levell temporarily forgot about the impromptu ménage a' trois show that he witnessed just hours earlier. Caliya had the look of a woman who needed some rest and some comforting. Whatever his wife wanted, he was obligated to provide the relief that she needed.

"Let me put Patrice to bed, and then I'll be on my way," he assured her as he picked Patrice up and carried her on his shoulders, while she giggled hysterically.

When they arrived to the room, Levell placed Patrice down on her bed. "So, did you have fun tonight?" he asked.

Patrice nodded vigorously, indicating how much she enjoyed herself. "But Daddy, all the big men kept running and hitting each other. Didn't it hurt them?"

Levell laughed. He didn't expect his daughter to pick up on the fine art of football. "Well baby, the big men had helmets on their heads, so whenever they run at each other, it doesn't hurt them. It's part of the game," he said.

Patrice smiled and gave a little nod to indicate that she understood what her father was saying, although he knew she really didn't understand.

"Can I play with them next time?" she asked.

No way. Pigs will start flying before I ever consider allowing my daughter to play football. "Maybe one day when you get older and bigger, but not now, okay?" Levell replied.

Patrice's face fell in disappointment, but it was only for a split second before Levell said, "Go to sleep now, okay? It's beddy-bye time," he added, covering his daughter in her sheets.

"Can you read me a story, Daddy?" she asked.

Levell smiled. He loved the fact that his daughter had a passion for stories and reading. In an age where technology played a factor in a child's development, Levell was very pleased that his daughter still desired to hear certain stories. Levell and Caliya would take turns reading to Patrice on certain nights.

"Sure, Patrice. Let's see what we have here," he replied as he searched through one of the unpacked boxes containing the children's books that were given to them as a gift by Mrs. Alreeda soon after Patrice was born. Reaching into the stash, he pulled out a classic book, *Green Eggs and Ham,* by Dr. Seuss.

As Levell read the book to Patrice, he made sure that he changed his voice to deviate the characters that he read. This was meant not only to entertain Patrice, but to help her define character development by making their voices different.

"I do not like green eggs and ham. I do not like them, Sam I Am," he read in light tones as Patrice repeated the words. The one aspect that Levell appreciated about Dr. Seuss was his ability to rhyme and still have profound life values through his words in a whimsical way that children understood.

As he neared the end of the story, Levell saw his daughter's eyes closing, and her breathing became steady. Finally, Patrice was asleep and Levell kissed his daughter on her right cheek before walking out of the room. Going into his room, he saw Caliya laying down on the bed, reading one of her romance novels. Rolling his eyes, he began to change out of his work clothes and he put on his tank top and boxer shorts.

"Tricey's asleep?" Caliya asked, her eyes emerging from the pages she was reading.

"Oh yeah. She's gone. She went to sleep pretty quick too," he replied.

"Oh yeah? Which book did you read to her?" Caliya asked.

"You know, the classic, *Green Eggs and Ham* by Dr. Seuss," Levell replied.

"Oh yeah, she loves those books. I think she loves 'em better than those other fairy tales we read to her," Caliya said. "I tried reading *Goldilocks and The Three Bears* to her the other night, and I promise you, it didn't do nothing for her," she added.

"I bet. She has the same taste in reading like you do," Levell said.

"You mean, like you do," Caliya corrected.

"Eh, I'm alright," Levell replied nonchalantly as he flipped off the room lights and went over to the bed to lie down next to his wife.

Caliya ran her smooth hand over Levell's cheek and shoulder. "I'm serious, baby. She gets her love of reading from you. Remember in junior high school when our teachers used to give us those boring summer reading assignments between grades, and we were only assigned to do a report for just two books? But you would read four books and do a report on those books?" she recalled.

Levell chuckled as he remembered doing extra book reports, not because he thought he would get extra credit, although he wouldn't have complained if he got any extra credit. But he had a love for reading since he was a child. Part of that love was due to the rough conditions that they lived in.

"Yeah, but that was the safest thing to do in the hood though. I made sure I was real discreet about it too cuz I didn't want my ass beat by Jimmy from down the street," he said, referring to an old bully who'd picked on him for a certain amount of time while he lived in the housing projects.

Caliya didn't grow up in the housing projects, but she still went to the same junior high school and high school as Jimmy and Levell. She laughed as the memory of Jimmy came back to her.

"I remember Jimmy Clarkson from the block," she laughed. "Wow, he gave you such a hard time, didn't he?" she pointed out as Levell shook his head, regretting bringing up Jimmy.

"Man, that dude neva' left me alone. I mean, I look at a guy funny, and he gets pissed off at me for four years," he said. "He never left me alone till about the tenth grade."

"Until you stood up to him for me," Caliya said.

Levell remembered the events profoundly. He was in the tenth grade, having been in high school for about a year and a half, and looking to establish a reputation at Jamaica High School.

At the time, Caliya barely knew Levell. She was reportedly dating a member of the football team, by the name of Gerald Monaco. But it was known that Caliya had plenty of suitors. One of them was Jimmy, a towering, lumbering fellow standing at about six-foot-seven, which was tall to Levell since he hadn't grown fully into his body.

One day, on the way to class, Caliya walked past Levell, busily talking with her friends, when Jimmy saw her from the opposite end of the hall. Determined to make his move on Caliya, Jimmy pushed the throng of classmates aside to approach her.

"Hey, girl, what's up?" Jimmy asked in his deep, graveled tones.

Caliya looked at Jimmy, staring at him as if he had some type of disease. "Hi," she said flatly, before turning to talk to her friends, hoping Jimmy would get the message.

But Jimmy was persistent and kept deriding Caliya. The more she ignored Jimmy, the angrier he got. "So, it's like that then, right?" he asked, raising his voice.

"It's exactly like that," Caliya replied firmly, turning to walk towards class.

But Jimmy wasn't done. He roughly grabbed Caliya by the right shoulder.

"Jimmy, get off me!" Caliya protested as kids stopped walking the halls to witness the drama unfolding. Looking around, Levell couldn't believe people were allowing the mistreatment to happen. He didn't know what he was thinking at the time, but he knew he couldn't allow it to go on.

"Yo, Jimmy, chill son. Leave her alone," Levell said, stepping in between Caliya and Jimmy.

"You talkin' to me, fool?" Jimmy asked angrily.

Levell could've sworn he felt the ground vibrate when Jimmy spoke. But as terrified as he was, he stood his ground.

"Yeah, I'm talkin' to you. She a female, man. You ain't got no right puttin' your hands on her," he said, secretly hoping that the school officials were on their way to break up the ordeal.

"How about if I put these hands on your mouse-lookin' ass, nigga?" Jimmy taunted Levell by goading him about his stature.

But Levell was determined not to be goaded to a fight, so he tried to diffuse the situation. "Just forget about it, man. I ain't got beef wit' you," he said. While Jimmy probably thought it was a cop-out by Levell, Levell turned to Caliya. "You good?" he asked her.

Caliya nodded, smiling slightly. She had never spoken to Levell before that day. "Yeah, I'm good," she replied, but Jimmy wasn't done.

Grabbing Levell by the front of his shirt, he slammed him to the lockers. "Listen mouse, I think it's time you walk or you gon' need life support in the next two minutes," he replied angrily.

At that moment, Levell decided he would no longer take Jimmy's abuse. He cocked his right hand back and punched Jimmy in the eye as the other classmates watched. The initial shot of pain from the impact went from Levell's hand up to his forearm. While Jimmy held his eye for a moment, Levell had hoped to use the time to make a quick getaway, but he wasn't so lucky.

Jimmy recovered, and although Levell tried to fight back the best he could, he endured one of the worst beatings of his life, ending up with a bloody lip, bruised ribs and a dislocated finger. He remembered how in the conversation that everybody had about it was the fact that he lost the fight to Jimmy. But there was something that Levell did win: respect. Caliya saw his courage, and they became good friends before they started dating. Jimmy was suspended for nearly a month and moved out of the district the following year but not before confronting Levell again, this time to apologize for what he'd done and to commend Levell for his bravery. Up until that time, Levell had never stood up to anyone as he stood up to Jimmy.

"Yo, man, my bad for what I did. You manned up that day, and you got heart. Much respect, kid," he said as they shook hands, ending their feud.

The event had occurred almost twenty years ago. While lying on the bed reflecting, Levell said, "You know, baby, if it wasn't for Jimmy, we probably would've never met, never gotten married, or experienced being parents."

"Yeah, you're right. If it wasn't for Jimmy, I wouldn't have met my knight in shining armor," Caliya said, rubbing Levell's right earlobe.

"Yeah right. Some knight I was. I got my ass whupped that day," Levell laughed.

"But you still put yourself out on the line for me, and I'll never forget that," Caliya said. Snuggling closer to Levell, she started kissing his neck and rubbing his bald head.

"And he also made you resilient. He made you battle tested. If you're able to deal with all the crap we've had to deal with up in New York, that makes you a real man in my eyes," she added.

Levell smiled. "Yeah, you're right. I guess a lot happened from that day," he replied. "Not to mention the fact that I swelled Jimmy's right eye shut for a couple days," he added, laughing.

"Oh, my God, are you really gonna be that petty?" Caliya laughed.

"Hey, hey, hey, come on now," Levell laughed. "He stopped calling me a mouse boy though," he added.

Caliya laughed even louder. "I ain't gonna lie. When he called you that, it was funny," she said.

"Yeah, real funny, till you realize there ain't nothin' small about me," Levell said slyly, his eyes gesturing toward his waist.

It took Caliya a second to realize that Levell was no longer talking about mice. She batted her eyelashes and lowered her hands until she started caressing his midsection.

"Show me then, boy," she challenged, and they began kissing more vigorously. As the bliss of love overwhelmed them, Levell slipped her nightgown straps from her shoulders, and he took his tank top off. As their bodies interlocked, he took the time to kiss her bare shoulders and her soft hands.

"I love you, baby," Caliya whispered in his ear as the temperatures rose, and heat radiated from their bodies.

Lost in their euphoric pleasure, Levell opened his eyes to look at

Caliya, but instead of seeing Caliya's brown skin pressed on his own, he saw white smooth skin with flowing black hair and blue eyes staring back at him. Raven closed her eyes in pleasure as she remained on top of Levell.

"What the...?" Levell asked in confusion before he blinked again and found Caliya staring at him, her eyes staring at him in concern.

"What's wrong, Levey?" she asked.

Levell rubbed his eyes. Had he just visualized himself making love to Raven? "Nothing, baby. I'm fine," he reassured her.

"Oh okay. I thought I was going too fast for you," Caliya teased.

"Oh no, never that. At least I ain't the one breathing hard," he added, laughing.

"Whatever, fool. You pantin' hard too. You know I worked you out," she said as she laid down on his body.

That next week, Levell continued teaching classes as the workload began increasing for the students. During this particular week, they began studying the epic poem of Beowulf. Although Levell attempted to block it out of his mind, every time he saw Raven in his class, he couldn't shake the image of her in the dark classroom with Tex and Ginger. He really couldn't get the image of her in his bedroom out of his mind.

It's gotta be unhealthy to be thinking of my students that way. C'mon, Levell, shake it off. She's a student like everybody here. She ain't no different from anybody else.

"Alright class, we discussed the journey of the hero Beowulf, and I've given you an assignment to read the first three parts of the story. So, before we continue with the story, who was the King of the Danes as was described in our epic tale?" Levell asked the class.

A few people raised their hand. Levell glanced at Raven and realized she didn't raise hers. Looking around, Levell selected another student named Amanda to answer the question.

"Was the King's name Hrothgar?" she asked.

"Right you are, Amanda," Levell confirmed. "Hrothgar was the King of the Danes, which is modern day Denmark. He approaches Beowulf because his kingdom was being attacked. And whom, might you ask, is attacking the kingdom? What was the name of that creature?"

Fewer people raised their hand this time. Raven still hadn't raised her hand. By looking at her, she didn't seem engaged in the classroom as she normally was. Levell decided to select someone else.

"Xavier, why don't you take this one?" he asked.

Xavier, who hadn't raised his hand, appeared stunned that Levell called on him. His book, which had been previously closed, was opened immediately as he frantically searched for the answer. From a student's perspective, it was cruel to call on anyone who wasn't prepared to answer a question, but as an instructor, Levell had to admit that seeing students frantically squirm for the right answer was one of his guilty pleasures. He was sure the other teachers felt that way, but if they didn't, he might just be twisted in a sense.

Finally, after skimming the story, Xavier answered. "Was it, uh, Grendel?" he replied.

"No, that's incorrect," Levell said abruptly, causing the other students to laugh under their breath.

"But it says on this page-" Xavier began to protest before Levell raised his hand to stop the student mid-sentence.

"I'm just joking, sir. No, that is the correct answer," he said as Xavier sighed in relief. "Grendel was attacking the hall of Heorot due to his jealousy of the Danes. Beowulf is sent to kill Grendel, and he succeeds before Grendel's mother comes out looking for revenge. Now to find out the outcome of the battle, please read the next two parts and answer the analysis questions at the end of those parts," Levell concluded before the bell rang, dismissing the students.

Everyone started to pack up and exit the room. Raven, still wearing the look of dejection across her face, packed her books into her book bag. While Levell sat to prepare for his next class, Raven walked up to him.

"Hey, Raven, what can I do for you today? Is everything okay?" he asked.

Shaking her head, Raven indicating that she was clearly bothered. A couple of tears fell out her eyes.

"What's wrong? You want to talk about it?" he asked.

Raven didn't answer for a few seconds. Levell glanced at the clock on his wall. If Raven didn't hurry she would be late for her next class. Finally, she spoke. "Tex and I broke up today," she said, between sobs.

At first Levell didn't know how to respond to the situation. He had an impulse to state the fact that any relationship with a man and another woman as the third wheel was always doomed, but he didn't want to be considered insensitive.

"I'm sorry to hear that. Was he playing you behind your back?" he asked as if he didn't already know the answer to the question.

Of course, he was playing behind her back. Actually, he was playing right in front of her, and she allowed it, even joined in. What did she think was gonna happen?

Levell stood up and hesitated for a slight moment, with the vision of Raven on top of him already coming back to his subconscious. Shaking it off, he patted Raven on the shoulder.

"He was seeing my best friend behind my back," she said.

Levell acted as if he was listening, but he knew there was more to this story. How could she not have known about his infidelity when she was in the same room where the act was taking place. "Was it Ginger?"

Raven looked at him with a look of surprise. "How did you know, Mr. Thomas?"

"To be honest, I know a lot more than that," Levell replied. "I know that you're not being entirely honest to me. I feel like you're hiding something."

Raven's eyes began shifting left to right. Levell knew he had hit a nerve because Raven was doing everything she could to evade his questions and his suspicion.

"I don't know what you're talkin' about," she said, fidgeting uncomfortably.

Levell eyed Raven, as if to tell her that she could really explain what was really bothering her.

Raven started to walk toward the door. "The next bell's about to ring, Mr. Thomas. I should really get to class," she said making her way out the door.

"So, you don't wanna talk about what happened this past Friday at the game?" Levell asked.

Raven stopped dead in her tracks. "What do you mean?" she asked in a tone that suggested she wasn't sure what he was talking about.

"I mean, when I saw you, Tex, and Ginger at the game, you guys seemed to be fine," Levell said. "As a matter of fact, it looked as if all three of you were having a ball, especially at halftime," he added, looking at Raven's eyes.

He saw Raven's eyes widen for a split second, as if she was in shock. *I got her.*

"We just went to get something to eat at the concession stand at halftime," she said, before beginning to walk away again.

I can't believe this girl is lying to me in my face. "Yeah, you and Ginger ate from the same guy, I see," he said.

Raven turned back around to face Levell, her face slightly red as she blushed. "How much did you see?"

"Oh, I saw just about everything," Levell replied, all pretense aside. "Raven what you, Tex, and Ginger were doing goes against the school by-laws and policies. Not only that, you guys are underage. I could've reported you three and gotten you expelled," he added flatly.

Raven, though recovering from her shock, began to walk to her next class as the late bell rang. Levell's next class was already in their seats waiting for class to resume.

"If you could've expelled me, why didn't you?" she challenged as she walked to her next period class.

Chapter 7

EVELL SAT AT THE FAR END OF THE BAR AT PINE mountain town grille, located off the corner of Pine Mountain and Kennesaw Due West Road. After a long school day, he needed to unwind. After learning about the bar from one of the other instructors at Kennesaw Mountain High School, a black Economics teacher named Cedric Hopkins, Levell decided to check the place out himself. He never considered himself an alcoholic by any stretch of the imagination, but he learned since teaching at Hillcrest High School that he even needed a beverage stronger than coffee sometimes.

I'm surprised I'm not an alcoholic already. Dealing with these kids all week gets to a brotha' sometimes.

Levell waited for his drink, a scotch on the rocks. Mr. Hopkins was scheduled to meet him at the bar in a few minutes, but he appeared to be running late. Looking at his watch, Levell hoped that his colleague wouldn't have him waiting too long. It wouldn't be long before Caliya worried about him and called him. Normally, Caliya, who worked in the Wellstar Health System at Kennestone Hospital, got off work before he did and would swing by the Primrose Early Start daycare program to pick up Patrice.

Waiting for his order, Levell thought back on his drama with Raven. He recalled the last question she posed to him. He also wondered why he never reported the teens. What caused him to hesitate on acting quickly when he saw one of his students in a compromising position? The worst part of the whole situation was Raven's nonchalant attitude upon finding out she was discovered that night. She did not seem to panic or did not appear to be apologetic about the situation. It shocked her initially when she found out he saw her, Tex, and Ginger playing around on the classroom floor, but she came across as defiant and challenging, not denying his claims at all. Levell hoped that his one moment of mercy wouldn't cost him his job. For that, he knew he had to tread softly because he didn't long for any unneeded drama.

The bar doors opened, and Mr. Hopkins walked in. He was slightly shorter than Levell, but whatever he lacked in height, he excelled in weight. Looking at him, Levell wouldn't call him overweight, but he just seemed to be slightly portly in shape. Sitting next to Levell, Mr. Hopkins ordered his own drink, a Coors Light.

"What took you so long, man?" Levell asked Mr. Hopkins, who smiled sheepishly.

"My fault, bro, I was grading some work after the bell, and I almost dozed off in my chair before I realized that I was supposed to meet you here," Mr. Hopkins replied. "So how these kids treating you?" he asked while the bartender looked to hand him a bottle.

"Man, these extra periods are killin' me dawg," Levell replied.

"I know how you feel. Well, I wouldn't hold on to them thoughts. I would take it out of my mind, bro, because if you don't do that, you couldn't wake up to teach another day," Mr. Hopkins said.

"Yeah, you right," Levell agreed as the bartender brought Mr. Hopkins's beer out. While sipping on their beverages and watching Sportscenter on ESPN in silence, Levell decided to break it.

"Man, sometimes I envy these ball players. I should've just tried to go to the league," he said, laughing to himself.

"I know, and you would've probably made it too," Mr. Hopkins laughed. "You definitely got the height. Lemme guess, you were one of them cats that wanted to play ball growing up, but yo' mama told you to stay in them books, huh?" he asked Levell.

"Something like that," Levell replied, laughing also. "See, my mama never had to force me to stay in them books. I loved reading, but I loved playing ball too. So, giving up one dream for another was hard at first, but you accept it," he added.

"I feel you," Mr. Hopkins said, taking a swig from his drink. "For me, it wasn't about just reading. My folks groomed me on how to save money. Since my first job, my mama started opening bank accounts for me, telling me about loans, bad checks, investments, stock options bonds and all that," he added, reflecting on his past.

"But look how you ended up though," Levell said. "You're one of the best Economic teachers in the county and from what I heard, you about a couple of years away from being a millionaire," he continued, before Mr. Hopkins hushed him.

"Damn, man, keep that on the DL," he said, laughing.

"Oh, I see," Levell replied. "You don't want people to know that you got a fortune in the works. Well whatever it is, cut me in," he said slyly.

"You know I got you, fam. Once that money starts rollin' in, and that pension kicks in, life will be lookin' up. But don't broadcast it. Remember, it's supposed to be a secret," Mr. Hopkins said.

"Okay, I got you," Levell replied. After more swigs from their beverages, Levell said, "Ced, I got something to tell you man, while we're on secrets."

But Mr. Hopkins didn't appear to hear him, as his eyes were still glued to the TV. "Yeah man, kick it to me. What's up?" he asked.

"Well this past Friday at the football game, I walked inside the school to use the restroom, and I looked inside one of the classrooms, and I saw some kids gettin' their freak on, on the floor," Levell said.

Mr. Hopkins tore his eyes from the TV and stared at Levell with surprise. "Wait, time out. Lemme get this straight. So, you saw students getting it in a classroom at night. What happened?"

Levell shook his head. "Nothing, man. I just saw it, and I didn't do anything about it. Shit's eating me up too."

"Wait, so you didn't report them or anything? They could've gotten into some trouble doing that at school though," Mr. Hopkins warned.

"I know, man, and trust me I would've reported them. But I held back for some reason, I don't know," he confessed.

"Levell, you really should've said something, man. You gotta recognize these kids grow up fast, and they're gonna get involved in relationships with others and all that, but they violated school rules," Mr. Hopkins said.

Levell looked around because he didn't want anyone else to hear what he was saying. "I know, man. I've been thinking about it. But what if I report it, and people don't take it seriously? Then I'm the one who gets axed, bro, and I just started out here. I ain't tryin' to start nothin'," he said. "The last thing I wanna do is get involved in some 'he said, she said' nonsense."

"Were you able to identify the students?" Mr. Hopkins asked.

"I recognized one of them. Her name was Raven Roberts. Does that name ring a bell?" Levell asked. Mr. Hopkins.

"Raven Roberts? Yeah, I know that girl. Taught her last year when she was a sophomore. I remember that girl had a smart mouth on her. From what I've heard about her, she got a lot of issues, man," he said.

"What kind of issues?" Levell asked.

"Well, you didn't hear from me, but I've heard stories about Raven and her family, and even though I can't confirm what I heard, I just have to tell it to you straight," Mr. Hopkins said.

"Her family, especially her pops, are bigots, bro. They would look down on certain people who didn't act like them or look like them, and they really hate guys like us," he added.

Levell sat back and thought about it. It explained why the man, who Levell assumed was Raven's father, ignored him when he first met her on the week he moved into the home. He hadn't seen any evidence of Raven herself being racist, but then he thought back to small behavior patterns that he noticed from Raven, from the careless way she replied to him earlier in the day, to the way she disregarded Caliya at the game.

But that doesn't mean she's racist. Her father may very well be racist, but I don't see that trait in her. All the same, I gotta keep an eye out on her.

Levell finished his beverage. "The worst part about it is that I live right across the street from her," he said.

"What? You mean to tell me that she's your neighbor?" Mr. Hopkins asked.

"Yeah, she is," Levell replied.

"Man, I don't know anything about your current situation, but if I was you, I would get up out of there," Mr. Hopkins warned Levell.

"Well my family and I only been here for about a month. We're still unpacking certain things," Levell said.

Mr. Hopkins shook his head slowly. "Levell, you don't know what her family is capable of. I've heard different things about her mother and her father. Her father is part of a white nationalist group, and her mother, well her mother has gotten a few of the teachers at Kennesaw Mountain High School fired. I guess it was for some crazy pointless reason, like they gave her daughter low grades that she didn't agree with. I saw all those brothers clean out their desks for the last time, and she didn't have no remorse whatsoever about it," he warned.

Levell looked back up at the television, hoping the images could drown out what Mr. Hopkins said about Raven and her family.

"Look, man, you don't have to take my word for it, but I'm just sayin', watch your back," Mr. Hopkins said as he stood up to leave the bar.

Early the next morning, Levell and Caliya were dressing to go to work. Levell, who just stepped out of the shower, was buttoning his blue pastel shirt and started putting his pants on when their doorbell rang. Caliya and Levell stared at each other questioningly.

"Who's that?" she asked Levell.

"I don't know, but I'll answer it," he replied as he walked downstairs to answer the door. "Looking through the side door window, Levell saw that it was Raven. She had the look of urgency all over her face.

What could she possibly want this early in the morning?

"Raven? What's up, is everything okay?" he asked.

Sighing, Raven said, "Mr. Thomas, I'm sorry to bother you so early, but my usual morning ride ditched me today. I was wondering if you could give me a ride to school?"

"Why, what's wrong with taking the bus?" Levell said, his eyebrows raised slightly. Mr. Hopkin's words still rang in his ears: *You don't have to take my word for it, but I'm just sayin', watch your back.*

"Mr. Thomas, I'm in the Beta Club and the Prom Committee, and we meet every morning at seven o'clock sharp. The buses don't even roll out till a quarter to eight. Please sir, I'm desperate," Raven pleaded.

"Where are your parents? Can't they give you a ride?" Levell asked. If Raven's parents were anything like Mr. Hopkins described, he knew they wouldn't be okay with him taking their daughter to school.

"My parents left to go to work early today. I ain't got a car yet. Please, Mr. Thomas, can you give me a ride to school?" she asked again.

Levell thought about it for another moment, studying Raven's face. There was no sign of trickery or bluff in her voice or her mannerisms. "Alright, I'll give you a ride to school today. But you're gonna have to set up an arrangement for going home after school," Levell replied.

Raven waved her hand dismissively. "Oh, I ain't even worried about that. My friends are gonna drive me back home," she replied.

Why couldn't you call those same friends to pick you up this morning? Levell thought, but he didn't repeat his thoughts out loud.

"Come on in," he said, inviting Raven inside. She sat on the dining room couch. "Do you want something to eat? I think we still got some cereal, bagels, and orange juice in the fridge here," he offered.

"No thanks. I'm okay," Raven replied as she looked at all the family portraits that hung on their wall. Her eyes fell upon a portrait of a young Levell with his mother outside of the housing projects. His mother was holding what appeared to be a flag.

"Oh my God, is that you?" she asked as she looked at the portrait.

Levell emerged from the kitchen to look at the portrait. "Yeah, that's me and my mother in Queens, New York."

Raven's eyes widened as she looked at the portrait. "What is your mom holding?" she asked.

"Oh, she's holding our national flag," Levell replied. "That's the Haitian flag cuz my mother and father came to America from Haiti many years ago," he added as he put on his work shoes.

"What about you? Were you born in Haiti?" she asked.

"No, I'm first generation American. I was born and raised in Queens before coming down here. I still visit Haiti often, and I do speak the language," Levell replied, knowing that he had just told a boldfaced lie. He hadn't visited Haiti in years.

"What language do they speak in Haiti? Swahili?" Raven asked.

At first, Levell took offense upon hearing the question. These were the same types of questions that he hated people asking him, just like those workers at Publix asking him about New York and the culture surrounding the Big Apple.

"Well, we speak Creole and French in Haiti, sometimes even Spanish too," Levell replied.

"That's so cool," Raven said.

At the same time, Patrice walked downstairs, aided by her mother, who saw Raven sitting on the couch. Caliya shot a quick look at Levell.

"Hi, Mrs. Thomas," Raven greeted bubbly, instantly prompting a smile out of Levell. Raven greeted his wife much better than she did the first time at the football game.

"Hi, Raven. How are you today?" Caliya asked politely, although Levell, who knew Caliya and her temperament, could sense a tinge of distrust in her voice.

"I'm doing great, thanks. Hi, Patrice!" Raven said as she greeted her.

Upon recognizing Raven's face, Patrice smiled and waved back.

Levell turned to Caliya. "Raven came by because she needs a ride to school today. She got meetings with the Prom Committee and the Beta Club," he explained.

"Okay, that's cool," Caliya said while going to the refrigerator to get some food for Patrice and herself. "Would you like anything to eat, Raven?"

"Uh, I already offered her breakfast, baby. She's not hungry," Levell replied.

"Oh. Well that's good. Anyway, I gotta go. I have to get Ms. Grown Madame over here to school," she said, walking Patrice over to their car in the garage. "By the way, do your parents know that we're dropping you off to school today?" Caliya asked.

"Yeah, they know I'm getting a ride from Mr. Thomas today," Raven replied.

Upon hearing that, Levell was internally debating whether to believe Raven when she said that her parents knew she was getting a ride from him.

If her parents were as racist as Ced would have me believe, they wouldn't have approved of this arrangement. Maybe Cedric was lying about the whole "racist" thing. Maybe her parents are just misunderstood. But then again, she could be lying about this too.

Whatever the case was, Caliya decided to trust her, so if his wife was all in, so was Levell. "Okay, well you two have a great day, and honey, don't give the kids too much homework today," she said, winking at Raven.

"He always does," Raven said, rolling her eyes in jest as Caliya laughed while walking out with her daughter.

After Caliya pulled out of the driveway, Levell turned to Raven. "Well, it's almost seven o'clock. Ready to roll?" he asked her.

"Yeah, I'm ready," Raven replied, grabbing her book bag and heading for the garage door.

A few minutes later, Raven and Levell were on their way to Kennesaw Mountain High School. At first, no words were exchanged between teacher and student, and the atmosphere felt tense. Raven reached over and abruptly turned the radio station from the jazz station to a contemporary pop station.

"Whoa, whoa, whoa, who told you to flip the station?!" Levell asked as they made the right turn at an intersection.

"Look, I have to listen to something on the way to school, and you ain't sayin' nothin' so I figured…" Raven started to explain.

"So, you figure you'd start messin' around with my radio, huh?" Levell replied, finishing the sentence for Raven.

"Hell, if you ain't gonna say nothin' on the way there, I might as well because that jazz or whatever just ain't cuttin' it for me. That's old people music," Raven said.

Levell looked at Raven as though she were crazy. *Old people music? This girl just doesn't understand what real music is nowadays.*

Levell loved the jazz station. It was his only source of real music. He could never understand the music of the current generation with their high overuse of autotuned, manufactured studio sounds and this new hip hop and rap genre that was being called "trap" music now. To Levell, those artists were nothing more than mumble-mouth individuals who probably wouldn't be able to play an instrument as simple as a triangle chime, much less other instruments.

As one of the lower forms of music started playing on the radio, Raven got into the song, rapping it verse by verse, even appropriating the profanity and slang included in the songs. She remembered all the lyrics to the song and was even trying to get Levell to dance to it.

"Come on, turn up!" she said, egging Levell on, but Levell simply wouldn't bite.

"Look, this may be music to you, but it's far from music to me. I can't dance to a whole bunch of empty rhymes over studio beats," he said.

Raven just looked at Levell, shaking her head. "Mr. Thomas, you look much too young to have a mind of an old man. You gotta get with the times," she said.

"No thanks. I'd rather stay stuck in the box of the 80s and 90s all day. I'll let you newer millennials enjoy this crap you call music," he chuckled.

"Whatever, Mr. Thomas. You're just a hater," Raven replied.

As the long building with the blue-domed top came into view, Levell was eager to change the subject.

"Hey, Raven, um, about yesterday...I wanted to apologize for what I said about the incident at the football game. I was out of line, and I could've addressed it better. I'm sorry," he said.

Raven looked at him, her smile widening. "That's okay. I'm sorry for what I did with Tex and Ginger. We were all stupid for that. I wanted to thank you for not reporting us to be expelled," she said.

"It's all good," Levell said. "Besides, I remember what it was like to be in high school. At the right time, in the right environment, I probably would've been caught doing the same thing. Lord knows, I was no angel in high school."

"See, that's what I like about you, Mr. Thomas. You're not like any of the other teachers around here. If any of them caught us, they would've already dragged our asses outta here," Raven said.

"Well, consider yourself lucky," Levell said. Finally pulling up to the parking lot, Levell parked his car and turned off the engine.

"Thanks for the ride," Raven said, grabbing her book bag as she opened the passenger door and stepped out. "Oh, by the way, you never really told me this, but how long were you watching that night? Did you just get a short glimpse, or did you see the whole show?" she asked slyly.

Levell froze for a full minute upon hearing the question. What was Raven insinuating? Did she know more about that night than Levell knew? Could she have possibly seen him spying on them that night?

"I was only there for a minute. Actually no, I was only there for a few seconds," Levell replied, but he could tell that Raven was skeptical of his response.

"Alright, bye, Mr. Thomas," she said as she waved at him and walked inside the school.

Later that day, Raven arrived home from school. Her mother was in the kitchen, cooking dinner, and her father was in the den, fixing a wooden stand. Raven was in her room on the upper level of her home. She stared out the window at the house across the street, writing in her diary. Currently, the window across the street was closed, and the blinds were down so she couldn't see what he was doing. She loved the way he cared for his daughter, reading her a bedtime story before bed. She loved the way he smiled as he laughed with his daughter.

The greatest view of all was whenever he taught the class and turned around to write on the marker board. She loved the firmness of his backside under the gray pants he wore. What she didn't love was the fact that he was still with Caliya. Caliya could never love him like she would love him. She would never appreciate the fine man that he was, and she knew she was threatened whenever she came by. It was time to get Caliya out of the picture for good.

Chapter 8

T IS ONLY PRUDENT NEVER TO PLACE COMPLETE confidence in that by which we have even once been deceived. Reading the quote by Rene Descartes, Levell shook his head in silent amusement. For all the quotes he pulled out of his pocket, that one was like a warning, almost an ominous prediction, if anything.

As he resumed his morning activities, Levell took the time to reflect upon his experience in Georgia. Almost two months had passed, and now in the first week of October, a slight wind chill affected the Kennesaw area, so Levell took out his North Face jacket. Normally, he wouldn't wear a jacket that heavy so early into the fall season, but he felt it was the right time. He felt the cold nipping, and although he started wearing long-sleeved sweaters, the garment just wasn't cutting it for him.

Caliya was still sleeping under the sheets, when Levell nudged her. "Baby, did you sleep past the alarm again?" he asked, laughing as he got all his school supplies together.

Caliya, only barely awake, glanced once at the clock. Then realizing that it was almost a quarter to seven, jumped out of bed and hastily headed for the shower, hitting Levell on the shoulder. "You know whenever I do that, you're supposed to wake me up at the same time you wake up. You know I oversleep," she said.

"My bad, baby. I thought you could use the extra rest," he

replied, smiling slyly at his agitated wife before leaving the room. Heading downstairs, his first thought was to head to the kitchen to make some coffee when his doorbell rang.

Not again. Since the first time he gave Raven a ride to school, she had visited their house every morning on many occasions, almost daily. For the past month, he had given Raven rides to school. Levell, who had always gone out of his way to help others, was getting fed up with having to help Raven almost every morning. Caliya noticed the many times Raven had asked him for a ride. Therefore, she became very suspicious of the girl who was seemingly taking advantage of her husband's generosity.

Sure enough, when he answered the door, there she was, standing on his welcome mat, smiling.

"Hi, Mr. Thomas. Ride fell through again. Can I get a ride to school?" she asked.

Man, doesn't that girl have anyone else that could help her this time other than me?

Sighing slightly, he reluctantly let Raven inside. "I was just making some coffee. I don't know if you drink coffee, but if you don't I understand," he offered as he started to fill the coffee maker with the ground coffee beans and hot water.

"Yeah, I would love some coffee," Raven replied, smiling.

"Alright, so it's brewing right now. Give it a few minutes, and I'll make you a cup before we go," Levell said. Excusing himself to go upstairs so grab the rest of his classroom supplies.

Caliya was already in the room, putting her clothes on. "Baby, I heard the doorbell ring. Who was at the door?" she asked.

"Who else?" Levell replied.

Caliya shook her head while putting on her hospital scrubs. "Why does that girl always come over every morning for you to give her a ride? Don't she got anyone at home that can help her?" Caliya asked in apparent exasperation.

"Baby, you know she's a student of mine, and I can't ever turn my students down when they need help," he replied.

"Well, she's needed our help for the past month taking her to school, and it seems that she's eager to go with you," Caliya said.

"Baby, I know what you're gonna say and believe me, no one's more tired of it than I am. But if she needs help, I gotta help her. Maybe her family's unable to help her get to school," Levell replied.

"Well that's on her and her family, Levell. I mean, it shouldn't have to concern us all the time," Caliya said. "She comes to get a ride from you, and there are days that she never talks to me. She just sits there waiting for you to give her a ride. And she barely acknowledges Patrice when she's there."

"Hold up, she's always been nice to Patrice, baby. Come on now, what would Jesus do?" Levell asked in jest, knowing such a statement would throw his wife off the scent of jealousy.

He laughed at his statement because he knew he wasn't even a religious person at all. Caliya would always invite him to come to church, but though Levell went with the family, he went grudgingly. Even though he spoke differently, it always seemed to be the same message to Levell and he would be too happy once service ended. He knew that God probably didn't like the way he looked at church, but maybe if God started to show himself a little more, he would show more of an incentive to go to church.

But to his surprise, Caliya responded, "Man, I think even Jesus would've been like 'Girl go on somewhere. Leave this family alone."

Levell laughed. He understood his wife to be the most senile and docile when it came to matters of spirituality. He saw the chink in his wife's spiritual armor and the chink had black hair. Walking downstairs, he saw Raven sitting down, looking at her cell phone, no doubt on Facebook or Instagram.

Why do kids invest in all those social networks? Levell had a Facebook account that he created, but he rarely used it due to his busy schedule.

"Coffee coming right up," he told her while the coffee was brewing.

Caliya came into the kitchen a few minutes later, holding Patrice's had as she normally did. "Hi, Raven," Caliya greeted as she headed out to her car.

"Hi, Mrs. Thomas," Raven greeted back. "Hi, Patrice!" she greeted gleefully as Patrice smiled, recognizing her friend.

When they left, Levell turned to Raven. "I swear every night, as I'm putting her to bed, all she saying is when she grows up, she wants to be like you," he said.

"Really?" Raven smiled. "It looks like I'm having quite the impact on your daughter, Mr. Thomas," she replied, laughing.

"Yeah, you are, but let's not forget who Big Daddy is," Levell replied jokingly.

Laughing even louder, Raven said, "Oh, it's you. It's you all the way. She has a great role model in her daddy, anyway," she crooned in her normal southern drawl.

Levell hated to admit it, but even he had to confess that when Raven spoke in the southern drawl tones, it sounded sensually submissive. He hated having those thoughts. Raven was not a grown woman. She was a student in his class. The personal interactions had to be at a minimum. If he stepped outside normal teacher-student boundaries, it could be disaster for him, not only for his career, but his marriage and family also.

As the time arrived for them to leave, Levell grabbed his briefcase and car keys. "Okay, Raven, you've had your coffee now, so I expect you to stay awake in class, right?" he asked, laughing.

He knew Raven never slept in his class, although he couldn't speak for the rest of her classmates, who were clearly bored with the class. He pitied those students come test time.

"Well, I can't promise anything. This coffee is kinda weak, to be honest," Raven said slyly.

Levell's eyes widened. "Hold up, so you got jokes about the coffee? Remember, who's giving you the coffee now. What you gonna tell me, you drink something stronger?" he asked.

"Yeah, I'm sure I have, and I got the empty beer bottles at my house to prove it," Raven said, confidently.

Levell did a double-take. "Raven, you ain't twenty-one yet. What you doin' drinkin' so early? Do your parents know you drink at that age?"

"Yeah, my parents know. It ain't a big deal," Raven replied, shrugging.

"Okay, just make sure you never come to my class drunk, and don't get caught by the police," Levell warned.

Raven started to walk outside to the garage, and Levell unlocked the door so she could enter his car. "Don't worry. I got it under control," she said, smiling.

Levell also got in and started to back out the garage. "Listen, I'm having a little get-together here at the house for Caliya. It's her birthday, and we're throwing a surprise party for her. All her relatives and my relatives are gonna be there. We just gonna have some music, food, and games, nothing too big. I just figured I'd invite you and your family, if ya want to come-"

Raven didn't even wait for Levell to finish. "Yeah, I'll definitely be there. But my family probably won't come cuz they got, you know, things to do," she said, awkwardly.

That's code for they don't wanna come because they don't wanna be around a whole bunch of black people probably.

But he didn't wanna assume that Raven was a racist or bigot because she seemed to enjoy being in the company of other black people, and he didn't want to hold her responsible for how her parents feel towards his family.

"Well, that's cool. I'll see you there. Now remember it's a surprise, so don't say anything to Caliya when you see her, okay?" he asked.

"I ain't gonna say nothin'," Raven said, as they pulled out the driveway and headed to school.

It wouldn't be until the party that Levell would notice how prophetic the literary quote by Descartes would be when the date of the party arrived.

Saturday finally arrived, and Levell checked his party inventory to make sure that he had everything: birthday banner, balloons, sandwiches catered by Subway and Chick-Fil-A, pizza, and nachos. And he came ready with drinks, the most important ingredient for all parties. He also dropped Patrice off at a babysitting service run by one of Caliya's friends at the hospital. Since he was positive that his uncle and friends would be coming with their children, he brought two separate coolers, one for the non-alcoholic beverages and one for the beer, wine coolers, etc. He also took care of the music for the event, mixing some old 60s, 70s, and 80s hits along with the New Jack Swing and early hip hop of the 90s. He also created a mixed CD of various Haitian music groups and acts such as Sweet Mickey and Carimi. Enlisting the help of Mr. Hopkins and a couple other teachers at the school, he hung the birthday banner on the wall above the kitchen arch so Caliya could see the banner as she was walking inside. They hung the streamers and set up the table with different board games but made sure the dominoes set was at the very top of the table.

From past experiences and previous parties, Levell knew how serious Uncle Max and the rest of his friends were when it came to Dominoes. They played the game as if they were in Olympic trials, often betting huge amounts of money. Last, but not least, Levell made absolute sure that he had the best *cremas* available. A fermented rum which had a cinnamon coconut flavor, it was the ideal drink for many Haitian adults. As they added the finishing touches, the doorbell rang. Levell answered the door, and Uncle Max came with Percy and Jennifer. Vicky trailed behind them, carrying three gift boxes and appearing winded. Levell offered his assistance by carrying one of the bags.

"Come on, Uncle Max, you couldn't even help Aunt Vicky with this stuff?" Levell said, indignantly.

"Well, I thought she could handle carrying all the packages since she wants to be a strong black female," Max replied with a shrug.

As Vicky passed Max one her way to the kitchen she whispered, "Dumb ass," in Max's direction.

Max didn't seem phased by his wife's angry reaction.

Based on her tone, Levell could tell that Vicky and Max had gotten into one of their petty arguments. Levell hoped that their bickering didn't ruin the occasion. He didn't want anything to get in the way of celebrating his wife and lifelong companion. But before any further words can be exchanged, the doorbell rang again. Levell ran to answer it. Raven walked in with a couple of her friends, and Levell noticed that Ginger wasn't among them.

"Hey, guys. welcome to Caliya's party. Glad you could make it. Please make yourselves comfortable," Levell said.

"Thanks, Mr. Thomas," Raven replied. She turned to her two friends. "By the way, this is Maria Hernandez and Amber Jackson," Raven introduced. "Ladies, this is my English teacher, Mr. Thomas. He's one of the coolest teachers at Kennesaw Mountain and better looking than all our other teachers too," she added as Maria and Amber giggled.

Levell wished he hadn't done so, but he felt a blush coming on. "Eh, I'm okay," he said, trying to downplay her compliments.

Soon, a few more guests arrived and sat in the living room, watching TV. As they sat in the living room, Levell looked outside, and as if on cue, he saw Caliya's car pull up. She immediately saw that she was unable to park in the garage due to cars blocking her driveway.

"Okay, guys, she's here. Take your places," Levell said.

Parking on the side curb, Caliya parked the car and entered her home.

"Levell, what are all these cars doing here…?" Caliya started to ask, but no sooner had she asked the question that she emphatically received an answer.

"SURPRISE!" Levell and all the other guests yelled as Caliya's eyes widened in shock.

"Oh my God, when did you all get here?!" she asked in shock.

"Well, we wanted to wish you a happy birthday, baby. You deserve all of this and much more," Levell said, kissing his wife.

"Aww baby, thank you for all this, but you didn't have to do anything for me," she gushed.

"Yeah, I do. It's not just your birthday that I appreciate you, but I appreciate you every single day of my life, from the time I wake up to the time I go to sleep at night," Levell answered. "You've done more than enough to hold your family down. You've done a great job, and this is to show you how much we appreciate you and your efforts. Happy Birthday, baby," he added, kissing her on the cheek again.

Caliya did her best not to break down, but she couldn't stop herself. Soon the tears began to fall. Greeting everybody, she made her way to the dining room where the food was set up, and the cake had the candle numbers 3-7 on the top of it. Once she blew the candles out, the party got underway. Bottles popped, and corkscrews were flying everywhere as the champagne flowed. The kids went in the backyard and played football, tag, and all the adults were inside watching TV, talking, or playing Dominoes. Max was dominating the game, as the other players grudgingly gave up their money once he slapped the final Domino piece upon the table.

About a couple hours later, tired, full and a little inebriated, Levell made his way over to the bathroom before heading back out and walking upstairs to his room. He knew the guests would have to leave at some point, and he would ask them to leave soon but not before he rested his eyes for a moment. With Caliya downstairs, talking to Vicky and the other female guests, Levell went up to his room, expecting to see only his empty bed, linen sheets, and pillows. But someone was already lying on his bed. Squinting his eyes, Levell slowly made out the image of a semi-nude white girl.

God please, no. Not now, please. This is a mirage. It's gotta be a mirage. There is no way Raven is lying on my bed like this.

Yet, there she was, unapologetic, and smiling ear- to-ear.

"Raven, what are you doing hea'?" he asked.

"Well, your wife is downstairs, and she's having fun, so I feel like it's my turn to have some fun now," she said in a slow, seductive voice. "I can tell I'm not the only one who wants to have fun," she said, staring at Levell's mid-section.

Levell tried his best to stay limp, but seeing the young girl lying there virtually undressed and with the alcohol circulating in his system, caused his blood pressure to rise slightly. He felt the blood rush to other places, including the spot where Raven was staring. Levell felt his pants tightening every second.

"Raven, I'm only gonna say this once. Put your clothes back on and leave my room. What you want isn't here. My wife is downstairs. I'm a happily married man, you understand?" he asked.

"I understand that you're tryin' to throw a party to appease Caliya but you're really thinking of someone else," Raven said seductively, starting to rise from the bed and walk towards Levell, her breasts fully exposed, and she was wearing a thong underwear.

Why does she have to be so developed? Come on, man, drop that bone in your pants. Think of something ugly or close your eyes. Do something.

Raven came closer. "So, I think I know why you didn't report me when I was in the room with Ginger and Tex. You were enjoying what you saw. Well, you ain't gotta window-shop no more, cuz I can give you the full experience," she said.

The next minute she was on him, attempting to kiss him, but he pushed her off.

"I don't want the full experience, Raven. As a matter of fact, I want you and your friends to leave now," he said firmly. He might have been a little inebriated, but he wasn't unconscious of where he was or the predicament he was in.

But Raven persisted. "You don't mean that," she said, attempting to caress him again.

But this time, Levell held her hands. "I don't mean that? Get your friends, get your stuff, and get the hell outta my house now," he said, raising his voice slightly.

Taking her cue, Raven rolled her eyes and went to pick up her clothes.

"Go to the bathroom, put your clothes on, and leave now," he repeated again.

After fully dressing, Raven went downstairs and stormed out of the door without saying goodbye to anyone else at the party. Noticing her rapid departure, Caliya asked, "Honey, what's wrong with Raven?"

Levell shook his head, trying to gather his thoughts over what transpired just a few minutes before. "Nothing, she just had to go home. Maybe her parents called or something," he said wildly, still trying to gather his thoughts.

"Really? She just left without saying goodbye or anything?" Caliya asked.

"Yeah, it probably was an emergency. She had to take off," Levell replied.

After another hour, most of the party guests started to leave, so Levell, Max, and Percy began to clean the dining room. While they were cleaning, a thought struck Levell. While it behooved him that Raven would try to seduce him with his wife just a level below them, she might have left a piece of clothing or garment in the room. If Caliya ever caught anything down there, it would raise suspicion, and he wouldn't be able to explain away the encounter. Rushing up to the bedroom, Levell opened the door to find Caliya on the bed, taking off her shoes.

"Baby, is something wrong?" she asked.

Levell internally hoped that he didn't sound nervous because he would be giving himself away. "No baby, nothing's wrong. Why?" he asked. *What a stupid move, Levell.*

"I don't know. You just bum-rushed the door like a New York Giant linebacker, like you expectin' the worst," Caliya said, concerned.

"Nah, it's nothing like that. I'm good," Levell lied. He knew he wasn't being completely honest with Caliya because his eyes were shifting through all corners of the room, hoping that Raven hadn't left anything in there.

"Well, okay, if you say so," Caliya said while getting up to walk to the bathroom. "Honey, aren't you going to go pick up Patrice?"

Levell, who had been lost in his own thoughts, snapped back to reality. "Yeah, I'll go pick her up now," he replied. Grabbing the car keys, he walked to the car and jammed the key into the ignition.

I just need to drive to clear my head. Yeah, that's what I need...to drive to clear my head. Damn, what the hell was she thinking, pulling that stunt? Just gotta clear my head.

Levell drove on to the babysitter's home to pick up his daughter.

Chapter 9

ON HIS WAY HOME FROM THE BABYSITTERS WITH Patrice sleeping in her toddler seat, Levell tried to shake off the image of Raven and her attempt to seduce him. Still stunned by the encounter, he pulled up to his driveway and parked inside the garage. Opening the back door and getting Patrice, he carried her inside the house, slowly walking upstairs before laying her down on her bed. As he looked at his daughter sleeping peacefully, Levell came across a horrible realization: Patrice was a little girl now, but she was steadily growing. Soon she would be going through puberty. She would also become a young lady—strong but impressionable, self-sufficient but dainty—and she would catch any boy's eyes. Levell feared seeing that reality one day. Soon his baby girl, stars lighting up her eyes, would bring little boys home, and she would be raving about them.

Lord forbid that she brings any of these bums home. If I have to murder for my little girl, I will go to jail for her.

Caliya did an outstanding job in teaching Patrice life values and behavior. Levell didn't want his daughter to grow up without values or with a low self-esteem. Most importantly, he didn't want Patrice to pick up the habit of drawing older men to her by sex. That meant he couldn't allow his daughter to be around Raven, as emotionally reckless as she was.

Walking into his room, Levell saw Caliya opening the last of her gifts, including a designer bag, new watch, cell phone case, and workout gear, complimentary of Vicky Thomas.

"Honey, this was the best surprise party I've ever been a part of. Thanks," she said as she reached over to kiss her husband.

But Levell only partially returned her kiss. Caliya was lying down on the same spot where Raven had just been lying down an hour earlier. Levell was surprised that Caliya couldn't sense another woman had been lying on her bed. He loved to believe that women had a sixth sense where they could literally smell the stench of infidelity, but Caliya seemed completely oblivious.

"You're welcome, baby," he said, going to bed.

"Levey, what's wrong?" Caliya asked, sensing how aloof and unenthusiastic Levell seemed.

But there was no way Levell was going to tell Caliya that the room had an unwanted visitor just an hour earlier.

"I'm fine, baby. I guess I'm just a little tired," he replied.

"Well, come to bed, baby. You've worked so hard today, putting the party together and what not. Come get you some rest," Caliya said, trying to coax her husband to bed.

"Yeah, I'll be there in a few minutes. I just gotta go downstairs and grade some assignments," he said.

"That can't wait for tomorrow?" Caliya asked curiously as Levell began walking out the room and into the hallway.

"No, baby. I gotta handle it now. I got a lot of papers to grade tonight. The party delayed it a bit, but hopefully it shouldn't take too long. I'll be in bed in a few minutes, I promise. Get you some rest," he said.

"Okay, well goodnight," Caliya said.

Just by Caliya's tone, Levell could sense the disappointment in her voice. It was her birthday. Despite all the gifts she had received, the one gift she wanted above all others was her husband to love her. Levell knew that fact very well, and he hated himself at that moment. While he really had some grading to catch up on, he also wanted to rid his mind of Raven.

Walking downstairs, Levell went over to his laptop in the living room and took all the ungraded papers from his bag. His classes had just completed the epic of *Beowulf,* and they were studying stories from the

Middle Ages. As Levell graded the papers, he had his laptop open for access to his electronic grade book. Normally, he preferred to keep the actual grade book where he would use a pen to mark the grade of a certain individual, but since technology improved its grading system, he now had to record the grades online, so students could access their grades with their school's intranet and login system.

As Levell began grading, he received an email notification on his instructor account. He normally used this platform to answer questions students had on assignments, test dates, and other notifications. Opening the email, he saw a polished, typed-out message. There was no name in the sender box, and when Levell opened the message to read it in its entirety, it read:

Dear Mr. (Levell) Thomas,

I wanted to apologize about my stupid behavior earlier tonight. I must've had one too many drinks at the party. I went too far when I tried to fuck you (excuse my French), and before you say anything about it, yes, I know I shouldn't be drinking right now. I'm underage, but seriously, what did you do when you were my age? Like I told you before, I've been drinking alcohol for a while now, so I'm not new to the buzz at all. I normally control my drinks, but today, I lost control, and I nearly made a horrible mistake. I know what I did was wrong, but I didn't know how else to approach you at the time. I think I have a thing for you. Yes, I know it sounds weird because of the whole student-teacher thing, and it's awkward, but I can't hide how I feel about you. Since the time we met, I've really been attracted to you, and I love the way you care for Patrice by tucking her in at night and reading her stories. I know Caliya's your wife, but how do you know if she really loves you? If we can just talk and try to sort our feelings out, maybe we can start over, and it won't seem as awkward. Please, Levell, give me just one chance. Every night before I go to bed, I think about you. Every morning, I look forward to seeing you so that you can drop me off at school. I know you probably think I'm crazy, but why bind ourselves and our emotions when we know how we feel about each other? I think love should have no rules. It should be wild and free, and we should let love do whatever it wants. At the end of the day, I still believe that love conquers all. If you receive this email, please reply back ASAP, or we can talk about it at school.

Signed, R.R.

Levell read the whole letter. At the end, he was stunned by it, but he knew who wrote it. *That girl just doesn't know how to take rejection. She got one thing right in that twisted letter of hers: she's out of her freakin' mind. If she thinks that we are gonna be in any type of relationship, she got another thing coming.*

Levell started to reply to the email. He typed:

Raven, this is a public-school email system, used for educational purposes only. This is an inappropriate letter that you sent to me that has nothing to do with the material that I assigned you, so please stop sending personal emails. This isn't the correct platform to express yourself this way. Besides, I am HAPPILY MARRIED, so please stop sending me these emails, and just focus on your school work. I do accept your apology, and I appreciate it, but what you're suggesting in your email is not only impossible, but it is also reckless and foolish to think that our relationship will be more than instructor and student. So please stop this immediately. I don't want to have to resort to disciplinary action if this correspondence continues.

Thank you. Instructor L. Thomas.

Levell went over the email before sending it to Raven. He knew he had sent the message loud and clear. He was neither interested nor would he ever be interested in Raven, and if she didn't understand when they were in the same room, she would eventually understand him. Unlike the previous time when he didn't report her, this time he would not hesitate to if she pushed the inappropriate relationship too far.

As he went back to grading papers, Levell received another email notification from the same anonymous sender. There was no message, just an attachment. He was leery of it because attachments from unknown senders could be a virus or malware. As he felt his stomach drop, Levell still opened the attachment. Before his eyes, a young nubile, white girl stared back at him, her eyes seemingly enticing him, her developed curves bent over so her backside became more prominent than it was. Raven smiled at him through the picture, and the caption below read: "Does your wife look like this? I didn't think so" in small, block letters.

Hearing footsteps walking down the stairs, Levell immediately closed the attachment and the email right before Caliya entered the living room. Noticing the scattered papers and graded assignments on his desk, she caressed her husband around his neck.

"You look swamped, baby. You need any help?" she asked.

"No thanks, baby. I'm fine," Levell lied.

He hated lying to his wife. He wasn't fine. This girl was complicating his life and his marriage. It was bad enough that she visited almost every morning to get a ride to school. On the mornings when she didn't get a car ride from him, she would see him after class every day and would engage in annoying small talk with him, so much that the students in his next block were becoming suspicious. Now she was trying to sleep with him and had sent him naked pictures. It was time to end this immediately. He was not going to be a victim.

After Caliya walked back upstairs to their room, Levell continued grading papers. He heard a couple more email notification indicators, but he didn't bother to reply to any of them. He closed his inbox and continued working. Finally, after another hour and a half of grading, an exhausted Levell walked upstairs to his bedroom and changed into his flannel pajama pants and tank top before going to bed. Caliya was already sleeping peacefully, no doubt full and satisfied by the birthday party that was thrown for her. Levell was overjoyed that she had a ball, and he would not let anyone get in the way of making his wife happy and their marriage healthy and fruitful, and that included the temptress who lived across the street from them.

That following Monday, Levell entertained his class by demonstrating a live chain mail of armor that soldiers or knights fought with during the Middle Ages. He had the suit of armor for years, since teaching at Hillcrest in New York. Through some connections many years ago, a friend who happened to be a museum dealer and a part-time historian, had given Levell the 12th century armor, and he used it as part of his lectures every semester. Levell wasn't even sure if what he did was against school policy, and he didn't bother to ask. As far as he was concerned, educating wasn't limited to books and just pointing at marker boards. Education was interaction, and it was innovative. Some students would understand and be engaged while others would still be struggling to stay awake in class, which didn't bother Levell. As far as he was concerned, he kept the class engaged.

As he passed the breastplate portion of the suit to a girl in the first row by the name of Briana Stamford, Levell glanced at Raven sitting in the back of the class. She didn't look the least bit entertained by the passing of the suit of armor.

"Did this actually belong to a knight back in old England?" Briana asked.

"That's right. This was actually worn by a knight during the Middle Ages, and he made sure he had his family seal, or his flag, engraved. You see it?" Levell explained as he pointed to the center of the breastplate at a large cross.

"Many of the knights who wore such armor fought in the Crusades, which were fought between Christians in Europe and Muslims in the Middle East between the years 1095 and 1291," he explained.

The students all raved at the parts of the suit of armor, especially the helmets worn during the period, although some complained that the helmet was too heavy.

"Yo, how can dudes wear this on their heads, man? This shit's heavy, yo," Xavier exclaimed while the other students laughed.

Levell turned to face Xavier. "Right you are, sir. They had to wear this heavy piece of metal over their heads, and this is what the footgear looked like," Levell said as he showed them the metal boots and metal shin guards the knights wore.

"But the only problem was that this armor barely provided protection to the knights. If you stabbed a knight in the right spot with a long broad sword and thrust it in there hard, it still caused massive blood loss and death," Levell added.

To begin the next story selection of excerpts from Thomas Malory's *Le Morte D'Arthur,* Levell's goal was to teach the culture of the times surrounding the literary works that he taught to his classes. He also planned on showing them the 1981 movie *Excalibur,* which was an excellent comparison to the story, give or take a few events that were exaggerated from the book itself.

As the bell rang for class to end, the students packed up and prepared to leave for their next period class. As the students handed Levell the pieces for the suit of armor, he placed them on his desk for display to prepare for his next class. As he continued working on preparing for next block, he knew she was behind him. He didn't even look up. "I have nothing more to say to you, Raven," he told her.

Raven stared at him intently, as if her stares could burn through lead. "So, I spill my heart out to you, and you turn me down? What's wrong with you?" she asked, although she kept her voice to barely a whisper so that the students coming in for the next block wouldn't hear her.

Levell let out a hollow laugh. "You're asking what's wrong with me? Seriously? I think I should be asking you that same question," he said smartly, erasing the content off the marker board.

Without warning, Raven started rubbing his arm, and Levell started to feel beads of perspiration form on his head. "C'mon, Mr. Thomas. I meant everything I said in that email. I don't know what it is, but I really like you. Why can't you just give me a chance?"

"I can give you a thousand reasons why I can't give you a chance," Levell said, more harshly than intended, pulling his arm away from Raven's grasp. "Let's start with your age. You're only seventeen years old, which means if I lay a hand on you, my ass is going to jail for rape," he said firmly, standing up emphatically.

Raven rolled her eyes, but Levell continued. "Then, let's move on to the part where I said that I was married, okay? I'm not looking for another relationship. I'm not moving on from my wife. It just ain't happening. So, I need you to stop this charade right now, or I will have no choice but to impose disciplinary action," he warned.

"Yeah, just like you did on game night, right? You really showed me up then, huh?" she asked sarcastically.

Levell started to feel himself getting angrier by the minute. Every time he tried to let Raven see reason, she allowed her teen adolescent infatuation to get the best of her.

"Raven, go to class, and please don't send any more emails to me. As a matter of fact, I think you and I really shouldn't be communicating outside of class at this point," he said.

Raven let out a sound that could only suggest her frustration that Levell was not responding to her advances. She stormed out of class, bumping a few students on her way out.

"Hold up, you mean to tell me that this chick was laying down on your bed, buck-naked?" Mr. Hopkins asked Levell after work later that day at the Pine Mountain Bar once Levell finished explaining his ordeal to him.

"Bro, I'm talking 'bout just nothing on. She was lying there spread-eagle, like she been waitin' on me," Levell replied.

Mr. Hopkins shook his head but also began to laugh.

"What's so funny, man?" Levell asked, not seeing what was humorous about the situation.

"I always knew that girl was cracked in the head, but she came at you that way? No rhyme or reason?" he asked.

"No rhyme or reason," Levell confirmed. "I don't know what happened, dawg. I always knew she was someone that was outgoing, and she had that horny streak about her, but I never thought she would take it this far, man. I should've reported her when I had the chance," he added.

"Levell, that's not gonna be enough at this point, man. She has a sick fascination for you. You might need to get a restraining order on her or something because if you slip up and find yourself in a compromising position with her, that's yo' ass," Mr. Hopkins warned.

"I know, man. I don't know what I'm gonna do. She sendin' me nude pics in my email and everything," Levell said.

"What?" Mr. Hopkins said in shock just as the bartender provided their drinks. "What did you do with them pics?" he asked, while taking a sip of his Bud Light.

"What you think I did, man? I deleted all of them. If my wife opened my laptop and saw all them pictures, she'd light me up," Levell replied.

"You erased them all? Why would you do that? You might need that as proof or something, especially when you're putting in that restraining order," Mr. Hopkins said.

"Damn, I didn't even think about that," Levell said. He was focused on getting rid of the photos so quickly because he didn't want Caliya on his case and didn't want her to get suspicious.

"You better be lucky that she's the only one after you and not her daddy," Mr. Hopkins said.

"Man, I don't care how her daddy feel about me, I gotta go tell him something," Levell said.

"You could try to talk to him, but I guarantee you he ain't gonna wanna listen," Mr. Hopkins replied.

Levell understood what Mr. Hopkins was saying, but he didn't know what alternative he had. As misguided and borderline insane Raven was, perhaps if Levell spoke with her parents, they might be able to speak to her and persuade their daughter to stop pursuing him.

"I'm gonna visit them this Saturday and explain what's going on," he said.

"Okay, just let me know what went down, and if you don't make it out of there alive, let Caliya know that she ain't gotta worry cuz Hopkins got her and Patrice!" he exclaimed with a wink, and Levell laughed while he fake-punched his friend in jest.

Early Saturday morning, Levell watched as Raven's friends picked her up as they normally did every weekend. He guessed that they were probably headed to the mall, so he figured he had plenty of time to discuss her behavior with her parents in hopes of diffusing the situation. He found it strange that since Monday's class, Raven had been absent Tuesday through Friday. She had not shown up to class, and this was another reason that Levell wanted to visit with her parents. He figured they would know what was going on with their daughter. After seeing the car turn around the intersection to leave the subdivision, Levell crossed the street and walked over to the Roberts' residence. He rang the bell. After a minute, a short frumpy white woman with long hair, a long t-shirt, and jeans answered the door.

"Hello, good morning. My name's Levell Thomas, and I'm your neighbor from across the street. I also happen to be a teacher at Kennesaw Mountain High School," Levell said.

"Oh, hello. Nice to meet you, Mr. Thomas. My name's Pat Roberts, and my husband Jerry is working in the basement," she said, smiling. "It's nice to finally meet you. Raven's been talking about a teacher named Mr. Thomas, who was 'one of the coolest teachers at Kennesaw Mountain.' She must have been referring to you," Mrs. Roberts said in a voice that Levell could only describe as flirting. She was giggling as she was describing the way her daughter talked about him.

"Is everything okay at the school?" she asked.

"Well, that's actually why I came to visit. I wanted to talk about Raven and her performance in school and her activities outside of school," he said.

"I see. Well, please come on in," Mrs. Roberts said, inviting Levell into her home. As soon as he looked around, Levell immediately felt like a fish out of water. Their whole dining room and living room area were covered in Confederate flags and emblems of southern pride and different propaganda signs, mostly political.

Wonder where they keep the long white robes at...

Mrs. Roberts asked Levell to sit down in the living room table.

"So, what brings one of Kennesaw Mountain's finest teachers to my home today?" she asked.

Levell took a deep breath. He had been involved in thousands of parent-teacher meetings throughout his career, but he had never felt as nervous as he did sitting before Mrs. Roberts. "Well, um, Mrs. Roberts, this is not easy for me to say. Raven is a great kid and a great student. She's very ambitious, very determined, and she's headstrong."

"Thank you, Mr. Thomas. Yes, my Raven is all them things. She gets that from me, of course," Mrs. Roberts said in her southern twang.

"I see," Levell said. "The reason for my visit today is to discuss a very serious matter. Despite Raven's brilliance, she has exhibited some behavioral issues recently, especially around me," he continued.

Mrs. Roberts raised her eyebrows, slightly. "Is that so?" she asked as if it was news to her also.

"Yes, I'm afraid it is, Mrs. Roberts. I hate to be the one to bring this to you, but Raven has been making some inappropriate advances toward me recently, and despite how adamant I've been about keeping the relationship strictly as instructor and student, she seems to believe there is something more in that relationship, and that's simply not true," Levell explained.

Mrs. Roberts appeared unfazed and nonchalant at first. Then, to Levell's surprise, she laughed. "So, you mean to tell me that Raven has a lil' ole crush on you, and you have a problem with that?" she asked.

"No, ma'am. That's not what I'm saying," Levell tried to clarify, but Mrs. Roberts was already calling to her husband.

"Jerry! Jerry! Come on over! I've got one of Ray's teachers in here, and he wanted to talk about Raven," she said.

"I'll be up in a minute," a deep voice boomed from somewhere under the basement.

Levell didn't know why, but he suddenly felt uneasy and nervous. Mrs. Roberts thought he was exaggerating his situation, and if she thought that way, what would Mr. Roberts think? "You know what, Mrs. Roberts, we can do this another time. I really have to get going," he said.

"Nonsense. Please stay. Would you like some water? Beer? I think we got some other beverage in here," Mrs. Roberts offered.

"No, that's okay," Levell said politely as one of the side doors of the kitchen opened, and a tall man with a bushy mustache and beard walked through the kitchen and into the dining room.

He had on gloves and was wearing overalls.

"Pat, have you seen my hammer?" he asked before his eyes fell on Levell. Then as if a light switched, his eyes narrowed in suspicion. "What you doin' here?" he asked Levell angrily.

Chapter 10

ERRY ROBERTS STOOD ACROSS THE DINING ROOM FROM where Levell and Mrs. Roberts were sitting. Levell hadn't expected such an unwelcome greeting from Mr. Roberts, but he wasn't going to let one of his student's father intimidate him.

"Good morning, sir. I don't believe we've met yet. I'm Levell Thomas. I live just across the street," Levell said, standing up to shake Mr. Roberts' hand.

Mr. Roberts looked at Levell's outstretched hand as if he was looking at a repulsive slug.

"Baby, this is Raven's teacher up at the school. He came to tell us about Raven and how she been behavin' in school the last few days," Mrs. Roberts explained.

"The way she been behavin' in school?" Mr. Roberts asked, his scowl beginning to dissipate. "What the hell she been doin' then?" he asked her, but Levell had an odd feeling the question was directed towards him.

He knew the game Mr. Roberts was playing right then. He was attempting to test his intelligence and his competence by insinuating he didn't keep track of his students. Meanwhile, Mr. Roberts never shook Levell's hand, so Levell withdrew his, not wanting to look foolish for having it sticking out.

"Well, I didn't say she wasn't performing well in school-" Levell started to say, but Mr. Roberts spoke over him again.

"Is this what you called me up for?" he asked his wife.

"No, honey, there's something else. Mr. Thomas said that Raven has been gettin' under his skin, if you know what I mean," Mrs. Roberts explained.

Levell just stood there, internally shocked at how Mrs. Roberts was spinning the situation by making light of the interactions between him and Raven.

Mr. Roberts stared Levell up and down as if he was judging him. "Really? Please, Mr. Thomas, explain how my daughter's been treating you. Can't be all that bad because she's bringin' good grades home every day," Mr. Roberts said.

Levell had a sinking feeling that Raven's folks were not going to believe his accounts of his interaction with her. "Sir, there's no denying that Raven is a great student. However, I'm receiving inappropriate emails from her, and seeing that we lived right across from each other, I wanted to let you know first," Levell said.

"Basically, he's sayin' that Raven been crushin' on him for a while," Mrs. Roberts said, laughing.

Levell looked between mother and father in shock. *Come on, no parent could be oblivious like this. Why are they glossing over the fact that their daughter stepped over the boundaries between teacher and student?*

Mr. Roberts stared at Levell, one of his eyebrows raised. "Is that so? Wondering what she sees in this one right here."

Levell felt his comfort level decrease again. Perhaps it was time to leave. Not only was Mr. Roberts' statement completely out of bounds, but it also showed a complete disdain for him as a person.

"Is that what you called me up here for, woman?" he barked at his wife.

"Yeah, honey, that was pretty much it," Mrs. Roberts said while Levell remained baffled at how lightly Raven's parents treated the situation.

Jerry Roberts turned to face Levell. "What, you can't handle a woman in heat, Mr. Thomas?"

"No, sir, that's not it. What I'm saying is that Raven has sent me certain emails that weren't appropriate between student and teacher-"

Mr. Roberts cut him off again. "So, my daughter's taking a likin' for you sir? Is that what you're saying?"

Levell noticed how condescending Mr. Roberts was towards him. He could never get a full sentence out before Mr. Roberts felt the need to cut him off. But Levell was determined to keep it professional and not fall for the mind games that the Roberts were playing on him.

"I don't know how she feels about me, Mr. Roberts, but all that I'm saying is those emails that she has been sending to me are not appropriate between teacher and student," Levell said. "My school email is strictly a tutorial tool meant to help other students with their homework or other assignments, and she hasn't been using the tool for that purpose."

Before Mr. Roberts replied, they all heard the front door open. Raven walked into the living room, accompanied by Ginger and another young woman. Upon seeing Levell, she gasped a little bit.

Mr. Roberts called his daughter. "Raven, your teacher Mr. Thomas here is saying you've been sending him some funny emails lately. Is this true?" he asked his daughter.

Raven looked between her father and Mr. Thomas as if she was unaware of the situation or was thinking of a way out. Levell was almost certain she was trying to avoid the question.

"Emails? I don't know what he's talking about, Daddy," she replied in her faux southern drawl. Levell looked at Raven, his eyes opened in shock.

I can't believe she would lie straight to her dad like that.

"It must've been someone else using my name or something like that," she said.

Liar. There was no way anyone else wrote that way.

"And he also says you ain't been to class in the last few days, but I seen you go to school with your friends," Mrs. Roberts said.

Raven and her friends laughed. "Duh, Mom, I've told you that I've transferred out of Mr. Thomas's class, and I'm in Mrs. Pitner's class now," she explained.

Levell knew Mrs. Pitner, who taught in the same hallway just a few doors down. Even while it explained why Raven hadn't been inside his class, it did not excuse the fact that she tried to seduce him and had sent him inappropriate pictures. But the damage was done, and he already appeared to have made a fool of himself in front of the Roberts.

"Oh, okay. I didn't know you transferred classes. I was wondering where you were. I thought speaking to your parents would give me some information," he told Raven.

At this, Mr. Roberts was over the visit. "Okay, Raven, you can go upstairs with your friends," he said to her, and they walked upstairs to her room.

Mr. Roberts turned to Levell. "So how many times do you get off lying to people about their children, Mr. Thomas?" he asked.

"Jerry!" his wife exclaimed.

"I wasn't lying to you, sir. I saw her email address as the sender, and I came to you hoping we could discuss this," Levell said, trying to keep the same attitude of class and decorum, but deep inside, he was losing his mind.

It was clear that the parents were pawns for Raven. Either that or they didn't know how nefarious their little girl was.

"Well, Mr. Thomas, I do appreciate you coming over and visiting us," Mrs. Roberts said. "We have plans throughout the day today, so we're gonna have to cut this meeting short," she added, and Mr. Roberts headed back to the basement.

Levell could not have been more relieved to leave the Roberts' residence. As far as he was concerned, the Roberts didn't seem to have a clue about their daughter or her activities. Walking to the front door, he looked back at the staircase. There at the top stair stood Raven. Her friends weren't with her, and as Levell walked out the door, he could've imagined it, but he could've sworn he saw Raven wink slyly.

Shaking his head, Levell continued and crossed the street to his home. He felt the anger build up inside him. Raven played him once again by acting oblivious about the emails. He was angrier with himself that he didn't mention the menage' a trois that she had with her friends the night of the football game. He was sure that her parents would've had a stern talk with her after hearing about that excursion. Then again, they probably would've thought that there was no way their little girl would participate in any sexual act.

While on the way back home, Levell came across Caliya, cleaning the kitchen and doing laundry. Noticing the strained look on her husband's face, she was concerned.

"Baby, what's wrong?" she asked.

"Well, I walked over to Raven's house to speak to her parents because she hasn't been in class for the last three days, and her parents, especially her father, weren't cool at all with me being there," Levell replied.

Caliya looked out the kitchen window across the street at the Roberts' house. "I've been really suspicious about them lately, Levell. They've never welcomed us since we've been here, now that I think about it. Only Raven has been nice to us, and that's because she's your student," she said.

Oh, you have no idea why she's been this nice.

Secretly hoping that Caliya never read the email that Raven sent to him, Levell walked into the small study room to work on grading papers. He needed to get his mind off Raven and her parents. If she decided to transfer out of his class, that was better for him. He didn't have to worry about her staying after class just to talk to him. He didn't have to worry about being caught up in her sexual escapades. He didn't have to worry about dealing with her parents. He could focus on teaching his classes and getting through the year.

Three months passed leading into the new year, and Levell had successfully completed his first semester at Kennesaw Mountain High School. Normally, he knew how to teach classes without losing control of his life or stressing out. The most encouraging part of his career was the appreciation that students showed for him. He couldn't count how many times he would pass different classrooms and hallways, and most of his students from his first semester already spoke about how much Mr. Thomas cared about his students and how much fun he made his classes.

Students loved his innovative style of teaching and his willingness to help them succeed. Out of all the classes that Mr. Thomas taught during the first semester, he only had three students fail his class. One of them failed because he didn't follow the withdrawal policy, which normally mandated a student to drop or transfer a course before a specific date. But overall, most of his students passed, and although it was a rumor, Levell started to hear rumblings that he was going to be one of the teachers nominated for Teacher of The Year. He didn't give much thought to that because he thought there were other excellent teachers and professors who received consideration, such as his good friend Mr. Hopkins. Mrs. Render, the biology professor, and Mr. John Anderson, the physical education professor, also received nominations.

Wrapping his jacket around him, Levell walked out into the cold January weather and headed to his car in the parking lot when he saw a figure in a huge black jacket standing by it. The figure's back was turned, and the hood was pulled up so Levell couldn't tell who it was at first. The strange person appeared to be hunched over as if they were looking for an object.

"Hey, sir, is everything okay?" Levell asked, but the figure didn't turn around. Walking over to the figure, hoping it wasn't a car thief, Levell addressed him again.

At the second address, the figure turned around to face Levell. Although the scarf was covering her mouth, there was no denying the person under the jacket. The green iris stared intently at him with her black hair blowing in the wind.

"Hey, Mr. Thomas, did you miss me?" Raven asked in a voice that oozed honey.

Levell shook his head in exasperation, sighing deeply. For three months, she had not had contact with him. She had left him alone, but now here she was in front of his car. "Raven, what are you doing here?" he asked.

"Well damn, I just thought I would come and say hi. It's been three months since we've seen each other, and I was just seeing how you were doing," Raven replied as she walked up to her former teacher.

Levell could feel his body heat rising, even in thirty-degree weather.

"I'm doing fine, thanks, Raven. And that's close enough," he warned as Raven stood about an inch from him.

Raven rolled her eyes. "C'mon, Mr. Thomas, are you still mad about what I did at that party?" she asked.

"What do you think?" Levell asked. "You tried to tempt me to sleep with you on my wife's birthday. Then you send me provocative email messages," he added.

"How many times do I have to say that I'm sorry?" Raven asked. "I know I messed that up, but I meant what I said. Caliya doesn't deserve you. I still think I can treat you better than she can. You just gotta give me a chance."

But Levell was not going to bend this time. "Raven, you're a very beautiful young lady. If I wasn't married, and we were about the same age, I wouldn't mind dating you. But that's not the case right now. We can never be together, okay? It wouldn't be right," he explained, but he didn't know how persistent Raven was when it came to getting what she wanted.

"You see how cold it is outside right now?" she asked.

Levell nodded. "It's pretty cold out here," he agreed.

"Well, that's how cold your heart is," Raven replied. "But I could warm it up for you, if you just give me a chance," she said seductively.

She took Levell's hand, which was cold and ashy, and placed one of his fingers under her jacket, where he could feel the warmth of her chest and the beating of her heart flowing through his fingers. What she did next was completely unexpected and almost drove Levell out of his mind. Raven took one of his fingers and placed it in her mouth, her tongue swiveling and wrapping around his finger.

Oh my God, this girl is crazy. She is a sex fiend. Come on, Levell. Be strong. You're the adult in this situation. He had to break away from this spell that Raven had him in. She had a look of longing on her face, and Levell started to feel himself getting aroused.

"Let's get outta here. Caliya will never have to know," Raven said as she continued to entice Levell.

Deep inside of him, there was a beast that was erupting from within, and it was goading him to take up Raven's offer. *Go ahead, Levell. She's virtually throwing herself at you. You know you want to do it. She's young, dumb, and full of cum. Nobody needs to know what you're doing, not even Caliya. Just take her inside the school, find some empty room, and make it happen. A few quick pumps... hit it, and quit it. Take it back to them old days.*

Levell closed his eyes and thought about the pleasures of going inside Raven and fulfilling her fantasies as well. But he also thought about the pain and the consequences that came along with those pleasures: jail on statutory rape charges, Caliya discovering the affair and filing for divorce, breaking up their family, and his reputation at Kennesaw Mountain being destroyed beyond repair. He couldn't afford to get another rape case thrown at him. At that same moment, he came to his senses.

It ain't worth it. It ain't worth it. I ain't goin' out like that.

At that same time, he broke away from Raven. "Nah, Raven. I can't do it. I love my wife too damn much," Levell said, unlocking the door to his car and getting inside.

Feeling spurned, Raven turned to Levell as he started his car. "You ain't nothin' but a fool then," she said angrily. "You scared that you can't handle me. That's your problem," she added furiously.

"Okay, whatever. Just keep on thinking that, and stay away from me and my family," Levell replied as he threw his car into reverse to back out of the parking spot hastily, not noticing another car driving right behind him, nearly causing a collision.

The driver of the other car honked angrily as he took off.

"That's what you get for being an asshole!" Raven yelled as she continued to follow Levell's car up to the traffic light intersection at Kennesaw Due West Road.

Turning right, Levell sped away from the scene. Still shaking slightly, he turned on the heat to warm his car up, but he didn't turn it up all the way due to the beads of perspiration that had formed on his head. He almost hadn't made it out of the parking lot. Raven had him trapped, and she had come close to getting what she wanted, again. Levell thought the first incident where she was on his bed unclothed was bad enough, but this time she was fully clothed, yet she was still able to come on to him. He had to go home, shower, and scrub off any evidence of that girl.

But what was most perplexing and somewhat amusing was her reaction when he fended her off. She was so hurt, she had to insult him to make herself feel less inadequate. She couldn't stand the thought of being hurt or rejected, so she had to find any type of mechanism to cope, even if it resorted to petty name-calling.

She needs help. Her parents need to get her to a psych ward. Forget the hospital. That girl needs a strait jacket, tied all the way up to her neck and put in a room with padded walls.

As he pulled up in his driveway, Levell opened the garage and entered his home. Running upstairs to his bathroom, he took a quick shower, changed his clothes, and went downstairs to his study. He had to pick Patrice up from daycare soon. The daycare normally allowed parents until five in the afternoon to pick up their children before they started charging extra for after hours. Levell needed to check his email for any updates from Kennesaw Mountain High School or any further questions from his students. He saw an email notification signal in his inbox. As he checked for the sender, he noticed it was under an anonymous email account. He didn't think anything of it at first because many creditors and third-party marketers normally sent notifications under anonymous names. Levell simply deleted the email. But no later than two minutes after deleting it, he refreshed his page, and to his surprise, over fifty messages had made their way over to his inbox, all under the same anonymous sender.

Feeling sick to his stomach, Levell opened one of the messages. In large bold letters, were the words, "I LOVE YOU!" in all capital letters with heart emoji characters stamped all over the page. The message was repeated on all fifty messages.

Stunned, Levell frantically deleted all except one of the messages, which he printed and had with him when he grabbed his keys and walked outside. It was the final straw. He had to end this. As soon as he finished picking up Patrice, he was going to go straight to the police department to file a restraining order against Raven. As much as he hated resorting to that option, he felt that he had no choice. The girl was becoming more incorrigible with every passing day. She just couldn't take "no" for an answer. Now he had no choice but to teach that little femme fatale a lesson, even if it cost her some of her freedom.

It was the second full week of May, and the graduating class of the year stood up at Kennesaw State University where the graduation commencement was taking place. Sitting on the third row, only a few feet from the stage, Levell beamed as he watched his students pick up their diplomas. Chuckling to himself, he thought about the same exact moment the previous year when he was still at Hillcrest High School in Queens, watching all the students pick up their diplomas. It was basically coming full circle for him, and he couldn't have been prouder of his students.

Most importantly, he had completed the academic year without any controversy, worries, or stress. Since filing the restraining order against Raven four months earlier, it had been one of the most unencumbering second semesters as he didn't have to worry about her popping up next to his car or appearing to him while he was all alone in his classes. The order constituted that Raven stay more than one hundred yards away from Levell, whether in school or out of school. From what he heard from other neighbors, the Roberts weren't exactly thrilled about the restraining order, and they were deeply resentful of Levell, and that was putting it kindly. There would be days when Mr. Roberts would walk out to pick up his mail while Levell would leave to go to work, and their eyes would meet for a split second, but that was all the time Levell needed to know that he was public enemy number one in their eyes.

But Levell didn't care about that. All he cared about was the fact that Raven finally left him alone. He barely saw her during the second semester, and he knew that the police force was working diligently behind the scenes, tracking her movements between school and home and making sure that her classes never included Levell as an instructor. And they were making sure that Raven didn't meet up with him after school.

As the school administrator stepped up to the podium in Kennesaw's Convocation Center, he made general announcements about the accomplishments of the graduates and how proud he was for the school and the county. Finally, he started to make the announcement for Teacher of the Year. Levell and others were nominated for it and voted for by their peers.

"And without further ado, we would like to present the award for Teacher of The Year to Mr. Levell Thomas!" the administrator announced, and the audience cheered as well as the student body, which roared raucously and blew catcall whistles in jest.

Levell couldn't believe what he heard. Petrified, he couldn't move from his seat, so he just remained still for a moment until Caliya and those who sat around him urged him to walk onstage and accept the award. Feeling the emotion of the moment overwhelm him, Levell wiped a tear from the side of his eye. Just less than a year ago, he was telling himself that he wasn't ready for the challenge that teaching an unfamiliar environment would bring, but based on student feedback and their grades, his students and other members of the Board of Education seemed to believe otherwise. As Levell made his way to the podium, he felt the familiar sense of nervousness from whenever he had to address a huge audience. Speaking in front of a class of students was no problem, but having to address a crowd with thousands of people made him nervous. The administrator handed him the award and shook his hand. Levell finally stepped up to the microphone as the applause ceased.

"Wow, um, I really don't know what to say. This year has been one of the most memorable years for me and my family, moving down here from New York, and we didn't know what to expect," Levell said, searching the audience until he found his wife and daughter, sitting next to the seat he just vacated.

"Winning this award wasn't because of my efforts alone. I thank all my students who came to class every day and put forth the effort to succeed. Some of them are sitting with caps and gowns, and others still have a year to go. But I thank Kennesaw Mountain High School and the Board of Education committee for this award, and I wish the best of luck to our graduates!" he said as the crowd cheered again.

Levell walked back to his seat, kissing his wife and daughter on the cheek. Handing his award to Caliya, he excused himself to use the restroom located just outside the Convocation Center. As he stood over the sink to wash his hands, he looked at his reflection in the mirror when, suddenly, as if she had materialized out of thin air, Raven's eyes stared back at him.

They were red and bloodshot, as if she had been crying. Wearing a blue blouse with sky blue jeans, she smiled as she took in the look of shock forming on her ex-teacher's eyes.

"Hi, Mr. Thomas. Did you really think a restraining order would keep me away from you?" she asked in a hollow tone.

Chapter 11

LEVELL SLID TO THE SIDE OF THE SINK WHERE HE HAD just been washing his face a few seconds earlier. He couldn't believe Raven followed him to the men's restroom and was violating her restraining order without apology. Four months had gone without seeing her, and now here she was, her eyes narrowing, and her confident lips formed into a pout in realizing that she had cornered her obsession once again.

"Raven, what the hell are you doing here?" Levell asked angrily, unable to control the edge in his voice. "Not only are you violating your restraining order, but you're in the men's restroom. Have you lost yo' mind?"

Raven didn't answer right away, but she took a step toward Levell, prompting him to slowly back away.

"Well, the last time we were together like this, things didn't go too well for us, Levell," she answered, removing the hair ribbon that kept her long black hair in a ponytail until her hair flowed wildly, freely.

Levell continued to back away slowly.

"Raven, there is no 'us'. You need to get some help. I'm a teacher, and I'm married. Don't you get that?" he asked.

But Raven continued to advance toward Levell and acted as if she didn't hear his words.

"I'm willing to look past all the distractions that prevent us from being together. Come on, baby, we can make this work," she said seductively.

Levell couldn't believe what he heard. The girl was delusional. There could be no way she believed they could embark on some type of relationship.

"Levell, don't you see? We can run away together and start a new life, away from Kennesaw and away from Georgia. I could be a better mother for Patrice than Caliya ever could," Raven said.

Levell looked around. The restroom was not very large, and with the door about five steps to the right of him, he had enough room to make a clean getaway. He had to get as far away from this girl as quickly as possible.

"I could be the one who reads to Patrice every night before she goes to sleep. I can tuck her in at 8:30, and I could sing to her," Raven continued, oblivious to Levell's protests.

"Okay, I get it…wait. How do you know what time I read to my daughter every night?" he asked, but while he was asking, he came across the answer on his own.

Raven had been spying on him every night. The very first night when he was tucking Patrice in for the night and he saw a streak of black hair flowing in night sky, he shrugged it off, thinking it was some type of crow or owl, but it was Raven all along.

This girl needs a psychiatrist.

A sly smile came cross Raven's face. "Remember that night at the football game?" she cooed in her southern drawl.

At that moment, Levell vaguely remembered that night, but he wasn't going to tell her.

"Why don't we get into some trouble right here, right now?" she asked, and contrary to their last interaction, Raven decided to skip all subtleties and went at Levell aggressively.

Levell was not prepared for the impact, and when Raven grabbed him by his shirt collar, she kissed him full on the lips. Levell broke the connection and tried to pry her off him, but Raven was uncharacteristically strong for her small stature.

"Come on Raven, get off me!" he yelled, looking at the door, hoping nobody walked in on them.

"Come on, Teacher of The Year. Teach me a lesson I'll never forget," she coaxed as he continued to back away, her body still pressed on him.

"Raven, look. We can't do this, okay?" Levell pleaded, hoping for a speck of sanity from this mad woman that had him in her clutches. He didn't want to resort to getting physical, but she was forcing the issue.

When she grabbed his face to move in for another kiss, Levell pushed her back into one of the stalls, more forcefully this time, and Raven fell back, stunned. Levell shook his head angrily. He had hoped he wouldn't resort to physical contact, but it was self-defense at that point. "Raven, I'm tellin' you. I'm not gonna say it again. Stay away from me, you hear me?" he warned her.

Just like a light switch, Levell saw Raven's face turn up and her facial features flashed signs of anger. "I'm not giving you up that easy!" she yelled.

When Levell made a dash for the door, she jumped on his back in anger, hanging onto his neck and chest, trying to subdue him, but Levell pried her hands away from him. Relieved that she finally got off, he thought the confrontation was over, but in the next split second, he felt a burning, electrical sensation through his body. With a grunt pain, he fell onto the linoleum surface hard, banging his head in the process.

His body still, he looked back at his attacker in shock. What had she done to him? Looking up at Raven, he saw the taser in her hand. She had taken it out of her pocket and shocked him while his back was turned. For the next couple of minutes while Levell floated in and out of consciousness, Raven got on top of him. He felt his belt being undone, and she was sliding his pants down. His ears still ringing from the impact, he couldn't hear the words that came out of Raven's mouth, but he knew he had to get away from her. She barely had time to pull down his underwear before he pushed her off him again with more force. With a yelp of surprise, Raven fell back, hitting her head against the stall post.

Pulling his pants back up, Levell opened to the restroom and ran as fast as his legs took him. Still groggy and experiencing blurred vision, Levell made his way back to the Convocation Center. He found his wife, who was holding his award.

"Baby, let's go. We're leaving," he said to Caliya who turned to look at him and was surprised as well as other people in the row to see Levell's clothes disheveled and his face red.

"Baby, what's wrong? What happened to you?" she asked as Levell took Patrice's hand and guided her outside to walk to their car.

Levell didn't answer right in front of the other parents and family members who attended the graduation. He didn't want to create any suspense.

"Baby, you're really scaring me. What happened? Why your clothes messed up?" she asked, but Levell didn't answer any questions until they reached the car.

As soon as he placed Patrice on her child seat and sat in the driver's seat, he finally explained Raven's aggressive attack. "Caliya, I barely got out of there. Raven came at me in the bathroom and tried to attack me," Levell said.

Caliya couldn't believe what Levell said at that time. "Wait a minute, she attacked you in the men's bathroom?" she asked in shock, yet her voice had the concealed skepticism that she spoke with whenever she doubted him.

"I know it sounds crazy, but that girl is cracked. She came in the bathroom to try to get busy, and when I turned her down, she lost it," Levell explained. He could see Caliya's look of concern, but he knew that his wife would probe around, searching records, validating her husband's claims.

"Is that what happened? So, Raven did this to you?"

Upon answering, Levell finally told Caliya what happened, from the time Raven laid down on their bed on her birthday, to the recent encounter in the restroom. Levell could see his wife's eyes seething in rage.

"Levell, why didn't you tell me none of this? Why you ain't say nothing to me earlier? I would've checked the little bitch. See, I knew I didn't trust that girl. Something was off about her," Caliya said, unapologetically.

"I'm sorry, Caliya. I didn't wanna drag you in this. I thought I could handle it, but she just kept coming back and kept getting me in compromised positions," he explained. "But she got worse and worse and kept coming back. This time, she had a taser on her, and she tried to get me down so she could abuse me," he said as he made a turn off Cobb Parkway.

"So not only did this chick violate her parole and lie on my bed, but she tried to hurt my man too? Uh-uh, turn around. We're going back," Caliya said furiously, but Levell felt exhausted and didn't want his wife to overreact.

"Baby, calm down," Levell said. "I'm on my way to report that girl. She violated her restraining order and tried to assault me. I'm on my way to the precinct right now," Levell said. "Time to show her ass a lesson," he added as he turned onto an intersection that would take them to the P.D.

As soon as they parked, they walked inside the precinct building. Many of the officers were in the office filing paperwork, addressing people that walked in with documents. They waited for a few minutes until Sherman Powell, the Kennesaw chief of police, addressed them.

"Yes, how can I help you today?" he asked.

"Officer Powell, how're you doing? My name's Levell Thomas, and this is my wife Caliya," Levell introduced. "A few months ago, I filed a restraining order against Raven Roberts, citing abuse, and today she violated the order," he reported.

Officer Powell appeared half-interested while listening to the account. "Okay, so she violated her order and attacked you?" he asked.

Levell started to sense the apathetic reaction from the chief. It was as if he couldn't be bothered by a student attack. "Yes, sir. She attacked me in the men's restroom, and she used a taser on me. Sir, I barely got away, but she should be charged," he replied.

Officer Powell reached into the files in one of the cabinets behind him and pulled out a file and the copy of the restraining order.

"Okay, Mr. Thomas, I do have a copy of the order you filed in late January. Now you're aware that if charged, she is a minor, so she won't be charged as an adult?" Officer Powell asked.

"The hell with that!" Caliya said vehemently. "If she grown enough to pull the shit that she's pulling, she grown enough for the big house!" she added emphatically.

As Levell tried to call his wife down, Officer Powell replied, "I understand your frustration, Mrs. Thomas. We spoke with her parents regarding those charges, and they have denied any evidence of contact or accounts of any contact from Mr. Thomas. Now we still upheld those charges out of respect for Mr. Thomas. Where is Ms. Roberts?" he asked.

"I don't know. She still might be at the Kennesaw Mountain commencement ceremony, but it's been a while, so she might be at the mall, the park, or at home," Levell answered.

"Okay, we'll put an APB out on her, and once apprehended, we'll take a statement from you," Officer Powell stated.

Reluctant not to leave the police station without assurance that Raven would be arrested, Caliya and Levell had no alternative but to go home and wait for the outcome. As they drove home, Patrice was in her child seat playing with her doll while Caliya and Levell didn't exchange a single word. Levell felt his wife's glare boring right through him. He knew Caliya was upset that he concealed what Raven had been doing to him, and he knew that his marriage could be in serious jeopardy. Pulling up to the driveway, Levell parked the car, went to the back seat, and unbuckled Patrice from her child seat. Caliya got out of the car as well, walking behind the two.

"Tricey, why don't you go upstairs to play with your dolls, okay?" she asked.

"Okay," Patrice said, heading upstairs.

Levell watched his daughter walk upstairs, knowing what was coming next. Caliya was about to start an argument with him. He never got into any huge arguments with Caliya in the past, but this time, she wasn't going to cut him any slack.

"So how long has this thing with you and Raven been going?" she asked.

"What thing? There's nothing going on with me and that girl. She made a couple passes at me in class, but I thought she would draw the line there," he replied.

"Oh really?" Caliya asked sarcastically. "And what about when she was lying down butt-ass naked on my bed on my birthday? Or when she was kissing up on you in your car? Did you draw the line there?" she screeched.

"No, she caught me off guard when she did all that," Levell replied.

"And you couldn't tell me? I thought we were a team, Levell. Your problems are my problems too. If you knew that child was coming after you, you should've told me," she said.

"You're right. I'm sorry, okay?" Levell apologized. "It's just a situation that just got out of control, that's all," he explained.

"Were you attracted to her?" Caliya asked.

"What?" Levell replied. He couldn't believe Caliya would ask him that question. "No, I wasn't attracted to her. I told you, she came at me," he insisted, although he knew deep inside that he was lying to a certain degree.

Raven was appealing to the eye, but to Levell, it didn't compensate for her instability. Before he protested further, there was a loud banging sound. Someone was frantically knocking on the front door. Levell excused himself from his agitated wife to answer it.

"Yes, who is it?" he asked the unexpected visitor.

"This is the Kennesaw Police Department. Please open the door, sir," the officer said sternly.

Why the police knocking on my door? Maybe someone heard what went down between me and Raven, and whoever it was, must've called the police.

Caliya emerged from the kitchen and had the same thought as Levell about the officer's intentions. "Well, open the door. They probably wanna get a statement from you," she said.

Levell opened the door and was taken aback when he saw two white officers standing in his doorway. Suddenly, a wave of nervousness fell over Levell. He would've been able to give a statement to one officer, but the presence of two officers seemed more ominous.

"Hello, officers, is there anything I could do for y'all?" he asked.

"Are you Mr. Levell Thomas?" one of the officers asked.

"Yes, sir, that's me," Levell replied.

What happened next completely took Levell by surprise. One of the officers held a small document in his hand with sloppy scrawled writing. While placing the document in his pocket, the other officer took out a pair of handcuffs and said the very words that Levell dreaded to hear since growing up in the hood: "Mr. Thomas, you're under arrest for sexual assault and battery of a minor."

The officer who placed the document in his pocket grabbed Levell's shoulders roughly and held his two arms behind him, while reading his Miranda rights.

"Assault from who? Hold up, I ain't assault nobody!" a stunned, angry Levell remarked as the officers slapped the handcuffs on him.

Caliya, who stood a few feet from the doorway, saw the ordeal, and naturally her instincts to defend her husband came out.

"Officers, wait a minute. This has gotta be a mistake. Levell wouldn't assault nobody!" Caliya said frantically as the officers walked Levell toward their police cruiser.

"Ma'am, I would kindly ask you to please retreat back to your home," one of the officers, an older man with gray sideburns and bushy mustache, said.

Nearby neighbors who arrived home early from work watched and witnessed Levell being taken away by the Kennesaw police officers. While he was being led to the cruiser, Levell glimpsed various people watching him taking the perp walk to the officer's vehicle. This was the type of publicity and attention he wanted to avoid. But Caliya did not retreat quietly, following the officers to their squad car.

"Officers, who charged my husband? I have a right to know that!" she screeched as the officers got inside their car. But Caliya didn't have to look far to figure out her answer as she glanced across the street at the only neighbors who didn't come outside upon hearing the squad car.

It was them. The Roberts charged Levell for assaulting their daughter when the slut was obviously trying to sleep with him, she thought, and she let the cops know about it.

"It was her! Wasn't it?" she asked. "Raven was the one that charged him, wasn't it?"

The officers didn't respond, avoiding her gaze. At the same time, Levell came to the realization that Raven set him up and accused falsely him of rape.

"Man, this is some bullshit!" he said angrily from the back of the car.

Caliya stood in the path of the squad car.

"Ma'am, I won't tell you again. Go back in the house," the officer repeated, more warily.

"Officer, please listen. My husband didn't rape or hurt nobody. That girl was stalking him, and she tried to attack him, and he's a rapist? That don't make no sense," Caliya said angrily, but Levell shook his head, asking Caliya not to provoke the officers any further because he was not ignorant to various reports on police brutality and knew that the police would look for any excuse to gun her down.

"Baby, it's okay. Just go back in the house. The last thing we need are more problems. I didn't do a damn thing to her. She's lying," he added, and Caliya walked back in the house, intending to call her lawyer once she got inside.

Glancing at the hallway window near her front door, she watched the car back out of her driveway. As soon as the officers left, an enraged Caliya crossed the street to the Roberts' residence.

Knocking on the door frantically, Caliya was at her wit's end. "Mr. Roberts, where are you?!" she yelled frantically, but no one replied.

Caliya knew that she had no right to just walk on other people's property only to behave belligerently, but she didn't care if Mr. Roberts came out with a shotgun or any other weapon. If she had to go to her grave defending her husband, she would go all the way for him. "Mrs. Roberts, answer the damn door! Ya know good and well my husband didn't rape that hoe you call your daughter," she said.

Nobody answered the door, and Caliya figured that they were still out. Maybe she might've been out of line, but at that moment, she was determined to expose her neighbors. Another neighbor from two doors down by the name of Angela Cartwright walked up to her. Angela, who was not only her neighbor, but also a co-worker at Kennestone Hospital, attempted to comfort Caliya, hugging her, trying to calm her down. Caliya, in her rage and anger, broke down crying in Angela's arms.

"I don't why they did that to us. We didn't do or say anything to them, and they're attacking us," she said.

Angela's face reflected the sorrow and regret she felt her friend going through. "I know it's hard, girl. Your husband is a good man, and I know for a fact he didn't do those things," she reassured Caliya, whose face was tear-streaked.

"The worst thing about it is that I should've known. I should've known that girl was up to no good, and she was after Levell," Caliya said.

"Honey, there's no way you could've known what their intentions were," Angela replied.

"They're evil," Caliya said. "They're evil, conniving, scheming racists. And trust me, it's gonna come back to them," she added.

"Caliya, you're not thinking of doing anything rash now, are you?" Angela asked in a concerned voice.

"Well they had no problem charging my husband on a false accusation, so I ain't gon' have any problems messing up their world," she replied, before thinking it over.

Levell wouldn't want her overreacting to situations beyond her control. At times when Caliya felt like blowing her top or whenever she felt she was cornered, she remembered what Levell told her: "Don't allow tough circumstances to lose your mind. Instead of panicking, use your mind."

It was a clever play on words but also useful advice. She had to calm down and decide what she was going to do. Then, as if a light switch went off, she knew. She was going to fight fire with fire. If the Roberts wanted to set her husband up, she was going to expose them through the law. To accomplish this task, she was going to need the help of a family relative who worked in the Marietta Police Department, but not before working in the NYPD for years.

Dialing a number on her cell phone, she turned to Angela. "I think it's time to call my cousin," she said.

Leon "Stuntman" Jones ran as fast as he could, leaping over ditches and fences as he tried to elude law enforcement. Leon was a drug dealer with a rap sheet that included assault, use of a deadly weapon, and intent to injure another citizen. What started out as a car chase, continued by foot as he abandoned his car and continued running through a path of trees with two to three officers hot on his trail. He was wanted for severely beating a man to a pulp at a local bar, and when law enforcement was called, Leon knew he couldn't stick around for the officers to pick him up. He couldn't understand why these big shots couldn't leave him alone when all he wanted was a drink. They always had to drag him into these types of situations. If the police hadn't been called, he probably would've killed the man. He always had a checkered past and couldn't allow the police to apprehend him or else it was game over for him. He could hear the footsteps of the other officers behind him.

Checking the sides of his pants, he had a small pistol that probably only had two bullets. He was covering a lot of ground, but he felt his lungs betraying him and fatigue starting to set in. He knew he couldn't keep this up. He was going to have to stop at some point. When he made an erroneous turn onto a dead end on Spire's Street, he knew the police were closing in. Shutting his eyes, beads of sweat started to form on his face. He took his pistol out of his pocket and pointed it at the direction of the street corner where the cops were expected to turn. He had a good head start after abandoning his vehicle and was a good quarter mile from the police at the start of the chase, but he knew that it would come to an end. Sure enough, three cops came into the clearing. The street was illuminated by one streetlight. Leon could see that all three officers had their guns out and pointed at him.

"Okay, Stunt, it's all over. Drop the weapon and put your hands up now," one of the officers ordered.

More officers came into the clearing, and before Leon could move, he was surrounded by eight officers. But Leon was resilient in his criminal resolve and was not backing away without a fight. Pointing his gun at all eight officers, he started laughing uncontrollably. The police officers looked at one another, almost certain that Leon was losing his mind, unaware that he was using his laughter as a diversion to slide over to a side street to escape. With guns still pointed between them, Leon held his head, his eyes began rolling, and spit began falling out of his mouth in an insane episode.

Orders were given to the police to approach the suspect calmly, as they tried not to trigger him to open fire on any of them. It was obvious that he was not heeding to their calls to drop his weapon. But a couple of officers rushed in too quickly, and Leon's gun went off. As soon as the officers heard the shot, they knew they had to fire back in self-defense, but before they fired, Leon crumpled to his knees, blood covering the top of his head. He had been knocked out by a blow to the head from an officer's gun butt. The officers moved in to remove the pistol from Leon's hand and handcuffed him. Leon, who was only semi-conscious was walked over to the police cruiser.

One of the officers, Charles Anderson, turned to the officer who knocked Leon out as the other officers made their way over to their squad cars. Charles said to the officer who walked just in front of him, "Smooth move, slick. Got him out without us having to draw any chalk outlines."

Turning around, officer and former detective Isaac Sands turned to face him. "Appreciate that, Anderson," he said, smiling.

Chapter 12

AS HE PARKED AT THE PRECINCT PARKING LOT, OFFICER Sands got out of his squad car and headed inside the building. He walked past a few officers who were booking two suspects on charges of drug possession and robbery.

"Hey, Chief, heard about Leon's takedown earlier. Good shit, man," Officer Anthony Rosales said to Sands.

"Appreciate it, Rosales," Sands replied.

"Yo, Chief, what's up?" another officer, Frank Temple greeted.

"Chief" was the nickname that every officer in the division gave Detective Sands since he previously served as a police detective and chief in Precinct 101, the Queens Police precinct, for twenty years.

Starting out as an officer in one of Queens' Juvenile Halls, Sands was lauded for his work with troubled teens and was soon promoted to detective of the Queens precinct where he continued solving crimes, from robberies to drug busts and gang activity. Sands caught and apprehended a dangerous gang leader named Tadarius and many members of his M.O.B. gang after one of the biggest gang busts in the history of the city. Afterwards, he relocated to Long Island, New York, where he worked for five years before moving down south to Marietta with his wife, Betty; twelve-year-old son, Bryce; and eleven-year-old daughter, Jalisa.

Noticing his background and his experience as a detective and head chief of the Queens division, the police commissioner offered Sands the head chief position at the Marietta precinct, but Sands declined the offer because he wanted to work his way up to the position. He didn't want to cause a stir among fellow officers who had worked there for years, only to have a new officer arrive from out of town and assume the position without earning the rank. As a result, Isaac Sands happily began his Marietta police tenure out on the field with other officers where he stayed. And although he wasn't a chief, the other officers in the precinct gave him the nickname "Chief."

Heading to the locker room to change shirts and remove his bulletproof vest, his partner Charles Anderson entered the locker room. "Hey, Sands, P. T. wants to see you in his office ASAP man," he said.

Sands looked at Anderson. P.T. were the initials for Paul Taylor, the real police chief of the precinct. Normally, when he requested to see someone, it was either for two reasons: disciplinary action or promotion. Very rarely did he call officers in his office for any other reason.

"Alright, tell him I'm on my way," Sands replied. After five minutes, he made his way over to Chief Taylor's office and began knocking on his boss's door.

Taylor opened the door for one of his top officers. "Close the door behind you, will ya?" he asked, and Sands closed the door.

Paul Taylor was a short, stocky white man with short hair that was balding rapidly. Some officers in the division weren't too fond of Taylor because he was known to be short-tempered and judgmental of others. But Sands and other officers didn't have an issue with Taylor because, while he was very strict, he was also fair and bipartisan of any officer, no matter his or her background, race, or gender. Sands believed that Taylor's rough, abrasive attitude came from service in the Gulf War in the early 90s, much like Sands' himself.

"Please, take a seat," Taylor offered, and Sands sat in the single chair facing the chief's desk.

Although he had been in this office before, Sands looked at the walls where Taylor's certificates from his training in the academy were mounted and his trophies for being Citizen of The County for ten years.

After three minutes of silence, Taylor asked, "Do you know why I brought you here, Sands?"

Shaking his head, Sands indicated that he didn't know why he was summoned to Taylor's office. "I'm not sure sir, but I have a feeling that you're gonna tell me why," he answered nonchalantly.

Smirking slightly, Taylor opened his desk drawer and took out a few yellow pieces of paper with ineligible writing. "Do you know what these are, Sands?" he asked.

"Yes, sir, those are police reports," Sands replied, internally wondering why Taylor asked him although he had been working law enforcement for years. It seemed like he was being undermined.

"Right, and do you know what's in those police reports, sir?" he asked.

Sands looked over the reports and noticed that the dates on the reports had passed, but they all were describing details about the previously arrested Leon. The many charges on those reports included robbery and drug possession charges as well as the most recent report on charges of battery.

"You may be wondering why I showed you these reports and why I've highlighted them," Taylor said.

Sands shook his head. "I'm not sure sir," he replied.

Taylor sat in his chair, now looking at Sands more intently. "Well, Sands, I wanted you to review these notes so it could be more apparent to you how dangerous this man was. Out there in the pursuit of Leon, was he not armed and considered dangerous?" he asked.

Sands lowered his head, shaking it slightly. He knew what was coming. "Yes, sir, he was considered armed and dangerous," he replied.

"Well then, why in God's name did you get in the way of your fellow officers, then?" Taylor asked.

This time, Sands did not know what his chief was talking about until he recalled what he did or didn't do. "What do you mean, sir?" he asked.

"I'm talking about your vigilante tactics, Sands," Taylor answered. "The man had his gun pointed at our officers, so at that point he is a danger to himself and a danger to our men, which gives us the right to take him down by force, before you interfered with your reckless actions," he said.

Sands looked at Taylor quizzically. What had he done wrong?

"Reckless actions? Chief, all I did was knock the guy cold so the officers could arrest him," he argued back.

"I mean, do you know how many of our men you put at risk? What if he was so coked up, he didn't feel anything, and he fired at the force? What would you say then, huh?" Taylor asked.

"Sir, I promise you, I was not trying to play super cop, but truth be told, I saved this division a lot of time, money, and possibly negative press," Sands replied.

"Oh yeah? And just how did you manage to do that?" Taylor asked.

"The man has a few drug raps and committed battery, but did he kill anybody? No, so why did that justify killing him?" Sands asked.

"So, what you're saying is that you'd rather have dead police officers than one dead suspect? Seems like your logic is twisted, Sands," Taylor said.

"So, my logic is twisted because I believe that every man should have his day in court? It was clear that the brotha' was out of his mind, and him having his gun pointed at us was beyond stupid. But it would've been more stupid to shoot first," Sands protested.

"Sands, I completely understand your stance on this issue, but this ain't the streets of New York. This isn't Queens, no matter how much you try to delude yourself that you're still there because you're not, and as long as I'm still here, you will follow chain of command. Do I make myself clear, Officer?" Taylor warned.

"Crystal, sir," Sands replied, but he wasn't done. "I know it's clear that you want your officers to shoot down armed or unarmed men and call it a day. It's clear that whenever we have a suspect that's, shall we say, a lighter complexion, we shoot to maim or injure. But when comes to people like me, you want us dead," he added.

"That's enough, Sands. I don't need a sermon. You may leave now," Taylor said dismissively.

Shaking his head, Sands left the chief's office. *Some people will never understand what they are and what they're doing.*

Looking at the other end of the precinct, he saw police bring in suspects, mostly for traffic violations and small misdemeanor crimes.

They were all young, foolish, impressionable, and very naïve to the world around them. But most of them were similar in another way: they were black, and just like millions of other black men, they were confused about their place in life and lost in this wayward country where they were taught to be reckless. They were taught to be criminals. They were taught to be violent. And just as the black men seemed programmed by the standards of society to wreak havoc in their communities, the white men and white police officers were programmed to eliminate all of them and those who were innocent even more than those who often got in the way. By no means was Sands defending the crimes of Leon, but he deserved to be tried in the court of law just as everybody else.

Walking outside the precinct, Sands took out a box of Marlboro light cigarettes. Lighting a cigarette that he had in his mouth, his mind flashed back to that fateful night in October 2003 back in Merrick, New York, during the stakeout of M.O.B., the gang accused of murdering a female high school senior. The victim's boyfriend, David Anderson—a former gang member—was initially accused of the murder but was acquitted in court after insufficient evidence and several witness accounts that didn't place David at the scene of the crime.

Upon his exoneration, David agreed to work with the NYPD to expose the whereabouts of M.O.B. whose leader, Tadarius, had them relocating to different areas of the borough to escape police. It was a high-risk sting operation, for when David located his former gang, Tadarius was a moment away from killing his old companion before Sands and members of the NYPD in SWAT gear emerged and raided the old apartment where the gang members hid, resulting in one of the most violent and bloodiest shootouts in the history of the city.

When the smoke cleared, two gang members who were young black men lay dead on the ground. Sands never forgot the overwhelming feeling of sickness that washed over him when he saw those bodies lying in the pool of their own blood. He would never forget it. Just a few months earlier, his wife had just given birth to their first son, and although their son's entrance into the world was a joyous occasion for them, it was also very bittersweet for Sands. He knew that he had a stern responsibility to teach his son how to act and discipline him accordingly. He couldn't allow his son to be caught up in the streets. Too many of boys who were in the gangs never experienced happy endings.

Sands was a tough man himself, but even he had shed a tear over the death of those two boys who were caught up in their element. Although they unwisely challenged authority, they were too young...much too young. Any of those boys could've been his sons. While people rejoiced that M.O.B. and its ringleader were finally brought down and brought to justice, Sands retreated from the spotlight. Knowing that he could no longer raise his family in that segment of Jamaica, Queens, he moved to Long Island where he spent the next five years. But the Long Island system was corrupted, and many officers in their division were either caught in scandals or doing heinous crimes behind the scenes.

At that point, Sands grew disenchanted with New York and decided to move to greener pastures in Georgia. But nothing erased the memories and the images in his head of the two boys. Even now his son, who was now in the seventh grade at Marietta Middle School, reminded him of one of the boys who lost their lives that day. Since then, Sands made an oath to himself: never again would he shoot another black man or child to kill, and he wouldn't let anyone else on the force take any black lives either, even if it cost him his job.

After smoking his cigarette, Sands went to his locker where he retrieved his cell phone. A blue light was flashing on it, stating that he had a missed call. In truth, he had three missed calls. As a habit, Sands never took his cell phone with him when he was on duty because he saw it as a distraction. Checking his voicemail, he noticed that it was his cousin, Caliya, who had called. He dialed her number back. After two rings, she picked up.

"Hey, Ike," she said, using his childhood nickname.

"Caliya, how you been? It's been a long time. How's everything going?" he asked.

There was a pause on Caliya's end. She didn't know where to begin. "Not good," she admitted. She went on to explain how the precocious girl next door was harassing Levell and how Levell attempted to quell the abuse, only to be charged of abuse himself.

Sands listened, but the more he did, the more it felt as if Caliya was blaming herself for her husband's arrest.

"I mean, I should've seen it sooner. When I tell you, this girl got a stank attitude about her...I knew there was something wrong. She just gave off this weird vibe," she explained.

"What vibe could a seventeen-year-old girl be giving out?" Sands asked curiously. "They're at the age where they're finding themselves, hooking up with other guys and what not. Now the only problem I see here is this sounds like an inappropriate relationship between teacher and student, and if her parents hire an attorney, they have the power to take this case to a state court," Sands informed Caliya. "If Levell is found guilty at the state level—hell, at the local level—he could be looking at ten to fifteen behind bars."

"Damn," Caliya sighed. "But the thing is, the whole scenario just wreaks of a setup. They're setting my husband up, and I just can't sit here and do nothing," she replied.

Sands knew his cousin long enough to predict that she would try to take on the system herself. But Sands advised her against taking such actions. "Okay, Caliya, let's see if more clues are revealed in this case because if they ain't got a paper trail, they can't charge Levell with anything. I will ask you this though. Was Levell intimate with this girl?"

He secretly hoped Caliya answered that he wasn't because if he found out that Levell was two-timing his cousin, a high school girl would be the least of his worries.

"No. he wasn't," Caliya said firmly, although in her mind, she was unsure.

Levell was known for having a wandering eye while they dated and even early into their marriage, but she never took him for a serial cheater or rapist.

Sands continued asking questions. "And did he tell you the girl was harassing him?" he asked.

Caliya paused again. "I don't know how long they've interacted with each other before today," she finally confessed. "She used to show up in the house every morning so that he could give her a ride to school because she didn't have a car yet."

"Okay, so aside from this interaction as well as in them school halls, was there any other time they had close contact?" Sands asked.

"Well, at my birthday party...you know I invited her to attend, and she came by with a friend. When the party was about to end, this little wench goes up to my room, strips down to her birthday suit, and tried to have sex with my husband. And mind you, I was downstairs," Caliya explained.

"Whoa, either this girl got daddy issues, or she need a man that badly," Sands said, laughing.

"I don't see what's funny about that," Caliya replied, and Sands felt the edge in his cousin's voice, so he continued more seriously.

"Okay, and Levell didn't do anything with her that time, right?" he asked.

"Levell said that she tried him, but to his credit, he turned her down. He didn't play that mess, but the girl kept trying since then," Caliya said. "She just wouldn't give this game up. She appeared at an awards event today, and she knew my husband was going to be there, and they had another confrontation in the men's room. My husband came out, and he was shakin', Ike. When I tell you, his clothes were ripped in some areas, he looked like he been through a tornado. He said that she tried to mess around again, and she attacked him, using a taser on him," she explained, taking a deep breath before continuing. "We rushed out of there, due to Patrice mostly, and once we got her home, we're contemplating calling the police to report assault, and this ain't the first time. Levell did put out a restraining order against her once the harassment got worse, so she violated her restraining order when she attacked him," she said.

"Okay, so we can start with that," Sands replied. "If Levell has a restraining order against her, it'll be on record, and y'all would have a case against this girl."

"I hope so, cuz. I know she is setting my husband up because he didn't want her skanky ass," Caliya said sharply. Then her tone softened. "I'm asking for your help in this situation, Ike. Please?" she asked earnestly.

Sands stared out into the clear May night. He had regular duty hours at his station, and he had to patrol his town. But this was family. Caliya and Levell needed his help. Although Sands did not know Levell too well, meeting him only on a couple of occasions, Caliya was in over her head. He knew the whole case could detonate in their faces if it was, indeed, discovered that Levell had an inappropriate relationship with a high school minor.

But on the other hand, Sands, just like Caliya, sensed that Levell was being wrongfully charged for other reasons. It didn't escape his mind that one of those reasons could be due to Levell being a black man. Although there were false perceptions that race relations have improved, Sands knew from history that men who were accused of false crimes ended up on the wrong side of the law.

"Okay, Caliya. I'll do whatever I can to get to the bottom of this," Sands replied.

"Thank you so much," Caliya replied gratefully before hanging up.

As he dropped his cigarette butt in the public ashtray, Sands couldn't help but wonder what he had gotten himself involved in.

As the squad car made its way through downtown Kennesaw, Levell stared out the partially-barrier window from the back seat. Never had he been in a worse predicament as he currently found himself in at that moment. During the first few minutes of the ride, he tried to argue his case to the officers that they'd gotten the wrong man, and he didn't have any prior offenses before they apprehended him, but his protests were ignored as the police continued to make their way towards the Kennesaw Police Department. After a while, Levell just gave up and remained silent. Although he found himself in dire straits, he still couldn't help but to find his situation humorous.

He spent thirty-four years in arguably one of the biggest cities in the U.S. and somehow managed to stay out of trouble with the law, but the moment he relocated to what was supposed to be a change of scenery and a positive career direction, he found himself a suspect under police custody. It didn't make any type of sense, but what happened over the course of a year didn't make any sense either. All of it could've been avoided if he had turned Raven in for the sexual misconduct that she displayed on the night of the game, but he hesitated and never went with his gut instinct. As a result, he allowed this strange individual to roam free and make himself prey to her. Shaking his head to himself, he couldn't believe he fell for the charm and the sweet, innocent look that Raven passed off. If he wasn't a stronger man, he might have taken the bait, and then it would've been ten times more controversial.

Levell wondered if the media was going to discuss it in the news. He was sure the local media outlets would've aired the story at six o'clock. If the police let him go, he might as well start thinking about cleaning out his desk at Kennesaw Mountain High School. He knew that the negative press was going to fall upon the administration, and they could not afford that type of media attention. Then he also knew the Board of Education would somehow launch an investigation regarding the interaction between Raven and him. It sure didn't help that he had given her all those rides to school in the morning, and students had witnessed those excursions. It didn't help that Raven's family lived across the street from his family. It didn't help that people heard Raven's screams as she insinuated the use of deadly force by Levell. And it's not going to help him explain his side of the story when they hand him the pink slip and tell him to hit the road.

But avoiding prison time was a battle in and of its own, and to fight this battle, he would need a lawyer. He was sure that Caliya was back home calling one of the attorneys from the Peach Law Group, the same firm that Uncle Max and other family members were utilizing. He hoped the lawyer would look at the case from an unbiased perspective and understand that it was self-defense. Levell was trying to defend himself. That was it. He was banking on the fact that his lawyer would focus on two factors: forensic evidence and the record of the restraining order that he filed against Raven back in January. He was sure that at some point, the doctors would run tests on Raven. He was positive that they were not going to find any blood, semen, or urine stains on her, and once they discovered the absence of Levell's DNA in her, they would know for sure that she was lying. The restraining order would just be the icing on the cake, and once the police department could cancel out any motive that they suspected Levell had against Raven, he would be in the clear.

The only question that remained unanswered was the length of time that it would take to accumulate the evidence needed to prove his innocence. As the car approached the station and parked, the officer who sat in the passenger seat exited the car.

Opening the back door, he addressed Levell: "Step on out, but no sudden movements. Let's go," he said in rushed tones.

Levell stepped out the squad car and gave both officers dirty looks.

What the hell am I gonna do while I'm handcuffed?

As they led him inside for due process and criminal booking, he looked at the clerk that sat at the other side of the processing window from him. He also saw other suspects, some with handcuffs and others who had already had them removed. Levell didn't have any time. He had to find someone who could locate a record of the restraining order. He looked around the station. One of the officers instructed him into the processing booth where photos were taken and handcuffs were removed for fingerprints.

As he was being processed, Levell asked the officers who processed him, "Look, I'll go through the process, but I haven't committed a crime. About five months ago, I filed a restraining order against my accuser for harassment. It should be on record, so can you check it please?"

The processor looked at one of the other officers, and to Levell's relief, the officer gave him permission to check the files for the restraining order. Levell sat and waited. He was confident that the evidence of the restraining order would release him.

Finally, the processing officer returned. Levell perked up, waiting to hear some good news. "Well, Mr. Thomas, after thorough searches through our records, unfortunately, we weren't able to find the restraining order file," he said.

Chapter 13

CALIYA ANXIOUSLY LISTENED FOR THE INTERACTIVE voice response system of the Kennesaw County jail system to prompt her to allow her husband to speak with her the next morning. Levell had not returned home, and Caliya feared the worst. Perhaps he was being held in a jail cell awaiting his court date in which she knew she couldn't contact him until he called from their phone system. She was sure the police had confiscated his cell phone, so he was unable to call her. And his battery must be dead because when she tried calling the night before, his phone went straight to voicemail. After a two-minute long hold, she finally heard Levell's voice.

"Baby, what happened? I tried calling you on your cell phone, and you didn't respond," she said.

"I know," her husband replied, and by his dull tone, Caliya could already tell that he was beginning to lose hope in the holding cell where he awaited his trial. "They couldn't find the damn restraining order that I filed against Raven, and now they think I'm making the whole shit up. This can't be happening right now, Caliya. It's like a bad dream that I can't wake up from."

He felt even worse because if he told Caliya or anybody what was happening, he would've avoided the predicament that he was currently in.

"Baby, listen. I looked online last night and found a lawyer: Allan Richter. He's part of a private firm in Acworth. I was thinking about calling him and asking him to take up this case for us," Caliya said.

Levell remembered upon moving down south how Max informed him to partner up with a lawyer, in the unlikely event that he faced legal trouble. At first Levell shrugged it off and told Max that he would find a law firm when he got around to it, but he procrastinated and had not carried out his own promise. Maybe this was karma for shrugging off his uncle.

"I'm willing to try anything right now, Caliya. I gotta get outta here. I don't belong here. I didn't do anything," he said.

"I know you didn't, Levell. It's not like you to take advantage of someone," she agreed.

Levell hung his head. He knew he had only a couple of minutes before his call time was up.

"Baby, I'm sorry I'm didn't tell you about Raven earlier. I was wrong for trusting that devil or anyone like her down here. I should've been upfront about her from the beginning," he apologized.

"It's okay, Levy. We all make mistakes. But believe me when I tell you, I'm gonna do whatever it takes to prove your innocence and get you outta this. What you gotta do now is to be strong, baby. I need you to be strong for me and hold on till the trial date. Can you do that for me?" Caliya asked, struggling to hold back her tears.

Her husband had never been locked up before although he had a close call back in college but was never found guilty of the crime that he was accused of back then. Caliya knew that there was a possibility that he could lose his mind in jail, if not his life.

"Yeah, baby, I got you," Levell answered before the phone system confirmed that there was no more time left in their call and that the call must end.

After hanging up the phone, the jail warden directed Levell back to his cell. There were no other convicts in the next cell over, so Levell felt the isolation and the cruel feeling of being truly alone as he sat on the jail floor, reminiscing on only a few days ago before his life took a turn for the worst.

Allan Richter paced up and down the front of the courtroom in front of the judge and one of the witnesses who was being cross-examined. There were only a few people at the trial. Max and Vicky attended, but their children stayed home. A few community members were also at the trial as well as Caliya, who sat directly behind Levell and waited anxiously for Allan to finish the cross examination of Causwell Peters, another teacher at Kennesaw Mountain High School and head of the English department as well, which made him Levell's boss.

Levell was starting to feel confident that he would be released. So far everyone who had taken the stand had glowing words about Levell and his teaching, which angered the prosecutor, who sat next to Raven and her parents. Levell did his best not to glance in their direction, but his eyes would wander over to them every so often, and he could sense their venomous stares at him.

"So, what you're saying, Mr. Peters, is that my client has no history of assault or abuse. Is that right?" Allan asked.

"That's right," Mr. Peters confirmed. "Levell Thomas has not shown any sign of abuse or physical aggression with any of our students. As a matter of fact, many of our students consider him the best teacher they had...hence, why we voted him the Teacher of The Year," he continued.

"Thank you, Mr. Peters. No further questions, your Honor," Allan addressed Judge Aaron Crawford, a middle-aged, stout white man with balding gray hair.

The prosecutor for the Roberts' family, John Covington, was a tall, thin man with a Southern drawl. He stood up from his chair. "At this time, I would like to call Ms. Ginger Grant to the stand," he said.

After a minute, Levell saw Raven's friend sit at the witness stand. After she swore on the Bible, John began his cross-examination.

"So, Ms. Grant, what is your current relationship with Mr. Thomas?" he asked.

"Well to me, he was just a teacher, but he was a very cool teacher," Ginger answered.

"Did Raven ever express any thoughts of infatuation, or shall I say, 'obsession' for Mr. Thomas?" John asked.

Ginger shook her head. "No, she never told me that she liked him liked that."

"Objection, your honor," Allan said, but it was overruled by the judge.

She's lying. I know she's lying. Levell stared intently at Ginger.

There was no way a girl would keep secrets from her best friend or "bestie" as they like to refer themselves at times. The same way they shared that unfortunate Tex fellow on game night, they were capable of sharing lies as well. John continued cross-examining Ginger.

"How close would you say Mr. Thomas was with his students?" John asked.

"Well, I never had him this year, but I had friends who were in his class, and all of them said that he was cool," Ginger replied.

Despite the seriousness of the atmosphere, Levell tried his best to stifle a grin. He knew he hadn't been Teacher of The Year for nothing.

"Is it true that Mr. Thomas would normally give Raven car rides to school each morning?" John asked.

Ginger lowered her head, slightly, and right away Levell knew that she was conflicted. He started realizing that John was going for the angle that he was a popular teacher who just found himself being too comfortable in the wrong place at the wrong time.

"Yeah, Mr. Thomas, would drop Raven off to school every morning," Ginger answered.

"And has he given car rides or any other types of favors to any other students?" John asked.

"Not that I know of," Ginger replied.

"And has she ever described any inappropriate behavior that Mr. Thomas may have displayed towards her?" John asked.

Levell held his breath at the question. Somehow in the back of his mind, he knew that public opinion of the jurors could swing toward Raven's camp by Ginger's response.

"Well, she did tell me that she would find him staring at her for minutes, staring at her body," Ginger replied.

Levell closed his eyes, rage coursing through him. He never looked at Raven that way, and even if he did, how did it prove that he molested the girl? He could hear the murmurs of the people in the courtroom.

"Well, no doubt Raven would make any young man happy," John continued with a sly smirk. "Please explain what happened on graduation night," he continued.

"Well, I went there because I had some friends who graduated this year, and Raven came with me. We sat through graduation and watched everyone pick up their diplomas," Ginger replied. "Then Raven tells me she was going to the restroom and that she would be back. So I waited, but she never came back. About thirty minutes later, I decided to go to the bathroom to check on her because I started to freak out a bit, you know?" Ginger continued. "When I go into the girl's bathroom, it was empty. I didn't see Raven at all. I looked in every stall, and she wasn't there, so I thought she might've went back to her seat, so I was gonna leave the bathroom when some kid comes to me and tells me that there's a girl in the boys' bathroom who looks like she's been hurt bad," Ginger explained, her voice breaking silently.

Levell shook his head. It didn't sound too good for him at all.

"Even if it was the boys' restroom, I had the worst feeling that it was Raven, and sure enough, there she was, lying in the corner of the bathroom wall, her clothes ripped, and she had bruises everywhere. I asked her what happened, and all she could say was, 'Mr. Thomas...Mr. Thomas,' Ginger said, tears started to stroll down her face.

Levell bowed his head. Ginger painted a vivid image in the minds of the jurors that he knew was irreversible.

Allan immediately stood up. "Objection, your Honor. Just because Raven was found with bruises does not mean my client was responsible for them. This crime could've easily been committed by somebody else," he argued.

"Objection overruled," the judge replied, slamming his gavel on his desk.

Levell glanced at Raven. Some of the bruises were still apparent on her neck and her shoulder, but he didn't do what they thought he did. He had to defend himself when she attacked him. After a few minutes of loud commotion, order in the courtroom was restored, and John continued.

"After you saw Raven and called for help, was Mr. Thomas still at the premises?" he asked.

"No, by the time I realized who Raven was talking about, he'd already left," Ginger answered.

"Thank you, Ginger. No further questions, your Honor," John said as he went to walk back to his seat next to the Roberts family.

Allan stood up and prepared his own cross examination of Ginger. "Ginger, how long have you been friends with Ms. Roberts?"

"We've been friends since we were still in diapers," Ginger said, smiling lightly. "Our parents knew each other for years, and we always went to the same schools in the same district, and we always celebrated each other's birthdays by throwing parties at each other's houses."

"So, it sounds like you and Ms. Roberts have known each other for years now," Allan said. "While growing up, did you know anybody that had anything negative to say about Ms. Roberts?"

"Not really," Ginger replied, shaking her head. "Well, the only knock she ever gets is that she's an overachiever. She works so much harder than everybody else."

Well, that was one thing I could agree with Ginger on: she does work hard. She's putting in overtime to make sure my teaching career's destroyed.

"That's great. So now let's get to the nitty-gritty of this trial," Allan said. "Has Ms. Roberts ever expressed any sort of infatuation towards Mr. Thomas?" he asked.

"No, she never expressed those feelings," Ginger answered, quickly.

"Okay, Ginger, remember you're under oath now. You just stated that you were best friends, and she normally would tell you certain things. So, are you one-hundred percent sure she did not admit some sort of crush on Mr. Thomas?" Allan asked.

"She didn't tell me any of that, I told you!" Ginger answered, more sharply this time.

"You seem like a nice enough girl, Ginger, but lying for your friend at this juncture's not gonna get you anywhere," Allan replied.

"I'm not lying!" Ginger yelled.

"Objection, your Honor," John said to the judge. "He's badgering the witness."

"Objection upheld. Please refrain from irrelevant cross-examination," the judge informed Allan, and he slammed the gavel hard to make a point.

"She has a boyfriend. Why would she be hittin' on somebody else if she got a B.F.?" Ginger protested, and the commotion grew among the other patrons of the courtroom, resulting in the judge slamming his gavel down harder than ever.

Allan smiled, knowing he had her rattled and that the events leading up to the supposed assault had become blurry.

"I would like to call Mrs. Thomas to the stand," he said, and Caliya walked up.

After Caliya took oath, she sat down on the witness stand. "Okay, Mrs. Thomas, can you tell the courtroom how long have you been married to Mr. Thomas?" Allan asked.

"Yes, sir. Levell and I have been married for nine years now," Caliya answered.

"Do you have any children, Mrs. Thomas?" Allan asked.

"Yes, I have one daughter. She's four years old," Caliya replied.

"And how would you describe Mr. Thomas as a husband and father?" Allan asked.

Caliya looked at Levell, their eyes seemingly locked together as if they were comforting each other's souls during the trial.

"Levell is a wonderful father. He loves his daughter, and we love each other. He is an example both at home and at school. His students have nothing bad to say about him at all," Caliya replied. "He is a positive example to students in his classes," she added.

"Has Levell ever been accused of inappropriate contact with any minors during the tenure of his teaching career?" Allan asked.

"Not at all," Caliya replied vehemently. "My husband wouldn't do anything to anyone because he has a great teaching career, and he wouldn't risk throwing it away for something this serious," she answered.

"Thank you. No further questions, your Honor," Allan said as he took his seat.

John stood up and paced the courtroom. "Mrs. Thomas, can you briefly describe the mood in the home whenever Raven comes over?" he asked.

"At first, I was indifferent to it because Raven was just another student my husband was teaching. But as time went on, the mood changed, and it became more awkward," Caliya explained. "She was coming over every day, and I'd be lying if I didn't say that I was feeling jealous because my husband had a big heart, and this girl was taking advantage of it. I felt pushed aside," she said.

"So, in essence, what you're sayin' is that Raven spent most of her time with Mr. Thomas, and it caused tension?" he asked.

God, he's playing that angle again. Is he ever gonna quit making me out to be some kind of sex-crazed boogeyman?

"So, during that time, did you ever witness Levell make any passes at Ms. Roberts?" John asked.

"I've never seen him make any passes at her. But she has tried to make a pass at him," Caliya answered.

"Okay, can you give me some examples?" John asked, although Caliya could tell by his voice that he was dismissing her claims that Raven made advances at Levell.

"Okay, well there was the night of my birthday party. My husband invited Raven to the party," Caliya said, before suddenly realizing her mistake. She might've opened her mouth about the party invitation too early and had now given the prosecutor more ammunition.

"So Levell invited Raven to your party? Pretty strange that a high school teacher invites one of his students to a party where there is sure to be alcoholic beverages...am I right?" John asked.

Levell lowered his head, wishing his wife never uttered words regarding those events.

"I mean she stayed across the street, and we invited other neighbors too. It wasn't meant to spite me. But then, that girl did what she knew was wrong. She went upstairs to my bedroom and waited for my husband to come up so she could have sex with him. My husband refused," Caliya said, strongly emphasizing the last three words, while staring at Raven and her parents.

There were deep mumblings in the courtroom, and most eyes turned to Raven.

Levell breathed a sigh of relief. *Maybe people will see Raven for the devious, scheming person that she really is.*

"Okay, Mrs. Thomas, even if that was true, why do you think Raven felt this comfortable around Mr. Thomas?" John asked.

"I don't know, sir. All I know is that he refused the little slut, and she left the house as she should," Caliya replied angrily, as the thought of her husband and Raven making love on her bed incensed her beyond the boiling point.

"My daughter is no whore! You watch your mouth there, missy!" Mrs. Roberts screamed at Caliya.

"Well, tell her to stop lying down nude on my bed then!" Caliya bit back.

"Okay! Order people! Order!" the judge exclaimed, slamming his gavel three times.

John paced the courtroom a few times. Every time he did that, Levell got nervous as he knew John would have an ace up his sleeve. Sure, enough he did.

"Well, it wouldn't be the first time a woman was found on his bed nude then," John said, pulling some old police reports from a package envelope on his table.

Please don't let that be what I think it is. Please God, don't let my past sins fall into this devil's hands.

"Ladies and gentlemen of the jury, in my hands, I have an old police report from June 2000, where a young nineteen-year-old, known to the public as "Levey" was arrested and indicted on charges of rape of a female co-ed at Queens College in New York," John said, slamming the report down in front of Caliya.

Levell never experienced asthma attacks before, but he suddenly found it extremely difficult to breathe, as if he was hyperventilating. Caliya seemed to be at a loss of words as well, her face pale at the sight of the information that was presented to her.

"Says here the girl was a victim of hazing that was done by a male fraternity group that your husband joined. She was found unconscious on one of the boys' beds, and guess whose bed that was?" John asked.

When Caliya stammered and shook her head, unable to utter a single word, John answered his own question.

"That's right, Mrs. Thomas. The young woman was found on your husband's bed. Not a good look for Teacher of The Year, eh?" he asked as he walked back to his seat.

Caliya stood up on the witness stand. She knew about the story, and even though her husband was arrested, it was never proven that he raped the young college co-ed. For many years they'd tried to forget about the incident and move on.

"My husband was never found guilty of that crime!" she exclaimed angrily.

"No further questions, your Honor," John said, ignoring Caliya on the witness stand while she continued protesting.

"My husband was a college boy and joined a fraternity like any other college boy would. He made the mistake of joining the hazing initiation, but he was never charged for anything!" Caliya argued, but it was futile at that point.

The judge once again restored order in the courtroom and called for a recess, where the jurors would take their time to deliberate on the testimony and the evidence presented.

Back at the Marietta precinct, Sands went to file the last of his police reports from morning patrol before heading back to the squad car. Although the news covered Leon's capture and arrest, it didn't do him any justice. With an intent to clear his mind and work out his frustrations, Sands went to the gun range located in one of the adjoining buildings beside the station. The facility was dark. Nobody was there yet, and that's how Sands liked it. He knew that in a few minutes, some of the other officers would make their way into the range to work on their shooting. It was nothing personal to his fellow officers, but he felt uncomfortable standing next to a white officer while firing at the same paper targets. He often wondered who the officers envisioned shooting when they were firing. Did they envision some unarmed, confused, wide-eyed black boy, or were they unbiased in who they were shooting at? Until he had a clear idea, Sands wouldn't turn his back on any of them.

Sands put on some noise-cancelling headphones, and as he loaded his Glock 22, he hit a switch on the pole next to him so that the metal hooks, guided by a long conveyer belt, made their way over to him. He selected a paper with huge round target circles and hung the paper onto the hooks. Then with another push of the switch, the conveyer pulled the paper target back as far as 150 yards before stopping. With his hand at ready, he aimed the firearm toward the target and fired one shot. With a loud bang, the bullet pierced the target directly in the chest. He shot a few more rounds, some towards the torso and two head shots.

As he readied his gun again, the images came back. With a blink of an eye, he was back in the abandoned apartment building, and members of the SWAT unit stood behind him. They crouched low, waiting for the signal from the decoy that had engaged in conversation with the dangerous suspects. Sands listened intently, and once the moment came, he emerged and demanded the suspects drop their weapons. But instead of listening, they fired. As Sands fired the target, the bullet ripped through paper, and the shells fell onto the floor. But with every bullet ripping the paper, all Sands could see was the bullet ripping through flesh, blood, bone marrow, and chest cavity, and bodies hitting the floor. Sands shot at the target again.

Why did they have to shoot at us? Why didn't they drop their guns upon command? Why am I seen as an enemy to my people?

It was only after the dust settled from one of the deadliest shoot-outs in Queens' history that Sands realized that he wasn't an enemy to his people. The badge and whom he worked for were viewed as an enemy to his people. The significance of law enforcement and their interaction in the black community was what citizens feared the most. For many black men, the badge was the very last image they saw before their life was snuffed out. As Sands continued to fire into the target, he heard the door of the range open. A few off-duty officers walked in and started to put their gear on to shoot their targets.

"Yo, Sands, what you doing here so early?" one of the officers asked.

Sands took off his headphones and put his firearm down. It was time for him to go. "Nothin,' just getting some target practice done. I'm on my way out," he said as he took his belongings and left.

Levell waited nervously for a verdict at the Kennesaw City Courtroom. He wished he knew what decision the jurors would make because the whole case was split into two public opinions: those who believed he was innocent based on earlier testimony and those who believed he was guilty, only affirmed by an old case that he thought was thrown out years ago because they couldn't tie him to the hazing back in college. But the fact that it was his bed the girl was found on, did no more than implicate Levell during the trial.

After two long hours of deliberation, one of the jurors came back out with the verdict. The people in the courtroom, who had been immersed in silent talks, finally came to attention. The juror began reading the verdict out loud. Levell and Caliya held their collective breaths, waiting to hear that the jury found him not guilty of the crime of raping and assaulting Raven Roberts.

But he would never hear those words. On June 20, 2015, Levell Thomas was found guilty of assault, battery, and rape and was sentenced to ten years behind bars.

Chapter 14

I T WAS A SCENE FOREVER ETCHED IN LEVELL'S MIND AS soon as the final verdict was given in the Kennesaw City Courtroom. Uncle Max and Caliya stood up in anger and protested loudly against the judge and the officers present and had to be quieted by the judge, who pounded his gavel to restore order. Caliya was ready to go after the prosecution, but the Roberts—the family of the girl who falsely accused her husband—was shoving Allan aside as he attempted to stand between her and them as they celebrated the verdict.

Levell could have stood between his wife and the accusers, but all he could do was stand there, shaking his head at the verdict that was given. All he wanted to do was take advantage of a teaching opportunity in Georgia, and when he finally had his chance and had shown some level of success, in one swoop, it was all taken away from him.

As the police proceeded to place handcuffs on Levell's hands once again, he glanced across the courtroom at the people he now perceived as enemies and glanced at Raven's face. Throughout the trial, she wore a fake, dramatic expression, appearing ready to break down into tears as if she was really traumatized. She played her role well, fooling everyone, especially the jurors, who were now responsible for his fate and made sure his life hung on a balance. At the delivery of the verdict, for a split second, Levell saw her expression change. The traumatic, fearful expression was momentarily replaced by a smug smile as she looked at Levell as if to say

"I finally got your black ass. This is payback for ignoring me, and now it's your turn to experience misery."

The most unsettling part about the scenario was that it could have all been prevented. Levell felt Allan's hand pat his shoulder lightly, quietly consoling him without saying a word. Levell couldn't place all the blame on his lawyer, but he really didn't want to be touched by Allan Richter. He had failed him in this case, and even though he would no doubt request a plea bargain for less jail time and possibly appeal for parole in the next two years, his future was bleak.

As the police led him away, Levell came away with another epiphany: his professional career was over. The local news would be covering his case, and once people viewed his face plastered on their television screens, they wouldn't take a chance to hire him. His career at Kennesaw Mountain High School was as good as finished. He imagined the head administrator and the principal going over to his classroom, cleaning out his desk and belongings and removing his name from the school website and the system. His name and his photo, which was taken after he won Teacher of the Year and was scheduled to be hanged just outside the auditorium, would be taken down immediately. Kennesaw Mountain had a reputation to protect in the Cobb County School System. Parents who were sending their kids to school would not want their kids to attend classes that were being taught by an accused pedophile.

Levell had watched his unfortunate fate befall so many professors and teachers back in his school days in Queens. Now it was a cruel twist of irony that he joined the nefarious list of perverted educators who taught their students more than what was on the curriculum. Not to mention, he would also be part of another dubious list: a list of registered sex offenders in Georgia. Caliya would be receiving countless visits from state officials, asking about his relationship with his daughter and who would probably allude to accusing him of having inappropriate activities with Patrice. Although, Levell knew that Caliya would defend him with a passion, her words would be taken with a grain of salt. They were not going to believe that her husband was a hardworking man who was accused by a psycho ex-student of his, but they would believe that he was unstable, violent, and lewd in every mention of the word.

Despite Allan's words telling Levell that he would do whatever it took to seek a retrial or to work on a plea bargain to reduce his sentence, Levell knew his life was over. His career was over. At that point, he came to terms with what he would be going through. He was determined not to show sorrow or weakness. He had to be strong and tough-willed at this point. He was heading to a prison where he knew he was going to be surrounded by other accused criminals, some of them possibly murderers—individuals who were dangerous and wouldn't hesitate to kill or rape those other prisoners they considered soft. Levell had witnessed, firsthand, the effects of prison life through his cousin Pernell, a son of his father's sister who was the same age as him.

Pernell was also a man convicted and charged with armed robbery and assault with a deadly weapon. He had spent three years in a high-security penitentiary, and when he was paroled for good behavior, Levell saw the change that took place with his cousin. Pernell, who was typically a jokester playing pranks on his siblings and joking around with Levell before his sentence, became deadly serious when he was released. Once an outgoing, social individual, Pernell later became reclusive and private. He revealed to Levell that he still struggled to sleep at night because he still heard the screams, the blood-curdling yells of inmates being violently tortured and raped by other inmates in the dead of night. He told Levell that after the guards performed their nightly checks of inmates before lights out, a couple inmates would sneak out of their cell blocks and head over to the cell of the weakened or feminized inmate, one they could easily take advantage of without fear of resistance. While the other prisoners slept peacefully as if nothing was wrong, the poor victim could be heard grunting and yelling in pain as two or three prisoners overpowered him and penetrated him anally. Pernell described the yells of pain as "foreign and unlike any sounds he heard from a normal man...the worst sound any man could hear: the sounds of his manhood being taken from him."

Levell also noticed that half the time his cousin visited, he would smell his cousin's body odor. When he asked about it, Pernell confessed that he would sometimes go days without showering, a habit that he unfortunately picked up while he was locked up. Showering with other prisoners almost guaranteed them being violated. He would tell Levell that he would often wait for the other prisoners to finish showering before he got in the showers himself, and if he managed to take showers with the other prisoners, he made sure that he kept his head up and his back straight. The worst part of the whole experience was what Pernell experienced psychologically.

Being in an enclosed cell for hours had Pernell deep into his thoughts, and the more he thought about his extended stay, the more hope he lost in life. He would often tell Levell that prison tested his sanity. It wasn't a secret that prisoners would lose their minds and became so mentally unbalanced that they would do anything to leave their current situations, which included committing suicide. Pernell witnessed more than a fair share of inmates who hanged themselves, cut themselves with sharp wall objects, or overdose on crack cocaine, which was smuggled to them by friends who often visited them.

One horrific death that Pernell witnessed was when a prisoner by the name of Jermaine Shawley, nicknamed "Shaw" by other inmates, fought a guard during one of the night checks before lights out. Shaw was 6'4" and weighed about two hundred and twenty-five pounds and easily overpowered the smaller guard. But what baffled Pernell was that right after Shaw knocked the guard out, he grabbed the guard's firearm, and Pernell thought for a split second that Shaw would shoot the guard. But by this time, the prison alarm, which rang whenever there was a prisoner attempting to escape or whenever fights broke out, went off, and Shaw, probably realizing that he would soon be subdued by the other guards, took one last look at Pernell, as if to say, "Stay strong, brother" right before he blew his own brains out with the gun. Pernell still envisioned the bullet entering Shaw's skull and the blood that splattered from the exit wound before his lifeless body hit the floor.

Pernell admitted to Levell that he never showed remorse or concern for any inmates who were locked up with him, but Shaw was a prisoner that he had befriended. They would share a comradeship before that horrendous day. Shaw was the one that strengthened and encouraged

Pernell from within the cell blocks and told him to keep his guard up every day. "Never turn your back on 'em, pup," Shaw would tell Pernell, addressing him by a personal nickname he gave Pernell from the time they met. He called him "Pup" because of their difference in age. Pernell was twenty-one when he met Shaw behind bars while Shaw was entering his forties, having been in prison for over ten years. Pernell remembered struggling not to cry that night after they removed the body and wiped up all the blood. He described to Levell that if any of the prisoners heard him crying, he feared that he would be perceived as soft and would be ripe prey for other prisoners to rape him.

Although Pernell was relieved when he was finally released from prison, the nightmares never ended. He never stopped reliving the horrors that he witnessed while in prison. The most chilling image was his friend and mentor's head snapping violently to the side from the force of the bullet that entered his right temple. He cried at his home for many weeks, unable to sleep, eat, or live a normal functioning lifestyle. The last time Levell saw Pernell, he only had a few weeks before moving to Georgia. Pernell had lost close to seventy pounds and was almost frail.

"So, you're moving down south, huh?" he asked Levell when his cousin told him about his job opportunity.

"Yeah, man. It gives me a chance to experience life outside of New York, you what I'm saying?" he remembered telling Pernell.

"Yeah, I feel you. I hope you make some noise down there in Atlanta," Pernell said in his Jersey accent. "But remember, they don't play down south though. Remember what it was like for guys like us forty years ago?" he asked.

"Yo, come on, man. That's history son. This is the new millennium, man. This ain't the antebellum South anymore, and it ain't Jim Crow-" Levell replied, but his cousin cut him off almost immediately.

"So, what?" he replied harshly. "Ain't nothin' changed, man. Not for us, anyway. They still treat us black folk like shit down there. You think what I went through at the pen was bad? Imagine what jail's like down south, man. If you get caught by them cracker cops down there, it's a wrap, son. They ain't gonna give you no type of chance. Them folks won't hesitate to throw yo' black ass in jail for nothin'. I'mma tell you what Shaw told me, and that's to keep your guard up. Don't turn your back on any of 'em," he warned Levell.

Now with the verdict that basically sealed his doom, Levell realized how prophetic his cousin's words had been. He'd underestimated the climate he was living in, and now he found himself in the same exact situation his cousin was in years earlier, all because of a white girl who couldn't keep her hands to herself and cried wolf to the police. Levell knew there was foul play involved because they couldn't even find the restraining order that he placed against Raven a few weeks ago. But he didn't heed the warning his cousin gave him. He turned his back on Raven and his other conspirators, and that cost him dearly. Levell knew he now had to harden his resolve and his attitude. He couldn't allow the other prisoners to view him as a pushover. He was going to fight to stay alive, even if he had to break an inmate's neck to do so. He took one last look at his wife before being led out of the courtroom by police.

A few hours after her husband was charged with rape, Caliya sat in her living room with Uncle Max, Allan Richter, and Vicky. Still reeling in shock at the final verdict, Caliya had almost lost control, threatening to leap over the railing to get her hands on the prosecutor, the Roberts, and their devious daughter, but Allan jumped in her way in the nick of time and prevented Caliya from making physical contact. Now, they were at her home trying to figure out how they were going to get Levell out of prison.

"Here's what we can do," Allan explained. "It was explained to me right after the trial that Levell still has a possibility of parole, but it won't be until October 2015, and he'll have to register as a sex offender-" he continued.

Caliya immediately cut him off. "Register as a sex offender? You gotta be kidding me, right? Levell teaches high school kids for a living. How is he gonna find another job in this town if he's a registered sex offender, which by the way is a damn lie?" Caliya said, pacing up and down her living room uneasily, although the other guests were sitting on her couch.

"I understand your anger and your frustration, Caliya, but that's the best plea bargain that I can get right now," Allan explained. "If he can do time for a little less than a year, he might be eligible for parole in six or seven months. Then he would be released."

"But he'll never work in this town as a teacher again though, right? Is that what you're telling me?" Caliya asked.

Allan put his head down, and Caliya knew that he didn't want to tell her that any hope of Levell resuming his teaching career was dashed. "So, we'll have to move again and start all over? Find a different line of profession?" she asked.

"It's more than what most people get from the judicial system now," Allan admitted.

"The judicial system..." Caliya repeated, chuckling dryly. "The system failed my husband because some crazy girl accused him of something he ain't do, and now he's got to throw away years of school and his teaching degree for this so called judicial system?"

When Allan failed to reply again, Caliya paced the floor again. How was she going to explain this to Patrice? Currently she was in daycare, but at some point, she was going to start wondering where her father was. Caliya couldn't bring herself to tell her daughter that he father was locked up.

"Caliya, I know you're shook up about this whole thing, and no one feels any worse about this than I do," Uncle Max said.

"But you didn't do anything," Caliya insisted.

"I'm the one who convinced Levell to come down here and take the job. Hell, I'm the one who advised him to buy this house," Uncle Max replied.

"It's not your fault, Max. This girl lives right across the street from us. I should've sensed that she was disturbed. From the way she looked at me when we met at the high school football game, I should've known this girl was cracked. She probably saw me as competition for Levell," Caliya said.

"A girl like that needs help. She probably got some mental issues she's dealing with. Maybe she's been abused by her parents. Perhaps she needs a psychiatrist," Vicky suggested.

"No, what she needs is a psych ward, with a strait jacket and shots that put her to sleep every damn hour. That's what she needs," Caliya replied cruelly.

"I mean, think about it, Caliya," Vicky explained. "She's probably been abused at home, and she saw Levell as male guidance and protection, but she mistook it for affection and infatuation."

Caliya stared at her relative in bewilderment. How could Vicky not see the manipulation? "Vicky, do you not understand what's going on here? Don't you see that they locked up your nephew because of the lies of a high school psych job? How can you defend that girl?" Caliya asked angrily.

"I'm not defending her. I'm just trying to find a rational reason for all this," Vicky argued.

"Ain't nothing rational about that girl, Vicky. Are you on her side, or are you on ours?" Caliya asked, and the two ladies went back and forth until Uncle Max whistled loudly, causing silence between them.

"Look, baby, Caliya's right about this girl. She knew what she was doing. Ain't nobody stupid," Max said.

"Thank you," Caliya said. "I think she planned this all along. I think her parents helped her set Levell up."

"But what proof do we have of that?" Allan asked. "I can't just present that theory to the judge without evidence that indicates he's being set up."

"Fine, but what I wanna know is how did the prosecutor get his hands on that old case back in college? That case was supposed to have been thrown away," Caliya said.

"I know, but somehow it must've been kept on his record. I'll get to the bottom of that right away," Allan promised.

"Please do," Caliya insisted. "He was found innocent that year. Some other frat boys placed the girl on his bed to implicate Levell, and he was the fall guy for it. I'm not letting them get away with it again," she added.

Before Caliya proceeded, she heard her doorbell ring. Peeking through the peephole, she saw that it was her cousin, former detective Isaac Sands. She opened the door for him, greeting him with a hug.

"Hey, cousin, thanks for coming," she said before inviting him inside.

"No problem. I was on duty, but I decided to stop by and check on you. My partner's still waiting outside, so I'm gonna make it real brief," Sands said. "I did some research and digging in this area, and I just happened to find out that this is not the first time the Roberts were involved in the public implication of a black employee. Look at this," he said, reaching into his pocket and pulling out a printed newspaper article dating back to the year 2004.

Caliya took a closer look at the article. Apparently in January 2004, a black man by the name of Jim "Sonny" Williams was arrested and charged for the murder of 62-year-old Charles Deneau, a former politician who ran for Georgia's seat in the Senate. Although Deneau lost the election, he continued to reside in his hometown of Alpharetta, Georgia, working as head of Deneau Deliveries, a postal delivery chain. Williams worked as a postal worker at one of Deneau's locations where all the employees described Williams as a "diligent, hard-working fellow who did his job and took care of his family as well as others."

But then, the article continued, explaining the events that led to the murder of Deneau. The week before Deneau was found dead in his office with multiple stab wounds to the chest and neck, there was a huge layoff of Deneau's employees, including Williams. Williams, who had a wife and three children, was especially affected by the lay-off, so he sent a letter to Deneau, expressing his frustration over losing his employment. When Deneau reportedly didn't reply to the letter, Williams took it upon himself to visit Deneau to discuss his employment status. Deneau's wife invited Williams inside her home. She'd recalled that he was, indeed, polite and only wanted to talk to Mr. Deneau and ask for a recommendation for future employment endeavors. But Mr. Deneau, who was known to be short-tempered, seemed to scoff at Williams before finally dismissing him from his home. Enraged, Williams left Mr. Deneau's home, and not too long after, Deneau's lifeless body was discovered by his wife.

Immediately, police officers were sent to Williams' home, and he was arrested and charged with the murder. Among those who accused Williams was one of Deneau's close friends and confidante Jerry Roberts. Roberts had served as vice president of Deneau Deliveries. He described Williams as a "big brute that deserved to rot under the jail" for the heinous crime.

After a trial in which the evidence did not tie Williams to the murder of Mr. Deneau, Williams was nevertheless found guilty of the crime and was sentenced to life without parole. Friends and supporters who disagreed with the guilty verdict stated that Mr. Williams was set up and that Mr. Roberts implicated Mr. Williams for no other reason than the fact that he was black who had been heralded as a model employee.

After reading the article, Caliya looked at Sands, her eyes widened in realization. "Jerry Roberts, isn't that...?" she started to ask before Sands answered her question.

"Raven's father, yup," he confirmed. "He was one of Williams' main accusers, and it was no secret that he harbored hatred for this man, or any man who worked there for that matter," Sands replied.

Before Caliya replied, Allan walked over and introduced himself. "Hello, I don't think we've had the pleasure of meeting yet. I'm Allan Richter, attorney at law for Mrs. Thomas," he said, shaking Sands' hands.

"Detective Isaac Sands, Marietta Police Department," Sands replied.

Allan's eyes suddenly widened. "Wait a minute. Isaac Sands? Weren't you the main investigator for the gang bust in Queens, New York, about twelve years ago?" he asked.

"Yeah, that's right. How did you know about that?" Sands asked. He thought the news of that event aired locally.

"I remember your name being mentioned on CNN and other news outlets the day after the shootout. Biggest gang bust in Queens history, huh? You must've been quite the hero up there," Allan quipped.

"Yeah, but I try to block that day out as much as possible," Sands replied, and Caliya wished Allan hadn't brought up the event because she knew from past talks with her cousin that he wished it never happened.

"Yeah, well I had called Detective Sands here because I wanted him to find out as much as he can about Raven and her family," Caliya said.

"And it seems, Detective Sands is onto something. So, this isn't Mr. Roberts' first go-around at accusing an innocent man for a crime, I see," Allan said.

Caliya shook her head. She had a feeling that her husband had been set up, and now her suspicions had been confirmed. She was convinced

Mr. Roberts coerced his misguided daughter to accuse Levell of rape. "So, what do we do now?" Caliya asked.

"Well, I actually intend on interrogating Mr. Roberts about this case, and I'll make sure to bring up this little detail here," Sands replied.

Caliya shook her head. If this scenario played out well, her husband may see freedom sooner than expected, but she knew that it all depended on chance. If only she had access to the article before Levell's court date, she would have countered John's hidden information with Mr. Roberts' hidden information. "Thank you so much, Detective. Find out what you can, and please be careful," Caliya said.

"No problem, cuz. You know I got this. We'll have Levell out in no time," Sands assured Caliya before stepping out of her home.

After closing the door behind her cousin, Caliya closed her eyes and secretly prayed that Detective Sands would soon crack the case and her husband would be exonerated.

Chapter 15

STARING THE POLICE GUARD STRAIGHT IN THE EYES, Levell reached for the orange prison jump suit required for each inmate to wear. As soon as the verdict was read in the courthouse, Levell had barely had time to bid his family goodbye before he was handcuffed once again and led out of the courtroom. He could hear his wife's angry protests and his uncle grumbling about how crooked the justice system was, but it wasn't going to change the jurors' decision to convict him of child molestation and rape.

He was taken to a small block cell no larger than a storage room where he was ordered to strip off his clothes and his belongings. His cell phone, belt, shoes, and car keys were immediately confiscated, and he was forced to change his clothes right in front of the guard. When he had stripped down to nothing but his underwear and prepared to put on his prison attire, the guard suddenly stopped him.

"Not so fast, my man. Take them boxers off too," the guard ordered.

Levell looked at the guard as if he was out of his mind.

"Come on. Hurry up. We ain't got all day," the guard continued impatiently, so right in front of the guard, Levell removed his boxer shorts.

Never had he felt more emasculated and humiliated in his entire life than at that very moment when he had to remove the last stitch of clothing he had on, exposing his buttocks and his penis. He always vowed that the only people in life that would see him completely naked would be his parents and the women that he was intimate with before meeting his wife. There was a strange feeling about stripping down in front of another man, a feeling of manhood being stripped from him. He immediately put on the prison briefs and orange jumpsuit, so the guard wouldn't start making lewd jokes about him.

After fully dressing, the guard took his clothes away and left Levell in the cell by himself. The room was dimly lit by a single light bulb, and as Levell sat on the small bench, he suddenly came to the realization of what he had to do. He had to show toughness in a place where toughness reigned. He didn't know where he was scheduled to be transferred, but he knew he would be going to a place where he would be in the same vicinity with murderers, rapists, and thieves—men without a conscience, fear of consequences, and mentally imbalanced. He would have to dig deep into the recesses of his soul and harden up immediately. Any sign of softness would be perceived as weakness, which would make him an easy target for other prisoners. Looking down, Levell saw a small piece of folded paper that fell out of his pocket while he was changing his clothes. Slowly unfolding the paper, Levell realized that it was one of his literature motivational quotes that he normally printed daily: *That, if I then had waked after long sleep/ Will make me sleep again/And then, in dreaming, The clouds methought would open and show riches/Ready to drop upon me, that when I waked I cried to dream again.*

Levell wondered if Shakespeare had ever been wrongly imprisoned during his lifetime because he seemed to echo Levell's wish at that very moment. He wanted to go back to sleep, permanently. His life was virtually over. Even if he was going to be eligible for parole, who would ever believe a convicted sex offender? He wanted to go to sleep and never wake up again. After about thirty minutes, which seemed like a couple hours to Levell, the guard returned.

"Alright, Thomas, let's go. Transport's outside and ready, and trust me there ain't gonna be no lil' kids where you're going," the guard said grimly.

Levell made sure he gave the guard the most piercing glare before exiting the small cell where they held him. Walking outside, Levell saw a white van with small bars covering the windows from the inside. As he entered the van, Levell saw three other prisoners, one white and two other prisoners who were black. All the prisoners had tattoos, but one of the black prisoners had more tattoos than the rest. He was tall, well built like a football player, and one of the tattoos on his right arm read "COLLEGE PARK CRIPS," in blue ink with a picture of two gangbangers with blue flags hanging out the back pocket.

This guy's a Crip. He probably killed someone, and now I'm riding with him. Well, I ain't gonna be his next victim.

Levell still made his way to the back of the van. The van made its way onto the road and the highway en route to the Smyrna State Prison. None of the prisoners spoke during the ride, so Levell entertained himself by staring out of the window although it was heavily barred. Watching cars with happy families go by made him extremely envious. He remembered when he took driving to work for granted because he had settled into a repetitive routine. He never once thought that the simple privilege of driving to a preferred destination would be taken away from him. Now that he was on his way to the big house, he longed to be one of the kids who would stare at prison vans, laughing while pointing at the van.

Levell was sure that the parents would tell their children, "See those men in that van? Those guys are pathetic losers and law-breakers headed to jail. They're not anybody to look up to for an example, and they won't amount to anything in society."

Levell wouldn't blame them at all if they described him in such a way. He thought he was above the system in ways only to find out that he was a wrong crime away from being part of the system. He found it ironic that he avoided prison one time during his life, and it was as if God, if there was a God, was playing a cruel game with him. No matter if it was three days or sixteen years, prison was always the end game for him. Eventually, his past transgressions would come back to haunt him.

Finally, the van pulled up to Smyrna State Prison, and the doors opened. With his hands and his feet handcuffed, Levell walked out with the other inmates inside the building, where they entered a huge corridor. The tunnel was empty, but there were doors on the left and right side of it.

Levell suspected that those doors were entrances to solitary confinement rooms or private work rooms.

As the head guard walked ahead of the four prisoners, he took out his key and unlocked about three locks. Upon the final lock being opened, there was a loud buzzing sound, and the door clicked opened. Levell saw that they finally reached the cellblocks, and each 6-by-8 cell had a toilet and a bunk bed on the opposite side. All of them had windows, which made Levell wonder if the city of Smyrna was purposely teasing prisoners with the image of what freedom was, as a reminder of what they lost. Looking up, Levell saw there were stairs leading to another level of prison cells.

Wow, consensus really wasn't lying. They're really trying to populate these prisons.

Levell didn't echo his thoughts out loud because it wouldn't have been significant. Besides, he was now a statistic, and there was nothing he could about it. The head guard finally stopped at the opposite end of the first level and ordered the prisoners to stand straight up, so they could read their prisoner I.D. Levell watched as the head police guard assigned the prisoners to their respective cells based on their I.D.

Finally, the guard walked up to him. "Inmate #02369, Thomas. You'll be over there," the guard ordered, pointing to an empty cell close to the middle of the second level.

Levell made his way over to his cell. As he passed scores of inmates, he heard them deriding him.

"Fresh meat," one inmate, a black man with two of his front teeth missing, said as Levell walked.

"Keep walkin', boy," another light-skinned black inmate told him as he walked to his cell.

Then, out of nowhere, Levell heard a whistling noise, almost like a catcall whenever men saw attractive women.

Not me. Ain't nobody touchin' me. I'd much rather die fighting everybody else up in 'dis bitch before I give myself up to any of 'em.

He continued to his cell. The guard pulled a small lever to open it shortly after another buzzer-like sound emitted from the speaker hoisted just under the ceiling, opening Levell's door. After Levell walked inside, the buzzer sound went off again, confirming the prison doors would lock up and prevent any inmates from entering or leaving the cell. Levell walked over to the bed, his prisoner attire, change of garment and bed sheets still with him. He had two other inmates next to him, one on both his right and his left side. One of the prisoners, an elderly black man, appeared to be sound asleep on his bed.

Well, he ain't worried about nothin'.

Levell placed his items on his bed, which wasn't really his. It was the state's bed, and the mattress smelled like urine, armpits and cigarette butts. He started to spread his sheet and blanket out to prepare his bed, but he stopped at the last minute because he realized that many eyes were on him. He couldn't allow them to see him act neat and prompt, as he would have normally acted at home since in the state pen, it might've been perceived as being soft or feminine. Instead, he carelessly threw the blanket on his bed.

The prisoner on his right, a young white man with a short buzz cut stared at him for what seemed like hours while Levell looked over his small surroundings. The man tried to get his attention. "What's up, brotha? What's up, man?" he kept asking, trying to make conversation, but Levell promptly ignored him.

His whole mission while incarcerated was not to strike any type of friendship with any inmate. He just wanted to serve his term in silence so that he could be eligible for parole. Only then, would he stand a chance to leave the hellhole that he was in. But the man wouldn't quit.

"C'mon, man, I know you hear me. What you in for?" he asked.

Finally, Levell decided to reply, only to get the man to shut up. "Assault and battery," he replied.

"No kiddin'!" the man replied enthusiastically as if Levell was a hero. "So, who'd you fuck up? How'd he piss you off?" he asked.

"It wasn't a dude," Levell replied instinctively.

The white man silently chuckled. It was apparent that he didn't take the hint that Levell wanted to be left alone.

"So, what'd she do? Screw another man behind your back? I don't blame ya.' I woulda' went off on her ass too if she played me for a sucker like that," he said.

"It ain't go down like that. She came after me and tried to kill me, but I fought back," Levell replied.

The man listened intently. "Damn, what kinda bitch did you get yo'self involved with?"

"The wrong kind," Levell replied, clenching his fists.

Every time he thought about Raven, he got infuriated. She'd ended his life and his career. There weren't enough words in the English language to describe what he wanted to do to her, but he just wished that all types of misfortune befell her.

The man laughed. "I hear that," he said. "Name's McKinley, by the way. Sam McKinley," the man replied, introducing himself.

Levell sighed. He didn't want to introduce himself to a stranger, but he found out that he had no choice. He was in the next cell over and eventually he would have to talk to him. "Levell Thomas," he said.

"Nice meetin' you brotha," McKinley said.

Levell didn't know why, but he found it annoying that this white man was calling him "brotha." As far as he was concerned, he was not related nor did he wish to be related to any one of them.

McKinley seemed to read the doubt on Levell's face and tried to break to ice to ease his tension. "I know what you thinkin' already. Don't let the white boy look fool ya. I got some black in me. I'm down," he said, attempting to use Ebonics to sway Levell's opinion of him.

Levell stared at him, and McKinley gave him such a cheesy smile that Levell had no choice but to laugh. "You corny as hell, man," he replied as McKinley laughed even harder. "So, what you here for?"

"Assault with a deadly weapon and armed robbery," McKinley replied.

Levell felt himself getting more nervous. Why did he bother asking?

"But I won't be here for long though. Spoke with my lawyer a couple days ago, and he's workin' some loophole to get me outta here," he continued.

"Lucky you," Levell replied.

"If you want, I can get him to look at your situation too. He can probably get you outta hea' too," McKinley offered.

"Thanks, but I already got a lawyer," Levell replied.

"Okay, cool. Lemme know how that works out for ya," McKinley said.

"Trust me, it's gonna work. I'll be outta here in a few months," Levell replied, but secretly he was worried.

What if it didn't work out? What if his lawyer couldn't prove that he didn't rape Raven? He would be looking at an extended stay in Smyrna State Prison, and he couldn't afford it, not when Caliya and Patrice needed him.

As Levell began serving his time behind bars, Detective Sands stayed at his desk in the Marietta Police Department looking up old articles online. He considered himself fortunate to find his first clue in his theory that Levell was implicated and framed in the assault case. After reading Sonny Williams' story, Sands knew that Jerry Roberts had to be a bigoted individual. But he also knew that he couldn't easily prove Jerry framed Levell. Still, the article was his first key to unlocking the plot. Sands attempted to look up Raven's police file and, unfortunately, Raven had never been accused of a crime in her life. Sands re-read the Williams article again, his face narrowed in concentration. Raven couldn't have acted on her own accord to lay false allegations on Levell. There had to be other players in the game. It was just like having two signs that pointed him in the right direction but not being able to discern which sign would get him to his destination swiftly.

As he worked, he felt someone's presence hovering over him. Turning around quickly, he saw Charles Anderson standing over him. "Damn, Anderson, don't you think you could give a brotha a little warning before sneaking up?" he asked.

"My bad, man. I saw you deep in thought and didn't wanna disturb ya, so I figured I'd step in with the stealth," Anderson replied. "What you doin'?" he asked as Sands took copies of past cases and police reports and stapled them together.

"I'm working on the Levell Thomas case," Sands replied.

"Levell Thomas? You mean the high school rapist?" Anderson asked.

"Don't play yourself, man. He didn't molest that girl," Sands replied.

"Says who? You?" Anderson asked slyly. "Look, man, that dude's a teacher, surrounded by thousands of kids. So, it didn't surprise me when he was charged with assault. He picked a little girl out the litter, got some ass, and thought he could get away with it."

"And how do you know he did it?" Sands asked.

"Evidence placed him at the scene of the crime-" Anderson started, but Sands immediately cut him off.

"So, what? You don't think evidence was planted on purpose to frame him for that?" Sands asked his partner.

Anderson shook his head, as if he agreed with Sands. "I mean, it's possible, but what would make you think it was a setup?"

"Look, we can never base our evidence on circumstantial grounds, but we can try to piece this puzzle early," Sands replied, showing the Williams article to Anderson. "Remember the Deneau case? Raven's father Jerry was a former employee and assistant manager of the postal service chain. They implicated this guy Williams, and not only did he lose his job, but he was also accused of murder. Williams was sentenced to serve life in jail because he was accused of killing Mr. Deneau, and Jerry was one of the so-called witnesses who accused Mr. Williams," he explained.

"Okay, but how does that tie him in this case?" Anderson asked.

"Raven had no prior record of arrest yet. What if her father told her to accuse Mr. Thomas of rape?" Sands asked.

"What would his motive be to accuse him?" Anderson asked, still unable to comprehend or gather his partner's claims.

"That's what I'm trying to find out. Maybe Mr. Thomas said or did something to him. I don't know," Sands replied. "But I do know that Levell Thomas did not assault Roberts' daughter. It's just not like him," he added firmly.

Anderson clearly saw that Sands would not be convinced otherwise.

"How do you know what he's like?" Anderson asked, before the answer revealed itself less than a minute later.

Sands had remained silent, not answering the question.

"You're related to Thomas, aren't you?" he asked, and when Sands didn't reply right away, he chuckled silently. "Look, man, we all would like to think our family's incapable of doing crazy heinous things to others, but we have to be unbiased as law enforcement officials," he added.

"Well, this ain't about if he's related to me or not," Sands replied. "It's about an innocent man spending years behind bars for something he ain't done, and it ain't right. I'm not gonna sit here and allow my cousin's husband to lose his life based on false accusations and circumstantial evidence. I'm gonna solve this thing one way or another. I made a promise to Caliya."

Anderson seemed to understand because he remained quiet for the next few minutes.

"What would you do if it was your family member that had a bogus charge on them based on racism?" Sands asked.

Anderson seemed to be pondering over the question. Sands knew that Anderson couldn't relate because he was a white man in America that never had to watch his back from any other race in society, and he never had to worry about being a statistic or a hashtag in someone's social media.

"I would probably be doing the same thing that you're doing," Anderson finally admitted, smiling sheepishly.

Sands smiled back at his partner. "Glad we on the same page, man," he said before looking at the clock over the office. Realizing that it was a little after two in the morning, he got up and placed all his papers in his desk. "Whoa, look at the time. We gotta get outta here," he said, closing the lights over his desk, before heading out to the parking lot.

Anderson walked alongside him.

"Okay, Chief, I'm with you on this. I wanna help you clear Thomas. I'll find out as much as I can," Anderson said.

"Thanks, man," Sands said, shaking Anderson's hands. "What are partners for, right?" Anderson asked as they walked over to their parked cars.

After ten minutes, Sands arrived at his home on Campbell Road, a few blocks away from Kennestone Hospital. Turning on the hallway lights, he did his best to tiptoe quietly past his children's bedrooms, where his daughter and his son slept. Walking into his own bedroom, he started to take off his uniform in silence, believing his wife to be asleep under the covers. When she suddenly stirred, Sands slightly jumped.

"Baby, what time is it?" Betty asked groggily as she turned around in her bed. Sands looked at the clock on their lampstand.

"It's 2:39, baby," he replied softly.

"Why are you back so late?" she asked him, her eyes still closed.

"Late night at the station, Bee. You know how it is," he replied, calling Betty by her childhood nickname.

"You've always came late before, but never this late. What's been going on lately?" Betty asked.

Sands sat down at the foot of their bed. He never liked to discuss his cases or his police work with his wife, mainly for safety reasons. And he was not a fool. He knew that he made more than a few enemies in his profession, and he did not want his family to be involved in his messes. It was bad enough that on the night of the horrific shootout in Queens, his wife, after giving birth to their son, almost cried herself to sleep every night after waking up from nightmares where Sands would fail to return home to their family. Although Sands was virtually unharmed in the shooting, Betty never felt confident about her husband going out in the streets every day where there were people without any conscience who would fire or harm her husband on sight. It took Betty many years to move on from the night where her husband's life could have ended, but it didn't stop her from being overprotective of her husband or extra clingy whenever he was home. At first the extra attention irritated Sands, but eventually he softened his expressions as he attempted to work through her extra attention.

"I'm sorry, baby, but something came up lately. You remember my cousin Caliya?" Sands asked.

"Oh yeah, I remember her. She always come to all the family reunions. It's been awhile since I've seen her though. She still in New York?" Betty asked.

"Nah, she moved down here because her husband got a new job. They've been here almost a year now," Sands replied.

"Really? That's great. So, what does she think about the South so far?" Betty asked.

"Well, right now, she's not likin' it too much cuz her husband was just sentenced to prison, and he started his time today," Sands replied, bluntly.

Upon hearing Sands' reply, Betty sat up in bed. "What? What'd her husband do?" she asked, suddenly causing Sands to regret spilling the beans about the case.

"He was accused of molesting one of his school students, and he was tried yesterday in court, and they found him guilty," he replied.

"That's terrible. I feel so bad for Caliya. I don't have any respect for a man who touches any child inappropriately," she said.

"But I don't think he did it. There's gotta be more to this story," Sands said.

Once those words came out of his mouth, Betty knew what was about to happen. Her husband was going to get involved. "Baby, I think you should let someone else prove his innocence. Don't get yourself involved in this," she said.

But Sands shook his head. "Can't do that Betty. She's my cousin, and they have a daughter who's gonna grow up without her daddy. I can't let this one go. I promised Caliya I would prove Levell innocent," he said.

"And what about the promises you made to us?" Betty asked, her voice slightly elevated. "You promised you would spend more time with your family. What about that promise? Jalisa had a school recital last week. You couldn't make it because you had to work. What about that promise? Bryce had an AAU basketball game earlier today and asked you to be there, but you couldn't come because you had to work. What about that promise?"

"Look, Betty, calm down," Sands said, trying to stem his wife's anger. He regretted not being able to attend his children's events, but he was out making the world a safer place for them. He thought his wife understood his job description. "Look, baby, I know I didn't keep my promise this week, and I promise I'll make it up. But I can't ignore this. Levell's life is hanging in the balance," he replied.

"I'm sure Caliya has lawyers and her own private investigator that can help her. You don't have to get involved in this. Please," Betty pleaded.

"I'm already involved," Sands said firmly.

Betty sighed. "Isaac, I've watched you solve cases and save lives but risk your own life. I'm just afraid that if you get mixed up in this, you won't make it back to us," Betty said, turning off the lights before laying back down, leaving Sands in his own thoughts in the dark.

Chapter 16

THE NEXT MORNING, THE EARLY PRISON ALARM sounded, emitting a buzzing noise that woke Levell out of his brief, somber slumber. As the other prisoners woke up on his cell floor, Levell reflected on what went down as the most miserable night he had ever endured. He was surprised by how quickly McKinley fell asleep, but Levell figured that he wore himself out by talking incessantly. Unfortunately, all Levell could do was lie down on his small prison bed, or cot as he saw it, and stare at the ceiling for hours, his mind racing.

So, this is how my story's gonna end. I'm gonna be locked up, caged like a primitive beast, uncivilized, and unrecognized.

As soon as his thoughts began running away with him, Levell knew he was in for a sleepless night. Not to mention, he didn't want to fall asleep in his current surroundings. The inmates that he was locked up with were dangerous, at least in his mind. These were men who were serving not just years, but decades, some for theft, but others, as McKinley pointed out to him earlier, for murder. These men could kill a fellow inmate if they were provoked and not give it a second thought or feel any type of remorse. It didn't help that Pernell told Levell that in the prison where they'd locked him up, inmates would stuff their beds with blankets and pillows during the evening prison check, while they hid out in the bathroom stalls. The place was too secure for them to make an escape. But they would wait until all the lights were turned off and with the aid or assistance of a master petty thief (or crooked officer), they would open the prison door of a fellow inmate who'd provoked them earlier, and while the poor fellow would be in a state of peaceful slumber, oblivious to what was going on or what was about to happen to him, the inmates would slit his throat.

Pernell once described to Levell that one of the inmates who'd suffered that fate had begun gasping short breaths all throughout the night, and Pernell could hear him struggling to breathe as he gargled blood and saliva. The very next morning, the victim would be found dead in a pool of his own blood. So as a result, Levell kept his eyes open because although the Smyrna State Prison appeared to be more secure than the prison system in New York, he knew that among all the creatures of this world, the human was the most cunning. If anyone was going to slit his throat, he wasn't going to make it easy on him. He was going to fight for his life, and if he went down, he was going to bring them down with him. Fortunately, Levell saw little rays of sunshine through the steel-caged windows and barely drifted off in comfort before hearing the alarm.

"Alright, ladies, get up!" the head warden yelled as the prisoners woke up.

Levell, who had covered his body up to his chin with the prison sheets, threw them off as he got to his feet.

"Okay, most of y'all already know the drill around here, so I'mma say it again for all the newbloods," the warden continued. "When the cell opens on your section, you will all follow Officer Camden to the toilets. You'll be handed a small brush if you ain't got one and some toothpaste and soap. Those who choose to shower, those stalls are located behind the urinal walls. Be at the mess hall at 8 a.m. sharp for breakfast," the warden concluded, before walking off to speak with Officer Camden.

Levell sat up on the foot of his bed, rubbing his groggy eyes. He looked to the cell on his left. McKinley was still under the covers, and it was obvious to Levell that he was too familiar with the facility to the point that he didn't feel he had to wake up. But he knew that, eventually, one of the officers would force him awake.

Meanwhile, in the cellblock to his right, the older black inmate was wide awake. He had been sleeping for over twelve hours because he wasn't awake when Levell initially arrived at his cell. The old man curiously stared at Levell for a few minutes before finally speaking.

"New blood?" he asked.

Levell shook his head to confirm the man's suspicion.

"Yeah, I thought so. This block been empty since Luis got transferred up north somewhere," he added, leaving Levell to wonder who Luis was.

Maybe another poor guy who was accused of rape by a white psychopath...

"Name's Wesley Marlon. Most cats call me Wes," the man said, introducing himself.

"Levell Thomas. So, what you in for? You look like you been here a minute," Levell replied, instantly regretting the extra remark. He spoke too much sometimes, to his detriment.   But Wes answered the question directly. "Cash fraud. Cheated this couple out of thirty-two grand. I used to be a sports agent for Clay Robinson. D'you know him?"

Levell heard the name before. Clay Robinson was a well-known veteran NBA player, and he was a journeyman, which meant he traded from team to team, never having a place to call home. Most recently, he'd played for the Orlando Magic in the past season.

"Wait a minute, you knew Clay Robinson? That's what's up, man," Levell said.

"Yeah, but I lost out. Robinson saw a huge chunk of his earnings gone, and what did he do? Throw my ass under the bus. Robinson, who had an entourage of about ten people, did not once consider that it might have been one of his boys. Naturally, the agent becomes the fall guy, so he called the po-po on me, and I've been on lockdown eva' since," Wes explained.

"Damn, sorry to hear that man," Levell said.

Wes shrugged it off. "Eh, it was gonna happen someday," he said.

"I ain't even know Robinson got down like that," Levell replied.

"Well, it's that money, mayne," Wes said, pronouncing the word "man" with a southern twang. "It be changin' folk."

"You ain't neva' lied about that," Levell agreed.

"So, what's your story, youngblood? How'd a young nigga like you end up hea'?" Wes asked.

Levell shook his head. He knew the question would come up, but that didn't stop his anger from building inside him. "Over some bullshit, man. I'm a teacher at Kennesaw Mountain High School, and I had a student pushin' up on me. When I told her I wasn't feelin' her like that, she jumped me and had the nerve to accuse me of rapin' her."

When Wes looked Levell straight in his eyes without blinking, Levell figured it was probably to see if his new cellmate was lying. "Damn, so that really did happen, huh?" he asked.

"Yeah," Levell confirmed.

"Fo' a hot minute, I thought you got locked up for beatin' someone or killin' someone. You got a bit of size on you, mayne," Wes said.

Levell looked at his own body. He always thought he was average when it came to his weight. He was once skinny in junior high school and high school, but he figured that he may have gotten more muscle while in college. The fraternity brothers put all that extra weight on him with all the workouts, heavy lifting during initiation, and carrying sorority sisters.

"Nah, I ain't killed nobody, man. I would like to kill the chick that got me in this though," Levell replied.

Wes waved his hand dismissively, as if Levell had nothing to worry about. "You'll be iight. Yo ain't gonna do a damn thing to that lil' girl. Only someone stupid does something to get they ass back up in here, and you don't look like you stupid."

"Thanks, dog," Levell replied.

"But you do look green," Wes added.

Levell wondered what he meant by that term. His confused expression must've spoken for him because Wes laughed.

"You don't know what that mean?" he asked.

"Nah, what you mean I look green?" Levell asked.

"Like this your first time you eva' got locked up. You know, the first time you eva picked up a rap sheet, did some time. You lookin' wide-eyed," Wes explained, laughing.

Levell looked around. McKinley was starting to wake up, and the prisoners on the lower level were already being dismissed to the bathrooms and the mess hall. He was about to tell Wes that it wasn't the first time that he was arrested but decided to let it go. Wes beckoned for Levell to approach him, so he could whisper to him from his cell.

"Trust me when I tell you that you don't wanna look wide-eyed in this hell-hole. See some of these cats around me?" he asked gesturing to the other prisoners.

Levell followed his gaze and saw prisoners who looked as if they bench-pressed at least three-hundred pounds. There were others who looked even more skinny than Levell and Wes, including those that came with Levell during prisoner transport.

"See, you don't wanna look like that. Ex-cons and killas can see fear just by lookin' at yo' face. Guys like Treg and Joey B. ova' there," Wes said, pointing to the far end of the cell, where two huge black men were sitting, glaring at every officer or inmate that passed within their vicinity.

They fit the description of those prisoners who looked as if they bench-pressed Aston Martins for fun. One of the inmates had a long scar on one side of his arm and tattoos across his chest. His prison garment was partially unbuttoned, so Levell could see the different tattoos that spread upon his chest. The other man was also black, slightly darker than his heavily tattooed counterpart.

"The one with the scar across his arm and the tattoos is Treg. The other guy is Joey B.," Wes explained. "Now, I'm bout to tell you what's finna happen because it happens to every new blood that roll up in here. Treg and Joey's gonna try you by breakin' you in," he added.

Levell's eyes widened. "By what?" he asked in horror.

"During one of the meals, either breakfast, lunch or dinner—hell, even in the showers—they're gonna drag yo' ass away from everybody else and start beatin' yo' ass. Only for a few minutes. Some guys fight back. Others start cryin' like they mama whooped 'em and shit," Wes said. "The last thing you wanna do is cry. Fight back and show 'em that you ain't no punk ass bitch. If you do that, they not gonna mess wit' you while you still here."

Levell looked at Treg and Joey B. and felt a lump rise in his throat. But he was determined to maintain his edge and remain calm and collected.

"Hopefully, the officers step in and stop it before they end up killin' dudes, and they normally send 'em to the Hole," he said, pointing downward. "It's an isolated cell, no windows, little food or water, where they send people that be actin' a fool. Treg and Joey been down in the Hole damn near every month, and they still do what they do. Tells you about they mindset, huh?" Wes asked, patting Levell on the arm.

"Did they get you?" Levell asked.

"Hell yeah, they got me," Wes answered, slowly rolling his prison garment sleeve up, revealing several cuts and a long thin scar, running from his shoulders to his elbow. "Got my ass right after dinner one night. They waited till the mess hall was clear, and they dragged me over the mess hall floor before lettin' off on me. Oh, don't get it twisted, I held my own. Even gave Joey B. a nice lil' shiner and cut over his right eye, so he'll remember me," Wes said, laughing at Levell's concerned look.

Before he could ask any more questions, the floor prison doors opened, allowing Levell and everyone on the floor to head to the bathroom. An officer handed Levell a toothbrush and regular toothpaste. Walking to the bathroom, Levell made sure to keep his face in constant scowl mode. While brushing his teeth, he saw a few inmates undress and head to the showers.

I probably need a shower cuz my pit's probably stinkin' Levell thought, and he was right.

After brushing his teeth, Levell took a quick impromptu shower, quickly dispelling any thoughts of impurity or insecurity. There were about twenty men in the stalls, and none of them were paying him any attention, at least not at that moment. Then it was on to the mess hall after dressing back up. Levell walked slowly to make sure that Wes caught up with him. After two minutes, Wes walked with Levell to the dining hall where the prisoners were fed three meals a day.

Breakfast was typically at 7:30 every morning, and lunch was at noon. Dinner was served at five in the afternoon, and there were no meals in between. Guards were placed on duty to make sure that no prisoners snuck into the mess hall to steal food from the kitchens. As they stood in line to receive their trays from the conveyer belt that rolled out the tray from the kitchens to each prisoner, Wes continued conversing with Levell.

"The food here ain't bad though. I mean, it ain't no five-star shit, but you get what you can," he said, but Levell was barely paying attention, as he was busy looking around the mess hall.

Wes laughed as his cellblock neighbor's eyes darted east to west. "I know you ain't trippin' on Treg and Joey B., man. You best wipe that scared look off your face, or else Treg and Joey B. are gon' be the least of your worries."

Levell shook his head, knowing how right Wes was. He couldn't allow fear of anyone to overwhelm him in this place. Shrugging his shoulders, he picked up his tray. Breakfast was a few sausage links, grits, and scrambled eggs with a small biscuit on the side. The tray resembled the ones the school system served kids in elementary and middle school, where they were split into rations.

Levell followed Wes over to the table on the opposite end of the hall. McKinley soon joined them, and they ate their food in silence although the mess hall was loud with other prisoners talking amongst each other. Officers walked around the mess hall, giving the prisoners small pints of orange juice. Levell looked down at his tray. The eggs were runny, the grits tasted like stale Cream of Wheat, and his biscuit was hard as a rock. Levell tried to muster an appetite to eat his meal, but after a couple spoonfuls, he couldn't bring himself to do it.

So, this is what my life's been reduced to: eating soggy, nasty food off kid trays. I feel worse than my students.

At least his students had better food to eat. As many times as he walked the hallways, whether it was at Hillcrest High School or Kennesaw Mountain High School, he often heard complaints about the school food. Now Levell understood their complaints. He had also been critical of the school lunches or breakfast, but now he felt his students should consider themselves lucky that they didn't have to eat the standard straight-out-the-can or box product that he was relegated to consume.

Breakfast time was only thirty minutes. Levell saw that time was almost up, so he attempted to eat a couple more spoons of grits when two figures approached him. He didn't see them at first, only their shadows when they hovered over his back. Levell didn't even have to look behind him to know that Joey B. and Treg stood there.

"What up, Wes?" Joey greeted as Wes gave the men a half-hearted head nod.

"So, who's the new nigga sittin' next to you? Don't think I've seen him befo'," Treg said, deviously eyeing Levell.

"New blood. Name's Levell," Wes replied.

"Levell? Sound like a bitch name to me," Treg replied. "So, what you for here for, mayne?"

Levell was ready with his reply. He didn't want to give off the image that he was a schoolteacher who got sentenced to jail by alleged rape. He would've been considered a soft individual, which would just paint the bulls-eye in his back more prominently.

"Aggravated assault and use of a deadly weapon. A dude was givin' me hell in my job, so I went off on him. Real shit," Levell replied.

Treg looked Levell up and down to see if he was fidgeting or lying about his account before looking back at Wes. "Brother ain't never been broke yet, right?" he asked.

"Hell, if I know," Wes replied.

"Looks to me like this nigga needs to be broken into," Treg said.

Although Levell maintained his stoic attitude, he was secretly petrified. What if he didn't survive the initiation? What if the police were resorted to using deadly force and ended up shooting Levell as well as Joey B. and Treg? So many questions, but Levell was not going to budge for anyone.

Getting close to Levell's ear, Joey B. whispered ominously, "Watch yo' back cuz we comin' fo' yo' ass," he said, before walking away with Treg.

Although his heart was pounding furiously, Levell resumed eating.

After checking to make sure Joey B. and Treg were out of earshot, Wes whispered to Levell in short tones. "Okay, lemme holla at you," he told Levell.

Levell listened.

"Okay, so I'm gon' tell you how they normally get down. They gonna start with a right cross to yo' cheek, so hold both hands and arms up to your face to prevent any hits there, and make sure you duck and stick and move. You might walk out of it alive," Wes continued.

"What? You mean to tell me that they've killed other people?" Levell asked.

Wes laughed out loud. "Nah, man, they ain't killed anyone yet. Just keep away from their right hooks, and you'll be alright," Wes reassured. After a brief silence, Wes spoke again. "And make sure you say 'hi' to Nurse McGee for me."

"Nurse McGee? Who the hell's that?" Levell asked.

"She has a little clinic offsite here for wounded inmates. Believe me, when Joey B. and Treg get through with you, you're gonna have to see her," Wes said.

Levell looked at McKinley. "Did you ever get messed up by Treg or Joey B.?"

"Oh yeah. None of us can avoid that. They didn't do much damage to me though. Just had a black eye, swollen chin, and that was about it," McKinley replied.

Levell suddenly wished he kept the question private.

"The only negative part about it is that you'll never see it coming. They're gonna pick spots in between meals to get you. Be ready at all times," McKinley warned.

As the officers gave the order for the men to head back to their cell, Levell hoped that he wouldn't run into them anytime soon.

Detective Sands drove down Cobb Parkway early that morning to avoid traffic that was heading southbound towards Atlanta. His first point of investigation would be Sonny Williams, who'd made parole after a re-trial and insufficient evidence not tying him to the murder of Charles Deneau. From other sources, Sands found out that Williams currently lived on Windy Hill Road and had found another job at UPS shipping. Sonny remained low-key, and Sands understood why he chose to be very discreet about his location. He knew Deneau's associates still thought Sonny was guilty of the murder.

As he reached the UPS shipping and receiving dock, Sands parked his car in the visitor's section and went inside the building. When he presented his badge, and requested to speak with Sonny, the head crew member asked him to wait in the break room as he went to retrieve Sonny. After five minutes, a tall broad-shouldered black man entered the room. He wore his UPS uniform, and his work badge was clipped to his right shirt pocket. He looked older than the old mugshots of him that appeared in the newspapers more than ten years ago.

"Mr. Williams, I presume?" Sands asked.

"Who wants to know?" Sonny asked suspiciously.

Detective Sands chuckled slightly. He wanted Sonny to be as comfortable as possible. If Sonny felt uneasy, Sands knew he would never divulge any information that might help him in the investigation.

"My name is Detective Isaac Sands. The reason for my visit today is to ask you some questions about a certain individual that's in the center of our investigation."

"How do you know if I even know the person that you're talking about?" Sonny replied. "Look, sir, I've been clean the last few years. I ain't got into any trouble or nothin' like that," he started to explain, but Sands held up his right hand to silence Sonny.

"Don't worry. It's not about you. But I want to ask you about a man that you might be familiar with...Mr. Jerry Roberts. Does that ring a bell?" Sands asked.

The effect that the name had on Sonny was instantaneous. Sands saw Sonny's face grow pale as the recognition set in, but he still didn't budge.

"I don't know who you're talkin' about," Sonny lied.

"Yeah, you do," Sands replied. "I know all about you, Sonny. I know that you were falsely accused of murdering your old boss, Mr. Deneau, and I know that you were locked up for it. And I know that Mr. Roberts was one of the chief instigators who accused you of the crime," Sands reeled off.

Sonny shook his head. "So, you think you know everything, Detective?" he asked.

"I'm not the one being interrogated Sonny," Sands replied.

"So, you think you know everything, huh?" Sonny repeated. "Lemme tell you something, detective. You don't know shit. You don't know Mr. Roberts, and you damn sure didn't know Mr. Deneau. Both were the biggest racists that you'll eva' find."

"I know, but I have to prove that in court," Sands replied. "Another man was accused of a crime he didn't commit, like you were, and he led the charge too. That man's behind bars, Sonny, and he's innocent."

"Nothing personal, sir, but if I were you, I would drop this case and let the man do his time. You don't want to be mixed up with Mr. Roberts. Man's got a lot of pull in Kennesaw and Marietta," Sonny said.

"Son, I'm part of the police force. Getting mixed up in messy shit's my business as well as proving guys innocent. Now I need you to tell me what you know about Mr. Roberts," Sands said.

Once he realized how persistent Sands was, Sonny gave in. "After Mr. Deneau was murdered, and they arrested me for doin' him in, Mr. Roberts made a statement revealing everything I did leading up to the man's murder...going to his house, to ask for my job back, and how I left in such a rage that I had no choice but to kill him, which was a damn lie. Ever since I was working at Deneau Deliveries, Mr. Roberts was after me, my job, my reputation, and my family," he said.

"Your family?" Sands asked.

"Ever since I was paroled, my family's been getting death threats, both from former employees of Deneau Deliveries and members of some white supremacist group. I've had my water turned off, even though I paid my bills. I've had racial slurs written on my mailbox, small wooden crosses burned on my yard," he explained.

Sands listened intently.

"Finally, I just got up and got out of there. My life was on the line. If I had stayed there, I probably woulda' gotten lynched," he continued.

"I understand, brotha, and I apologize for what your family went through. But Levell Thomas' family could be going through the same thing unless we work together. All I wanna do is help an innocent man stay out of prison," Sands replied.

Sonny reached into his pocket and pulled out a small piece of paper, no larger than an index card. He handed the paper to Sands. "Here, man, this was one of the letters I received after they set me free. Even when they remove our chains, we're never truly free," Sonny said, before getting up to walk out of the break room.

Sands read the message on the paper, which stated in large block letters: *I WILL KILL YOU AND YOUR BASTARD CHILDREN, YOU MURDERING NIGGER!!!*

Sands folded up the paper and placed it in his pocket. *We're never truly free,* he thought as he left the UPS shipping dock.

Chapter 17

*A*FTER BREAKFAST, THE WARDEN AND THE OFFICERS assigned the inmates into two separate work groups. The first group would be taken to the side of Interstate 75 where they would be doing irrigation, lawn mowing, and shrub trimming. The second work group would work in the industrial facility, doing laundry, equipment and machine maintenance, and running assembly lines for car body parts for Smyrna City. Levell was assigned to irrigation. He couldn't have been more thankful for that because Treg and Joey B. were assigned the industrial duties, which meant he would be far away from them for the day. Levell knew they would eventually find him without the blanket of law enforcement to protect him, and whenever that day came, he would be sure to get ready to defend himself.

Three prisoner vans drove around the penitentiary to the front entrance where the first group started loading into them. Wes and McKinley were assigned to perform industrial duties, so Levell felt alone and isolated although he was surrounded by other inmates. As he entered the vans, he saw that each had a separate wooden loading dock that included shovels, pickaxes, large shearing scissors, and four lawnmowers. Looking outside, Levell saw the bright rays of the sun shining.

Looks like it's gonna be a very hot day. Hopefully, the wardens brought water.

They made their way into I-75, and to Levell's surprise, the ride was only three minutes long. Once they'd reached their destination, one of the officers handed Levell and the other inmates shovels. After listening to the officers' instructions on irrigation, each prisoner was handed bags of grass seeds to throw down after digging up small tufts of dirt. Levell took his bag and walked over to the secluded area where a few tufts of green grass remained. The rest of the area contained brown, dead grass. He began working, digging up holes about two centimeters wide. Slowly, he opened his bag of grass seed and scattered about a dozen of them inside the hole.

After the first hour and a half, the sun was beating down on Levell's back. As he wiped the perspiration off his face and forehead, he looked over his work. He was no stranger to irrigation work. He'd irrigated and mowed his yard back in New York and in Kennesaw. As the officers handed out water to the inmates, including Levell, they sat under the shade and rested for fifteen minutes. While they were resting, Levell saw other cars driving by them, and he immediately felt envious, just as he'd done the first time the van had taken him to Smyrna and he'd seen men and women driving with their children.

Free men and women were living their American Dream and didn't have to worry about waking up to a nightmare such as the one he was currently going through. They didn't have to worry about a psycho girl taking away everything he once held dear, including his career. Levell had managed to save his marriage, but Lord knows what might have happened if Caliya had chosen not to believe him when he revealed Raven's nefarious actions and advances toward him. Many women would not have stayed with their husbands. Thankfully, Caliya had been a rock throughout the entire ordeal.

While he worked outside, Levell wondered what Caliya was up to. He didn't doubt that she was working hard to prove his innocence, while also working hard to maintain for herself and Patrice. He knew that her burden had increased twofold because, without Levell's income, Caliya wouldn't be able to pay most of the bills for their home. It wouldn't be long until the bank foreclosed and repossessed it. Levell hoped that Allan Richter was working on a parole date. His hope for freedom and a second chance remained in his hands. Levell just had to believe that Allan was going to find a way to free him.

Looking at the other inmates working, Levell thought back periods and topics that he often covered during the lessons in his class: the slavery era, the post-slavery era or Reconstruction and the Gilded Age, which began in the late 1800s and rolled on into the early 1900s. He thought about books such as *The Adventures of Huckleberry Finn, Uncle Tom's Cabin,* and *The Narrative of the Life of Frederick Douglass.*

To him at the time, it was all just another period in American history that was part of the curriculum. He wouldn't necessarily gloss over it, but he would not spend more than a few days on that period. Now he wished he'd spent more time covering those sections to his students because society had not changed, but Levell had underestimated the bigotry that still existed.

Raven used the strategy that so many of her forefathers have used on black sharecroppers or slaves during the period. But what was most unsettling to him was what would happen once parole was granted and was set free. How would people respond to him? He knew that he would be perceived as a sex offender and a child molester. Who would trust him with a teaching job after his time in Smyrna State Prison? He was going to have to move out of Kennesaw, perhaps out of Georgia, and start over somewhere else. Even that prospect was not guaranteed because his record would follow him, and once other schools viewed it, they wouldn't take a chance on him.

The most frightening prospect for Levell was feeling hopeless because teaching was all he knew. In a twisted sense, Levell's mind wandered back to the individual who created this mess: Raven Roberts. He often wondered how her life was going, now that he was out of the picture. Certainly, she felt invincible now, since she could do whatever she wanted and knew she would get away with it. No doubt, the community was holding her up as a hero for getting big bad Levell Thomas behind bars so that no other kids could be hurt by this monster.

White privilege must be nice, he thought as he continued to work.

Unbeknownst to Levell at that moment, the privilege that he assumed was working for Raven was beginning to work against her. Since the arrest was made and the days leading up to the trial, Raven was considered the helpless victim of a man who took advantage of his position and forced himself upon her. She was on the nightly news, and every newspaper and Internet news source in Georgia followed her story. Raven went along with her testimony, although she knew deep in her heart that Mr. Thomas was innocent. But there was no way she could relinquish her newfound fame, and there was no way she could turn away from the large amount of money that she was offered to tell her story as a battered, underage girl. To the white contingent, she was the victim who deserved justice, and they were overjoyed to see it finally happen for her.

But there were those people of other contingents who were not flattered by Raven and did not appreciate the extra buzz she'd received since the trial. Raven was still enrolled at Kennesaw Mountain High School. Despite being with her friends, she knew deep down that there were other people eyeing her as if they knew she had lied about that day in the men's restroom and that she was benefitting off an innocent man. Raven could feel her fellow classmates' eyes looking down on her, from the black students, to Hispanic students to Asian students who she encountered at Town Center Mall in Kennesaw. Nobody outside of her circle thought Raven was innocent and believed she played a part in the arrest of the former Teacher of the Year. Raven secretly hoped that the situation would blow over in a couple of weeks and that people would forget about her situation with Mr. Thomas. Some students didn't forget, and it all came to a head one morning in the food court at Town Center Mall.

Raven was greeted by her friend Ginger and another student, Gloria Ramirez, who sat across from her in the crowded mall food court. After ordering chicken biscuits from Chick-Fil-A, the friends sat down at the table across from a group of black kids who knew Raven from Kennesaw Mountain High School. The kids were throwing dirty looks at Raven whenever they had the chance. For the first two minutes, Raven ignored the stares that were thrown at her. But finally, after receiving the eye roll of Octavia Jones, a particularly brash and outspoken black girl who was a part of the group, Raven finally snapped.

"What are y'all starin' at?" she asked angrily.

"I'm starin' at you, bitch," Octavia replied angrily.

"What'd you call me?" Raven asked.

"I ain't stutter. I called you a bitch," Octavia repeated, standing to her feet for emphasis. "Don't act all innocent wit' me. I don't play that. I ain't the news. Everyone here knows you set Mr. Thomas up," she added.

"What the hell are you talking about?" Raven asked.

Octavia turned to look at her friends, who were shaking their heads, obviously not buying Raven's cluelessness. "This Becky must think I'm stupid," Octavia told them before turning to Raven again. "I said, 'you set Mr. Thomas up.' Everyone knows yo' hoe ass was tryin' to fuck him, and when he turned yo' skinny ass down, you dimed him out. Tell me I'm lyin'," Octavia challenged.

Raven laughed to herself as if Octavia's claim was preposterous, even though it was spot-on. "You weren't even there, so you don't know nothin'," she replied.

"I ain't gotta be there to know how yo' type gets down," Octavia bit back. "Whenever ya don't get what ya want, ya cry and bitch to everybody till you get yours, like a big-ass baby. People here knows you wanted Mr. Thomas. Even yo' dizty ass boyfriend knew that, but you couldn't get him, so you had to lock the man up on some bullshit."

"He attacked me. He raped me, and he tried to kill me. He had a history of doing this. Weren't you watchin' the damn news?" Raven asked.

"Mr. Thomas ain't do shit to you. You was tryin' to give him some, and he turned down yo' flat chested ass, and you came after him. He was tryin' to defend himself," Octavia repeated firmly.

"Whatever. Why don't ya' mind yo' own business and focus on not being broke-ass baby mamas and deadbeat baby daddies?" Raven retorted, not realizing the seriousness of what she said.

The group of friends that accompanied Octavia now stared at Raven, anger flashing in their eyes. Octavia walked over to the table where Raven and her friends sat. Raven, determined not to show fear, stood up from her seat. The mall, which had been noisy and abuzz with other adults and students, abruptly fell silent with everyone watching the drama unfold between the two girls. They both eyed each other, daring one to strike first.

"What did you say, white trash?" Octavia said, inching closer to Raven.

Raven suddenly realized that Octavia stood an inch or two taller than her. However, she wasn't going to give Octavia the pleasure of backing down, so she stood up to face her. "You heard what I said," she replied defiantly. One lesson her father had taught her was to never back down from people who were inferior to her.

"You know what? You just a sad little po' white girl who couldn't get off from her own people, so you had to chase some black dick, and you couldn't even get that. No one would want to be with a triflin', trailer-park tramp like you. You just like yo' dime-droppin' daddy," Octavia said, despite her friends telling her to calm down.

Raven's blood boiled when the girl mentioned her father.

"Ya' don't like us, but you listen to our music. You do yo' hair like us, and you try to take our men. Ya' jealous of us, and you know it, real talk," Octavia added, before allowing her friends to usher her back to the other side of the room.

But Raven wasn't done. She was not going to let Octavia get the last word. "And you ain't nothin' but a horse-hair weave wearing, loud-mouth bitch that no black man would wife up if ya were the last woman on earth. That's why they run to us," Raven replied, not expecting what came next.

"OH, HELL NAH!" Octavia yelled as she lunged for Raven's throat.

Both girls fell to the ground, Octavia's weight knocking Raven to her backside. Both girls were wrestling on the ground, pulling each other's hair. Octavia grabbed Raven's throat, and Raven began scratching her face in retaliation. Raven's and Octavia's friends both attempted to separate the two girls, but Raven's friend John Whitfield and her ex-boyfriend Tex were confronted by Michael Bellamy and Shawn Turner, two of Octavia's friends. It wasn't long before the boys began shoving one another. Soon mall security arrived and separated the fighting teenagers. All six were eventually arrested by the Marietta Police Department and were taken to the precinct.

It wasn't long before news broke out about the brawl at Town Center Mall later that evening. While the story was still being presented to the public, Mr. Roberts drove to the Marietta precinct after receiving the phone call that his daughter was involved in a fight with another girl. When he arrived at the jail, he saw his daughter sitting on a bench outside the police chief's office. Because both girls were under eighteen years of age, they were charged only as minors and had to await the arrival of their parents to post bail for them. Raven's neck was still red in spots where Octavia's fingers had squeezed when she was attempting to choke the life out of her. Octavia had sustained a small bump across her head and a bruised arm. She sat on the bench across from Raven, and it became clear to Raven that if Octavia had another chance to attack her, she would take advantage of the opportunity. Octavia had the look of pure hatred on her face.

Mr. Roberts walked to his daughter and checked her neck and her face. Steaming with anger, he took one look at Octavia, whose parents had just arrived after receiving the call from the officers at the precinct. Mr. Roberts turned to face Officer Phil Coates, one of the lead officers who led the arrest of the girls.

"Who did this to my lil' girl?" he asked, trying to contain the fury in his voice.

"We received a call from a member of Town Center security who informed us that these two young women were fighting," Officer Coates replied, looking at Raven but also pointing at Octavia.

Mr. Roberts stared at Octavia and her parents. *These savages got some nerve,* he thought. Walking over to Octavia, Mr. Roberts gave her a fiery look.

"You the one almost killed my baby girl?" he asked.

"After all the heinous things your daughter said..." Octavia's father

Phillip Jones replied, standing up to look Mr. Roberts in his eyes.

"Maybe you oughta teach your daughter that savagery doesn't pay," Mr. Roberts told Mr. Jones.

"And maybe you oughta teach your daughter something about tact," Mr. Jones replied.

"I don't need advice on how to raise my daughter," Mr. Roberts replied. "Especially from people like you," he added as he beckoned his daughter to stand up, and he walked over to the bursar's desk to pay the bail.

"People like us?" Mr. Jones replied, facing Mr. Roberts. "Can you please clarify that, sir?" he asked.

"Not too bright, I see," Mr. Roberts said, chuckling dryly. "Well lemme see if I can clear it up for you to understand. Next time your daughter or any other members of your tribe touch my daughter, it'll be the last thing you do. Do you understand now?" Mr. Roberts asked rhetorically.

"All right, that's enough, gentlemen. If you've finished signing them out, please exit the premises," Officer Coates said, quelling the tension between the two fathers.

"I don't believe you can sit there as an officer and allow this man to threaten me. Didn't you hear what he just said to me?" Mr. Jones protested, but Officer Coates ushered him away from the waiting area in the precinct and directed him to go his separate way.

"Let's go," Mr. Roberts said to Raven, who shot one last look at Octavia, and Octavia continued to glare back.

As Raven and her father entered their car, Mr. Roberts turned to his daughter.

"You mind tellin' me what the hell you were thinkin'?" he asked her.

"What? Daddy, she started it. She ran and tackled me first. I was defendin' myself," Raven protested.

"Why didn't you call me when it was happenin'?" Mr. Roberts asked as he pulled out of the parking lot and onto the busy freeway.

"I thought I had it under control. I didn't know she would lose it like that," Raven explained.

"They always lose control like that. That's what makes them savages, like that ole' teacher that put his hands on you," Mr. Roberts said. "They got no control over their actions. They all need to be dealt with, if you ask me," he added.

Raven looked at her father. She always knew that her father was an outspoken advocate for the NRA and a staunch supporter of the Alternative Right political party. Many people labeled it as racism, but Raven dismissed those notions. Her father communicated with black people and people of color every day, so it couldn't be racism. She agreed that many of them were agitators and needed control to reign them back in.

What America labeled as racism was surely not racism in her eyes, but she reflected upon her treatment of Mr. Thomas. He wasn't like the other unruly black men in society. He was educated, well spoken, and he was attractive. But he hurt her, and she had no choice but to make him pay for what he did, according to her father. *When blacks don't follow the code, they get what they deserve.*

She still replayed the events in the men's bathroom that day, when Mr. Thomas fought her off and left her on the bathroom floor, crying and pouting. She knew she had to put on a great act so her family, the police, and surrounding witnesses could see that she was the victim, not him. It would be nothing but another black man in jail, where most of them were anyway. There were a hundred guys named Mr. Thomas, so she could easily find herself another black man to call her own. But she could never let her father know how she truly felt about them.

"Daddy, what if we were wrong about Mr. Thomas?" she asked.

Mr. Roberts looked at his daughter as if she was crazy.

"He tried to force himself on you. Where did we go wrong about him?" he asked.

Raven had not told her father that she fabricated the rape incident. She didn't think that it would've gone over that easily, especially without any type of medical evidence, which she knew she couldn't provide at the time.

"Nothing," she replied.

"Cupcake, my job is to protect you from harm. These men only want one thing from a purty lil' thang like you, and it damn sure ain't your smarts," Mr. Roberts said.

Instead of replying to her father, Raven sat in silence as they drove home. By this time, she had grown accustomed to her father making sly comments about her beauty compared to her intelligence, so she didn't think twice about it. However, she was starting to think twice about what she did to Mr. Thomas. Was it possible that she went too far in falsely accusing her former teacher?

Later that evening, Caliya and Patrice returned from Vicky's house where Vicky had been helping Caliya by babysitting Patrice after daycare and lending her money to help pay for some of her utility bills. Without Levell's contribution, keeping up with the payments on the house became a daily challenge. Patrice normally stayed in the Primrose School for Early Education between eight in the morning and three in the afternoon. She would use her hour-long lunch break to pick up her daughter and drive her over to Vicky's house, where Vicky would be waiting to watch Patrice for her with Percy's help. Caliya couldn't help but to be extremely thankful for Levell's family because, if it hadn't been for them, she would've lost her mind, what with Levell's case.

Caliya called Allan Richter to check on his progress in the case and the status of early parole, but he was not available, so she resorted to leaving him voice messages. She knew that Allan was working as hard as he could to set up a date where Levell would be eligible for parole.

With a heavy heart, she continued her duties, bathing Patrice, tucking her in her bed, kissing her goodnight. While leaving the room, Caliya reflected on how hard life without Levell was for Patrice. Not having seen her father for over a week, Patrice would ask every day, "Where's Daddy, Mommy? Is he still at work?"

To ease Patrice's mind as well as her own, Caliya would often lie to her daughter and confirm that her Daddy was still at work. For the first three days, Patrice seemed to accept it. But eventually, a four-year-old child would notice the absence of a parent. It didn't take long for Patrice to ask questions about Levell's whereabouts and why he still hadn't returned home from work.

One night, Caliya read Patrice a children's book, *Danny and the Dinosaur*, and although Caliya couldn't capture the same engagement from Patrice like whenever Levell read to her, her daughter didn't seem to mind her mother's reading at all. She drifted right off to sleep as Caliya tiptoed out of the room and walked into her own room.

The master bedroom seemed empty without her husband's presence. Caliya put on her nightgown and just settled in her bed when she heard her daughter yelling, "MOMMY!"

Jumping out of bed, Caliya ran to her Patrice's room and found her sitting up in bed, face streaked in tears.

"Patrice, what is it, baby?" she asked.

"I saw people hurting Daddy," Patrice said.

Caliya hugged her daughter tightly.

"Oh no, baby. You had a bad dream, that's all. Daddy's fine. He'll be back soon, okay? It's okay. It's okay," she said, comforting her daughter.

"When is Daddy gonna come back?" Patrice asked.

Caliya looked at her daughter's brown eyes, still wet with tears.

"Daddy will be back soon. I promise," Caliya replied, although she knew she was lying to her daughter again. What choice did she have? She couldn't bring herself to tell her daughter that her daddy might be locked up for years and may never see his family. She couldn't break Patrice's heart that way. "He'll come back home one day, I promise," Caliya said as she got into the bed next to Patrice, knowing that she wouldn't be able to sleep until Patrice was asleep in her arms.

At least I won't sleep alone tonight, she thought.

A few days passed as Levell and the other inmates dragged themselves out of the prison transportation van after working outside Interstate-75. Every part of Levell's body ached, and he longed for nothing but his bed. Wes caught up to him after he walked into the facility.

"Looks like you dead on yo' feet, young buck," he said, laughing.

"I am dead," Levell replied, his eyes unfocused around him. "I don't know if I can keep this up every day. I might have to do indoor industrial with you tomorrow," he said.

"Iight bet," Wes replied as he veered off towards the right side of the corridor into the washrooms. "We'll chop it up lata," he said as he walked off.

Levell continued to make his way to his cell, wondering where McKinley was.

He's probably still in the laundry room gettin' high on the soap detergent, he thought lazily with a chuckle, not realizing that he was the only one walking through the corridor on the way to his cellblock at the time. Without warning, his right cheek vibrated violently as Joey B.'s closed fist shattered the side of his face. He never saw it coming.

Chapter 18

EVELL STAGGERED BACK, GRUNTING IN PAIN AS JOEY B. and treg stood over him. Joey B. was massaging his knuckles that had just been buried into Levell's face just a few seconds ago.

"Yeah, boy!" Treg exclaimed as Levell rubbed the side of his face, where a huge lump was beginning to form.

It was severe, but fortunately no bones were broken.

"Wes ain't around to save yo' ass now. Come get some," Joey B. said.

The corridor was still dark, and Levell found himself desperately wishing that one of the guards would walk through the corridor and see Treg and Joey B. assaulting him. No one came.

Okay, Levell, this ain't high school no more. You can't wait for teachers to come and save you. This is a dog-eat dog world, and to survive, you gotta fight for your life.

As the two burly inmates closed in on their wounded victim, Levell closed his eyes. He had to bring himself back to the streets. All the books in the world couldn't save him when he fought Jimmy in high school, and they weren't going to save him in this corridor. Levell gathered all his anger and his rage that coursed through him and, without warning, he unleashed on his attackers, in a furious whirl of fists.

Remembering his self-defense boxing tricks his cousin had taught him, Levell caught Joey B. in the face with a square jab. To Levell's delight, Joey B. grunted in pain, and in the split second it took Joey to massage his eye, Levell swung again and caught Treg in the midsection. Unfortunately, his fist bounced harmlessly as Treg's heavily muscled abdominal muscles deflected his blow. Treg shook his head, as if to say "Nice try, slick, but no dice" before advancing onto Levell.

He swung at Levell again with a left hook, but Levell anticipated the punch, ducked, and came back up with an uppercut on Treg's chin. This time, injury was inflicted as Treg staggered back, holding his chin. Out of the corner of his eye, Levell saw the lights opening in the corridor. The noise caused by their scuffle was beginning to draw attention. But Joey B. recovered from being hit in the eye and, with extreme force, he tackled Levell in the upper body, driving him back into the corridor wall. Levell felt his head snap back and hit the brick corridor wall.

Lights popped in Levell's head, and he felt all the wind go out of him. Judging from the moisture on the back of his head and neck, Levell knew he was bleeding profusely, but he continued swinging wildly. Treg had recovered from the chin shot he received, and he charged into Levell. At that point, Levell knew it was all over. The men were going to overpower him. He knew if he couldn't hold on much longer, he was going to slip in and out of consciousness, and he wasn't going to make out of the corridor alive. He was never going to see the light of day again. He was never going to see his wife and daughter again.

As Joey B. and Treg landed more punches to Levell's body, he felt his heart pumping rapidly, but it was only a matter of time before his heart would give out, and Treg and Joey B. would kill him. Levell thought of his wife's loving embrace and his daughter's toothy smile. Caliya's gentle caress and her lips were all Levell longed for. He could feel her lips on his own lips. He was in a place of bliss, the corridor no longer surrounded him, and he was no longer relegated to prison bars, tasteless meals and forced labor. He was at home with his wife, and he was finally in a place of rest. The last scene Levell remembered was one where four guards rushed in and pried the two inmates off him, but by the time they were removed from his body, he already slipped into unconsciousness.

When Levell opened his eyes, the bright lights caused his vision to blur for a few seconds. Closing them again, he tried opening them a second time. His eyes finally adjusted to the lights of the room he was currently lying in. Observing his surroundings, he realized he was in an all-white room with drawers and cabinets filled with gauzes, stethoscopes, a weight scale, and a package of vaccination needles. He appeared to be in a hospital room. When he attempted to sit up, he felt a sharp pain on his right side.

"Ay, take it easy, bruh. You'll be iight," a familiar voice said.

Looking for the source of the voice, Levell saw that Wes was sitting beside him.

Smiling broadly, Wes stood and walked over to Levell and shook his hand. "Welcome back, L.," he said.

"Thanks, dog. Where we at?" Levell asked, looking around.

"Ward Clinic. This is where they send us when we get checkups, injury treatment, and all that," Wes replied. "It's about two miles from county."

"How long you been here?" Levell asked, realizing that talking took him a great deal of effort.

His chest was still throbbing in pain, and he felt the golf-sized lump on the right side of his cheekbone where Joey B. initially hit him.

"Came here with the officers. You know they don't let inmates out the pen for nothing, but they trust me. I wanted to roll with you, man, just to make sho' nothin' happened," Wes replied, hanging his head in shame.

Levell looked at him. "What, man?" he asked.

"Man, I feel responsible fo' what happened back there. They beat the shit out of you in that hallway, and they coulda killed you. I should've walked down there with you," Wes answered.

"What you talkin' about, man? If you did that, they would've beaten yo' ass too," Levell said.

"Nah, they wouldn't have fucked wit' me the same way. They know what time it is wit' me. But they ain't doin' much better though. You handled your own, man!" Wes exclaimed excitedly, shaking his fellow inmate's hand again. "They both down at the Hole, but Treg lost a few teeth, and his jaw is hella jacked up. Joey B., ole' raccoon face ass, got a huge shiner in his left eye. You proved yo' guts man," he added.

"Word?" Levell asked.

He knew that those two men were going to test him, and what a test it had been. Still, he never knew what to expect after receiving such a beating.

"You got heart, man. I know fo' a fact, you gonna make it outta here," Wes said.

"Out of the hospital?" Levell asked, absentmindedly.

"Nah, man. Outta the pen. They gon' set you free soon, man. I know it," Wes replied.

"I hope so. They'll set you free though too," Levell said.

"I wouldn't bet on it, but we'll see," Wes replied.

Looking outside the door, Levell saw two officers standing outside the clinic room door. *If only I was free this very minute...*

At the Marietta Police precinct, Detective Sands arrived at his desk. After interviewing Sonny Williams, he focused on investigating the alleged assault that took place in the men's restroom at Kennesaw State University between Levell and Raven. The investigation seemed to have him running circles. He interviewed Kennesaw State staff and the custodial department responsible for cleaning the restrooms, but they had not noticed any sign of a struggle in the restroom. To find out more information, Detective Sands examined the bathroom stall doors, the sinks, and the urinals. As dirty as the job was, he needed to find a clue or get a break in the case that might lead him to believe the whole assault account was fabricated.

As he sat at his desk, his partner Officer Anderson walked over to him. "Welcome back, man. Enjoy your vacation?" he asked slyly.

"Very funny, Anderson. You know there ain't no such thing as breaks for me," he replied.

"Well, I got some information that might help you out," Anderson said.

"What's up?" Sands asked, sitting up.

"Well, yesterday, there was a huge brawl at Town Center Mall, and six teens were apprehended and brought over here where they were later picked up by their parents," he explained.

Detective Sands shook his head. How did that information help him? "So, what?" he asked.

"Guess who was one of those kids that was arrested?" Anderson asked, and without waiting for a reply from Sands, he took out a copy of the previous days' citation report and handed it over to Sands.

"It's our girl," he added.

"Raven Roberts," Sands read from the ticket, secretly scolding himself for not coming to his office the previous day.

He could have interrogated Raven, maybe forced a confession out of her. "Who came to pick Raven up?" he asked.

"Her father, Jerry Roberts," Anderson replied.

Sands shook his head. He could have interrogated both Raven and Mr. Roberts in connection to the rape allegations accused against Levell.

"Okay, appreciate it, Anderson. It's time to go get somethin' out of 'em now," he said, but Anderson stopped him.

"C'mon, Sands. If it's true that Mr. Roberts and his daughter framed Levell Thomas, do you think they're gonna admit that?" he asked.

Sands thought about it for a moment. "Nah, you're right. It wouldn't make sense. But we can interrogate her friends."

"My thoughts exactly," Anderson replied. "There were two other subjects with her, John Whitfield and Tex Brown. Both were apprehended along with Raven during the scuffle."

Sands looked up the reports for Tex Brown and John Whitfield on the database and discovered that it wasn't their first time being in trouble with the law. They both had been previously arrested for the same reason— drug possession. Both were released after they made bail.

"Let's interview this Tex Brown guy. He might give us a good lead to go on," Sands said.

"Alright, let's get 'er done!" Anderson said in his southern drawl that caused Sands to look at him as if he lost his mind. "Sorry, it's a southern thing," he replied, grinning sheepishly.

"Right," Sands said, rolling his eyes as they walked to his car.

After fifteen minutes, the two officers arrived at Tex's one-story house in North Marietta. Parking on the side of the road to make sure they didn't block any pedestrians, Sands and Anderson exited their vehicle, thinking that they would have to knock on the door or ring the doorbell. As they walked closer to the home, they saw Tex in his garage fixing his tire rotation and brakes under his car. They also saw three red gasoline containers tied on the top with a black zip-tie. At first, Tex didn't realize that two individuals approached him. When he finally saw two pairs of feet walking towards him, he stopped working and slid out from under the car.

"Can I help you guys?" he asked with an unflattering tone.

"Tex Brown, I presume?" Detective Sands asked.

"Why? Who wants to know?" Tex replied, still suspicious about the men who just appeared in his driveway.

"My name's Detective Isaac Sands, and this is Officer Anderson. Mind if we asked you some questions?" Sands asked.

Still suspicious of his guests, Tex walked back to his open garage, wiped his hands on a small towel, and walked back to the two men in the driveway. "Questions about what?" he asked.

"Well, we wanted to ask about you and Raven-" Sands began before Tex cut him off.

"Look guys, if this is about what happened at the mall, I didn't do anything," he said immediately before Sands put his hand up again.

"No, this isn't about the mall incident. This is about Raven's rape allegations against Mr. Levell Thomas," he replied.

To Sands' surprise, Tex chuckled. "You mean that sick teacher who fucked around with Raven before taking advantage of her?" he asked.

"Wait, so are you saying that they'd been intimate before that incident?" Sands asked.

"Of course. That sick bastard always had his eyes on Raven. Why the hell do you think we broke up?" he asked.

"Hey, we're the ones asking the questions here," Anderson said.

Tex glared at him before turning back to Detective Sands. "I don't owe you any explanation. That girl rushed Raven first, and I was just backing her up when the other guys jumped in. We broke up, but that don't mean we're not still friends," he said.

"Okay, thanks for tellin' me that," Sands replied. "But now I need to get some more information about Raven. How long have you known her?"

Tex shifted nervously, and Sands knew it. All the tell-tale signs of an individual who was lying or covering up for someone were showing, from the eye pupil darting left and right, the pacing of the steps, or the slightest tremor and body movement from the individual. Sands was certain Tex would withhold information from him, and he did not disappoint.

"I've only known her for a couple years," he replied.

"Has Raven been known to exhibit any type of suspicious behavior, especially when it came to Mr. Thomas?" Sands asked.

"Okay, you know what? I'm not sayin' another damn word anymore. I know my rights. I don't have to sit here and answer your questions. I didn't do anything, and if you ain't got nothin' on me, then that means you're trespassing on my property," Tex replied, clearly agitated.

To Tex's surprise, however, Sands smiled. He knew Tex wouldn't cooperate willingly. "Okay, Tex, I'll leave," he replied calmly. "But I will tell you this. I know you ain't tellin' me the whole truth, and I know Raven didn't tell the truth about what happened that day. You're involved in something with her and her father, and boy I'd hate to be you when the Roberts get charged with falsely accusing a man of a crime he didn't commit cuz you'll most likely be charged as well if it's discovered you aided them in this farce. You understand?" Sands expressed firmly before signaling to Anderson that it was time to go.

Tex just stood there and watched as they pulled out of the driveway. He made sure that they were out of earshot before he took out his phone and made a call.

That cop knows too much. Gotta call Roberts now, he thought as he dialed Jerry Roberts' number.

Four days passed, and finally Levell was completely at full strength. Although he was still bruised in some places, he was still alive and grateful that his organs had not failed him, and he was able to recover. The awful news was the fact that he had to return to Smyrna State Prison as soon as he completely healed. He was not looking forward to the return. For all he knew, Joey B. and Treg might be out of the Hole by that time and would no doubt be ready for another encounter with him. But Levell was determined not to let those men enjoy another beatdown at his expense. He was going to workout while in prison, doing leg and strength exercises, followed by five sets of twenty pushups, to attempt to increase his muscle mass. If Treg and Joey B. had another initiation planned for him, he would be ready.

When prisoner transport took Levell back to Smyrna State Prison, two officers walked him back to his cell. It was a few minutes before noon, so Levell knew that all the other inmates were either outside working the highway or were in the manufacturing room working on textiles and windowpanes or performing laundry duties. Once he got back in his cell, Levell saw that Wes and McKinley were not in their cell, but looking at McKinley's, he noticed a medium-sized bag with white powder semi-buried under his pillow. Levell had to do a double take because he couldn't believe what he saw.

So that's why McKinley acts the way he does. He's snorts cocaine all the time.

Generally, the officers never allowed alcohol or drugs inside the prison or the cells, and for any inmate that was found with either or the both, the guards would not only confiscate belongings, but they would also make absolute sure that the inmate wouldn't be paroled or released anytime in the near future. Levell wondered how McKinley had managed to smuggle it so the guards couldn't get to it and how he'd hid it under the crack in his bedside and pillow. He must've been using some because there was a small tear in the side of the bag. What else explained his erratic behavior?

After settling for a few minutes, Levell headed to the manufacturing room where the other inmates were cleaning floors. Production must have finished because most of the inmates lounged back. When Levell walked inside the room, it only took the other inmates a split second to recognize him.

Suddenly, most of them chanted, "Level up!"

The cheerful shouts caused Levell to stare at them with a blank expression. *Level up? That's the best they could come up with on a name like mine?*

But Levell would've been lying if he didn't admit to liking the attention he received, and it was obvious that it came from their reaction to his fight with the two massive inmates. Wes walked up to him, grinning.

"What's so funny, man?" he asked.

"You da man of the hour, bro!" Wes said. "Nah, but I told a few cats here what you did, and even though you got yo' ass beat like a ragdoll, you got 'em."

"I ain't do nothin' special," Levell said, shrugging, "I was just defending myself when they came at me."

"I know, and believe me it ain't gonna be the last time, but it's good to know that you got some fight in you," Wes said. Then he looked around, as if to make sure nobody was listening. "Think about it, bro. Half these dudes were thinkin' you was soft anyways. You don't wanna end up like Lew," he warned.

"Who's Lew?" Levell asked as the rest of the inmates made their way back to their cell or towards the back of the prison, where there was a huge yard that stretched about five acres, only to end up inside a huge gate with barbed wire across the top.

Inmates went outside during their free time to walk around, exercise with the few weights and dumbbells that the prison contained. Wes pointed at a man about fifty yards away. His complexion was a light brown, as if he was mixed or a "mulatto" as most people referred to mixed children.

Lew wasn't very big in size, and that was the first red flag that flashed for Levell.

"Why, what happened to Lew?" Levell asked.

"Well, let's just say, Lew had a run-in with Treg about a week before you got here, and he wasn't a fighter like you were. Let's just leave it at that," Wes replied, waving his hand as if he didn't want to continue the story.

"Why, he lost?" Levell asked.

"Yeah, he lost the fight, but that ain't all he lost. Check out the way he walk," Wes replied.

Levell observed and noticed the skinny inmate walked with a slight limp.

"You know why he walk like that?" Wes asked.

Levell could've probably guessed what happened next, but he inquired anyway.

"Brotha's manhood was taken from him, man. Treg had his way with Lew. After the beatdown, he penetrated every and any hole he could find. Sodomy doesn't even begin to describe what happened to Lew. He ain't eva' gonna be the same," Wes said, solemnly.

Levell looked at Lew as he gingerly walked back inside. He felt deep pity in his heart for Lew, and he knew that if Lew could, he would probably try to end his suffering. Levell had held his own that night, but he still ended up unconscious and probably would've ended up suffering the same fate as Lew. Even showering with the other inmates had Levell paranoid. Although the guards did their best to keep inmates in line, he knew they couldn't be everywhere. It was only a matter of time before Treg and Joey searched for new meat.

I gotta get outta here. Levell desperately hoped that his lawyer was working on a parole hearing.

Later that week, Max Francis walked inside Lucky Pub, a bar just a few short miles from Highway 41. Sitting in front of the serving counter, Max called the bartender.

"The usual?" the bartender asked.

"You know it," Max replied as the bartender went to fetch Max's normal beer.

As he awaited his order, Max sat back, wondering what he was going to do next. His nephew had been behind bars for over three weeks, and he couldn't do anything about it. Caliya was waiting for Allan Richter to call and discuss the date for a possible parole hearing, but despite the countless messages that she left, Allan had yet to call her back. Now she was starting to feel the tug of pressure on her shoulders, and she'd had to rely on Levell's family.

As the bartender brought Max his beer, he sipped in peace and watched the sports network on the small television set mounted just over the corner of the serving counter. At the same time, two men walked inside the pub. They paid no attention to Max or the other patrons at the bar, but they sat at the table directly adjacent to where Max was. He couldn't help but listen to their conversation. Max didn't turn around right away, but he recognized the voices of the men who spoke behind him with the strong southern twang. He'd heard those voices in one other location: the courtroom where his nephew was convicted. One of the men was prosecutor John Covington, and the other man was Jerry Roberts.

"Hey, girl, lemme get shot of jack and some whiskey for my comrade here," John said to the bartender.

As she went back to grab the orders, Max heard the men whispering as if they did not want to be heard.

"For God's sake, man, couldn't he have met us someplace else? Why does he want to meet us here?" Mr. Roberts asked.

"Why not? He wanted a drink, and hell, I wanted a drink too. Relax Roberts, you'll be okay," John replied.

"It's too public. We should've held our meeting elsewhere. C'mon let's take drinks to go," Mr. Roberts suggested.

But then the bar door opened again, and a third man casually walked in. Joining the other two men at the table, the third man made his order.

"Can I get some Jack Daniels over here, please?" he asked. Noticing the expression on his comrades' faces, he decided to lighten the mood. "Why ya' starin' at me for? We're here, right? Let's talk," the man said.

"Okay, I'm gonna ask you what I asked John. Why are we meeting here? Why not go somewhere more private, like my house?" Mr. Roberts asked.

Max could tell by the slight trembling of his voice, he was either nervous, or he was not trying to be seen.

"Why not? I figured the only way to talk about parole denial was over some drinks," the third man laughed.

Parole denial? Max couldn't believe what he heard. He hadn't taken too many law classes in school, but he was certain that they couldn't discuss court proceedings out in public. But what shocked him the most was that he found out that the voice of the third man that spoke was none other than Caliya's attorney, Allan Richter.

Chapter 19

MAX COULD HARDLY BELIEVE HIS EARS WHEN HE discovered that his nephew's lawyer was in cahoots with the opposition. A wave of rage and shock hit him. Here was the man who was supposed to be defending Levell, and he was working with the enemy the whole time. Why didn't he see it coming? Max clenched his beer bottle in anger, and he was thankful that there were other people at the bar. Had he been alone with Allan, he would have smashed the bottle over Allan's head. Fortunately, Max was concealed from the three men because his back was turned, and he was wearing a black UGA cap on his head. Max did his best to drown out the noise of the other bar patrons as he continued to listen to the conversation of the three men.

"I gotta tell you, Allan, you gave me quite a scare in that courtroom though. For a minute, I thought you'd forgotten what team you played for," John said with a chuckle.

"Well I might not be a great actor, but I do play my part well. Levell's wife still believes that I'm defending her big oaf of a man," Allan replied smugly.

Max laid his head down to act as if he was already inebriated, but he peeked at the men from under his left arm and saw the smug, confident grin on Allan's face. The smile of betrayal. The smile of man who violated and disregarded the attorney's code to stand up for his client. He wanted to wipe that smile from Allan's face with his fists.

"I bet she is," John laughed. "And you came right on time with his background record of his prior arrest in college. I don't think we could've nailed that spook if we didn't have that information. The man is so damn noble, it's disgusting," he continued as the three men continued drinking their beverages, unaware that one of Levell's family members was keenly listening to their conversation.

Max shook his head. Somehow, in the back of his mind, he'd suspected that Levell was set up by the police, the D.A., and the plaintiff, and now his suspicions were confirmed. Allan had been the one who supplied John with Levell's prior records, even after he was eventually cleared of any wrongdoing. They'd succeeded in painting Levell as a black serial rapist who deserved to be locked up and the key thrown away at their disposal.

"Teacher of The Year...how did he ever win that?" Mr. Roberts asked, while shifting his head from left to right as if he was making sure that he wasn't being heard.

When Mr. Roberts turned his head towards Max, Max made sure to keep his head down, so he wouldn't recognize him.

"Out of all the great teachers in that school, and they had to pick him. Makes no goddamn sense," he continued.

"Easy now, Jerry. It's just one man. With Allan and Stanley, Paul, and Cromey, we got him right where we want him," John replied.

"Paul and Cromey did their part in tearing up the restraining order and wipin' it from police records, so Raven lucked out. I remind her every day about it. What did she see in that guy anyway?" Mr. Roberts asked.

"Well, he's a high school professor from New York, has street smarts, book smarts, hell, every type of smarts you could think of," Allan replied. "You're still under the impression that they're all big and stupid and good for nothing except sports and music," he added, replying to Mr. Roberts.

"Cause that's what they all are. It's not bad enough they take sports and music from us, now they're starting to take degrees too. The next to go is gonna be our women, and most of them already fantasize about them," Mr. Roberts said, and although he spoke in a voice barely above a whisper, Max could hear his hate in every word that came out of his mouth.

"Well, what if we start fantasizing about their women?" John asked.

"Well, I speak for myself when I say this, but I've had my eye on Levell's wife for a while. She's no Marilyn Monroe, but she's still a knockout. If Levell stays behind bars for ten more years, I might be tempted to try tasting that fruit, if you get my drift," Allan answered, laughing.

Now Max was really starting to steam. His right hand, already turning red as he angrily gripped the neck of his beer bottle, was at the point of shattering in his iron grip.

Tell me this grimy, treacherous bastard did not just admit to lusting after the wife of the man that he is supposed to be defending.

One thing was for sure, he was not going to stay silent about what he heard. He was going to tell Caliya everything. Afterwards, he was going to make sure that she cut ties with Allan immediately and hire a new lawyer to work with Levell, but not before pressing charges on Allan for conspiracy against his client.

"Oh well, she's still payin' me like I'm still doin' something for her husband," he continued.

John and Mr. Roberts laughed. As the laughter died down, Allan asked, "So, if they deny his parole, does that mean I can join the URA?" Allan asked.

Max shifted slightly as he continued to eavesdrop on the traitor and his two comrades. *What the hell is the URA?*

As the men finished drinking, they stood up and prepared to leave the bar. "Same time next week, gentlemen?" John asked the other two men.

"Yeah, but let's meet over at the compound," Allan replied as the three men exited the bar and walked their separate ways, each of them heading over to their cars.

When Max made sure that they drove out of the parking lot, he got up from his stool and prepared to leave. The bartender made his way over to him. "You sure you don't want one for the road?" she asked.

"Nah, I'm good. Thank you," he answered while paying his tab, and he made his way out the bar, his mind still replaying the treachery and betrayal that he'd witnessed only a few minutes ago.

After fifteen minutes, Max safely returned home, as he was able to drive because he was not fully drunk. One bottle of beer was all that he could stomach after what he had witnessed. He already knew that Caliya was at his home by her car parked in his driveway. As he opened the garage, he felt conflicted. Caliya was already going through a rough patch with her husband being in prison and with her being unable to pay most of the bills in her home. Just the other day, Caliya had described to Vicky how her cell phone service was suspended due to non-pay. She had explained how she had to make sure her mortgage and utilities were paid for and that her food was paid for. She also had to continue paying for Patrice to go to daycare and preschool. After all those bills were paid, Caliya barely had enough for herself, so she had to sacrifice her home phone service because it just didn't seem important.

After trying to call Allan to get an update of Levell's scheduled parole hearing, Caliya decided to visit Allan's office the next day to confront him for not calling her with an update. She knew he was a busy man, but it was ridiculous that he couldn't even follow up with her. It became another stress factor.

Max knew how stressed Caliya was, and the news that he was carrying to her was not going to do anything but cause more stress. When he opened the garage door to the kitchen, he was greeted by his son, daughter, and Patrice, who were all watching TV in the living room. Meanwhile, Vicky and Caliya were in the kitchen, discussing visiting Levell in Smyrna State Prison. Vicky was on her I-Pad, checking visitation hours.

"Okay, Caliya, it says that visitation is between two in the afternoon to six at night. We better go early because these visitation halls tend to get full, and they have to check us for drugs and weapons," Vicky pointed out.

"Whatever it takes, we'll do it. I just gotta see Levell to make sure he's okay. I still die inside thinking about where he's at," Caliya answered as Max walked over to the kitchen sink to wash his hands.

"Hey, baby, I didn't hear you coming in the kitchen. Is everything okay?" Vicky asked as Max sat down on one of his kitchen chairs.

After a moment of silence, Max replied, "No. Everything's not okay."

"What's wrong?" Caliya asked.

Max looked Caliya in the eyes. Where does he even begin? "Caliya, what I'm bout to tell you right now, you may wanna stay seated for this," he replied.

Caliya agreed and Max began to tell them about Jerry Roberts, John, and Allan at the bar.

"So, there I was, minding my own business just gettin' a drink after work, and then I see Mr. Roberts with John, the prosecutor. I didn't think nothing of it at first, but then when I heard them talk, I felt burned up inside because I've never heard such hate, such anger coming from those two degenerates," Max explained. "But that wasn't it. Allan walked in the bar and joined them."

Even before Max could utter another word, he saw Caliya's eyes widen in shock. "Allan? What does he have to do with those two?" she asked.

"Ain't it obvious? He's workin' with them two bastards," Max replied.

Caliya back away from Max, shaking her head as if she couldn't believe what she was hearing. "Uh-uh, that's not possible, Max. Allan is my lawyer. He wouldn't play me like that. Vicky, you need to get your husband," Caliya replied.

"It's true. I heard every single word in there. It was all a setup from the very beginning. They used Raven as a trap because he won some award. He played you, Caliya!" he said emphatically.

"Come on, Max. You gotta be lying. There's no way that was Allan. He hadn't returned my calls in damn near a week. He's probably busy working on other cases. Are you sure you just didn't see someone who probably looked like Allan, maybe? I mean, you were in a bar drinking, after all. Maybe you ain't see straight," Caliya said.

"I know who I saw, okay?" Max replied, slightly louder than he originally intended. "Allan was in that bar, he wasn't wearing no suit like he was at work. He was wearing this blue, short-sleeved, buttoned down shirt with some khaki pants and wing tip shoes," he added, describing Allan's full attire.

Caliya waved her hand dismissively at him. "Okay, I didn't come here for this," she said.

But this time Vicky turned to Caliya. She had been silent during the exchange, but she decided to speak up. "Caliya, what if Max is right? What if he really saw Allan in there?"

Caliya scoffed, as if she couldn't believe such a notion. "Vicky, be serious. Lawyers have a code that they follow. It's Allan's obligation to see me through this ordeal. Otherwise, why the hell am I paying him?"

"Because the man's a snake," Max replied. "They're part of this group, called the URA, or something like that, and they got members of this so called 'group' within the police force. They're the ones that arrested Levell. They took out the restraining order from their records, and now they're planning to make sure Levell's parole gets denied," he explained, wishing that Levell's wife understood that she was being used as a pawn in the justice system.

"That's it. I can't hear any more of this," Caliya said, standing up from her chair and grabbing her purse. "I came to y'all because you're the only family, besides my cousin, who lives down here. You're Levell's uncle, and you come to me with this BS?" she asked Max angrily.

"Okay, Ms. Thing, if you think I'm just blowin' smoke up yo' ass, why don't you find out for yourself? Why don't you ask Sands to investigate URA? As a matter of fact, why don't you ask your snake of a lawyer where he got Levell's prior record from?" Max asked firmly, causing Caliya to stop in her tracks.

"Excuse me? If you're talking about the whole college incident, that was the prosecutor who found his way to those records," she replied.

"How do you think he got them?!" Max exclaimed. "Allan searched through those records and gave them to John before the court date. So obviously he has some connections to NYPD also. Don't you get it? It was all a setup," he added, but he knew the argument was lost when Caliya already started to leave.

"Patrice, let's go," Caliya said, gesturing for her daughter to accompany her to her car, despite her protests of wanting to stay with her cousins.

Turning back to Max and Vicky, Caliya said, "Max, we're supposed to be a team that works together to get Levell out. If we start turning on each other, we'll only be failing Levell instead of helping him. So, unless I see proof of Allan doing these things, I can't align myself with you. I need an uncle, not a conspiracy theorist." With that, she closed the door on her car and pulled out of the driveway.

Early the next morning, the inmates were awakened by the normal buzzing signal that signaled the assignments of cell blocks into showers. However, Levell had been awake for more than an hour. While the sun's bright rays still peaked through the windows and the prison bars, Levell, who couldn't sleep, decided to exercise to improve his upper body strength. He was not a skinny man to begin with, but he felt that there was nothing wrong with getting stronger. He did one hundred pushups in five sets of twenty repetitions. He realized how difficult it was, since it had been years since he had done any type of vigorous workout. He was also aware that Joey B. and Treg would be gunning after him as soon as they left the Hole they were confined to as punishment for fighting. But it was nothing new to them, and he knew that he had to be ready. If they were going to ambush him again, he was determined that it wasn't going to be as easy as it was the first time.

After working on pushups, Levell's face and body drenched in sweat. Yet, he managed sixty sit-ups in three sets of twenty repetitions. Chuckling to himself, he often found it funny how he used to struggle with pushups and sit-ups whenever he was at home or at the gym, but here he was, in a place where nobody else wanted to be, and he got more out of his body in a desolate cell block than he did in the throes of freedom. After thirty minutes, he realized that he wasn't the only one awake. Looking at the cell block to his left, he saw McKinley hunched over in a corner, his back turned to the jail bars.

Based on the motion that his head moved, which started from the right side and gradually moved over to the left side, Levell immediately discovered that McKinley was snorting a line of cocaine. And the noise that emerged from McKinley's nose and mouth as he inhaled the white powder was comical. He would look around quickly to ensure that no guards passed by the cells. Then whenever the guards came, he would quickly stuff the contents under his bunk bed mattress and would patiently wait for the guard to walk past his cell. As soon as the guard was out of earshot, McKinley would pull out his small dime bag and resume snorting.

Noticing how quiet it was, McKinley turned around again, and this time, his eyes met with Levell's eyes. Walking over to Levell, McKinley offered him some cocaine.

"Nah, McKinley, I'm good," Levell replied.

"Whatever, man. More for me," McKinley said as he started back snorting.

Looking at the next cellblock over, Levell saw Wes reading a book, at least that was what it like from a distance.

"Yo, Wes," Levell whispered, so he wouldn't wake up the other inmates or draw attention to the police guards currently watching outside the door.

"What's up, young G?" Wes replied, not looking up from whatever he was reading.

"Yo, what you readin' over there?" Levell asked.

"You might be surprised by this, bro, but I'm reading the Bible. See?" Wes replied holding up the thick book, much to Levell's dismay.

Levell wasn't a stranger to the Bible. From an early childhood, his parents were devout Christians who hammered the Bible into him every day. On Sundays, it was church nonstop, and there was more than just one worship service. There were three. At times, Levell had to stay for all three of them. As a child, he never thought so much about it because it was about obeying his parents, which he always did. But as soon as Levell reached adolescence, he began to rebel, since it seemed that all his parents cared about was church. Levell got sick of it. He could still hear his mother's voice saying, "Li la Bib' ou chak jou," which meant "Read your Bible every day," in Creole.

But Levell was tired of it, and by the time he'd finished high school and entered college, he had begun to question the existence of Jesus Christ or God. It led to him majoring in English and education. It was his chance to learn about more literary works than just the Bible. To his family, they lived and died for a book that Levell saw little to no credibility in because it had been translated and modified over the course of more than a thousand years.

Levell was determined not to think the same way his parents thought. Therefore, he took more interest in social studies and courses in humanities, which focused on worldly cultures and their literary works. His parents always lamented about him not taking the words of the Bible seriously, but Levell figured that it was his life, and he had to figure it out on his own.

The irony of the matter was that he still hadn't figured life out because he found himself trying to figure out how to get out of prison. After speaking to Caliya over the phone for the past two days, Levell found out she had communicated with his family back in New York. She expressed to Levell how devastated his parents were when they heard their son was in prison for a crime he didn't commit. But how did they respond to Caliya?

They told her that they'll pray for me and keep hope that the truth will reveal itself.

Levell shook his head. It was a joke. Any logical parent would have either flown down to help their child or pitch together to raise money to bail him out. Instead the Bible had warped their minds. Therefore, logical thinking was replaced with hopeful wishing.

Sorry, Mom and Dad. It doesn't work in the real world.

"What, man?" Wes asked, obviously seeing the disapproving look from Levell.

"Nothin' personal, bro, but you wastin' your time reading that," Levell replied, expecting a standard lecture about the Bible.

To his surprise, Wes laughed. "Lemme guess, you one of them cats that probably grew up wit' church folk, and when you got up in age, you thought that this was nothin' but BS."

Bingo! Levell thought, but dared not say aloud.

"Lemme school you on something, son," Wes began, and Levell rolled his eyes.

Here it comes...the lecture. I bet he's gonna tell me something that I've heard from my parents already.

"Everything that's around us, from the air that we breathe, to the water that we drink and food we eat, all that comes from somewhere. God is real, brotha. His Word is real. Now I ain't perfect in my ways. God knows I screwed up many times in my life, and he could've took me out, but He kept me alive," Wes continued.

"Well, look around you, dawg. God didn't seem to save you from this shit, now did he?" Levell asked.

Wes lowered the Bible and looked at Levell, his old wrinkled tired eyes staring deeply into his young counterpart. "You an educated man, college educated at that, and you can't even fathom the possibility of God existing?"

"I've read the Bible inside and out, and it always seemed to be a book of stories. Like the Greek myths or the Arthurian legends. Stories that were fixtures of its time, not to be taken seriously," Levell replied.

"Okay, answer me this, young brother. Why did you come down here? Why did you move to the A?" Wes asked.

Levell rolled his eyes again. This old man was just as delusional as his parents, perhaps more so. "I moved down here so I can teach and educate kids, the same way I educated them in New York. I saw an opportunity, and I took it."

"That's my point, brother. You saw an opportunity, and you took it. When man sinned by eatin' that daggone fruit in that forest, mankind was doomed to die forever. Well, God through His son saw an opportunity to save us, and He came down here and took that opportunity," Wes explained, but Levell felt he was over the whole conversation.

"Yeah, yeah, I know the story...the whole dying on the cross for our sins thing. I get it. But here's why I have a problem believing. If he'd done that, wouldn't we have been better off?" Levell asked. "If He supposedly 'saved' us, why did He continue allowing evil to reign in this world? Why did He put people like Raven and her family on this earth? We're told to forgive all the time, but they don't forgive us. We are the most hated people on the face of this planet. So much for Him dying on that cross...He ain't did nothin'. Ain't nothin' changed. Matter of fact, it got worse. So, He wasted his time. Besides, why would an Almighty God give a damn about us?"

"This world doesn't belong to us. God created this world, but He's not of it. This here's the devil's playground," Wes replied.

Levell saw that it was pointless talking Wes out of his beliefs, but he was not going to allow Wes to talk him into passiveness. He'd already allowed his kind nature to override his better judgment, and it gave Raven an opening to rain all types of misery on him. Wes returned to reading and Levell continued sitting in his cellblock until he was called for the showers.

Chapter 20

As he finished his affidavits from other cases, Allan Richter stood up from his desk inside his office. Working within the Peach Law Firm Group in Acworth was excruciating because it prevented him from raising up stock to start his own firm. He was not too fond of the head of his firm, Jimmy Lee Jones, a staunch supporter of the whole affirmative action by-law that saw different attorneys—some with less training and a much lesser score than his own at their bar exams—handle bigger profile cases, the cases that would net people tens of thousands, if not millions, of dollars. Yet, he remained in the smallest office in the building, with the smallest desk in the building, and he was handling these worthless domestic cases that he loathed with a passion. If there was no money involved in those cases, he would have thrown them out many years ago.

He saw the messages left by Levell Thomas' wife and knew she wanted information about the date of his parole hearing. He managed to secure a date in September that would determine Levell's fate. Allan played his part too well, and he knew that the decision by the parole board would determine his entry into the URA, where he would finally be accepted for his credentials and commitment, with an organization that would be the key to getting the high-profile cases that he wanted.

As he placed all his papers in a folder, Allan packed his briefcase and glanced at the clock one last time. It was a little after seven o'clock, and his security, Pam Fields, had left for the evening. Believing that he was the only person in the building, Allan opened his office door and turned around to leave when he saw someone sitting in the waiting area outside his office. At first, he couldn't identify the visitor. Pam made sure she'd turned off all the lights in the office before she'd left an hour earlier.

Maybe Pam came back to retrieve something that she forgot.

Allan walked to the other side of the room to turn the lights on. To his surprise, it wasn't Pam who sat in a waiting room chair.

"Caliya!" Allan exclaimed, unable to hide the obvious tones of surprise and guilt.

He could see that Caliya was seated and her facial expressions were calm for the moment, but he knew it would only be temporary. If there was anything he knew about people such as Caliya, he knew that they could get irritated and irascible if they didn't get what they wanted.

"Leaving so soon?" she asked him.

"Mrs. Thomas! What a pleasant surprise-" he began, but Caliya abruptly interrupted him.

"Save me the BS, okay? What's going on with you? Do you know how many times I tried to call you, and all I got was your voicemail or your ditzy secretary tellin' me you ain't in the office?"

By the steady rise of her tone, Allan could see that Caliya was clearly upset over the lack of communication from her attorney. "Okay, Caliya, I know you're upset, but please let me explain," he said, but Caliya seemed determined not to allow Allan to get a word out on his own.

"Is it true?" Caliya asked.

"Is what true?" Allan replied, as if he was clueless on what Caliya was preparing to interrogate him on.

"Did you really give the Roberts' lawyer undisclosed information from a closed case just to implicate my husband?" Caliya asked slowly.

Allan looked at Caliya's face innocently. "Mrs. Thomas, I'm afraid I have no idea what you're talking about," he replied.

To his surprise, Caliya didn't react as quickly as she had a few seconds earlier. She laughed, which began to make Allan feel uneasy. "You know what's so funny? I actually knew you were gonna say that. You guys always stay on code, except when it comes to us," she replied.

"Mrs. Thomas, I'm working on a date for a parole hearing for Mr. Thomas, and I actually have one coming up this September. I still haven't been given a date yet, so you will be notified as soon as a date becomes available," Allan explained frantically, but Caliya interrupted him again.

"Don't bother, Mr. Richter. Since you have more pressing issues on your mind, let me help you ease it. I'm relieving you of your duties, and I'm terminating my contract with you," she said as Allan's face started to grow paler by the second.

Caliya thought it was very comical, but she was determined to remain serious. "In other words, you're fired," she added.

"So, this is how it ends, huh?" Allan asked and Caliya noticed a change in his tone, from a sunny southern accent to low, dulcet tones. "To be quite honest with you, Mrs. Thomas, your husband is a violent man who goes around violating other women while women like you are left wondering where the love has gone. Do you think your husband gives a damn about you or your daughter? I did him a favor by getting him less jail time, and if some historical legal documents fell into the wrong hands, well I'm not responsible for that."

Caliya just stood there, looking at her former attorney in disgust.

"And unfortunately, in the good ole USA, you need something called evidence to prove that I set Levell up, and since you can't produce any sort of physical evidence, it's just your word against mine. I think I'm a little more equipped than you are when it comes to the court system," he added smugly.

"Funny you should mention that, Mr. Richter," another voice replied in the left section of the room. Detective Sands had received the phone call from Caliya upon the advice from Max and had followed his cousin into the law office.

"Detective Sands, what brings you here this time of night?" Allan asked, his voice slightly shaking as he had a strange feeling that his charade was about to come to an end.

"According to these documents that I pulled from AT&T phone records, which happens to be your cell company if I'm not mistaken, we have several points of contact between yourself, Mr. Roberts, and his attorney," Sands said, holding the papers that contained phone records.

The look on Allan's face was priceless, as Sands could barely suppress his laughter.

"Now it's funny that you can be Caliya's lawyer, but you communicate more with her husband's accusers than with her. I mean, I'm not a lawyer, but I'm sure the Georgia State Bar and the judge would have few things to say about that, now would they?" he asked rhetorically.

Beads of perspiration started to form on Allan's head as he realized he was looking at the disbarment of his license and jail time. Slowly backing away, Allan started to make his way towards the back exit, but Sands, who was no sloth, caught him before he could make his escape.

Sands started to read his rights to him. "You're under arrest for conspiracy and fraud," he said, while leading Allan outside where his police car was parked.

"You have no idea what you're getting into," Allan threatened. "Jerry and John are not people to be played with. They will find you, and you'll wish you never put your hands on me," he continued.

Sands merely smiled at his face. "Oh yeah? Well your friend Tex actually told me the same thing a couple days ago, and guess what, sunshine? I'm still here," Sands replied as he guided the head of the false lawyer inside the police vehicle.

Caliya, who had been watching the scene unfold, shook her head. It turned out that Max was right all along. Allan was just pulling her along and had never planned on creating a strategy to ensure her husband's parole from prison. Was there anybody within the judicial system who she could trust?

Levell stared deep into his wife's eyes the next day during the Smyrna State Prison's visiting hours. The friends and relatives of inmates were checked for weapons, drugs, or alcohol before being allowed access inside the prison. Caliya had to wait for about an hour until the police brought her husband out. The sleepless nights that began with her daughter had somehow been transferred to her. Although Allan had been apprehended and charged with fraud and conspiracy, his threat to Sands was still fresh on Caliya's mind. She hoped her cousin remained prepared. She didn't know how many connections Allan or Jerry Roberts had, and she was afraid that one of their friends would try to avenge the arrest of a fellow comrade. Patrice still asked for her father, and it cut Caliya deep in the heart whenever she had to lie to her daughter because she still couldn't bring herself to tell her daughter that her father was a convicted felon.

Finally, Caliya saw the police bring out the inmates from the opposite doorway to greet their family members. Levell walked out, and upon seeing his wife, he couldn't hold himself back. Running to Caliya, he hugged her, and suddenly the outside world disappeared. Time seemed suspended as Levell held his wife for over three minutes before he finally let go. Sitting down at a table across from each other, Caliya noticed the cuts and gashes across her husband's face as he explained Joey B. and Treg's ambush and how he managed to survive. Caliya, fighting back tears, listened as her husband described how much of a struggle it was to wake up every morning, knowing he couldn't be with their daughter.

"Baby, it's just a struggle getting motivated every day to wake up, knowing I'm in here. I gotta get out. Hopefully, Allan got a plan up his sleeve," he said.

Caliya's face suddenly hardened, and she became tight-lipped. Levell immediately recognized the face his wife made whenever she was angry.

"There is no more Allan," she replied coldly.

"What? Why, what happened?" Levell asked before Caliya explained Allan's intention to sway the judge into denying his parole and his association with Jerry Roberts.

As she explained, she saw her husband's expression change instantly from shock to fury. For Levell to learn that even his own lawyer was against him was devastating. The one person that he trusted to get him out of his current situation was in cahoots with his enemies. Levell had to do all he could not to break the legs of the table where they were sitting. He was so furious.

"Ain't there anybody out here that I can trust anymore?" he asked, echoing the same thoughts Caliya had the previous night when Allan was arrested.

"Baby, you can still trust me," Caliya replied. "And you can trust Uncle Max and his family. He tried to warn me that Richter was two-timing us, but I didn't believe him," she confessed.

Levell sighed. "I'm never gettin' outta here," he said, coming to the realization that he just might be fighting a losing battle.

"Well, I hired a new lawyer, James Gentry. I brought the case over to him this morning, and he was appalled by how Allan treated me and how he ultimately betrayed me," Caliya explained.

"Well, how do I know I can trust this guy?" Levell asked.

He didn't want to plant the seeds of doubt on Caliya's mind, but if Allan was a crooked lawyer, how was he going to trust any other lawyers with his case?

"Believe me, he's on our side, and Sands referred me to him," Caliya replied.

Levell sighed. All he wanted was to get out of prison. He didn't care how it had to be done. If it took old men who read John Grisham's *A Time To Kill* as their only introduction into the legal system as their training, he would take them, as long as they were honest and sincere.

"Well, since I ain't got no other choice, might as well bring Mr. Gentry into my mess," Levell replied. "How's my princess doing?"

"Patrice is doing well. She's gettin' smarter every day. I think she may be ready for school soon. But I don't wanna start that without you," she replied.

"I wish I could be there when she starts, but..." Levell began.

Caliya quickly said, "You will be there when she starts. That's a promise."

The police guards gave the signal that wrapped up visiting hours, so Levell hugged his wife again before being separated by bars, windows, brick, mortar, and the outside world.

A few days later, on Saturday morning, Caliya took Patrice to the Swift-Cantrell Park in Kennesaw. It was a moderate summer day where temperatures peaked at about eighty-two degrees with a light breeze. Recently, Caliya had taken Patrice out to various places on weekends to enjoy her childhood. She enjoyed those moments with her daughter, not only for Patrice's sake but for her own also. She needed to keep her sanity, and leaving her house was the best way to take her mind off her husband, if not just momentarily. Not to mention, she wouldn't be reminded of the house across the street where those other people slept. Caliya had taken Patrice to the pool, Marietta Square, and Chuck E. Cheese. She did her best to go sparingly to actual establishments, such as Chuck E. Cheese because it was money out of her pocket, which had become scarce in Levell's absence.

Caliya enjoyed going to the park. There were swing sets, seesaws, monkey bars and other playground amenities that her daughter could enjoy, and it would be completely free. She always packed fruits and juice cups as snacks whenever Patrice was hungry and tired from playing. Caliya was also pleased that Patrice started to make friends at the park, hanging out with two other black girls and a white girl. She also spoke with the parents of those children and found out that they were very friendly and open, especially the mother of the white girl. She remembered the mother introducing herself as Amanda after Patrice had introduced herself, which Caliya was always reluctant about because she feared that people would make the connection to her husband. But her last name was so common that it wouldn't be an issue. She found that out very quickly.

I wish everyone was like Amanda. No judgment or bias. Just good all-around.

But Caliya knew it was an impossible wish because of people like the Roberts—people who enjoyed watching her struggle and wallow in her misery rather than reach a certain level of happiness or respect.

One day when Caliya arrived at the park, she realized Amanda hadn't arrived with her daughter yet, and there were only a few kids at the playground. Caliya checked her watch. It was 11:20. She figured that Amanda must have arrived at the park before anyone else. While Patrice started out on the swings, Caliya took out a small book that she just started and picked up from the chapter she'd left off previously.

Caliya found herself so deeply immersed in the book that she didn't notice a presence standing behind her. When the figure moved slightly to her right, the sun was blocked by her shadow. Caliya turned around to see who was blocking the sun from her view of the book, and the person she saw was the last person she'd expect to see. Her black hair was tied back in a ponytail this time. It wasn't flowing freely the way it had been when they first met at the football game.

Raven looked as if she hadn't been sleeping well either. As Caliya looked closer, she could see those visible bags under her eyes that were all too telling. She also appeared to have lost some weight, and it wasn't as if Raven ever weighed over 150 pounds. Caliya would have had pity for her if she hadn't put her husband through the nightmare that he was currently living through.

"Hey, Mrs. Thomas," Raven greeted nonchalantly as if she was greeting a friend or a family member.

But Caliya was determined not to fall for Raven's schemes or games. "Raven, you got a lot of nerve coming over to me after the hell you put my family through. What do you want?" she asked sharply.

Raven proceeded to walk around the bench that Mrs. Thomas was sitting on and attempted to sit next to Caliya, but Caliya shifted to the far left of the bench. She didn't want anything to do with the girl who cried wolf on her husband.

Sighing deeply, Raven said, "Look, Mrs. Thomas, you have every right to be pissed off at me, and I don't expect us to be friends or anything, but I wanted to tell you something."

Caliya suddenly stood up from the bench. "This conversation's over, Raven. I have nothing more to say to you."

But Raven was persistent in trying to communicate with Caliya. "Mrs. Thomas, please don't leave yet. Look, I know what I did or tried to do with

Levell was wrong-" she started.

Caliya cut her off. "You damn right it was wrong!" she exclaimed. "First, you tried to seduce my husband behind my back. Then you tried to sleep with him on multiple occasions, and then you accuse him of assaulting you, which landed him in prison and away from his family. So, your little schoolgirl apology routine ain't gon' fly wit' me today."

"Please just hear me out for a minute. Just one minute, and I promise I'll leave you alone," Raven pleaded.

Caliya rubbed both sides of her temple as she attempted to stem a possible migraine that this girl was giving her.

The damage is done, Caliya. What else can this girl say or do to put you through more misery?

Finally, after a moment of reflection, Caliya decided to listen to what Raven had to say.

"I'm not gonna lie to you. I really did like Mr. Thomas as more than a teacher. He listened to me, we joked around, even when I wasn't in the mood, and he was always there for me," Raven said.

Caliya wished she could turn Raven off like a bad radio station, but the teen continued.

"My parents are...well, it's hard to explain it, but they never understood me the way Mr. Thomas did. Even my boyfriend didn't understand me, but Mr. Thomas was the only one that got me. It was the best feeling, and I was afraid of losing that feeling," Raven explained, her eyes starting to well up with tears.

Caliya listened, and although she still resented Raven, she began to understand why Raven acted the way she did towards her. She saw her as competition and as a woman as she thought back to her own days as a girl.

"Raven, I was your age once, and believe me, I've had more than a few shares of crushes to men who were much older than me," Caliya said. "But I had to learn that there were boundaries that I couldn't cross, and you crossed it with me and Levell."

"I was scared. I thought that I needed to prove that I could be with a sensitive, hard-working man like Levell, someone who didn't care too much about looks," Raven replied.

"But Mr. Thomas is married, Raven. He has a daughter, so how do you think that makes me look?" Caliya asked.

"I know, I know. I was wrong, and I put your family through so much. I'm deeply sorry," Raven apologized.

Somehow it seemed all too easy for Caliya. Raven was too crafty to be taken for granted. Caliya was certain Raven had a devious plan under her sleeve, and she did not want to converse any longer.

"Thank you, Raven, for your apology, but what good does it do for Levell? He's still in prison because of you. Now you have to live with that on your conscience, and believe me, even if I have to fight the court system with my bare hands, I'm gettin' my husband out of jail," she said firmly.

Feeling that the conversation had reached its peak, Caliya stood up and prepared to call her daughter to head home, but Raven spoke again. "I know about Allan Richter," she said.

Caliya stopped dead in her tracks. Turning around to face Raven, Caliya asked, "What do you know about Allan Richter, exactly?"

Raven took a deep breath, and by the way she looked around, it was as if she was about to disclose a sacred piece of information that she obviously didn't want anyone else to hear. Soon Caliya would be confirmed in that theory...

"Allan was trying to get into this organization called the URA. It stands for the United Right Association. My daddy and another man started this organization, and it was meant to be a group that talked about power and independence, but recently, they've been talking..." Raven started but was unable to finish her statement.

"Dominance, supremacy, and hate," Caliya finished.

Raven hung her head, which answered Caliya's questions. "Allan wanted to be a part of this group, so he agreed to take your case but to make sure he gave my defense team information that would charge Mr. Thomas. Everyone from members of the police force, to certain lawyers were in on the setup," Raven explained. "After Levell fought me off in the bathroom that day, and he ran off, I was so hurt that I cried, and when my daddy, along with his friends came along, they wanted me to say that Levell raped me."

"But you went along with them!" Caliya exclaimed, her temper rising.

"I had no choice. You don't know my family, Mrs. Thomas. You don't even know my father. He has dangerous connections to other...groups," Raven said.

She meant to say the Ku Klux Klan. She definitely knows her daddy's on that KKK tip.

"Okay, Raven, well thank you for warning me. I got it," Caliya said, putting her thumb up while rolling her eyes.

But Raven wasn't finished yet. "No, I don't think you get it," she said, surprising Caliya with her tone.

"Look, as far as Allan's concerned, we took care of him. I exposed him for the lying fraud that he is, and I'm hiring a new attorney," Caliya said.

"Yeah, I know. But the problem is that my father knows and so do the other members of the URA. They will find a way to retaliate. If you have friends, family, or anybody that you know, you better check up on them," Raven said.

Now she was making Caliya nervous. *What did she mean when she said to check on them?*

"Raven, what are you saying?" Caliya asked.

"Anyone who gets in the way of URA is headed for trouble. Trust me when I say my father will not rest until he sees Levell in prison for life or until things go his way," Raven replied.

"I'm sorry, Raven. You must've gotten me confused with someone who's scared of your daddy or his little friends. Well, they got the wrong woman, and I will go so far as to say that I dare them to try anything on me," Caliya said defiantly.

Raven shook her head. "You don't understand, Mrs. Thomas. Nobody plays with the URA and gets away with it. I'm tryin' to warn you. Please just be careful," Raven said, and without warning, she slipped a piece of paper into Caliya's hand.

The paper was folded, almost to origami levels, and when she unfolded the paper, Caliya saw that it was a photocopy of a portrait of twelve men smiling, posing for a picture. All the men wore suits and were standing side by side. Based on the image, Caliya could tell that the photo was at least ten years old.

"There's my father in the middle," Raven pointed out to Caliya.

Looking closer, Caliya saw that it was not only Jerry Roberts who looked familiar, but she recognized two of the men who resembled the cops that arrested Levell in front of their house. Another member was John Covington, the lawyer for Raven and her family. It appeared to be a regular portrait, except for two factors: there were four of the members holding rifles, three of the members holding the Confederate flag, and one of them was holding a swastika flag. Caliya couldn't believe what she was looking at. With this evidence, she had enough to expose the secret group.

"Why are you helping me? I mean, this is your father," she told Raven.

Raven looked toward the swingset where Patrice was swinging without a care in the world. "I'm helpin' you because of her. She loves her daddy, and I don't want her to grow up without him," she answered before walking away, leaving Caliya at the park.

$\mathfrak{Chapter}$ 21

AFTER GINGER DROPPED HER OFF IN FRONT OF HER house, raven took out her keys and opened the door. *Thank God, my daddy's not home yet,* she thought after glancing inside the garage and noticing her father's car not parked inside.

Normally, her mother worked Saturdays, and her father would be home, working in the garage, where he did part-time carpentry work. His hands would be calloused from the blisters he would receive from sawing a wood plank or hammering nails between two wood board pieces. He made chairs, benches, and signs among other items and would sell them on the side, in addition to his regular day job at the post office. Speculating that her father was working overtime hours, Raven walked to the fridge to grab a bottle of grape juice, but she couldn't locate a bottle in the refrigerator door shelf, where she normally placed all her beverages.

Where's all the damn juice? Daddy must've drank the last bottle.

Disgusted, Raven settled for a cup of water. Making a mental note to go to Walgreens to buy another pack of juice, she poured the water from the kitchen faucet, unaware that she was being watched. When she placed the cup down, she gasped in surprise as Mr. Roberts stood at the kitchen doorway, intently watching her. Judging by the slight smirk on his face, he had obviously been watching her actions the entire time.

"Daddy! I didn't know you were already here. I didn't see your car," she said.

Mr. Roberts continued staring, his eyes deadpanned on his daughter.

"Car's at the shop. I'm having them check the battery," he finally replied.

"Oh okay," Raven replied, giving her father her best phony smile.

As she turned around to walk up to her bedroom, he asked, "So where have you been?"

Raven froze where she stood. She certainly couldn't let her father know that she was speaking with Caliya, tipping her off about the dangerous society in which her father was a key member. "I went to the mall with Ginger, like most kids my age do, Daddy," she replied to her father.

But Mr. Roberts continued to stare at his daughter with an odd expression on his face.

"Why do you ask?" she said.

Mr. Roberts continued to stare at his daughter sternly. "Well, I just wanted to know where you were. A man's got every right to be protective of his little girl, right?"

Yeah, that's true," Raven agreed.

Where was he going with this?

"Especially after what happened at school, right?" Mr. Roberts asked, waiting for another response from Raven, but she sighed, much to his disdain.

"Daddy, I have something to tell you, about what happened that day," she said, but her father dismissed her.

"What you got to tell me that I ain't already knew?" he asked, smiling at his daughter.

Raven knew his smile was phony. She knew her father was lying about what he knew, and she also knew exactly what her father was thinking that very instance.

"Now you wouldn't happen to be playing both sides of the fence, are you?" Mr. Roberts asked.

If any stranger had sat between Raven and her father, they wouldn't have had a clue what he meant by that saying, but Raven did.

"What would make you say that?" she asked.

Mr. Roberts continued to give Raven the same deadpanned look for about ten more seconds before replying.

"Well, I'm sure you remember Allan Richter, right?" he asked.

"Yeah, that's Levell's lawyer. What does that have to do with me?" Raven asked.

"Seems that Mr. Richter was relieved of his duties by the spook's wife, so that causes a bit of a problem with our whole little operation," Mr. Roberts said.

Raven knew what her father meant by "operation"—from the plan to accuse Levell, an innocent man of raping her, to setting up the lawyer that planned to purposely provide them with information needed to bring a conviction and prolonging his parole hearing. But in that very moment, Raven decided that she wanted no part in her father's games. She had experienced nothing but misery throughout the ordeal, and the media attention that the case brought had people questioning teachers and educators everywhere.

"Well, that sucks that Allan got fired. But again, what do that got to do wit' me?" Raven asked.

She noticed her father losing patience, and he had the glint in his eyes...a look that Raven only saw during the beatings.

"Don't play stupid with me, girl. I ain't raise no damn fool. I know you had something to do wit' Allan getting' fired. You're helpin' them mud people, huh?" he asked, walking over to Raven.

"I don't what you're talking about," Raven said, before a sharp blow to her face from Mr. Roberts' caused her to stumble back against the kitchen countertop.

Rubbing the side of her cheek, Raven glared at her father. It wasn't the first time Mr. Roberts hit her. Some days, the pain wouldn't endure. Other days felt like years of pain under his roof.

"I told you, I ain't stupid!" Mr. Roberts, bellowed loudly, his voice full of fury. "You knew that Allan was gonna make sure that uppity nigger stayed behind bars, and you went and screwed it up. His license got revoked. Now what you got to say to that?"

"I told you, I ain't got nothin' to do with Allan losin' his damn job!" she protested.

"Stop lyin' to me, you stupid bitch!" he yelled, grabbing her arm while dragging her across the kitchen floor.

"Let go of me, Daddy!" Raven yelled as her father slammed her against the living room wall. "I told you, I had nothing to do with Allan gettin' fired. He played dirty, and he got done dirty," she replied angrily.

"Shut up!" Mr. Roberts exclaimed angrily.

With his only connection to the D.A., police, and the judge out of the picture, Mr. Roberts was forced to create a back-up plan, all because of his meddling child. Softening his facial features, he held his daughter's chin. "It's funny. I don't remember the mall being located at the park," he said with a sinister smile as the realization dawned on Raven.

Somehow, her father found out that she was at the park and had spoken with Caliya. "But how…who saw...?" she stammered nervously.

"You didn't think you would possibly pull one ova'on me, now did you?" he asked. "I told you before that I got eyes everywhere. I see everything, and I take note of everything. And please correct me if I'm wrong, but where in our plan did it involve talking to that black wench?"

"I don't want any part of this anymore. I don't wanna be involved with this anymore," Raven said.

"Too late, sunshine. You're involved, and you're part of this. We're gonna make sure that he never sees the light of day," Mr. Roberts said.

Raven looked at her father. She always knew her father was racist, but never in her wildest dreams could she expect her father to be unhinged about one man. "Levell's not the enemy. He cares about his family. Caliya cares about their family, and I respect anyone who defends their family. I don't care what color they are. What you're doing is wrong," Raven said.

Her father stepped away from his wounded daughter and began pacing around the kitchen. "Don't forget who you are. They are beneath us. It's time for us to reclaim and take back what belongs to us," Mr. Roberts said.

Raven couldn't believe what she was hearing. Her father was completely delusional. She was convinced that he was losing his mind. "And what exactly belongs to us?" Raven asked.

"Everything that the sun touches belongs to us. Those savages shouldn't get a thing here. If they were smart, they'd pack up and take their black asses back to Africa," Mr. Roberts replied.

"And if you were smart, you'd learn not to be a racist asshole," Raven bit back, but she realized she spoke too soon.

Without warning, Mr. Roberts swooped over to Raven and grabbed her by the throat, cutting off her airway. Working fervently to disengage her dad's hand, Raven scratched, kicked, and clawed at it, but his grip was too tight.

"Now that's no way to talk to yo' daddy," he replied in low tones. "You brought this problem to us. If you didn't have any feelings toward that coon of a teacher, we wouldn't go through all this trouble. Remember, we're doing this all for you," he said maniacally, keeping a tight grip on his daughter's throat.

Raven continued to struggle and thrash around like a fish out of water, but she slowly felt her consciousness slip. With the air being cut off, her body went limp in her father's tight grip. Finally releasing his hold, Mr. Roberts watched his daughter's motionless body slide to the ground.

She just had to do it. She had to make me go crazy and lose it. Now I got more work to do.

Mr. Roberts picked up his daughter's pale body. Checking for a pulse, he found nothing. He proceeded to take a shovel and walked over to the backyard of his home.

If I could get away with doing that old fart, Mr. Deneau, I could get away with this one too. She should've listened to me. She betrayed me. She betrayed our cause, our movement. We have no time for traitors. We must eliminate those who betray us, family or not. It's about the greater good.

He continued digging in the backyard. Staring at the Thomas house across the street, he only had one thought. *Time to turn up the heat...*

Two months passed since Levell had seen the outside world, and in an environment where other prisoners tended to lose hope, he was determined not to lose his resolve. He knew that one day the evidence wouldn't add up, and they'd realize how they'd made a monumental mistake. He felt more at ease after finally meeting his new lawyer, James Gentry, a young man who only had a few profile cases under his belt but felt that he could appeal for a parole hearing. The reason Levell trusted him was because he did not mince words with him upon their meeting when he came during visiting hours with Caliya.

The first order of business was to sue Allan Richter for fraud and conspiracy. Richter's estate agreed to pay back over fifty thousand dollars in damages for settling out of court. When Gentry confirmed that he secured a date for a parole hearing, Levell was beside himself. Here was a man who was barely on the job a week, and he had managed to accomplish more than what Richter had accomplished.

With the parole hearing approaching in the next two weeks, Levell continued his daily exercise in his cell. It was all he could do to remain sane. The most difficult trial for a male inmate was the absence of female companionship, and Levell missed it more than anything. Whenever he managed to sleep in his dreadful surroundings, he dreamed of being in bed, his arms wrapped around Caliya, and her arms wrapped around him.

He missed her smell, her touch, her passionate lovemaking, and the sweet sensation of release once the peak was reached. It was easy to understand how his cousin and so many other black men lost their minds once they were locked up. Many of them spent years without touching another woman. It was easy to see the repercussions just by staring at poor Lew, who was the repeated victim of prisoners taking their sex depravity out on him in the showers.

Levell did his utmost best not to be in the showers when Lew was in there. Even without Treg and Joey B., many of the bigger inmates would take turns pleasuring themselves on him. Levell considered it a miracle that he hadn't been touched again since Joey B. and Treg had brutally beat him to unconsciousness, and he took it as a sign of respect. Although they were released from the Hole, they had been keeping to themselves, even though they still shot Levell dirty looks as he passed them during breakfast and lunch.

But Levell no longer feared them or anyone. He worked to become an intimidating individual determined to defend himself if attacked or provoked. Wes had warned Levell that Joey B. and Treg would attempt to attack him again, but Levell would be ready for them. As they were eating dinner later that evening, Treg and Joey B. walked into the mess hall, greeted by other inmates as they took their seats. While Levell was watching the impromptu reunion unfold, Wes turned his head around.

"Don't look at them directly, son, or they'll come wantin' to start somethin'," he warned.

"So? Let 'em come ova hea.' I want them to come over here," Levell replied defiantly.

"Look, man, you got a wife and a kid back home. If you wanna make it outta here alive to see them, do what I say. Don't provoke 'em, because they will kill you," Wes said.

Levell finally turned around and focused on eating the Hamburger Helper meat and bread slice that was on his tray until he sensed the presence of two people behind him. Their large shadows loomed over the table, and Levell knew exactly who stood over him.

"Guess who, muthafucka?" Treg asked, holding Levell's shoulder roughly.

"Yeah, you thought this was ova'?" Joey B. asked.

Did they always have to speak in unison?

Levell turned around to face the two massive inmates. With all the other inmates watching, he stood up from his chair and stared them in the eye.

"Don't get it twisted, fam. I don't sweat either one of you clowns, so if you wanna throw down again, I'm wit' it today. Trust me, you don't wanna catch these hands again," Levell replied.

Joey B. pretended to laugh as if he was amused by this smaller man, but a second later, his fist went flying, aiming to hit Levell in the jaw. But this time, Levell was ready, and he ducked. Joey B.'s fist swung nothing but air. Treg ran toward Levell's body with the intention of tackling him, but Wes jumped in and smashed his head with the metal tray. A gash opened across the top of Treg's head, and while the blood poured down the side of his face, Joey B. stepped back, staring at Wes, who was panting heavily.

"So, you want some of this too, old man?" he threatened.

"I'll give you all you want, youngblood, but as long as I'm here, you ain't touchin' this man anymore, you feel me?" Wes replied.

Joey B. started to make his way toward Levell and Wes, but at the same time, the officers ran to them and separated the four men before the situation escalated.

Noticing Treg bleeding profusely from his head, one of the officers asked, "Who's responsible for this?"

He turned to Levell. "Was it you, Thomas?"

"No, suh, it was me," Wes said, raising his hand slightly.

The officer hung his head, as if he instantly regretted what he had to do next.

"Well, you know the rules, Wesley. Initiating life-threatening injury to another inmate means ten days in the Hole. Let's go," he said, motioning for Wes to follow him.

Levell stood, shell-shocked. He had been ready to defend himself, knowing that he would've risked going down to the Hole as punishment, but Wes took his place. He took it upon himself to defend Levell when the time came. But Levell knew that Wes was an elderly man, one already showing early signs of emphysema. Ten days in the Hole where it was an enclosed space in the dark with no sunlight, no windows, and the cell was filthy, and that was putting it politely. Solitary confinement would be heaven compared to the Hole. Wes would not make it five days, let alone ten. Levell had to do something.

"Officer, wait please. Don't take Wes down to the Hole. Please, let me go for him. I started the fight. I was the one that busted Treg's head with the tray," he explained frantically, but Wes waved him off.

"Stand back, son. It's okay. I'll be iight," Wes said as the officer led him away.

Levell watched his friend take a walk to the dark corridors that led to the Hole.

"And I don't wanna see any more fightin' between you three, or you will all be confined to the Hole," the other officer warned before walking to his post.

The other inmates resumed eating and talking, as if nothing occurred. Treg walked away, leaving a trail of blood on the floor. The officers took him to the clinic to apply stitches to his head. Joey B. walked to a table on the opposite side of the mess hall. Levell sat down and pushed his tray away from him. He no longer had an appetite anymore. Why did Wes stand up for him? Why would he defend someone who had little to nothing in common with him?

After a sleepless night, Levell was still lying in bed that morning when one of the officers called him.

"Thomas, you got a phone call. It's from a Mr. Gentry," he said.

Levell looked at the clock. It was twenty minutes after six, so breakfast wasn't scheduled for another hour. Why would his lawyer call him so early? Accompanied by the warden, Levell walked to the phone center, a small room in the side of the prison. "Hello?" he asked.

"Hey, Levell, what's up? I just wanted to touch base with you again and give you an update on the case and the parole hearing," Mr. Gentry said.

"Thanks, man. Yeah, ain't nothin' goin' on here," Levell replied.

"Okay, listen. I only have ten minutes on this call, so I'm gonna make it quick," Mr. Gentry said. "We've contacted the alibis that you've mentioned in your statement from Kennesaw State University where the alleged assault took place. So, we got that as good news."

"What do you mean, you got that as good news? Is there bad news?" Levell asked.

He heard silence on the other end of the line for a few seconds. Levell was perceptive in identifying whenever people were not being forward with him and were dancing around an issue.

"Yeah, as you remember, we had an investigation led by Detective Sands on Raven for possibly giving a false account of the assault, but we haven't been able to locate Raven to get another statement from her, so we have another issue," Mr. Gentry said.

Levell started to grip the phone angrily as if it was a lifeline for him. *What was Detective Sands doing the entire time? Why couldn't he get to that girl? Was he also working with the Roberts?*

"What issue is that?" Levell asked with a sigh.

"Raven has been reported missing for the last two days. She was reported missing by her parents who stated that she left for the mall, and that was the last they heard from her. Her friends also stated that Saturday was the last day she was seen," Mr. Gentry said.

"What?" Levell replied in shock.

No, that girl's not gonna do this to me. She's not gonna get away with framing me and then getting out of dodge.

"Come on, man, there has to have been someone who saw her, unless she fled the state," Levell added.

"Detective Sands is investigating her disappearance right now," Mr. Gentry replied.

"I know damn well she didn't run to another state," Levell said furiously.

"Well, her teachers have her on their rosters for her senior year, and her friends said the last time they spoke with her, she was planning on staying for it," Mr. Gentry said.

Levell still held the receiver in his hand. Although he heard Mr. Gentry speak, he barely listened to him. He couldn't get himself to wrap his mind at the thought that Raven was going to get away scot-free, while he stayed rotting in prison.

"We have begun investigating her parents. There is a strong possibility that her parents may have had something to do with her disappearance," Mr. Gentry said.

"It wouldn't surprise me," Levell replied. "I remember visiting Raven's house to tell her parents about her behavior. I mean, the girl was a total psychopath. I thought the best thing to do was to approach her parents about it, but when I got to the house, they just had a weird vibe about them, almost as if they were hiding something that they didn't want me to see."

"Well, you're right about that," Mr. Gentry confirmed. "Turns out that Raven's father is involved in a group named United Right Association or URA. Although it was set up to be a political group, there had been reports of terroristic threats and attacks from members of that group," he added.

"So, we're talking like KKK now?" Levell asked.

"They're often referred to as a sub-culture or a branch of the Klan. Jerry Roberts was one of the founders of this group. Many of their members are policemen, doctors, lawyers, and even judges can be members of this group," Mr. Gentry said.

"Policemen and lawyers?" Levell asked.

In his mind, he began to do his own detective work. Hearing about the group left no doubt in Levell's mind that Mr. Roberts set him up, using people from the organization to carry out the plan.

"Detective Sands believes that Raven didn't run away. She may have fallen victim to her mother and father," Mr. Gentry said. "Her father has consented to be questioned and brought in," he added.

Levell shook his head. "I'll bet you anything Mr. Roberts had everything to do with his daughter's disappearance," he said.

"Detective Sands has interrogated Mrs. Roberts, and she is still shocked and saddened that her daughter is missing," Mr. Gentry said. "Anyway, the date that we had for parole hearing has been rescheduled until further notice. I'll keep you posted," he added before hanging up.

As Levell walked back to his cell, the feeling of hope that he held on to through the promise of exoneration began to dissipate.

Where could that girl be? She's not gonna deny me my freedom...

Levell had walked back inside his cell and was punching his pillow angrily. What made it even worse what that he couldn't express his anger to anyone. McKinley was on a parole hearing for his case, and Levell was positive that he would be granted it. Meanwhile, Wes was still down at the Hole for nine more days and counting. Looking up, he wondered, if there was a God, why would He make him go through misery?

Caliya was on her way back home from picking up Patrice from daycare. She thought about dropping her over at Max's house because she was invited to a girl's night out by some of her co-workers, and she needed a night where she could forget about what was going on with Levell, Raven, Allan, and the Roberts. She thought that a drink or two would give her the ability to forget what was going on around her, but she remembered Patrice. She couldn't abandon her daughter at a time when she needed her. So, at the last minute she changed her mind and decided to head home to cook dinner for herself and her daughter. She also thought about calling Levell, although she knew it would cost about seven dollars for five minutes. But she missed her husband, missed hearing his voice, and missed feeling him next to her at night.

As she entered her neighborhood, she noticed a black cloud ascending to the sky. *Someone must be burning wood or something,* she thought at first, but when she got closer to her home, she saw the black cloud thickening. When she turned onto her street, she saw a crowd of people gathering at the source of the blaze. It would be difficult for Caliya to enter her driveway once she realized the black smoke ascending upward came from the raging fire that was consuming the inside of her house.

Chapter 22

ITHOUT BOTHERING TO PARK HER CAR OFF THE SIDE of the road, caliya quickly threw it in park and ran out frantically, scarcely believing what she was witnessing. She saw nothing but black smoke emerging from her living room and kitchen windows. Looking up toward Patrice's room, she saw the flames consuming her precious, multi-colored flower designed drapes that she had bought only a few months ago. Unable to suppress her emotions, Caliya burst into tears as she watched her home disintegrate. Caliya tried to rush inside her home to save all her valuables, but Mrs. Laura Whitberg, the neighbor who lived right next door to her, held her back.

"Calm down, Caliya. It's okay. I've called the fire department. They're on their way right now," she said comforting Caliya, who was beyond frantic.

Everything that she worked for, all the blood, sweat, tears and money she and Levell paid for the house, was gone.

"Why me?" she cried looking upward.

God certainly didn't care for her, not when He allowed this to happen. She didn't leave the stove on before work, because she certainly would've smelled the gas. Then her mind fell upon another possibility.

Arson. Somebody must've broke into my house and started the fire, but who?

Her eyes glanced across the street and stared at the Roberts' house, untouched and unblemished. When she found out that Mr. Roberts was part of the conspiracy to frame Levell, she was upset, but she'd always had the feeling that her husband was set up. But Caliya would've never imagined that Mr. Roberts would retaliate by setting her house on fire.

He won the case. My husband's in jail, and he has the whole city of Kennesaw in his back pocket. Why would he burn my house down?

Furiously, Caliya broke away from Mrs. Whitberg's embrace and headed to the Roberts' house. She knew that she was insane for heading to their house without any type of weapon or protection, but at that moment, she didn't care. She wanted to rip Mr. and Mrs. Roberts from limb to limb and bury them where nobody would care to look. Caliya wouldn't shed no tears for the family she saw as demonic and evil, from Raven to Mr. Roberts and Mrs. Roberts. All of them deserved to pay for the misery they caused her. She walked over there with one intent: to harm and destroy.

"Caliya! Wait, stop please!" Mrs. Whitberg yelled as Caliya ran toward the Roberts' house.

"Mommy, what's that huge orange floaty thing coming out the house?" Patrice asked from the passenger window of the car, unaware that those were not colorful playful toys but was a deadly blaze.

Caliya was oblivious to her daughter as rage coursed over her.

Banging on the door, Caliya yelled, "Roberts! You better bring yo' racist ass out hea'! I'mma kill you! You think this is a joke? I know who you are and what you are. Best believe, I'm gonna call the cops on you and your wife and everyone else associated with you, psychopath!"

Mrs. Whitberg ran behind Caliya to grab her as she attempted to break the door down. Caliya knew her actions would get her seriously injured, if not killed. But she was determined to show Mr. Roberts that he was not dealing with a weak black woman. When nobody answered the door, Caliya knew that the family wasn't home.

They're in their little supremacist meeting.

She finally ceased knocking on the door. Her knuckles were red from the constant banging on the door, but she didn't care. Suddenly, she heard the sirens from the fire truck as the city firefighters turned the corner to rush over to her house.

It took the firefighters over two hours to subdue the fire. By the time they'd extinguished the flames, the house was destroyed. Whoever started the fire had done a thorough job in ensuring that there was nothing left. With the fire completely washed out, the firefighters and chief investigators searched the damage in hopes of discovering the source of the fire. Detective Sands and Officer Anderson also pulled up on the scene and after exiting their vehicle, Sands put his arms around a stunned Caliya.

"I'm so sorry that this happened, cuz," he said.

Caliya, her eyes wet with tears, looked at Sands. "It was him," she said, turning her head and then not removing her eyes from the Roberts home. "It had to be him. Somehow, he knew that I was gonna expose him for who he was."

Sands followed his cousin's eyes to the Roberts' home. His next step would be to head to the station and get a search warrant to search it. He believed Caliya, but now he needed the evidence to tie Mr. Roberts to the crime of arson. After thorough investigation, the other officers concluded that the arsonist broke into one of the living room windows to get access inside the house. Once inside, they proceeded to set the house on fire. One of the firefighters emerged from the charred foundations of the house with a small, plastic black zip-tie, which surprisingly was not destroyed by the fire.

"We found this near the side yard, just a few kilometers away from the broken window," he told Sands, who started to put on latex gloves so he could take the zip-tie.

"What's this?" he asked curiously.

"I think it's one of those zip-ties that wrap around gasoline gallon container lids. I've seen those before," Anderson replied. "And I've also seen someone who had those containers."

Sands closed his eyes as he racked his mind to recall where he had seen a gallon of gas with a black zip-tie across the top. Suddenly, he remembered. It was at Tex's house when they'd interrogated him.

Sands' eyes met Anderson's for a few moments as they both came to the same conclusion.

"Okay, let's go," Sands said running over to his police car, and

Anderson followed closely behind him. "Go to Max's with Patrice and stay safe," he told Caliya on his way to his car. "Don't go outside or take Patrice anywhere until we've gotten Mr. Roberts and his associates apprehended."

Caliya only nodded as Sands and Anderson got in their car and quickly peeled out into the streets, with their sirens blaring.

In the house of Sprayberry High School senior Chris Rider; Tex Brown and best friend Charlie Atkinson were laying back on the couch, drinking beers and watching TV. What started out as watching Clint Eastwood's western movies, turned into watching the "Mission Impossible" movies. Tex was in the house with Barbara Kendall and Sarah Broadside. Both girls were college freshmen at the University of Georgia. Tex was currently out of school, but he had his mind set on bigger goals: building and owning a compound on the outskirts of town and moving in with some friends and roommates, while waiting for his membership status with the URA.

After a busy night, Tex had nothing else on his mind but to relax and not think about what he had just done a few hours earlier. Mr. Roberts was very clear in the instructions he gave to Tex and Charlie.

Don't leave nothing behind. Get it done, in and out.

While Tex was internally celebrating his guile, he heard the sound that no man who'd just committed a crime wanted to hear: the sounds of police sirens. And it sounded as if they were coming closer and closer. Still, Tex shrugged it off. Just because he heard police sirens outside, it didn't indicate that those sirens were for him. He'd made sure he covered his tracks and no one, not even his mother, knew where he was. The sirens stopped, and Tex breathed a sigh of relief.

Is this how life's gonna be for me now? Am I gonna be paranoid every time I hear cops nearby?

But after a few more seconds, bright headlights were shining outside Chris's driveway.

"Who the hell's that?" Charlie asked.

Little did he know, his question would soon be answered. After hearing two doors slam, they heard the doorbell, followed by sharp door knocks.

"Who is it?" Chris asked, getting up to answer the door.

"Marietta Police Department. Open up right now," Detective Sands demanded as Chris unlocked the door.

Shit, how did they find me? Tex felt his palms getting sweaty, and his heartbeat elevated. Frantically, he looked for a backdoor to exit. Slipping out of the family room area, Tex heard as Chris opened the door, and Sands and Anderson walked into their home.

"We have a warrant for the arrest of Tex Brown for connection to an arson. Where is he?" Sands asked, as Anderson began searching the house.

Tex hid under the kitchen table. Glancing at the back door, he knew that he only had a split second to make a dash for it, which would lead him to the backyard. From there he could try to make his way to another friend's house. He knew he couldn't go back to his own house. For all he knew, the other cops would be there, waiting on him. Fortunately, he'd told his friends about his excursion, so he knew they would cover him.

"I don't know what you're talkin' about, sir, but Tex ain't here," Chris replied.

"Look, don't bullshit me, alright? I got a tip already that he was hiding out in this location. Now you will tell me, or all of you will be arrested for aiding and abetting. How would you like that on your record?" Sands asked.

Tex closed his eyes. Chris was only in high school, and he didn't want a police record of arrest under him. Would Chris sacrifice his own freedom for that of a friend? Hanging his head, Chris pointed to the kitchen, exactly to where Tex was hiding. Furious that his friend betrayed him, Tex made a dash from under the table to the kitchen door.

Anderson saw him running for the back door. "Sands, he's back here! Let's go!" he said, gesturing to his partner.

But Sands was in no hurry. He knew these homes very well, and he knew that most of them had backyard doors. He knew that in a matter of seconds, Tex would run out through the back door, only to be confronted by two more units that he'd called for backup and already had stationed behind the backdoor. Smiling, Sands followed Anderson into the kitchen, and sure enough, judging by Tex's grunts when the other two officers tackled him to the ground, his theory was proven. After being read his rights, Tex was handcuffed and taken to a squad car in the front of the driveway.

"Hey, Tex, nice to see you again, albeit in another circumstance," Sands said sternly.

"You think you've won?" Tex replied angrily, his eyes trained on Sands. "I'll get my lawyer, and he'll get me outta this, and after that, we're coming for you and your family. This ain't over," he added, as the officers placed him inside the car.

Walking to the door next to Tex, Sands shook his head. "We, huh?" he said to Tex, who'd just realized that he had implicated others involved too. "Well, we're gonna find out who 'we' is, and on top of arson, let's add threatening an officer to your list of charges. How about that?" Sands asked rhetorically.

In reply, Tex spat at Sands' feet on the ground as the door closed.

As the car sped away, Sands looked at Anderson. "That's one down, but we still got a long way to go," he told his partner.

"Exactly, we still have to locate Raven and her father. Something definitely tells me that they're tied to this," Anderson replied.

"Oh, I know they're tied to this," Sands confirmed. "But I'm not waiting for Raven to just reappear in front of us. She might have already left the state with her family, and they could be on the run."

"What do you suggest?" Anderson asked.

"I say we go back to the Roberts, and we do a complete search of the place, inside and out. We gotta pull out all the stops too...metal detectors, search dogs, all of that," Sands replied.

Anderson shook his head and headed back to the car to make the call to all units to appear at the Roberts' residence for a search to be done. Sands hoped that some clues would turn up while they performed the search.

After obtaining a search warrant, Sands and two other units made their way to the Roberts' house early the next morning. Sands parked just outside the driveway and walked over to the door. Looking around, he saw their grass had grown nearly a foot tall, indicating that the house had been vacated for a few weeks.

"Mr. Roberts, are you inside? This is the Marietta Police Department. We have a search warrant. Open up now," Sands said firmly, but no one responded.

After knocking the door again, Sands turned toward the other officers. "Go ahead," he said, prompting them to break the door down with the battering ram they held.

After three huge thrusts, the hinges of the door finally flew out. With gun in hand, Sands and Anderson cautiously proceeded into the house and looked around, as if they were expecting Mr. Roberts to jump out into the open with a firearm of his own. But Sands knew that the Roberts family hadn't been home, based on the accumulation of dust, grime and dirt that had settled on top of their furniture.

Okay, it's clear the Roberts didn't move out, because their furniture is still here. They simply fled after setting the fire.

Sands knew that if it was discovered that Jerry Roberts had fled with his family, it would place more pressure on police to locate them and communicate with other police districts in Alabama, South Carolina, Tennessee, or even Florida.

There was always a possibility that Mr. Roberts was still in the state of Georgia, but four days had passed since Raven was previously seen by friends. After talking with Mr. Roberts' former employees and informants, police found it was the same amount of days that Mr. Roberts had not been seen. After Tex was interrogated, even though he was uncooperative at first, he eventually informed police that he, Mr. Roberts, and two other suspected members of the URA, were responsible for setting the fire that destroyed the Thomas's home.

"Let's search upstairs," Sands instructed the officers and he followed Anderson, who walked upstairs.

There were three bedrooms upstairs. Sands walked inside the first one to the right. Turning on the light, he saw the wallpaper of the room appeared to be sky blue. There were different posters of several musical stars plastered on the wall. Apparently, he was in Raven's room. Searching through the dresser drawers, small cabinets and closet, he saw different garments and shoes.

Girl had quite a collection...

Sands continued searching. Walking over to Raven's window, Sands noticed that one of the curtains was drawn back widely, and sitting on the windowsill was a small notebook with a pen on top of it. Looking at the contents of the book, he realized that he was holding was her diary. Sands walked back towards the hallway with the intention of placing it into a bag as evidence, but instead he skimmed through the pages. Sands' mouth gaped open in shock. Raven not only admired Mr. Thomas, but she also had a very sick obsession with him. The first entry of the diary was back in August of 2014, where Raven had written about a dashingly, dark handsome beauty that lived across the street from her:

Dear Diary, I was just lazying around enjoying my last few days of summer before going back to school (ugh!) when I saw this great looking black man walking outside, just a beautiful specimen. I've never seen anyone like him around here before. It's always just immature high school guys or immature guys, period, like my boyfriend Tex. Anyway, I introduced myself to him, and he said his name was Levell. I remember thinking, "What kind of name is Levell?" Must be one of those exotic names. But I didn't care what his name was. He was really attractive. We were just having a conversation, then my stupid dad came out and ruined everything. I never understood why my dad never liked black people. I mean, sure a few of them are obnoxious, like most of us white people, but not all of them are bad. Levell seems to be one of the good ones. I definitely can't wait to see him again.

When the entry finished, Sands continued skimming through the diary. Although he didn't take the necessary time to go through every page, most of them seemed to revolve around one person: Levell. She had gone on to talk about how sweet Levell was whenever he dropped her off to school, how he was her favorite teacher, and there were a couple of pages that were disparaging, mainly because Raven appeared to be hurt that Levell was not responding to her advances. The diary had more than a few derogatory terms and threats that were aimed at Caliya—the woman married to the man of Raven's dreams.

God, this girl is beyond sick. She needs to go to a psych ward.

Sands' eyes then landed on one month in particular: May, the month of the alleged rape. Turning through the pages, Sands found an entry from May 22nd, a day after Levell Thomas was arrested for rape and assault.

Dear diary, how long do I have to play the victim? Yesterday I was so close to getting what I wanted, which was me and Levell, all alone to have a little fun. Did I take it a bit too far? Maybe I did, but he doesn't understand. He doesn't understand that I need him. I depend on him, and I love him more than he will ever know. Of course, he denied me again because he's so worried about his precious wife, but I can tell she doesn't love him. When a woman ain't hittin' it right, you can always tell by her man's demeanor, his attitude, his mood. Maybe she works too much. I don't know. Anyway, I was trying to get Levell to relax, then he pushed me out of the way and he tried to leave. Luckily, I had ole reliable Betsy (that's what I named my taser). I know, I know...it's lame. Anyway, I gave him a couple zaps enough to slow him down, but he was stronger. My God, he was so strong! Before I could get to him he got out of the bathroom. I might have attacked him, but I couldn't help it... Sometimes, when a girl is in love, she does some crazy-ass things. I was so hurt that I started crying. Then someone came in the bathroom and asked me what was wrong. I said, someone tried to hurt me, even though it wasn't entirely true. So, they called my daddy, and he came in and asked who tried to hurt me. I was so hurt and angry, so I said Levell raped me, even though it wasn't true. I just knew Daddy had so many connections, and he would make sure Levell paid for what he did to me. But in the back of my mind, I can't help but wonder, did I make a mistake?

Closing the diary, Sands walked out of the room. He had seen enough. The entry proved what Levell testified and what he had suspected—that

Levell was innocent the whole time. Sands' focus now shifted from searching for Mr. Roberts to searching for Raven. If she attacked him, she needed to be questioned by the authorities. Fortunately, he wouldn't have too far to look.

One of the officers brought in a K9, a police dog, to sniff for evidence. While the officers searched inside, the dog and one of the officers went outside to the backyard. Sniffing intently as though on a mission, the K9 moved towards a secluded area in the backyard where there was a patch of bushes and shrubs. It circled the area for a moment and then let out a soft whimpering noise before barking to the other officers.

"Let's go!" Anderson said to the other officers, and they all walked outside where the dog was.

Sands placed the diary in a plastic bag before following the other officers outside.

"What'd you find, boy?" Anderson asked the dog.

The dog continued to circle the same area, barking excitedly while the officers stared at the shrubs questioningly. After a few moments, Sands figured out what the dog was barking about. There had to be something, or *someone* buried under the shrubs.

"Good boy. Grab me a spade!" Sands ordered the officers.

One of the officers retrieved a spade from inside the garage and handed it to Sands. He began digging at the same site the dog had been hovering over just moments earlier. Anderson and the other officers watched intently while Sands dug. A minute later, a pungent odor filled the air as Sands staggered back, and the other officers backed away as well. It was a smell so unnatural—a smell that only emanated from that of a dead organism. After shoveling away more dirt, a human torso appeared in plain view, followed by legs. Before long, the officers found themselves staring at a grisly scene.

The remains of a young teenage girl were discovered, and judging by the odor and the few patches of skin that remained on the corpse, the identity of the body became clear to the officers at once.

Anderson walked up to Sands. "Looks like Raven never left with her parents," he said grimly.

Sands wiped the sweat from his forehead and covered his nose to block the overpowering odor. "Apparently not," he confirmed as he stepped back from the site. "I want the coroner and the toxicologist here, ASAP," Sands ordered as Anderson rushed back to the car to make the call. "I also want the backyard taped. No access to this site at all, except for law enforcement and the coroner," he added as he stared at the partially consumed corpse of the girl who'd cried wolf.

It became clear to Sands that Mr. Roberts was not only suspected for arson, but now he was wanted for murder.

"What?!" Levell yelled in surprise and anger over the phone later that day. Speaking with Caliya, he had just found out that his house, the house that he'd earned his living for and that he was raising his family in was burned to the ground. Now, even if he was paroled, he had nowhere to go.

"I'm gonna find the lowlives who did this, and I'm gonna kill 'em myself," Levell warned through clenched teeth.

"Baby, look, I know you're upset, but the police are working to find the suspects responsible for this. Don't get yourself in any more trouble. My focus is to get you outta there," Caliya said.

"But then what?" Levell asked. "Where's my family gonna go after it's all over?" he asked angrily.

"Calm down, baby. Look, I've spoken with Uncle Max, and he promised he'll take us in until we figure something else out," she reassured him.

Levell hung his head. It wasn't enough that Raven and her family took away his freedom and his reputation. Now they'd taken away his home too. Levell was at a loss, and more than ever, he missed Wes, who was still in the Hole. McKinley had been granted parole, so he was no longer an inmate. Levell felt isolated and desperate. If he'd never taken the teaching job, maybe he would've avoided the storm of trials that overwhelmed him.

"Baby, I'm sorry about all this. I should've listened to you at first. I should've listened to my students at Hillcrest. I should've neva' came down here," Levell said somberly.

Caliya sensed her husband losing hope, but she couldn't allow him to do that, not in the place where he was. "Baby, stay up. We'll get through this, okay. Don't give up. Stay strong for me and Patrice."

Eyes wet with tears, Levell shook his head. "Okay," was all he could muster before ending the call.

While the guards, walked Levell back to his cell, he wiped his eyes furiously and hardened his face. He couldn't let the inmates see him cry. He knew they fed on weakness. Sitting in his cell, Levell had his head between his hands when he heard a voice.

"C'mon, young buck, keep yo' head up! Ain't no bitchin' gon' happen on my watch."

Looking for the source of the voice, Levell saw Wes in his cell, beaming at him.

Chapter 23

EVELL COULDN'T BELIEVE WHAT HE SAW AT FIRST. HIS cellmate and prison father figure, was released out of the Hole, a place where many an inmate had lost their minds, and in other cases, their lives. Wes, who had difficulty breathing at times, defied all his odds and made it out of the desolate lower-level cell.

"Wes, what you doin' here? I thought they put you on lockdown for ten days," Level said.

"They did intend to lock me away for ten days," Wes replied. "But one of the wardens, ole Jack Kepler, had a change of heart. Me and him go back a ways, from when I was first locked up, and he got me up out of there early," he explained.

Levell looked at Wes in amazement. If he had the chance to do so, he would've hugged Wes if it hadn't been for the bars that separated them. The Hole had a nefarious history of changing the mindset of the prisoners that stayed behind its cages. Even Joey B. and Treg appeared to have been transformed by their most recent visit to the Hole, even though they'd been locked down there previously. Yet, there Wes was sitting across from him, smiling as though he still wasn't in a prison house, surrounded by misery from all sides.

"God was with me, bro," Wes said.

Levell rolled his eyes. *Here we go with the God thing again.*

Wes caught a glimpse of his sarcastic expression. "Shrug it off all you want, brotha, but one day you'll see what I'm talkin' about," Wes said.

Then he looked across his jail cell to the windowpane, where the sun's rays reflected inside the prison. Wes appeared to be reflective.

"During those three days that I was down there, I thought about a lot, man," Wes continued. "I thought about everything I did early on in life—cheatin', scammin', and bettin' people. You know, shit that be linin' up my pockets, you feel me?"

"Yeah, all the crap that landed you in hea'," Levell replied.

"It got me thinkin', could I have handled it differently? I found myself thinking about the times I should've kept up with my family, especially when I'm away at work, or when I'm too busy hustlin'," Wes added. "God has many ways of humbling folk, and he did a number on me those three days at the Hole," he continued.

"Maybe I need one of those moments," Levell replied.

"Don't worry, your time will come, as will mine. Just gotta keep yo' head up," Wes said.

"How can I keep my head when all hope is lost, especially after I leave this place?" Levell asked. "The same bastards that put me in here burned my house down. Everything I worked so hard for is now gone," he said, his anger starting to build up within him.

Wes hung his head, "I'm sorry they did you like that, son. Every last one of them deserves to be six feet under, and I'll be the first to say it," he said. "But you can't sit here and mope about what you had. You need to focus on what you have. You have a family, you educated, and you have plenty of potential. The way to get back at them is to prepare our generation's kids and tell 'em what they're facing."

"Who's gonna listen to me? To everyone around here, I'm still a sex offender and a pedophile. I'm everyone's worst nightmare. What makes you think they'll listen to me?" Levell asked.

"Because education and knowledge of self is a class all its own. Look around you, man," Wes replied. "They tryin' to fill up shitholes like this with our kids, and soon enough, these cells are gonna be filled with hundreds of young bucks, younger than yourself. Teach 'em their history. Light that path for 'em. You may not be able to control your past, but lemme tell you this: you can control your decisions that affect your future."

Levell thought about Wes's words. In a way, they rang true. He thought about his original goal when he moved to Georgia from Queens, and that goal was to continue educating children.

"Believe me, man, when you do right by them young'uns and by God, you'll see your situation change," Wes reassured.

At the same time, Cojack came walking down the cellblock hall and stopped at Levell's cell. "Thomas, you got a call from your lawyer, Mr. Gentry," he said, unlocking the prison door and then walking with Levell to the phone complex.

Grabbing the receiver, Levell greeted his lawyer. "What's up, man?"

"Well the parole hearing for your case has been bumped up by a week, so we're going to the parole board next week," Mr. Gentry said.

Levell looked up at the sky. Could God have possibly worked a miracle for him? It wasn't just great news, it was wonderful news. If the parole board for the state of Georgia granted him the parole, he would be free. Although he was still bothered by his house burning down, his wife and daughter, who were currently staying in Uncle Max's house, were still safe. But he wanted to be sure of that assessment.

"Have they found the people who burned my house down?" he asked.

"They arrested a suspect connected to the arson," Mr. Gentry confirmed.

When Mr. Gentry informed Levell that Tex was one of the prime suspects in the arson, Levell clenched his fists harder.

Raven's ex-boyfriend. I knew I didn't trust that guy. Maybe that's why she was so eager to come to my house every morning. She was scoping it out so her on-again off-again boyfriend could do his damage.

But what if Raven and her boyfriend weren't on again? It certainly appeared they were on the same page that night in the classroom when their naked bodies were on top of each other.

"But we found out that Tex wasn't alone," Mr. Gentry continued, snapping Levell out of his thoughts. "He implicated two other suspects. One of them was Mr. Roberts. Both men are fugitives of the law by now," he added.

"What you mean? Like they on the run now?" Levell asked angrily.

If Mr. Roberts was responsible for burning his house, he wanted to make sure that the man and his companions were arrested immediately.

"Yeah, but Detective Sands informed me that they've alerted every police department in Georgia, Alabama, Tennessee, and South Carolina. He's on everybody's radar. If he slipped by them before, I guarantee you he won't slip by them again," Mr. Gentry replied.

Levell lowered the phone and stared at his reflection through the window glass. An angry black man stared right back at him. He wasn't sure whom he was more incensed with: Raven or her father.

"There's something else, too," Mr. Gentry said.

"What is it?" Levell asked.

"When all clues led back to the Roberts, we searched the property, where Raven was found dead, buried in their backyard," Mr. Gentry replied.

"What?" Levell said, taken aback. He was not prepared to hear the news that Mr. Gentry gave to him. His accuser finally met her end.

"Yeah," his lawyer confirmed. "Her body was taken to the lab for forensic research, although people at the scene stated that the cause of death was by strangulation."

With a mixture of feelings, Levell shook his head as he struggled to take in the news. Why did he suddenly feel guilty? He expected to be overjoyed by Raven's death. After all, she singlehandedly ruined his life, his career, and his reputation around town by falsely accusing him of rape. If anyone had any reason to rejoice, or at least breathe a sigh of relief, it would be him. But Levell was just numb to any feeling. He still saw her jet-black hair flowing down past her shoulders and her blue eyes as they often stared intently into his own. She was a mystery, her life was a mystery, and it appeared that her death would become an unsolved mystery, unless she was killed by someone she knew. Then it hit him.

Mr. Roberts. It had to be Mr. Roberts from the very beginning.

Reminiscing the very first day when he moved into the neighborhood and met Raven for the first time, Levell recalled the look of disdain that she gave her father before she made her way back across the street. But could Mr. Roberts harbor so much evil inside of him that would cause him to harm his own daughter?

"So, Mr. Roberts is currently being sought out by police departments across the Georgia State line for arson and suspected murder," Mr. Gentry said.

"Ain't nothin' suspect about this. He killed Raven. I'm almost positive of it," Levell replied. "I've had a bad feeling about her father since I walked inside their home at one point to discuss Raven's grades. They seemed out of touch with reality, especially Mr. Roberts," he added, remembering the night he visited with Mrs. Roberts.

Did she also play a part in killing their daughter? If so, it meant that Mrs. Roberts was a fugitive and knew even more.

"So, what'll happen to them?" Levell asked.

"Well, once they are apprehended, they will be extradited back to Kennesaw to await trial for the death of Ms. Roberts," Mr. Gentry replied.

Levell looked behind him straight through the open door to the police phone compartment. He stared down the corridor that led to the upper level cellblock, he had called home for almost four months to the day.

"I'll keep you posted if any more information arrives," Mr. Gentry said before ending the call.

As the officers walked Levell back to his cell, all he could think about was how his parole hearing was only a week away, and he was much closer to freedom. But did it come at the cost of a human life?

A few hundred miles away at a rest stop near the Georgia state line, a huge cargo truck stopped, and the driver got out. He walked inside to use the bathroom. After washing his hands thoroughly, he wiped them with a few sheets of paper towels before walking back to the truck. His wife was sitting in the passenger seat. The couple were on their way to South Carolina, where other members of the URA awaited him.

"Need anything?" he asked his wife roughly.

"No, I'm fine," his wife answered stoically from the seat.

She had been ailing with an unknown disease. It pained Jerry to see his wife deteriorate in front of his eyes. He figured that the main reason for her condition was stress over losing her only daughter under what Jerry labeled as "mysterious circumstances." It took a few days, but once the sorrow subsided, Jerry finally revealed the truth, that he killed his daughter. Pat never recovered psychologically after learning what Jerry had done, but Jerry explained that he did it to protect their way of life. Raven was going to betray them, and Jerry simply couldn't let it happen.

There had been plenty of screaming, grabbing, holding, and threatening. Finally, because she didn't want to lose her own life, Pat remained silent as she helped Jerry pack their things to flee the state, knowing it would be just a matter of time until they discovered Raven and pursued them. They drove for days, only stopping for food and gas. Jerry walked inside the convenient store and picked up a couple of cigarette boxes, a bottle of Dr. Pepper, and some honey buns.

Walking over to the counter, he proceeded to pay for his items. While he was paying, he had no idea that Georgia State Patrol officers had begun circling the convenience store. From the moment Jerry exited his truck to use the restroom, a store clerk had recognized his face from the news reports, so he quietly ran behind the store to contact the police department. Responding swiftly, the officers surrounded the place and waited for Jerry to walk out. He never saw the ambush, nor had he suspected anyone would recognize him.

"Hands up, Jerry!" one of the officers shouted upon Jerry leaving the store.

Jerry looked at the truck where his wife still sat and knowing that his escape from the law had come to an end, he finally gave up and put his hands up. The police confiscated his items and handcuffed him. When they inspected the truck, they also arrested Pat Roberts in connection to the murder of Raven Roberts.

Waiting inside the chief's office, Sands gathered all his paperwork and files from Levell's case, which was given to him by Mr. Gentry. Although his face displayed that of stoic determination, deep within himself he felt a twinge of joy. He almost couldn't believe it when he got the call from the Dahlonega County Department stating that wanted fugitives Jerry Roberts and his wife Pat Roberts were held after they were identified at a rest stop nearly thirty miles north. They were on their way to being transported back to Marietta. Sands breathed a sigh of relief. His worse fear had always been the possibility that the couple might have fled the state. He was only fortunate to have caught them before they could cross the state line.

Apparently, Jerry's wife was with him. Sands doubted Pat would have had anything to do with her daughter's murder, but she was with him while fleeing the state, so in Sands definition, that placed her as a primary suspect too. Finally, the precinct doors opened, and four police officers entered, two of them guiding Jerry Roberts to the interrogation room and two others guiding a disheveled, pale faced Pat Roberts into the adjoining room.

Sands stood up, and Anderson walked alongside him. "All right, we got both Jerry and Pat Roberts in the rooms. Do you wanna interrogate Pat first or Jerry?" he asked.

"Let's start with Jerry," Sands replied as they both walked into the interrogation room where Jerry Roberts was held.

Jerry looked at both officers, rubbing his wrists, which were previously handcuffed. As Sands looked at Jerry, he saw what hid behind the scruffy beard and wide frame: *hate.* The initial thought would only be confirmed as the interrogation proceeded.

"Congratulations, detective," Jerry said sarcastically, pretending to clap his hands. "Looks like you caught the bad guy. Do you wanna know what the grand prize is?" he asked, maniacally.

Sands knew that Jerry was attempting to get him rattled, and he knew that he would stoop to any tactic, from intimidation to mockery, so he prepared himself to take the brunt of Jerry's attitude.

"No, but I can name your grand prize. How does fifty to life sound?" Sands replied.

"How does it feel?" Jerry asked, but he wasn't addressing Sands. He spoke to Officer Anderson. "How does it feel to know that you're workin' for a monkey? Gives real meanin' to the phrase 'monkey see, monkey do' eh?" Jerry said as if in jest, but he had a nasty edge to his voice.

Anderson didn't flinch. Leaning closer to Jerry, he replied, viciously. "How does it feel to know that you're a lying, cold, murderous bastard who doesn't give a damn about no one, not even his own daughter?" he asked rhetorically.

"Well, we all know who runs this station. Be careful with that because before you know it, they gonna end up running us hard-working people outta here," Jerry replied.

The nerve of this man. Does he know where he is?

Sands knew he couldn't afford to get into small talk with Jerry. It was important that he received a statement from him. "So, Jerry, we've been looking for you for quite a while. Using your daughter as bait to accuse an innocent black man wasn't good enough, huh?"

"You have no proof that I told Raven anything. You're a lousy cop, you know that?" Jerry replied, smartly.

"And you ain't slick, Jerry," Sands replied. "The false accusations, the fire, and last, but not least, the demise of your meal ticket..."

Technically, Sands never intended to us those terms to describe Raven, but he used that opportunity to decipher his suspect. Many parents would be outraged if Sands referred to their children as "meal ticket," but Mr. Roberts seemed unfazed, yet defiant. Sands was finally convinced that he had his man.

"You can't prove a goddamn thing! You're a fraud, and those who work with you are frauds," he said looking from Sands to Anderson and then back at Sands.

"Well, actually we can prove that it was all you, sir. Do you like stories, Mr. Roberts?" Sands asked, but Mr. Roberts ignored him and only stared directly at him with the same glare.

"Raven kept something that most girls her age normally keep. It's called a diary. We happened to find her diary at the scene of the crime," he continued, pulling the small notebook out of his pocket. It was still wrapped in its plastic.

Mr. Roberts continued glaring at Sands, but Sands started to notice Jerry's body movements. He was shifting in his chair, as if he wanted nothing more to do with his case.

"Well, if a father had any type of relationship with his daughter, he would've known that his daughter kept diaries, journals, or at least, disclosed it to you. I know we're in the technology age now, but Raven's quite the writer. Let's read one of the excerpts, shall we?" Sands offered, flipping through the pages of the diary. "Ah, here we go," he said, before reading from one of Raven's entries a few weeks before her death:

Dear diary, Ughhhhhhh! I hate my father so much!!!!!! I never like to say anything about the people that gave me life, but my father hurts me so much. All I did was ask him if I could use the car to go out with Ginger and Emily, but he said no. When I asked why, because he sure as hell wasn't using it, he told me to get out of his face. So, I called him a jerk and walked away. Next thing I know, I feel him tugging the back of my hair and he slams me into the ground. No bones were broken or anything, but there was no reason for him to do that. Maybe this is why my life is shit right now...because I have a mom who doesn't give a shit, and I have a dad who's too blinded by the color of his damn skin that he could care less about me. At least he didn't pull out the extension cords or the beer bottle, this time. He just shoved me to the floor. I should call the police on him, but I already ruined one man's life by calling the police on him, for just defending himself. I don't want to ruin my daddy's life because he's all my mama's got right now and even though I hate it, I have no choice. But I have to do something. I gotta get to work on leaving this house, but I want to talk to Levell's wife. I'm responsible for her husband going to jail and even though the town sees me as a hero, Daddy sees me more like a punching bag than his daughter. It's not as bad as it was before, but it still hurts.

After reading the entry, Sands closed the diary. "Just answer me one question, Mr. Roberts. Why Raven? Why kill your only daughter?"

With his cold eyes staring at Sands, Jerry showed no remorse. "She was in the way of progression for me. Nobody gets in my way when it comes to this war, not even my family."

"So, it's a war now, huh?" Sands asked.

"You damn right it's a war," Jerry said defensively. "Too many of your kind are runnin' things, so now it's up to us to put an end to this scourge."

Is this man legally insane, or is he just that delusional?

"By 'us' you're referring to the members of URA, is that correct?" Sands asked.

Jerry remained quiet, so Sands continued. "I get it, you're staying on code. Wouldn't want to implicate all your fellow Klan members, huh? Well, you don't have to worry about that, Mr. Roberts. We got a full confession from Tex, and he identified each and every member of your group, including those who committed arson. They're now in custody, and now you get the privilege of joining them behind bars."

"Believe me, one of these days, you're gonna be sorry that you ever crossed me. Do you realize who you're messing with?" Jerry threatened.

"Yeah, I do, and unfortunately, not everyone who's had the misfortune of shaking your slimy hand knew you were a snake, especially Mr. Deneau," Sands answered.

Jerry's eyes widen in shock for a split second. Sands sat closer to Jerry, and he knew that if left to his own devices, he would've tried to kill Sands, but the feeling was mutual for the detective.

"Mr. Williams never killed Mr. Deneau, did he?" he asked quietly as Jerry closed his eyes. It was all over. "Get him outta hea," Sands ordered the other officers as they led Jerry out of the interrogation room. It wouldn't be long before Jerry was locked up, awaiting trial for arson and murder in the first degree.

Clarke Hooker, the head of the Georgia State Parole Board, stood up to address the parole board. In unison, the rest of the attendees in the parole hearing stood up as well. Levell sat across from the parole committee, and seated next to him was Mr. Gentry. Levell's palms were sweaty, and his heart was beating a hundred miles an hour. But he had waited for this moment to arrive for weeks. Finally, after three dreadful months behind bars, a crooked lawyer, a burned down house, and a murdered girl, the day had finally arrived. Caliya, Max, and Sands all attended the parole hearing and sat in the adjoining seats across from Levell.

"Today, the parole board for the state of Georgia is scheduled to hear the statement of inmate number 02369, Mr. Levell Thomas, who was tried and convicted of battery and sexual assault of a minor and is currently registered on the Sex Offender List. If Mr. Thomas or a representative would like to make a statement or read a statement, they may proceed," Mr. Hooker said as the people in attendance sat down.

Mr. Gentry stood up. "My name is James Gentry, attorney at law for Mr. Levell Thomas, and he has given me permission to read this letter to the parole board. Permission to proceed?" he asked.

"You may proceed," Mr. Hooker replied. Mr. Gentry cleared his throat and read:

"To the parole board in the state of Georgia. My name is Mr. Levell Quincy Thomas, and I taught tenth and eleventh grade English at Kennesaw Mountain High School. Prior to my teaching career, I earned my English degree at Queens College in New York, and I have been teaching for ten years. In my duration of teaching more than eight hundred students in a decade long span, I have not had any prior criminal record, and I can attest that the previous record that was pulled up by the prosecution on the court date was false due to that case being thrown out, and the documents were falsely procured," Mr. Gentry paused to clear his throat.

"Furthermore, it was proven by my defense team as well as the Marietta Police Department that a plot by members of a white nationalist organization was exposed. The prosecution had members of this organization serving in the Kennesaw Police Department as well as the attorneys of this case, both of whom were confirmed as being members of this organization. I have displayed good behavior at the Smyrna State

Prison, as can be attested by the warden. I have continued to uphold and maintain my innocence in this case, and to this day, I still hold my stance that I did not commit the crime of which I was accused. I am not a sex offender. If granted parole, I will continue to teach, educate, and equip our students for the next level. I hope and I pray that the parole board will make the right decision on this case. Thank you," Mr. Gentry folded the letter and sat down as he waited for the decision.

The parole board spoke among themselves as Levell waited for what seemed like an hour, although it was only a few minutes. Finally, Mr. Hooker stood up.

"Today, the parole board in the State of Georgia has decided to grant parole to Mr. Levell Thomas," he stated as the attendees listened, waiting attentively before celebrating Levell's exoneration.

Chapter 24

A WHIRLWIND OF EMOTIONS RAN THROUGH LEVELL'S body the moment he heard the words from Mr. Hooker's lips. He was free. It was finally over. The days he spent in complete misery, working from sunup to sundown, were over. Caliya, who had been sitting in the hearing with Max, ran to hug her husband, tears streaming down her face. Levell looked up at the ceiling. The board could have negated his appeal and looked the other way and in doing so, would not have been much different than those who had twisted the system against him.

He thought about everyone who came after him: Raven, Jerry Roberts, the officers in the police department who were secret members of the URA, along with Allan Richter, who sought membership by betraying his own client. In the back of Levell's mind, *revenge* was the word that flashed in his subconscious. A part of Levell longed for payback against those who'd attempted to take his life away from him, to separate him from his wife and his daughter and destroy his reputation.

Unfortunately, Raven, whose actions ironically set off the chain of events that followed Levell in the state prison, paid with her life. After hugging his wife, Levell walked outside to the prison transport. He would only stay for a few more hours, then he would be free to go. It was a relief that he was leaving immediately. He did not want the inmates to know that he was leaving prison on parole, except for one individual. He was the one who'd supported Levell from the first time they met. Levell could not leave without bidding him goodbye. When he arrived at his cell, Wes was in his reading. He looked up, beaming widely. It was as if he already knew the outcome.

"So, how'd it go, man?" Wes asked.

Levell hung his head for a moment, as if he was prepared to give Wes the worst news, and for a moment, Wes felt that Levell hadn't made parole. But after a minute, Levell smiled at Wes.

"You shoulda seen the look on you face, man," Levell said.

Wes laughed, shrugging his shoulders. "So, did you get off?" he asked.

"Yeah, I got off, man. I'm going home. I was just gathering some of my stuff before I bounce," Levell answered.

"That's what's up," Wes replied, reaching under his cot mattress. Looking around to make sure the guards didn't see him, Wes handed Levell a small King James Version Bible.

"I've been prayin' fo' you, brotha, and God answered my calls," he said.

Chuckling, Levell took the Bible. If there was one aspect of Wes that Levell would miss, it was the faith he had in God, despite his surroundings.

"Thanks, man, but isn't this the same Bible you read every night?" he asked.

"Nah, I got a couple more here. Proof that my family never gave up on me, and now I'm giving this to you. Don't give up on yourself, and never give up on our young kings," Wes said.

"When you head back to the classrooms, teach them to be more than just followers. Teach them to be leaders, to go out into society with their head up, and their guard up. The responsibility is yours, Levell. Teach our boys right, and keep 'em out of places like this," he added.

"I definitely will, man. If anyone'll still hire me after this..." Levell said, shaking his head.

"Man, trust me, someone's definitely gonna hire you. I predict that by year's end, you'll have another teaching job," Wes said.

"You're real confident about that, huh?" Levell asked, laughing.

"Yes, sir, and you better be Teacher of The Year next year too, cuz if not, I'm getting' outta here, and I'mma whup yo' ass," Wes joked.

As the doors of his cell closed for the final time, Levell turned to look at Wes. "Thanks, man. I won't forget you. I promise, whenever I can, I'll try to get you outta here," he vowed.

"Never make promises you can't keep, brotha," Wes replied. "I'll be all right. Just remember what I told you. Educate the next generation. When you get a chance, read Proverbs chapter three, verses five and six. I know how you is wit' them quotes. Them verses right there? These are my quotes to you," Wes said.

Deciding to read the verse, Levell looked at the glossary in the back of the Bible. It had been so long since he opened a Bible, and he had to find the book of Proverbs. Finally locating the verse, Levell read it:

Trust in the Lord with all your heart; do not depend on your own understanding; Seek his will in all you do, and he will direct your paths.

Turning to Wes, he shook his hand. "Thank you," he said, after reading the verse.

Walking out of the prison, Levell looked straight ahead. Out of the corner of his right eye, he saw young boys, different ages, sizes, and skin tones. Every time he saw a glimpse of those men, he saw himself. He was those boys, and those boys were him. Many of them were locked up for small misdemeanors, felonies, and other petty crimes. Many of them were caught up in the same system that he was caught up in. Many of them weren't fortunate enough to be paroled, and their sentence was longer than his own. But Levell knew he had a job to do and a mission to fulfill.

A few weeks later, Levell was at Uncle Max's house, where his family was more than kind enough to take them in. It took one look at the smoldering wood and rubble that used to be his home, and instantly Levell's anger had raged again as if he was still in the prison. Jerry Roberts was tried and convicted of second-degree murder, and he was charged with arson. He was sentenced to life in jail without parole. Thanks to Tex's testimony, the remaining members of URA were currently under investigation for their part in conspiracy, racketeering, and other cases of racial violence.

Allan Richter's law division office was under investigation, and in subsequent months, the office was shut down due to charges of unlawful practices. Allan was dishonorably disbarred by the state, and he would never practice law again. Raven's mother Pat Roberts was also charged for conspiracy and the murder of her daughter. Although she had no direct part of the murder, the argument against Pat was that she was negligent and knew Jerry committed the murder and failed to bring him to justice. Therefore, it made her an accomplice to her husband. She received ten years in a women's correctional facility in Mississippi.

Detective Sands was promoted to head sergeant at the Marietta precinct for his efforts in exposing the secret society and uncovering the truth behind Levell's wrongful arrest. Although the Thomas' home insurance covered natural disasters and damage caused by fire in addition to the thousands of dollars in damages that were paid to the Thomas family from the Roberts' estate, Levell found himself contemplating his next move. He was no longer employed by Cobb County Board of Education. Although his record cleared him to apply at other school districts in Georgia, Levell made a crucial decision.

On that day, Max came out of the guest room, holding the last of Levell's travel bags and suitcases.

"Nephew, how are you gonna get all this to fit in your car?" he asked as he placed the bag down by the front door.

"Don't worry. I'll find a way to make it work," Levell answered, laughing as he took the bag from Max and headed outside to the little minivan that was parked on their driveway.

During their stay at Max's house, Levell and Caliya decided to trade their cars in exchange for a 2017 Chevy Ventura. It made for more comfort during travel and contained more trunk space. Shifting through Caliya's bags, which were no doubt filled with miscellaneous beauty products, shoes, and old jeans, Levell stuffed the bag between the other two bags. He shut the truck door and headed back inside the house. All the bags were finally in the car.

"Alright, Caliya, Patrice, let's roll. Gotta step out now if we wanna beat that interstate traffic," he said.

Caliya emerged from the bathroom, still tying her hair into a neat bun. It had been a few weeks since she had decided to go the natural route for her hair care. After making sure Patrice was dressed up, the Thomas family was ready to leave.

Levell shook his uncle's hand. "Thanks for everything," he said.

Max shrugged it off. "Don't worry about it. It's all good. We family, and that never changes," he said as offered the Thomas family a case of water for their travels.

"You sure I can't convince you to stay though?" he asked furtively.

Levell laughed. After he told Max, Vicky, and their children that his family was planning to move back to New York, they were taken aback at first, but given what they had experienced, they fully understood why they'd come to the decision.

"You can convince me to do a lot of things, Uncle, but I have to go back. Figure some things out while I'm up there... And I feel like I have much more to teach and learn up there," he replied.

"You have so much to teach and learn down here also," Max said.

"That's true, but if my time down here hadn't taught me anything, it's taught me that the grass ain't always greener on the other side. Sometimes we gotta go through some stuff to realize where we really belong. Maybe one day I'll come back down hea'," Levell said.

Max shook his head. He couldn't believe his nephew wanted to go back to the cold, crowded, streets of New York, but Levell had already made up his mind.

"Okay, well I think we got everything packed up. Are you sure you wanna drive up there? It's an eighteen-hour drive, I mean. I think flying would be more quick and efficient-" he started.

"I'm sure, Uncle. Okay?" Levell cut him off. "Drivin' back up to the Mecca will be more fun anyway. We'll pass D.C., take in some sightseein', and we'll be cool," Levell reassured Max.

As Levell, Patrice, and Caliya loaded up the car, they thanked Max and Vicky for their hospitality.

"Make sure you call us when you arrive in New York," Max said.

"No problem," Levell replied and backed the car out of the driveway and headed toward the freeway.

It was January 2017, the first day of a new semester at Forest Hills High School. Students were frantically rushing to find their classes before the late bell rang. In his classroom, Levell Thomas was prepared for the day. His daily agenda was written on the marker board, and he had the planners on each of the desks waiting for the students when they arrived. Upon arriving in New York a few weeks earlier, Levell had spoken to his landlord and re-signed a rental agreement for his old duplex home.

No one was more thrilled about their return than Mrs. Alreeda, who shrieked in joy when she saw Levell and his family return to their house. She even made them her special apple pie that Levell immensely enjoyed whenever he was in her company. Fortunately, no one had rented the home since the family had left a year and a half ago, and it was still in good condition. After settling in, Levell applied with the Board of Education and was offered the English teaching position at Forest Hills High School, since Hillcrest had replaced him with a different teacher. The transition was nothing short of smooth, and Levell was back in his element, grateful for another chance at teaching his favorite subject.

As the warning bell rang and students started filing in, Levell took a slip out of his pocket. The quote was from none other than Malcolm X. It read:

The future belongs to those who prepare for it today.

With Wes's message in mind, Levell turned to address his class. "Good morning class, welcome to American English. My name is Mr. Thomas, and in this class we will discuss, not only literature but also influences to literature, which will include both American folklore and African folklore."

Staring at the attentive faces, Levell smiled. *There's no other place I'd rather be...*

THE END

About the Author

"Marc A. Beausejour"

Marc A. Beausejour was born on July 28, 1987 in Queens, New York to Haitian parents Jean and Lineda Beausejour. He discovered his passion for writing at the tender age of twelve, with poetry becoming his initial artistic expression. Beausejour showcased his poetic talents in various school talent shows and poetry reading events during his time at North Cobb High School and later at Kennesaw State University after moving to Kennesaw, Georgia in 2001.

Throughout the years, Beausejour continued to hone his craft, writing poems for diverse occasions such as weddings, funerals, and church events. In 2011, he took a significant step by self-publishing his first book, "Words on High," a compilation of spiritually inspired poems from his formative years. Building on this success, Beausejour released his second poetry book, "Rising Higher Than Ever," in 2015.

In the same year, he ventured into a different literary landscape by writing and publishing his first urban novel, "The Preacher's Web." This gritty morality tale marked a departure from his earlier poetic works, showcasing Beausejour's versatility as an author. Expanding his literary horizons, he created the *BlackCyrano* series, demonstrating a wide-ranging creative skill.

While continuing to share his literary work on blogs and social networks, Beausejour remains committed to his education and promotions, earning his associate degree in marketing management from Chattahoochee Technical College in 2018. As a multifaceted writer, Marc A. Beausejour continues to captivate audiences with his words across various genres and platforms.

Also by, Author

"Marc A. Beausejour"

Title: The Preacher's Web | Publisher: SHE PUBLISHING LLC | ISBN: 978-1-953163-91-2 (paperback) Publication Date: February 2024 (*Second Edition*)

Set in the heart of the city, "The Preacher's Web" unfolds a gripping narrative of former All-City quarterback turned pastor, Mike Hillman, whose dedication to preaching love and forgiveness in Queens, New York is challenged by the return of an old friend seeking revenge. Amidst a community grappling with the scourge of drugs and gangs. As Mike puts his reputation on the line to testify for a young man accused of murder, the story converges with the adolescent struggles of Jamal Samuels on the basketball courts of New York City.

Now, standing at the crossroads of faith, family, and societal challenges, Mike faces a pivotal choice. Will he risk more than his reputation to uphold justice and fulfill his role as a public servant and father? The pages of "The Preacher's Web" beckon you to explore the complexities of morality and redemption. Can Mike Hillman rise above, or will he be consumed by the web of his past?

Title: Street Retribution | Author: Marc A. Beausejour | Publisher: SHE PUBLISHING LLC | ISBN: 978-1-953163-96-7 (*paperback*) | Publication Date: February 2024 (*second edition*)

New York City attorney Edward Reed harbors a secret. He was once known as Antonio Franks, a member of M.O.B., the most dangerous gang in Queens, New York. He was also the key witness in the trial that exonerated another ex-gang member, David Anderson, when he was falsely accused of murdering his girlfriend, Loree McAfee. But years later, both men's lives are in danger, as other former gang members are slain under mysterious circumstances by a femme fatale, prompting rumors that M.O.B.'s ruthless gang leader, Tadarius Hill is seeking revenge on those that turned on him and his organization. Will Edward and David survive the bounty, or will they fall victim to the code of the streets?

Title: Adia's Ballad | Author: Marc A. Beausejour | Publisher: SHE PUBLISHING LLC | ISBN: 978-1-953163-92-9 (paperback) | Publication Date: February 2024 (*second edition*)

From the author of "The Preacher's Web", this coming-of-age story explores the life of young Andrea McAfee who struggles to cope with the tragic murder of her older sister. Then a chance opportunity lands Andrea into the music business where she shares a bond with other artists in the hip hop industry and learns she has more in common with them than she realizes. As Andrea immerses herself deeper into the life of recording, touring and partying as Adia, the new R&B princess, she begins drifting away from her family and her loved ones as her star rises too fast for her to absorb. With fame corrupting her relationships with those she loves, will Andrea find the inner peace and closure she seeks, or will she succumb to the draw of money and celebrity?

Title: Split Decision | Author: Marc A. Beausejour | Publisher: SHE PUBLSIHING LLC | ISBN: 978-1-953163-94-3 (paperback) | Publication Date: February 2024 (*second edition*)

Prepare to enter the ring as cultures clash in this adrenaline-filled drama! Under the tutelage of experienced trainer Jim Shaw, young boxer Sylvio Dominique has taken the middleweight class division by storm, winning bout after bout. Nicknamed "Wolf" for his boxing style and aggression in the ring, Sylvio works hard in the ring and plays even harder out of the ring and there is no shortage of women. Reuniting with childhood friend Valentina Cruz, the two become involved in an intense romance. But as Sylvio falls deep in love with Valentina, he realizes that she is more than what she seems. With a fight against the undefeated Dominican champion Felipe Maximo looming, secrets are revealed, and friends turn to foes as Sylvio later discovers that he may not be fighting only for the middleweight crown, but he may also be fighting for his life.

Title: Split Decision II - The Comeback | Author: Marc A. Beausejour | Publisher: SHE PUBLISHING LLC | ISBN: 978-1-953163-95-0 (paperback)| Publication Date: February 2024 (*second edition*)

After Sylvio Dominique's sudden retirement from middleweight boxing following a close brush with death, the former champion hangs up his gloves to continue running the Shaw-Dominique Community Center in Queens, New York. When Sylvio's hometown rival and current middleweight champion Barry Taylor; asks him to help train for his title defense against new contender and former MMA fighter Jun Zhang, Sylvio agrees to the proposition. But Taylor is defeated handily, and when Sylvio suffers a tragic death in the family and the center struggles financially, he makes the decision to return to the ring. Meanwhile, his girlfriend, Valentina Cruz find success as an actress and her relationship with Sylvio begins coming apart at the seams. Sylvio's trainer, Jim Shaw is reluctant to help Sylvio, as he finds himself struggling with his own personal demons. Jun Zhang then challenges Sylvio to fight him for the crown. As he prepares for his toughest ring battle yet, can Sylvio and Jim find the fortitude to emerge victorious while putting all their struggles behind them?

Title: Divine Vengeance | Author: Marc A. Beausejour | Publisher: SHE PUBLISHING LLC | Publication Date: COMING SOON!

After the murder of David Anderson, LaToya Richardson awaits her day in court while attorney Edward Reed receives a warning from Tadarius Hill, the gang leader of M.O.B. and sexy femme fatale Tina, who gives him an ultimatum. Realizing that he cannot use conventional methods to combat the tactics of his former gang, Edward pulls out all the stops to prevent Tadarius from wreaking havoc in the city. LaToya's son, Chris adjusts to his new home and new school while staying with David's family. Andrea McAfee's relationship with her boyfriend Quentin comes apart at the seams as lust and infidelity threatens to tear the couple apart. Can Edward, Chris, and Andrea summon the strength amidst the chaos in their environment to secure their futures?